"ARE YOU CALLING ME A LIAR, CAPTAIN?"

Nassir, unmoved by the Klingon's display of indignation, replied in a calm, even voice, "I don't believe that's what I said, Commander. What I requested was the record you or someone else surely sent to your superiors, who in turn would have relayed that information to your diplomatic envoys for transmittal to their counterparts within our Federation Diplomatic Corps. This procedure was put into place when it became apparent that both our governments expressed interest in exploring the Taurus Reach, so that incidents such as this apparent and unfortunate miscommunication might be avoided."

Standing at the rear of the bridge, Terrell forced himself not to smile. The captain was known for his enjoyment of spirited debate on a vast array of topics, and relished laying oratorical traps for any opponent foolish enough to accept his challenge.

"Somehow," Terrell whispered, his words audible only to Theriault, "I don't think this guy's in the mood for cunning wordplay." A quick look over the shoulder of Lieutenant Commander Bridget McLellan at the information displayed on her tactical console told him that both the *Sagittarius* and the Klingon scout ship had raised their defensive shields, but he felt a twinge in his gut as he noted that only the enemy vessel's weapons were powered.

I hate when that happens.

This title is also available as an eBook.

STAR TREK®
VANGUARD

DECLASSIFIED

DAYTON WARD
KEVIN DILMORE
MARCO PALMIERI
DAVID MACK

Based upon *Star Trek*
created by Gene Roddenberry

POCKET BOOKS
New York   London   Toronto   Sydney   Traelus II

Pocket Books
A Division of Simon & Schuster, Inc.
1230 Avenue of the Americas
New York, NY 10020

This book is a work of fiction. Names, characters, places, and incidents either are products of the authors' imaginations or are used fictitiously. Any resemblance to actual events or locales or persons, living or dead, is entirely coincidental.

First Pocket Books paperback edition July 2011

POCKET and colophon are registered trademarks of Simon & Schuster, Inc.

For information about special discounts for bulk purchases, please contact Simon & Schuster Special Sales at 1-866-506-1949 or business@simonandschuster.com.

The Simon & Schuster Speakers Bureau can bring authors to your live event. For more information or to book an event, contact the Simon & Schuster Speakers Bureau at 1-866-248-3049 or visit our website at www.simonspeakers.com.

Cover design by Alan Dingman
Cover art by Doug Drexler; station design by Masao Okazaki;
    Ptolemy-class design by Franz Joseph

Manufactured in the United States of America

10 9 8 7 6 5 4 3 2 1

ISBN 978-1-4516-0691-1
ISBN 978-1-4516-0698-0 (ebook)

ALMOST TOMORROW

Dayton Ward

For Addison and Erin:
You always make me look forward to tomorrow.

HISTORIAN'S NOTE

The events of this story take place in early 2265, several months prior to the completion of Starbase 47's construction and the station's being declared fully operational (*Star Trek Vanguard: Harbinger*; *Star Trek: Corps of Engineers—Distant Early Warning*), and before the *U.S.S. Enterprise*'s first voyage to the edge of our galaxy ("Where No Man Has Gone Before").

THE TAURUS REACH

2265

1

Commander Clark Terrell stepped onto the bridge of the *U.S.S. Sagittarius,* pausing at the entrance to take stock of the situation before him. Doing so took only a moment, as the *Archer*-class scout's command center was smaller than the room Terrell had shared with two other cadets at Starfleet Academy more than a decade earlier. Of course, the bridge was more tastefully appointed.

And it definitely smells better.

Sitting in the command chair, which along with the tactical station was situated at the center of the compact bridge, Captain Adelard Nassir turned to regard his first officer with a deadpan expression. "What took you so long?"

"I got lost," Terrell replied as he stepped away from the door and allowed it to close behind him. "You know, that joke doesn't get any funnier the more you try it." Given the size of the *Sagittarius,* one could travel between any two compartments in under a minute, and that included any movement requiring the use of either of the three ladders connecting the ship's three decks. Terrell's cabin was next to the bridge, along the port bow. He could traverse the distance in seconds should an emergency situation present itself, but the first officer otherwise preferred to spend a few minutes making a circuit of the ship's interiors before reporting to the bridge for his assigned duty shift.

Nassir asked, "But you know I'm just going to keep trying it, don't you?"

"At least until someone throws you out the airlock," Terrell countered, stepping farther onto the bridge and pushing up the sleeves of his olive drab jumpsuit—the standard duty uniform worn, without rank or other insignia, by every member of the *Sagittarius* crew.

Eyeing the first officer as he drew abreast of the command

chair, Nassir chuckled. "I assume that was said with all due respect?"

"Oh, absolutely, sir," Terrell replied. "You've even got my word as an officer that I promise to salute when I push the jettison button."

Nassir nodded. "See that you do." Despite the Deltan's bald pate, fair complexion, and slight build, the captain carried himself with the confidence of an experienced leader who harbored no doubts as to his authority. Though he had little use for the pomp and circumstance that so characterized much of Starfleet's various protocols and regulations, when the situation called for it Nassir could be the very model of by-the-book efficiency and expertise. Terrell knew that it was the captain's easy willingness to toss that book when a situation warranted such action that endeared him to subordinates and superior officers alike. Even Commodore Reyes, the commanding officer of the starbase to which the *Sagittarius* currently was assigned, not only respected Nassir's unorthodox leadership style but welcomed it, giving the captain whatever latitude he needed to carry out his mission.

Terrell moved to take up a position next to Ensign Vanessa Theriault, who sat at the bridge's science station. Studying the image of the lush, green world that dominated the upper third of the main viewscreen, slowly rotating from left to right as the ship maintained its high orbit, Terrell asked, "What's the story?"

Looking up from her console, the young, red-headed officer said, "The story is that Traelus II may well be the proverbial gold mine."

"Dilithium?" the first officer asked.

The science officer nodded enthusiastically. "Dilithium, pergium, rodinium. This planet's a buffet."

"That'll make the folks back home happy," Terrell said.

Rising from his seat, Nassir moved to stand to Theriault's left, opposite Terrell. "Or, it might just give them all bellyaches." He shook his head. "Considering how close we are to Tholian space, you know Starfleet Command's going to throw a fit when they hear about this."

Terrell's brow furrowed. "What were they expecting? Isn't this the reason we're out here in the first place?" Traelus was one of three solar systems in this region—a distant corner of the area that stellar cartographers had dubbed the Taurus Reach on Federation star charts—assigned to the *Sagittarius* for detailed surveys. All three systems shared three common traits. First, they so far had been mapped only by unmanned reconnaissance probes. Second, those preliminary sensor scans had raised enough questions that a further study was warranted. Planets in each of the systems were determined to possess at least some measurable quantities of the vital minerals Theriault had cited, making them potentially valuable from a mining as well as strategic point of view. In particular, the presence of dilithium and rodinium made completing mapping surveys of all three systems a top priority for Starfleet, at least so far as operations in this area of space were concerned.

This aspect also dovetailed with the third factor, in that all three systems were located along what laughingly passed as the territorial boundary claimed by the Tholian Assembly. Verifying that any of the planets did in fact contain important natural resources was a paramount concern, particularly in light of Federation expansion into this region of space.

For all the myriad reasons we're doing that, Terrell mused.

Turning from the science station, Nassir directed his attention to the Andorian officer seated at the helm, Lieutenant Celerasayna zh'Firro. "Sayna, what do the navigational charts show us about traffic in this area?"

The young *zhen* shook her head. "Not much, sir. Other than our own mapping probes and the odd civilian transport ship—probably smugglers hoping to avoid security patrols—I haven't been able to find much evidence at all that anyone cares about anything around here."

"You have to wonder why the Tholians didn't expand their territory to include this system," Nassir said, folding his arms across his chest. "Or the others, for that matter. Considering how averse they are to interacting with their interstellar neighbors, you'd think they'd claim these systems if only to keep anyone else from doing the same thing."

Terrell had no answer. Unnatural restraint seemed to characterize the Tholians' attitude toward the entire Taurus Reach, a wedge of space sandwiched between the areas claimed by the Tholians, the Klingon Empire, and the Federation. Starfleet vessels had only begun investigating the region two years earlier, but those initial forays had prompted an accelerated program of exploration and colonization here, all spearheaded by the construction of a massive, state-of-the-art space station, Starbase 47—or Vanguard, as it was informally known—which the *Sagittarius* and two other Starfleet vessels called their home port while tasked to this sector. Despite that activity, as well as the proximity to its borders of several systems and resource-rich planets, the Tholian Assembly appeared uninterested in moving in this direction, for reasons known only to them.

They may end up being the least of our problems.

"It's not the Tholians I'm worried about," Terrell said, "but you know it's only a matter of time before the Klingons start sniffing around out here."

"We already know the Klingons have been making their own ventures into the region," Nassir said. "The reports I've read from Starfleet Intelligence indicate it's just the beginning."

Theriault nodded. "If they were to plant their flag here, or some other system so close to Tholian territory, that might be enough to spook the Tholians into doing some poking around of their own." She sighed. "Tholians and Klingons, both with short tempers and hair triggers. That spells fun for everyone."

"Those are issues for Commodore Reyes and Starfleet Command," Nassir said. Reaching out, he rested his right hand on Theriault's shoulder. "Let's get started with the complete sensor sweep of the planet. The sooner we're finished here, the sooner we're on our way home."

Terrell chuckled. "Any chance they'll be finished building home by the time we get back?" Starbase 47 had been declared operational on a provisional basis for mission-essential tasks. Although primary support and defense systems were on line, the station still lacked many of the creature comforts it would boast once construction was complete.

"One can only hope," Theriault replied. "Just so long as I can get a hot shower, a decent meal, and a bed someone else hasn't been sleeping in when I'm not looking, I'll be happy." As though anticipating a retort from either Nassir or Terrell, the science officer looked up from her station and directed a scathing glare at both men. "With all due respect, gentlemen, any comment you might be considering will be avenged in your sleep."

"I wasn't going to say anything," Nassir countered, offering an expression of mock surprise. To Terrell, he said, "Were you going to say something, Commander?"

Terrell shook his head, schooling his features so that he did not smile. "My mother raised no fools, sir."

A series of beeps from the science station drew Theriault's attention to the array of status displays before her, and Terrell noted the change in the young officer's expression as she studied the readouts. "Something else, Ensign?"

Theriault replied, "Just more mineral deposit readings, Commander. This planet has it all: a temperate climate, beautiful oceans, and more raw materials than any of the planets we've charted so far." She paused a moment before adding, "I've got half a mind to retire early and build a house down there."

It took Terrell an extra moment for the statement to register, but when he glanced down to Theriault's console he saw that the ensign was tapping one blinking red light with her left forefinger, and realization dawned. Struggling to school his features, he turned to Nassir, who was already regarding him, the question evident in his eyes.

Is she saying what I think she's saying?

Looking up from her console, Theriault offered an almost imperceptible nod first to Nassir then to Terrell. The first officer glanced at the other stations, confirming that none of the other bridge personnel had caught their silent communication.

The science officer had invoked the code phrase that she, Terrell, and Nassir had agreed to use upon the discovery of any evidence of the Taurus Meta-Genome.

Entering Nassir's quarters and finding the captain and Ensign Theriault already waiting for him, Terrell waited for the door to close before thumbing the control panel to engage the door lock. The trio now enjoyed all the privacy there was to be found aboard the diminutive *Sagittarius*.

"So," Terrell said, leaning against the locked door and crossing his arms, "it's true?"

Theriault nodded. "Most definitely, sir. I triple-checked the readings, and there's no mistake. It's the meta-genome, all right."

"Well, how about that?" Nassir said, his face breaking into a wide smile. Terrell knew that despite the missions to which he and his crew were assigned, Adelard Nassir was first and foremost an explorer, having joined Starfleet for the express purpose of pushing outward the farthest limits of known space and discovering what might be waiting beyond those boundaries. For Nassir, the Taurus Reach and the mysteries it contained were like the seductive calls of the Sirens from Greek mythology.

Discovered more than two years earlier during a science survey mission in a system near the opposite edge of the Taurus Reach from the *Sagittarius*'s current position, the meta-genome had been determined to be a DNA sequence, apparently of alien origin, that possessed far greater complexity than any life-form previously encountered. Samples of the gene sequence had subsequently been located on several other worlds in scattered systems throughout the region in proximity to the initial find, with the possibility of further discoveries across the Taurus Reach.

The meta-genome, essentially a carrier of raw genetic data contained within a biochemical matrix, was believed to be hundreds of thousands of years old and carried with it the potential to revolutionize current understanding of life and evolution, provided its Byzantine composition could ever be fully understood.

If, as was believed by some experts at Starfleet Command, the alien DNA sequence was the product of artificial genetic engineering, then it suggested a level of technological prowess far above that of any known civilization. Investigating the meta-genome as well as its origins—and preventing rival powers such as the Klingons from doing the same thing—was the foremost priority for Starbase 47 and the starships assigned to it, and the reason the massive space station had been rushed into service in the first place. Support operations for the ongoing exploration, colonization, and merchant shipping efforts overseen by Vanguard would provide cover for that mission.

Terrell said, "Now, hang on a minute. The initial meta-genome samples were found in the Ravanar system, on the other side of the Taurus Reach. Everything found after that was still a long way from here." Until now, no such clues to the existence of the enigmatic gene sequence had been found so far from the original discovery. "If what we're saying here is true, then whoever cooked up that damned thing—"

"—had even greater influence than was originally theorized," Nassir said, cutting off Terrell and smiling to soften his interruption. "That alone is a rather interesting discovery, don't you think?"

Theriault chuckled. "Your gift for understatement never fails to impress me, Skipper." Glancing to Terrell before continuing, she said, "The preliminary sensor readings are very similar to what was found on Ravanar IV, but we'll need to collect samples for further, more detailed study and comparison back on Vanguard."

Nodding, Nassir said, "Agreed. They've already got a cadre of scientists champing at the bit for anything we might find out here." In addition to the team of specialists already assigned to Starbase 47 and given the task of studying the meta-genome, Terrell knew that Starfleet was dispatching a first-rate archeology and anthropology officer with advanced training and experience in the investigation of long-dead civilizations. That officer—currently en route from Earth—was not due to arrive at Vanguard for several more weeks.

Looks like we'll have a present for him when he finally gets here.

"Since the three of us are the only members of the crew who know anything about this," Nassir said, reaching up to rub his smooth, angular chin, "it looks like the two of you draw sample collection duty. We'll have to concoct a story to tell the others, but considering how long we've been running fast and hot, I imagine Master Chief Ilucci will welcome the opportunity to give the ship a once-over. That'll keep him and his people busy, and we can find other tasks for the rest of the crew. Just make your survey a quick one."

Terrell replied, "Copy that, Skipper." Then, with a small smile, he added, "You sure you don't want to go?"

"I'm absolutely certain I *do* want to go," the captain said, "but I figure that'll only raise questions among the crew."

Theriault nodded in agreement. "So, what do we do in the meantime, sir?"

Shrugging, Nassir offered a whimsical smile. "The first thing we need to do is call home. Commodore Reyes is going to love this."

2

The doors to Diego Reyes's office parted, allowing the commodore to enter his private sanctuary without breaking his brisk, determined stride.

That was what was supposed to happen. Instead, only the left door slid aside while the right door maintained its position, the result being that the entire right side of Reyes's body from his forehead to his boot slammed full speed into the barrier.

"What the hell?" Reyes snapped, feeling the sting where his nose and right cheek had caught the edge of the door and trying to avoid stumbling as he maneuvered his body through the blocked threshold leading to his office. Attempting to affect a demeanor communicating that he had with singular purpose intended to walk headlong into the door, the commodore directed his gaze out across the main deck of Starbase 47's operations center. He noted that every member of the operations staff within his field of vision seemed to be concentrating with unwavering intensity at workstations, viewing screens, data slates, or even the walls or the deck—anywhere but the entrance to his office.

Yeah, it's going to be one of those days.

"Where is Lieutenant Ballard?" he called out, referring to the station's chief engineer.

From where he stood on the operation center's raised supervisor's deck, Lieutenant Commander Raymond Cannella, Starbase 47's fleet operations manager, replied, "At last report, he was down in sensor control, sir." Cannella was a burly man, with dark, thinning hair swept back from his forehead and a neck so thick it seemed on the verge of bursting through the ribbed collar of his gold tunic. He spoke with a pronounced accent that betrayed his New Jersey heritage and made his every word sound as though he were issuing a challenge. "You need him up here, sir?"

Reyes considered the question, reasoning that the length of time required for Ballard to make the transit from sensor control to the ops center might just be sufficient for the commodore to reassess his current desire to reassign the engineer to the station's waste reclamation center. "No, that's all right, Commander. I'll just call him." Crossing to the desk positioned outside his office and intended to be occupied by his yeoman—should one ever arrive from Starfleet—the commodore reached for the computer terminal positioned near its left edge and thumbed the intercom control. "Reyes to Ballard."

There was a brief pause as the request was routed through the communications system before the lieutenant's voice replied through the panel's speaker grille, *"Ballard here, sir. What can I do for you, Commodore?"*

"Mister Ballard," Reyes said, "I was just body-blocked by my own office door. You wouldn't by chance happen to know anything about that?"

Ballard replied, *"That's probably my fault, sir. I had to take some of the internal sensor hubs off line to make some modifications. Very sensitive components, you know."*

"So is my *nose,* Lieutenant," Reyes said. "How long before systems are back up?"

"Half an hour or so, sir," Ballard said. *"It's just settling in adjustments more than anything else—the same kinds of things we've been dealing with for a while now."*

Sighing, Reyes nodded even though the chief engineer could not see him. Ballard's report about the internal sensors was but a variation of status updates Reyes had been hearing for more than a month. Ballard and his people had been fighting a rash of minor, annoying glitches and other assorted anomalies while working to bring Starbase 47's formidable array of internal computer and control systems on line and get them working in concert. All of this, in addition to the already rather long list of tasks to be completed before the station could be declared fully operational.

"Understood, Mister Ballard," Reyes said after a moment. "I don't suppose you have any good news for me?"

"You'll be happy to know we fixed that bug in the food replication systems for the officers' quarters," the engineer replied. *"Now when you order dinner, you won't be getting anything from Ambassador Jetanien's personal menu."*

Reyes chuckled at that. "Okay, you're forgiven for the sensors." A Rigellian Chelon, Jetanien had special dietary requirements, most of which were incompatible with human digestive systems. Some of the diplomat's favorite dishes had emerged from the food slot in Reyes's quarters, in response to the commodore's request for a simple steak with steamed rice and vegetables. As for the noxious liquid that had substituted for the iced tea he had wanted, it remained as yet unidentified. "I won't keep you from your duties any longer, Lieutenant. Keep Commander Cannella apprised of your progress."

"Will do, Commodore. Ballard out."

As the connection was severed, Reyes turned back toward his office, noting that the door remained open even though no one was in proximity to register with its sensor. He eyed the door as he entered his office, half expecting it to attempt cutting him in half as he passed through the entrance. When that did not happen, Reyes shook his head in mild irritation.

It's always something.

Moving toward his desk, the commodore took stock of the image on the viewscreen built into the wall to his right. At present it was programmed to provide him with constant, real-time updates as to the status of Starbase 47's construction as well as progress being made on the installation of numerous internal components. Most of the station's exterior was in place, along with essential onboard systems as well as ship maintenance facilities, cargo storage, and crew living areas. While the main civilian residential complex also was completed, many of the aesthetic features, such as the "terrestrial enclosure," were still under construction. A massive domed area within Starbase 47's primary hull, the enclosure formed a "habitat shell" designed to mimic Earth-based exteriors, complete with an extensive park and even an artificial sky that could be programmed to simulate day or night. Once finished, the enclosure also would be home to Stars Landing, a commercial and residential district intended to offer a wide variety of shopping, dining, and entertainment options to the station's crew, civilian merchants and travelers, and other visitors. The initiative was unique to Watchtower-class space stations such as Starbase 47, and unlike anything currently available to Starfleet personnel not assigned to a planet-based starbase.

Along with the status updates was a view of the station's exterior, generated by sensor imagery and illustrating where several sections of the starbase's internal skeletal structure remained visible as final outfitting tasks continued unabated. Much like Vanguard itself, the crew who soon would call this installation home also was incomplete. At the moment, the station's complement consisted of construction teams and engineers, with approximately one-third of the starbase's actual crew also on hand, though a report Reyes had read while eating breakfast informed him that a capable young man, Commander Jon Cooper, was en route and due to arrive within two weeks. The new second-in-command was being ferried by the *U.S.S. Endeavour,* the third of three Starfleet vessels permanently assigned to Starbase 47 under Reyes's overall command. Despite the seemingly unending stream of irksome problems to be dealt with when undertaking a project of this magnitude, he knew that things were shaping up in fine fashion.

"Commodore Reyes?"

The soft voice made him turn from the viewscreen to see a female officer standing in his half-open doorway. She wore a gold tunic with captain's stripes on her sleeves and carried a data slate in her left hand. Her hair, darker than even her uniform trousers, was styled in a short, feminine bob that—in Reyes's opinion, at least—did an admirable job of framing her gentle, slightly rounded features. He guessed from her appearance that she was of Indian descent and was perhaps in her mid to late thirties, and quite attractive, he decided.

Stow it, Commodore.

"Yes?" he asked.

Stepping into the office, the woman said, "I'm sorry to disturb you, but there was no one at your assistant's desk. We've not yet had the chance to meet, but I'm Captain Rana Desai, from the Judge Advocate General. Starfleet's assigned me to this station's JAG office, and I only just arrived yesterday morning." She spoke with a crisp London accent possessing an almost lyrical quality Reyes found soothing, though he noted that the captain radiated the proper bearing and confidence of a seasoned, accomplished officer. Of course, he knew Desai was such an officer, having reviewed her personnel record—and apparently forgotten about reading it—upon learning she would be serving aboard the station.

Reyes nodded in recognition. "Of course, Captain. I'm sorry

for not putting two and two together, and for not meeting you when you came aboard. One of the many reasons I'm supposed to have an assistant is because I'm lousy at remembering those sorts of things." He gestured toward the pair of chairs positioned before his desk as he made his way to his own seat. "Please, sit down. You were previously at the JAG office at Starbase 11, weren't you?"

"That's correct, sir," Desai said, taking one of the proffered chairs. "I was only there a year, but it was good duty." She glanced around the office before adding, "It was a planet, after all."

Dropping into his own thickly padded chair, Reyes chuckled as he leaned forward and rested his elbows atop his desk. "Fair enough, but I think you'll find some of the amenities here will help compensate for not being able to breathe fresh air. As for the work you'll be doing, this station's at the edge of Federation territory. New colonies, new trade routes, new friends *and* new enemies. You'll have your hands full from both the Starfleet and the civilian side of things."

And that's just the regular, everyday stuff.

Desai cleared her throat. "Actually, sir, it's something along those lines that's brought me to see you this morning." She paused, using a stylus to tap the data slate that now rested in her lap. "My office has received a few complaints from some of the station's civilian merchants who will be operating retail venues in Stars Landing. It seems you reassigned several cargo and administration areas that had been designated for them and reallocated them for Starfleet use."

"That's correct," Reyes replied, offering a single nod, "though substitute facilities were allocated elsewhere in the station."

"Smaller facilities," Desai countered, "and located farther away from Stars Landing."

Reyes shrugged. "The larger facilities they originally had were deemed necessary for security reasons."

"May I ask what those reasons might be, sir?" Desai asked.

"You may ask to your heart's content, Captain," the commodore said, "but I'm afraid the answers involve classified security matters." The areas in question, located within the station's secondary hull, had been reclassified as administrative and support spaces, at least according to the internal schematics and other unclassified records. In truth, that entire section was in the process of being reconfigured to serve as a secure research facility in which a team of specialists would operate in secret. Each member of the team would be listed on the starbase crew roster as serving in a variety of roles and responsibilities throughout the station. In truth, they would be working almost exclusively to study the Taurus Meta-Genome, as well as examining and testing any data or other materials that might be acquired during their investigation of the mysterious and highly complex strain of artificially engineered DNA. Indeed, Reyes had already received and approved a request by the captain of the *U.S.S. Sagittarius*— another of the vessels attached to the station to provide ship-based support—to conduct a survey mission on the second planet in the distant Traelus system, which apparently was home to newly discovered samples of the meta-genome.

How about that, the commodore mused.

As for the team's true purpose and even the existence of the clandestine facility, already dubbed "the Vault" by the officer overseeing its construction, those would remain closely guarded secrets, hidden from anyone without a direct "need-to-know." This included Captain Rana Desai.

"A few of the merchants said you were rude," Desai said.

Frowning, Reyes replied, "I told them that I realized this reshuffling of assignments might be an inconvenience to them, and thanked them for their cooperation."

Desai's eyes narrowed. "Did you say it nicely, or how you just said it to me?"

"That was me saying it nicely," Reyes replied.

As if in response to his question, the door to his office chose that moment to slide shut, its pneumatic hiss causing both Reyes and Desai to look in its direction. Reyes was sure his befuddled expression matched the one clouding the JAG officer's features.

"Does that happen a lot?" she asked.

"It's moody," Reyes said. Feeling his patience with the larger topic beginning to ebb, he leaned back in his chair. "They came to you because they didn't think I was nice?"

Shaking her head, Desai said, "They came to my office because they feel you didn't listen to them or take their concerns seriously."

"Captain, I did listen to them," Reyes countered, his interest in continuing this conversation now at an end. "I then balanced their concerns against this station's operational needs, and made a decision. They came to you because they didn't get what they wanted." Before Desai could respond to that, he tapped a finger on his desk and indicated the computer terminal positioned to his left. "All of this is in my report, so why are we here?"

Desai's expression hardened. "Sir, one of my jobs is to address grievances put forth by any member of the station's complement, Starfleet or civilian. I'm just following up on the report they filed and making certain their complaints are given their due diligence. You'll find I can be quite thorough in that regard."

"I wouldn't have it any other way, Captain," Reyes said. "You wouldn't be doing your job if you did anything less. I can respect that, even if you and I disagree on a particular point, which I imagine we'll do from time to time. I'm funny, that way."

Pausing a moment, Desai regarded him in silence, as though weighing the virtue of saying whatever else might be on her mind.

Sensing her hesitation, Reyes said, "Say what you want to say, Captain. I promise I won't bark."

"Thank you, sir," Desai replied. "Are you always this way? This direct, I mean."

Reyes nodded. "I am when I'm in charge, which I am a lot these days." Then, feeling the need to lighten the mood, he smiled. "But, I'm really quite pleasant when everybody just does what I want them to do."

Despite her composed demeanor, Desai released a small laugh before shaking her head. "Commodore, it's not my intent to tell you how to run this station, at least so long as all applicable laws and regulations are being followed, of course. But as Starfleet's senior representative to what looks to be a large number of civilian residents and visitors, I might suggest exercising a bit more diplomacy when dealing with such matters."

Shrugging again, Reyes replied, "That's why I have you, Captain: to take care of these things for me. You get to be polite, so I don't have to." Though he kept his tone light, he forced himself not to smile again. For reasons he could not quite understand—or, more likely, was unwilling to admit even to himself—he was enjoying the banter with Desai. The captain obviously took her job seriously, and he knew from her service record that she was not above mixing it up with superior officers if she thought she had the facts, truth, and justice on her side and with no apparent regard for any potential consequences. Reyes could definitely respect such an attitude.

This could be fun, he decided.

As though weighing the ramifications of what her new duty assignment would mean for her, Desai sighed. "It's going to be a long tour, isn't it, sir?"

"Not at all, Captain," the commodore replied. "Any tour's what you make of it." Tapping his desk again, he asked, "So, are we done here?"

"I suppose we are," Desai said, rising from her chair. "We're going to be having a lot of conversations like this, aren't we?"

Reyes nodded. "I expect they'll be the highlight of my day." Though he intended the remark to be sarcastic, he could not deny that there was more than a grain of truth behind the words.

Eyeing him with a quizzical expression, Desai finally said, "Thank you for your time, Commodore," before moving toward the door.

The door did not open at her approach.

Desai turned to look back at Reyes, who still sat behind his desk. "Still moody?"

Damn you, Ballard. Reaching for his desktop intercom panel, Reyes thumbed the activation switch. "Reyes to Ballard."

"Ballard here, sir," replied the chief engineer.

"My office door won't open, Lieutenant."

"Sorry about that, sir," Ballard replied. *"It's tied in with the problems we're having with the internal sensors. I should have it working in half an hour or so, sir."*

Without bothering to reply to the report, Reyes severed the comm link and drew what he hoped was a calming breath before returning his attention to Desai. "Well, Captain, it looks like we're stuck with each other for a little while longer." Rising from his chair, he started moving toward the food slot at the rear of his office. "Can I get you some coffee?"

"Yes, thank you, sir," the JAG lawyer replied as she made her way back to her seat.

Reyes input his request to the food slot's control panel. "No sense wasting this opportunity to get to know each other a little better. So, I hear you're from out of town." He could not stifle the chuckle that escaped his lips when Desai rolled her eyes, shook her head, and laughed.

This might end up being a good day, after all.

3

Irritated that he had not considered this course of action any sooner, Ronald Hanagan crossed the cargo bay of the civilian merchant freighter *Bacchus Plateau* to a tool kit he had brought with him. It took him a moment to rummage through the kit's contents until he found the item he sought, a P-38. Though the device normally was used to open magnetically sealed hatches as well as access panels on a starship, Hanagan figured the tool should serve his purposes quite nicely.

It's either this, or a phaser.

With a grunt of satisfaction, Hanagan made his way back to the oversized cargo container sitting near one corner of the storage bay. It was the last item on the shipping manifest to be unloaded from the *Bacchus Plateau* and into the internal transport system, which would move the container's contents down to one of the Starbase 47 cargo lockers currently assigned to Lauren Everett, his employer on the station. According to the manifest, the crate housed a plethora of merchandise and other supplies Everett would use to stock the store she soon would be opening in Stars Landing. Unlike its companions, this container was too large to transport on its own, so it had to be opened and its contents offloaded. Hanagan therefore had saved it for last.

Fool.

None of that mattered any longer, he decided. All he wanted now was to offload this bothersome container, which had of course further vexed him by being the only such container in the entire cargo shipment to have a malfunctioning access hatch. Several tries at forcing it open had failed, including one attempt in which Hanagan used a crowbar he had found on a nearby storage shelf. Why he had not remembered the P-38 before now was a mystery to him, but he did not care. Once he got the crate's contents unloaded and moved to where they belonged, he would be free to go and enjoy a decent meal, some fine spirits, and—with any luck—the company of an enchanting female.

All in good time.

Placing the P-38 on the cargo container's main access hatch, Hanagan pressed the control on the unit's embedded keypad, which instructed the device to send out a small pulse wave to break the magnetic seal currently keeping the hatch locked in place. It took only a moment before Hanagan heard a satisfying hiss emitted from the seal, at which time the P-38's status indicator shifted from red to green. He reached for the hatch's recessed handle and pulled, and the door slid aside with little effort to reveal darkness inside, along with the shadowy forms of a number of smaller containers of varying shapes and sizes.

"Finally," he said aloud, even though he was alone in the cargo bay.

Or so he thought.

His first indication that someone else was in the chamber came in the form of something clattering on the deck plating near his feet. Hanagan looked down and saw a bright red square, a nondescript Federation-style computer data storage card, resting on the deck near his left boot. Something in his peripheral vision caught his attention and he looked up to see a lone woman standing less than ten meters from him. How had she come so close without his having heard her?

"Are you Ronald Hanagan?" the woman asked. She was slight of build, though Hanagan noted the toned yet still slender musculature of her legs and arms. Wearing tan overalls, she looked to be a member of the *Bacchus Plateau*'s crew. Her hair, light red in color, was held in a bun at the back of her head, leaving her neck exposed.

Nodding, Hanagan replied, "Who wants to know?"

Rather than offering her own name, the woman instead said, "I've heard that the brothers, they fight one another."

After speaking the words, she held his gaze, and Hanagan forced himself not to offer any outward reaction as he considered what she had said. It was the challenge phrase he had been instructed to use when attempting contact with the other covert agent known to be working aboard the starbase. Though he had been on the station for more than three weeks, he had not yet had opportunity or reason to seek out his fellow mole. Had she sought him out, or was this some kind of trap engineered by Starfleet forces who had discovered spies in their midst?

There was only one way to find out.

"*Vaj Duj chIj,*" he said, offering the pass phrase—which translated to "navigate a warrior ship" in Federation Standard—in his native language as he had been instructed. Once spoken aloud, he had exposed his status as a Klingon. If this person was not his contact, then she would have to die, quickly and quietly.

To his relief and in flawless *tlhIngan Hol,* the woman replied, "*jaj qeylIS molar mIgh HoHchu'qu'.*" Hanagan smiled with longing as he recalled the words to the ancient drinking song he had enjoyed along with his fellow warriors while consuming far too many tankards of firewine or bloodwine, in the days before he had become a deep cover operative for Imperial Intelligence.

In those days, Ronald Hanagan had answered to the name bestowed upon him by his parents, Komaleq.

"You must be Lurqal," he said.

The woman's eyes narrowed. "Never use that name. I am Anna Sandesjo."

Hanagan knew this, of course, having been given this information by his handler, Turag, who soon would be serving as part of the diplomatic entourage invited to take up residence in the Klingon Embassy housed aboard the station. "Fine, Anna Sandesjo," he said, glancing about the cargo bay to ensure they were still alone. "What can I do for you?"

By way of reply, Sandesjo gestured toward the data card still lying at Hanagan's feet. "You can explain that."

Frowning, Hanagan bent to retrieve the card, holding it up and studying its surface. "What is it?"

"It's a recording of an encrypted message you dispatched to our mutual acquaintance." By that, Hanagan knew she meant Turag. "Rather, the message you attempted to send."

"What are you talking about?" Hanagan asked, confused. How dare this female question his competence?

Sandesjo shrugged. "I'm talking about your carelessness. You did a fine job encrypting your report and embedding it within the station's outgoing transmission feed, but what you didn't count on was the engineering staff disabling the communications array in order to make some adjustments to the equipment to address some technical issues. The array was off line for nearly six hours, during which all outgoing message traffic was held in a transmittal queue and subjected to a further round of scans and validation checks."

For the first time, Hanagan realized the severity of what Sandesjo was describing. If indeed the starbase's engineers had deactivated the communications system in order to perform some maintenance work, it had not been announced. In his role as a civilian merchant, he did not have access to any such information passed among the station's Starfleet contingent. It was without question a potentially devastating oversight on his part.

"If I hadn't been aware of this procedure taking place and acted to remove your message from the queue," Sandesjo continued, "it would've been discovered by security personnel and set off a stationwide search for you. In the event this explanation's beginning to tax your comprehension abilities, I'll reduce it to this synopsis: You jeopardized our mission here. Such flagrant disregard for security is inexcusable."

Ronald Hanagan saw the small dark object in her hand an instant before a high-pitched whine filled the air and a bright red flash engulfed everything around him.

Idiot.

Anna Sandesjo allowed the single word to repeat in her mind as she watched the last vestiges of Ronald Hanagan—Komaleq—dissolve into nothingness even as the echo of the disruptor blast faded. As his body disintegrated, Sandesjo raised her right hand to inspect the dull metal finish of the compact disruptor she held. She had purchased the weapon from a civilian dealer on the *Omari-Ekon,* an Orion merchant vessel operating in nearby space. The arms broker had been content not to ask questions, likely owing to the sizable number of Federation credits she had deposited in his account. As for the disruptor, it was an efficient weapon, small enough to be concealed on one's person yet possessing sufficient power to be of inarguable use in combat. It had also demonstrated its value to a covert agent needing a means of wiping away evidence of an inexcusable blunder.

Releasing a tired sigh, Sandesjo shook her head. She had not wanted to kill Komaleq, of course. Such actions were not within the normal scope of her assigned mission. Her duties as a covert agent aboard Starbase 47 involved straightforward tasks. She was to listen and watch; read and collect data by any means available; learn and report to her superiors; repeat as required. Anything more risked discovery, and finding a Klingon agent aboard a

Starfleet space station—an operative surgically altered to appear human, no less—would trigger a manhunt for other spies across the quadrant. Such a reaction could prove disastrous for the Empire's still-evolving plans for finally engaging its longtime rival, the Federation.

She had been here long enough, Sandesjo decided, taking an extra moment to reseal the cargo container Hanagan had opened and return the P-38 opening device to his tool kit, which she then secreted within one of the storage lockers lining one bulkhead. An inspection of the area revealed no other sign of the man's presence or of her having been there. There were no security video feeds in this area of the ship, and given her wardrobe she should be able to make her way without incident back to the station. The last thing she wanted now was to encounter a member of the *Bacchus Plateau*'s crew or Starbase 47's security contingent.

Despite her standing orders to remain a passive observer while embedded as a member of Ambassador Jetanien's diplomatic cadre, finding Komaleq's message in the outgoing communications feed had necessitated extreme action in order to protect the larger mission. Removing all traces of the communiqué from the transmittal queue had been a straightforward if time-consuming task. That aside, if Komaleq had made one error, he may well have made others, either in sufficient quantities or of such scope that Sandesjo would be unable to take corrective action before someone else discovered what he had done. The only sure way to prevent further errors was to remove its potential cause with surgical precision and dispassionate efficiency.

Covering up *that* action, however, required somewhat more ingenuity.

Fortunately, Sandesjo was used to working several steps ahead when planning a task. She already had transmitted a message—ostensibly from Hanagan himself—to his employer on the station, informing her of his intent to end his tenure with her small company and return to Earth, having acquired passage aboard the *Bacchus Plateau,* which was due to leave later in the evening. As for the freighter itself, another message had been dispatched to its captain, asking her for passage back to Federation space. Playing the role of Hanagan would be another human male who, through a notable lack of skill and judgment, had amassed a sizable gambling debt aboard the Orion vessel currently docked at the station. The human had expressed no small amount of enthusiasm at the idea of adopting Hanagan's identity and acting in his stead in exchange for Sandesjo's seeing to his debt with no questions asked. The deception might be detected one day, but only after weeks if not months had passed—more than long enough for Sandesjo to find a way to deal with the issue.

Her next order of business would be relaying a report to her superior, Turag, informing him that Komaleq was out of the picture. Sandesjo was certain her handler would be displeased at this development, regardless of any explanation she might provide for her actions and how she had in fact preserved the integrity of the larger mission. She did not care, for now she had other concerns. Regardless of how Turag might respond to what she soon would tell him, Sandesjo's immediate priority was ensuring that neither Komaleq nor Ronald Hanagan had done, said, or left behind anything that might endanger her presence on the station. With the potentially dangerous Komaleq now out of the way she was—so far as she knew—the only Klingon operative on the station, at least until Turag arrived. Until then, she was on her own here.

Sandesjo rather liked that.

4

"Let me put this as diplomatically as I know how, Ambassador. Your Klingon friends are really starting to piss me off."

Positioned to the left of Commodore Reyes, Lieutenant Commander T'Prynn said nothing as the station's commanding officer stood before the desk of Ambassador Jetanien, the diplomatic envoy assigned to Starbase 47 with the task of overseeing Federation political interests in the Taurus Reach. For his part, the Rigellian Chelon appeared unmoved by Reyes's comment, opting instead to reach for the oversized bowl of dark brown broth sitting atop a matching saucer on his desk. Grasping the bowl in his oversized manus, Jetanien raised it to his beaklike mouth and proceeded to slurp. T'Prynn forced herself not to react to the rancid odor emanating from the bowl, but rather concentrated on identifying the vessel's contents.

She failed.

"What have the Klingons done to test your patience this time, Commodore?" the ambassador asked as he returned the bowl to its saucer.

Reyes said nothing at first, his expression neutral as he watched Jetanien eat, and T'Prynn could see that the commodore also smelled the broth's pungent odor. Unlike her, Reyes had no problem voicing his likes and dislikes. "Are you sure someone didn't switch your lunch with a tub of lubricant from down in engineering?"

"Quite sure, my friend," Jetanien replied before uttering a series of clicks and chirps along with a rumbling gurgle that T'Prynn had come to recognize as a Chelon's equivalent to laughter. "Now, about your mounting irritation with the Klingons, I trust you're referring to the diplomatic envoy?"

Nodding, Reyes replied, "That's them." He held up the data slate he had brought with him. "We received their latest communiqué this afternoon, which includes their updated list of demands. They're asking for more floor space in their embassy office section, and they want us to dedicate one of the main docking bays for their exclusive use. Failure to deliver on any of these requests is considered a deal breaker for being able to enjoy their company here in Shangri-La."

"The way I see it," Jetanien said, clasping his hands before him and tapping the extremities that passed for his thumbs in a rhythmic manner, "at least some of these issues most definitely fall within your purview as this station's commander."

Reyes released a low grunt of irritation. "So far as I'm concerned, all of it's within my purview, but I'm pretty sure the reason the Diplomatic Corps sent you all the way out here was to talk to the Klingons so I wouldn't have to."

"A fair point," the ambassador said, "though I'd like to think my role has more substance than that. After all, my career ambition really isn't to simply keep you from starting an interstellar war, despite whatever levels of enjoyment such activity might bring me from time to time."

T'Prynn listened with patience to the verbal joust in which Reyes and Jetanien always indulged before turning to whatever matter required their attention. Despite their disparate backgrounds, the commodore and the diplomat had established an easy rapport, which had facilitated their ability to work together as Operation Vanguard continued to evolve. Jetanien had been given a most demanding assignment, acting as the senior diplomatic adviser not only to Commodore Reyes but also the Federation Council. With Starbase 47's presence in an area of space bordered by both a known rival and a potential adversary, the Federation had no choice but to tread lightly with respect to its own exploration and colonization efforts. Given the Klingons' ongoing aggressive territorial expansion efforts in all directions, many of Starfleet's leading political and tactical minds were predicting an eventual confrontation should the Empire extend its reach to the Tholian border, with the Federation possibly caught in the middle. The Taurus Reach was a delicate buffer preventing that from happening, and Starbase 47 had been inserted into that wedge in order to quell a possible flashpoint situation.

That was the official story, anyway. Whether Vanguard's legitimate if arguably secondary mission had any tangible effects on its primary objective remained to be seen, and it was T'Prynn's job to see that such consequences were mitigated if not altogether avoided. It went without saying that the Klingons most likely would be interested in the station's activities, and expending considerable resources in attempts to ascertain what other goals it might be pursuing. With the levels of operational security surrounding the mission to learn the truth behind the Taurus Meta-Genome and its creators, diligence at every turn would be required. Indeed, T'Prynn was certain that the Empire had already dispatched covert operatives here in hopes of gleaning any kind of useful information. She had been conducting her own clandestine investigations for weeks, some of which were beginning to show results. Though she had no hard proof to corroborate her suspicions, T'Prynn was certain that obtaining such evidence was only a matter of time.

Far above and beyond her own role on Starbase 47, and in the interests of working to maintain whatever fragile peace existed between the three powers, the Federation had seen fit to authorize the establishment of full, formal embassy facilities aboard the station for all three governments. It was hoped that having diplomatic representatives from all involved parties in one location would serve to effect quick, agreeable solutions to any conflicts that might arise. In T'Prynn's opinion, it was a noble goal, though putting the idea into practice had proven to be a formidable challenge. Whereas the Tholians had yet to even acknowledge the Federation's offer, the Klingons had tempered whatever enthusiasm they had managed to manufacture with the sorts of conditions and demands Reyes found himself addressing on a near daily basis.

"You know I'm always happy to provide you a cheap laugh or two," Reyes said, "but do me a favor and talk to these people, would you? Tell them they can't have a dedicated docking bay, but we'll reserve one of the lower docking ports, and we'll move any ship to an available bay if it requires maintenance, repairs, or resupply."

Jetanien nodded. "That seems like a fair compromise. There may yet be hope for you as a diplomat, Diego."

"Don't push your luck," Reyes countered, though he did offer a small laugh to punctuate his reply.

"And what of their request for increased space in their embassy?" the ambassador asked.

Shrugging, Reyes replied, "They can have as much area behind their rear bulkhead as they want." T'Prynn recognized the humor in the statement, given that the embassies occupied areas along the outer ring of the station's primary hull, and "behind the rear bulkhead" was nothing but open space. The commodore, from her observations, derived some measure of amusement from the employment of sarcasm.

Even Jetanien laughed, emitting another series of clicks and grunts. "That's more like the Diego Reyes I know. I should've guessed that you wouldn't easily submit to such petulant whining."

Submit.

The command came unbidden, lunging from the depths of T'Prynn's consciousness and forcing itself into the forefront of her awareness. It was Sten, at one time her fiancé, calling to her as he had since that day more than five decades ago when he was gripped by the temporary near insanity that characterized the *Plak tow,* the blood fever, which was the culmination of the ancient Vulcan mating drive, the *Pon farr.* As his betrothed mate, T'Prynn had rejected him and demanded the rite of ritual combat, the *kal-if-fee,* in order to free herself from the marriage bond. It was during that death challenge that Sten, sensing his impending defeat at T'Prynn's hand, forced into her mind his *katra,* his own consciousness. Even as he faced death, he attempted to bend her to his will, demanding that she subject herself to him. As always, she defied him, and her hands snapping his neck punctuated what she believed was to be her final refusal.

Submit.

The calls for subjugation had not ceased with Sten's demise. They had instead continued unabated during the ensuing 52.7 years, his *katra* haunting her waking moments, her dreams, and even her attempts to assert any degree of mental balance and control via meditation. She had sought the assistance of Vulcan *Kolinahr* masters and even the revered Adepts themselves, who had taught her techniques for managing her unique condition. Those methods only served to treat the symptoms, however; as to ridding her mind of whatever remained of Sten, for that there seemed to be no cure.

Submit!

From the tormented depths of her own mind, T'Prynn conjured her all too familiar response to Sten's challenge. *Never.*

"Commander, are you quite all right?"

It required an extra moment for T'Prynn to realize that Jetanien was speaking to her, and that both he and Commodore Reyes were regarding her with their own particular expressions of concern. Had her own features or bearing betrayed her inner turmoil? Unsure of the answer to that question, T'Prynn clasped her hands behind her back and nodded.

"I apologize for my momentary distraction, gentlemen. I was giving thought to some issues I plan to address once our business here is completed."

"You look tired, Commander," Reyes said, his eyes narrowing as he frowned.

T'Prynn offered another nod. "I have had some trouble sleeping in recent days, Commodore, though you can be sure it will not affect my ability to carry out my duties."

Reyes replied, "I trust your judgment, Commander, but feel free to take some time for yourself and go visit Doctor Fisher, if you think it's necessary."

"I will do that, sir," T'Prynn replied, hoping to put the matter to rest and move on with other, more pressing concerns.

Appearing satisfied with her answer, Reyes returned his attention to Jetanien. "All right. Where were we?"

"You were asking me to speak to the Klingons on your behalf," Jetanien replied, "in the hope of staving off total war between the Federation and the Empire."

"Right," the commodore said, nodding. "Can you help me out here?"

Tapping the nail of one large, scaled finger on his desk, the ambassador uttered a seemingly random string of clicks and pops. "I shall do my level best, my friend."

A beep from the diplomat's desk made him reach for the intercom panel situated near his left hand. "Yes?"

In response to his query, a feminine voice replied, *"It's Anna Sandesjo, Ambassador. I have those reports you wanted."*

"Excellent," Jetanien replied. "Bring them right in."

His office doors parted a moment later, and T'Prynn turned to see a young human woman enter the room. She wore conservative gray pants with a matching jacket over a white blouse, and her red hair fell loosely about her shoulders. Her eyes were a startling shade of green, and when T'Prynn met her gaze she sensed tremendous intelligence and confidence. There was an additional, unquantifiable reaction, and another moment passed before she comprehended the feeling she was experiencing as she beheld Anna Sandesjo.

Desire? Yes, T'Prynn felt that, but there also was something else, which she could not yet identify.

Their momentary contact was broken as the woman made her way to stand before Jetanien's desk. Extending her right arm, she offered the ambassador a data slate. "Here you are, sir. Everything I could find on all diplomatic exchanges between the Klingons and the Tholians. There's not really much there, I'm afraid."

"A little light reading?" Reyes asked.

Pausing to scan the data slate's display, Jetanien uttered a snort of disapproval. "Very light, as it happens. As I'm sure you've already surmised, diplomatic relations between the Klingon Empire and the Tholian Assembly can probably best be summed up with a synopsis which reads, 'Don't bother us, and we won't bother you.'"

"And here we are," Sandesjo replied, "doing what we can to annoy both sides."

Again, Jetanien laughed. "It's what we diplomats do best, my dear." Looking to Reyes, the Chelon asked, "How else may I be of service, Diego?"

Reyes shook his head. "I think I've bothered you enough for one day. Thanks for your help, Jetanien." As he turned to head for the door, he glanced toward T'Prynn. "Commander?"

"Aye, sir," T'Prynn acknowledged, moving to follow Reyes. As she turned, her eyes once more locked with Sandesjo's, and this time T'Prynn saw something new in the human's expression. What was it?

Submit, challenged Sten, interrupting her thoughts.

Die, she countered, rallying her mental skills and forcing her long-dead fiancé's consciousness back into the dark hole from which it had emerged. Then there was merciful silence, and she had time for one last fleeting glance in Sandesjo's direction as she left Jetanien's office. Though the human said nothing, the corner of her mouth turned upward, and T'Prynn registered the other woman's all but imperceptible nod.

Fascinating.

5

"Are you done yet?"

Though he asked the question with a smile, Clark Terrell still received one of Vanessa Theriault's trademark glares from where she knelt at the bank of the massive lake. Positioned next to her on a large rock were her science tricorder as well as a specimen collection kit, which Theriault had already filled with samples of the lake water as well as nearby vegetation and even some of the small, minnowlike creatures she had found near the water's edge. As interesting as those examples might prove to be, it was the vial the science officer now held in her hand that had Terrell's undivided attention.

"Almost," Theriault replied as she sealed the vial and returned it to her kit. "This algae sample is loaded with the meta-genome, but none of the surrounding vegetation has it. Neither does any-thing else, for that matter."

Terrell nodded. "Just like Ravanar IV, and the other planets where it was found." Whoever or whatever was responsible for the apparent scattered seeding of the complex gene sequence on so many disparate planets across the Taurus Reach, their choice of a dispersal pattern was as much a mystery as their reasons. "And no rhyme or reason to the target planets, either, even though this planet seems to be a lot like Ravanar." This region in particu-lar reminded him of what he had reviewed of the survey reports from the first system where the meta-genome had been discov-ered. The lake selected by the landing party for their survey was surrounded by mountains, which in turn were situated in the midst of a vast desert. The water here—fed to the lake by under-ground streams running through the mountain range—was crys-tal clear, affording the first officer an unfettered look at the sand and rocks forming the lake bottom. After determining that the water was safe for human consumption, he had dipped his hands into the lake and drunk from it, relishing the taste. It was cool but not, he suspected, so cold as to preclude swimming.

"Think we could convince the skipper to authorize a few hours' shore leave?" Theriault asked, smiling as she returned various instruments and collection containers to the kit. "Don't tell me you haven't been thinking about it."

"Only since we beamed down," Terrell replied. Captain Nas-sir had opted to keep the *Sagittarius* in orbit above Traelus II, unwilling to sacrifice the greater effectiveness of the ship's sen-sors while in space for the sake of landing in this idyllic location, even if only for a short while. Of course, his keeping the rest of the crew aboard ship made it easier to maintain Terrell and The-riault's cover story of transporting to the surface to collect sam-ples of dilithium and other raw minerals, which they had done while acquiring specimens found to contain the meta-genome.

Checking the chronometer display on her tricorder, Theriault said, "Well, I'm done, and according to this we've got about twenty minutes before our next scheduled check-in. Did you bring your swimsuit?"

Terrell's reply was cut off by the telltale beeping of the communicator in his jumpsuit's hip pocket. Smiling, he shook his head. "Right on cue. I told you the captain knows everything." He extracted the device and flipped open its antenna grid before announcing, "Terrell here."

"Clark," said the voice of Captain Nassir, *"we've got company up here. A Klingon scout ship is coming around the far side of the planet. We don't know yet if it just warped into the system, or if it's been here all along and hiding from us. Right now I don't care. Stand by for beam-up."*

"Klingons?" Theriault said, her expression a mask of concern. "All the way out here?"

Frowning as he gestured to the science officer to hurry up with collecting her equipment, Terrell said into the communicator, "Are their weapons hot?"

"Affirmative," the captain replied, *"but their shields are down. I think they know you're down there and they're trying to bait me into raising shields so we can't beam you back. So, get your asses in gear."*

Terrell knew that a planet like Traelus II, with its vast deposits of valuable minerals, would not escape the notice of anyone scouting for such materials. The Klingons required elements like dilithium, and their needs were perhaps even greater than those of the Federation. What concerned the commander now was whether the Klingon ship currently in orbit had any other reason for taking an interest in this particular planet.

Let's hope not.

"Understood, Skipper," Terrell said. Seeing that Theriault was ready to go, he began to report that they were ready for transport when a flickering light in the corner of his eye caught his attention. He turned to see four columns of coarse ruby-red energy appear out of nothingness. Within seconds each of the columns coalesced into the form of a bipedal figure.

"Clark," Nassir's voice called out from Terrell's communica-

tor. *"Be advised that sensors are picking up the Klingon ship's transporters."*

"Um," Theriault replied, "we know, sir."

Terrell's hand was already moving to the palm-sized Type-1 phaser in his right hip pocket when the figures completed the materialization process and the Klingon at the front of the formation drew a sidearm from the holster at his waist with startling speed, leveling it at the first officer.

"Do not move, Earther." He was tall and muscled, his dark uniform tunic and pants stretched tight across his physique. The disruptor pistol wavered not one iota as its muzzle pointed at Terrell's chest.

Freezing in place and holding his arms away from his body to demonstrate that he carried no other weapon, Terrell asked, "What's the meaning of this? We're on a peaceful scientific survey mission here, and pose no threat to you."

"You're trespassing, Earther," the Klingon snapped. "This world has been claimed by the Klingon Empire."

"Since when?" asked Theriault, and when Terrell glanced at her he saw the ensign's features cloud with uncertainty in the wake of her bold challenge.

The Klingons snarled as they regarded her, and the leader replied, "Since I said so, but if you wish to dispute that, I would welcome the challenge."

"Goading an obviously inferior opponent into challenging you?" Terrell said, not even bothering to hide his scowl. "That sounds awfully dishonorable for a Klingon warrior."

"What do you mean, *inferior*?" Theriault asked, her words laced with indignation.

Turning so that he could offer a scathing glare to the ensign, Terrell replied, "Oh, I'm sorry, Vanessa. Were you *wanting* to challenge him to single combat?"

Theriault glanced toward the hulking Klingon before pursing her lips and shaking her head. "I think I'll just stand over here and be inferior."

Nodding, Terrell said, "Good plan." His encounters with

Klingons had been few and infrequent during his career, but stories of the Empire's supposed allegiance to the notions of honor and courage in battle were well known, dating back to Starfleet's initial contact with the militaristic race more than a century ago.

As though considering Terrell's words, the Klingon glowered at him, and for a moment the first officer was certain the disruptor would belch energy at any second. "You are fortunate that my orders do not afford me the luxury of showing you the errors of your arrogance." He shifted the weapon to point its muzzle at the communicator in Terrell's hand. "Tell your ship to retrieve you, now."

"Or what?" Terrell asked.

The disruptor moved again, this time to aim at Terrell's face. "Or I will disobey my orders and risk the wrath of my superiors."

From the communicator, Terrell heard Nassir say, *"That's enough, Commander. Stand by for beam-up."*

Angry that the Klingons appeared to be getting their way, Terrell nevertheless clenched his jaw to keep from exacerbating the already tense situation. It took considerable effort on his part to restrict his response to "Aye, sir."

Terrell and Theriault arrived on the bridge of the *Sagittarius* to see Captain Nassir standing before the main viewscreen with his arms crossed as he faced off with the image of another Klingon.

"All right, Commander," Nassir said, his voice low and clipped, "my people are back aboard. Now, perhaps you'd be so kind as to show me some record of the Klingon Empire laying claim to this planet?"

Seated in a high-backed chair that blocked most of the area to either side, the Klingon leaned forward until his swarthy visage all but filled the screen. *"Are you calling me a liar, Captain?"*

Nassir, unmoved by the Klingon's display of indignation, replied in a calm, even voice, "I don't believe that's what I said, Commander. What I requested was the record you or someone else surely sent to your superiors, who in turn would have relayed that information to your diplomatic envoys for transmittal to their counterparts within our Federation Diplomatic Corps. This procedure was put into place when it became apparent that both our governments expressed interest in exploring the Taurus Reach, so that incidents such as this apparent and unfortunate miscommunication might be avoided."

Standing at the rear of the bridge, Terrell forced himself not to smile. The captain was known for his enjoyment of spirited debate on a vast array of topics, and relished laying oratorical traps for any opponent foolish enough to accept his challenge.

"Somehow," Terrell whispered, his words audible only to Theriault, "I don't think this guy's in the mood for cunning wordplay." A quick look over the shoulder of Lieutenant Commander Bridget McLellan at the information displayed on her tactical console told him that both the *Sagittarius* and the Klingon scout ship had raised their defensive shields, but he felt a twinge in his gut as he noted that only the enemy vessel's weapons were powered.

I hate when that happens.

On the viewscreen, the Klingon—Terrell realized for the first time that he did not even know the commander's name—said, *"I am not a diplomat, Captain, nor am I a custodian of administrative minutiae. I follow the orders of my superiors, who directed me to this world which the Empire has claimed. If you wish to dispute that, then you may address your grievances to whichever bloated sack of useless skin and meat oversees such matters. For now, you are trespassing. Remove your vessel from orbit above this world and leave this system."* He paused, his stern expression fading even as his eyes seemed to go flat. *"I will not ask again."*

"Captain," McLellan called out from the tactical station, "their weapons are targeting us."

Theriault gasped. "They can't be serious."

"You don't know Klingons," Terrell countered, stepping into the command well and taking up a position behind McLellan. Another reading of her console's status displays and other gauges was enough to bring him up to speed. According to the sensors, the Klingon ship and the *Sagittarius* appeared to be evenly matched.

"Commander," Nassir said after a moment, his stance unwavering as he maintained his gaze on the Klingon, "there's no need for violence today. We already know from your landing party's actions on the planet's surface that the superiors to whom you've pledged your allegiance also wish to avoid such actions."

"My superiors are not here," the Klingon replied, before snapping his fingers. In response to his unspoken command, the communications channel dissolved into static. The image on the viewscreen shifted to that of the compact yet still formidable-looking Klingon scout vessel.

"That's not good," Theriault said, already moving toward the science station.

A Red Alert siren wailed across the *Sagittarius*'s compact bridge, and McLellan jolted in her seat, her head snapping to look first at Terrell and then at Nassir. "They're locking weapons, and I'm picking up energy surges in their forward disruptors."

"Full power to forward shields and weapons," Nassir said, his voice hardening for the first time since Terrell had arrived on the bridge. "Stand by for evasive."

"Ready, Captain," replied Lieutenant zh'Firro at the helm, her fingers moving across her console and inputting the commands to carry out the captain's orders.

"Incoming!" McLellan called out. "Brace for impact!" She barely had time to give the warning before something slammed into the ship. Despite the deflector shields and the internal damping systems, Terrell still felt the deck shift beneath his feet and he reached for the back of McLellan's chair to steady himself.

"Initiating evasive!" shouted zh'Firro from the helm even as Nassir was giving the order. On the screen, the image of the Klingon ship disappeared as the *Sagittarius* veered away, clawing for maneuvering room.

Bracing against the science station, Nassir looked to McLellan. "Damage report!"

The second officer shook her head. "Shields are holding. All systems operational." A beep from her console made her frown. "They're coming after us!"

"Of course they are," Nassir said, and Terrell heard the resignation in the other man's voice as the captain made his way back to the command chair. "Lock weapons and prepare to return fire. Sayna, give me a tactical plot." In response to his order, the main viewscreen changed again, this time to a computer-generated map showing the positions of the *Sagittarius* and the Klingon ship in relation to each other as well as Traelus II and even the planet's pair of moons. Text scrolled down the screen's right side, indicating distances, speeds, power levels, and damage.

It also displayed the second barrage of disruptor fire as the Klingon vessel fired again. Terrell gripped the back of McLellan's chair again, but this time zh'Firro's piloting skills prevented another strike against the ship's shields.

"Nice flying, Sayna," Nassir said, maintaining his trademark composure. "Bridy Mac, how about giving our friends a taste of their own medicine?"

"Aye, Skipper," McLellan replied, not waiting for additional instructions before her fingers tapped the firing controls on her tactical console. The bridge lights dimmed as power was drawn from other systems by the ship's phaser emitters, and Terrell looked up to see the information displayed on the main viewer's tactical schematic being updated to account for the damage inflicted on the Klingon ship's defensive shields.

"Continue firing!" Nassir ordered, and McLellan repeated the attack sequence.

Despite the erratic maneuvers being effected by the pilots of both vessels, Terrell noted from the information on the viewer that the second officer was still able to land another strike on the other ship's shields. Then the Klingon ship fired again, and everything around Terrell bucked, shuddered, and groaned in protest. Lighting and console screens flickered in response to the assault, and Terrell was sure he even heard the hum of the ship's engines shift in protest.

"Multiple hits!" McLellan called out over the renewed chorus of alarms sounding across the bridge. "Aft shields are down, and I'm picking up hull damage near engineering!"

"Get me some space, Sayna!" Nassir said. "And stop showing them our ass!"

Pointing to McLellan's tactical console and the sensor schematic of the Klingon vessel displayed upon it, Terrell said, "Target phasers here and here." He traced a finger over the readout, where the scout ship's warp nacelles were joined to the hull. "That's where the shielding and armor is weakest on this design."

McLellan nodded. "Got it. Sensors say the same thing." To zh'Firro she said, "Sayna, bring us about to heading 137 mark 91. I just need a few seconds."

On the viewer, Terrell saw the red circle indicating the Klingon ship gaining on the blue arrowhead depicting the *Sagittarius*, the distance between the two vessels closing with even greater speed as zh'Firro carried out McLellan's instructions. It took him a moment to realize he was holding his breath when the second officer's fingers stabbed at the firing controls, and he felt the reverberation channeled through the deck plates beneath his boots as the weapons systems unleashed their hellish power.

Seconds later, McLellan slammed a fist down on her console. "Yes! Their starboard shields are down."

At the science station, Theriault said, "Sensors are detecting fluctuations in their propulsion system, and I'm also picking up damage to their forward disruptor array." Then she turned from her console and regarded Nassir. "They're moving off, sir."

"That's unusual," Terrell said.

"Nice work, people," Nassir replied. "Keep an eye on them, Bridy Mac. I don't want them sneaking up on us again." Next, he tapped a control on the arm of his chair. "Bridge to engineering. What's the story, Master Chief?"

Over the bridge intercom system, Master Chief Petty Officer Michael Ilucci answered, *"Are we done getting shot at, Skipper?"*

"That's affirmative," Nassir said.

"That'll help, then," replied the chief engineer. *"We took a decent hit down here. I'm going to have to take the warp engines off line to repair some buckling in the antimatter containment system and the intermix chamber."*

"What about impulse?" Terrell asked.

Ilucci replied, *"That's still available, even though the engine took a minor hit, too. We can maneuver, but I don't recommend going anywhere too fast until I get a chance to look things over."*

"Captain," McLellan said, turning from her station to face Nassir, "I just picked up a transmission from the Klingon ship. It's encrypted, but from what I can tell, it's the same message being broadcast over and over. I think it's a distress signal, sir."

"I'm not picking up any other Klingon vessels or other traffic on long-range sensors," Theriault added, "but somebody has to know those guys are out here."

Nodding in agreement, Nassir said to his chair intercom, "Master Chief, how much time do you need to make repairs?"

There was not a moment's hesitation before Ilucci replied, *"About twelve hours, Skipper."*

Turning away from the tactical console, Terrell saw the captain already looking at him, and both men nodded as they reached the same conclusion.

"You'll need to work faster, Master Chief," Nassir said, doubting the Klingons would give them that kind of time.

6

Standing on the supervisor's deck of Vanguard's operations center with his arms folded, Reyes focused on several of the viewscreens arrayed around the room and watched their depictions of activity currently taking place around the starbase's exterior. A civilian merchant freighter was disconnecting from one of the lower docking pylons positioned around the station's secondary hull. On another screen, a pair of single-person work bees hovered at the station's bottom, maneuvering into place a replacement component for the massive sensor array Lieutenant Ballard had determined was defective. Other screens showed images of the outer hull and engineers, shrouded inside environment suits, standing on the tritanium plating with the aid of magnetic boots as they endeavored to complete the installation of one piece of equipment or another.

It was the sort of work that intrigued Reyes for reasons he could not explain, piquing his curiosity and compelling him to watch with rapt attention as his people carried out their duties in efficient, even mundane fashion. It was an interesting notion to ponder, he conceded, given the very real danger in which some of those in his charge presently had placed themselves in order to carry out such necessary tasks. Perhaps that was it; he felt beholden to observe those he commanded while they placed themselves in harm's way, keeping watch over them until such time as they returned to the station's comparatively safer confines.

That, or he was motivated by a desire to find something—anything—that might occupy his attention and prevent him from going back to his office and finishing the latest stack of incomplete status reports.

The first one sounds a lot better.

There was another reason Reyes liked to watch his people at work. It helped to ease his mind, particularly when he received a report or other news that was troubling, and about which he was powerless to do anything, such as what he now confronted.

"Any updates from the *Sagittarius*?" he asked, looking away from the screens to regard Lieutenant Judy Dunbar, the station's senior communications officer, who sat at one of the eight workstations set into the octagonal conference table situated at the center of the supervisor's deck. Nicknamed "the Hub," it was from here that nearly every aspect of the station's operation was overseen and directed.

Dunbar shook her head. "Not since their last message from this morning, sir."

Reyes had with mounting concern reviewed the transcript of the message sent to Vanguard by the *Sagittarius*'s captain. It was troubling that the Klingons had taken an interest in Traelus II, a planet in a system located on the opposite side of the Taurus Reach from Klingon territory. There were dozens of star systems between Traelus and the Empire's borders, and yet someone in their leadership had seen fit to send a scout vessel to investigate that planet and, presumably, the vast mineral storehouse it was now known to contain. Even more worrisome was the aggressive stance they had taken against the *Sagittarius,* which now was recovering from damage sustained during a brief skirmish with the Klingon ship. Though Adelard Nassir had made it a point to offer reassurances that his vessel should be repaired and moved away from the system before the Klingons sent reinforcements, Reyes still did not like being unable to send another starship to provide backup. The *Endeavour* was still en route to the station, and no other vessels in the vicinity were in range to be dispatched to the Traelus system in anything less than three days. For all intents and purposes, the *Sagittarius* and its crew were on their own.

Damn it, he thought. *To hell.*

"We're going to a lot of trouble dropping subspace relays all over the place," Reyes said after a moment. "I want them put to work. I want regular updates from the *Sagittarius,* even if they don't have anything new to report."

Dunbar replied, "Aye, sir," before returning her attention to her workstation.

The sound of footsteps on the stairs leading up from the ops center's main deck made Reyes turn to see Captain Rana Desai ascending into view. Her ubiquitous data slate was in her right hand, and the expression on her face told Reyes she was here on business.

"Uh-oh," he said, offering a small smile. "I know that look. To what do I owe the pleasure, Captain?"

Holding up her data slate, Desai said, "If you have a moment, Commodore, I have a question about a message I received from one of the civilian ships making requests to dock."

Reyes's eyes narrowed. Knowing that Desai would not bother him with matters that had not caused anyone problems or inconvenience, he figured he knew to which vessel the captain was referring. "Let me guess: the *Omari-Ekon*."

"That's right, sir," Desai replied. "You refused their request to dock at the station."

"Imagine that," Reyes said.

Desai added, "You discriminated against a civilian vessel, Commodore."

"Calling the *Omari-Ekon* a civilian vessel is something of a misnomer, Captain," Reyes said. "We're still talking about an Orion ship, right?"

Nodding, Desai replied, "Yes, sir, but as you know, the Orions officially have declared themselves a neutral body."

"Yeah," Reyes countered, "and if you pull on my other leg, it plays the Starfleet Hymn. We're talking about Orions, Captain. Pirates. Gunrunners. Slave runners. Gambling, prostitution, controlled and banned substances. They're a threat to the security of this station."

Desai said, "I'm not suggesting we allow any of that aboard the station, sir, but under current laws and treaties, any civilian merchant vessel from anyone who hasn't been officially declared an enemy has a right to dock or make port at any Starfleet facility that welcomes such traffic, so long as its crew is willing to abide by all applicable rules and regulations. Has the *Omari-Ekon* provided any evidence or other reason to suspect they're not willing to do that?"

"Are you seriously suggesting that I allow an Orion vessel to make port here?" Reyes asked, frowning.

"So long as they've committed no crime," Desai said, "that is precisely what I'm suggesting. Once they're here, if they get out of line, you're free to rescind their authorization to dock, but you cannot do so preemptively."

Glancing at the data slate in her hand, Reyes asked, "I suppose you're able to provide the proper legal and procedural references to support this?"

"Yes, sir," Desai replied. "I am."

Reyes released a deep sigh. "Assuming I agree with whatever precedent you can pull out of that thing, I want there to be no mistake about what they can and can't do while they're here."

"What about our people?" Dunbar asked, looking up again from her station. "Is the ship off limits to station personnel?"

Desai replied, "Declaring it off limits probably wouldn't send a very nice signal to the Orion government, or our own."

"But it'd make my life a hell of a lot easier," Reyes said, making his way around the Hub. He started down the stairs, gesturing for Desai to follow him.

"That's another thing," she continued. "The ship is sovereign Orion territory, so we'd have no jurisdiction there. Essentially, whatever happens there stays there."

Grunting in irritation, Reyes stepped off the stairs and began heading toward his office. "If this is your best sales pitch, Captain, you're not doing a very good job of convincing me." Crossing the ops center main deck, he entered the area designated as his outer office and assigned to his still-nonexistent assistant. "Okay, so the regs say we have to let them dock, at least until such time as they give us reason to boot their asses off. Fine, but here's how we're going to play it: I want every member of the station's crew briefed on what's expected so far as their own conduct is concerned, and I want that ship's captain told in no uncertain terms that if any of our people encounter any trouble there, I'll place it off limits until such time as I rescind their authorization to be here in the first place. Fair enough?"

Desai nodded. "I'll make the formal response a bit more diplomatic than that, sir, but otherwise I think that's more than fair."

Lowering his voice, Reyes added, "There's one other condition."

Her expression turning to one of confusion, the JAG captain asked, "What's that?"

Reyes paused, looking around to make sure none of the ops center staff might overhear him. "Have dinner with me."

The blunt statement seemed to take Desai by surprise, if the look on her face was any indication. "I beg your pardon, sir?"

"You, me, dinner," Reyes said. "Nothing fancy. Just a quiet meal away from all of this." He gestured toward the ops center. "It can be a bit overwhelming, and I like to get away from it at least for a little while every day." It was not like him to be so forward, but there was something about Rana Desai that fascinated him. He also considered whatever perceptions might be held by members of his crew if and when they observed him and Desai interacting in a social setting, but he decided there was no reason to worry. He was only talking about a simple dinner in the officers' mess.

For the moment, anyway. It was an addendum that surprised even him.

Despite her apparent determination to maintain her bearing, Desai eventually smiled, her features relaxing as she nodded. "Invitation accepted."

"In that case," Reyes said, "bring on the Orions."

T'Prynn sat in her office, staring at her computer monitor and the distressing information displayed on it. After careful review and examination of the data she had been compiling for the past several weeks, she had finally come to the point where only one conclusion could be reached.

Starbase 47 was harboring a spy. Of that much, T'Prynn was certain.

What remained a mystery, despite her best efforts to this point, was the identity of the clandestine operative, or even if there was more than one. She did not know to whom the agent pledged loyalty, or if he or she was simply a hired mercenary with no allegiances beyond the monetary.

Most distressing.

Discovering proof of covert activity had proven a challenge even for T'Prynn's formidable investigative talents, in itself another issue that gave her cause for concern. The spy was well trained and quite adept at concealment. The search protocols T'Prynn had created to monitor the station's main computer and communications systems had been working for weeks, hunting for references to any of the numerous key words and phrases she had included as search criteria. Additional **algorithms** had been deployed to look for signs of encryption, or **even** messages that appeared to contain nonsensical passages, which of course might indicate a low-level form of encoding designed to thwart attempts at eavesdropping. Every correspondence transmitted to and from the station, no matter its contents, was subjected to the audit. Even though other parties might balk at this infringement of their privacy, for T'Prynn the measures were both prudent and logical so far as maintaining the starbase's operational security was concerned. Safeguarding the truth behind Operation Vanguard was her paramount concern, and the station's presence in the Taurus Reach, situated as it was between two contentious Federation adversaries, invited all manner of clandestine activities. She had decided from the moment she undertook this assignment that she would make use of any and all resources and methods at her disposal—ethical and otherwise—to carry out that duty.

Despite the effort T'Prynn had expended in the development of the various search routines, she did not expect any of them to yield any tangible results. Any spy of worth would avoid such obvious routes for passing information, electing instead to utilize some other surreptitious means to contact a superior or to receive instructions. It was therefore surprising when one of her watchdog programs did in fact find something.

Her program had detected a single message, divided into multiple data packets that in turn were embedded within other messages transmitted from the station more than three weeks earlier. To the casual reviewer, such information components could easily be dismissed or mistakenly viewed as portions of the communiqués in which they were inserted. Only by piecing together several of the packets did a pattern emerge, and even then it was but a portion of the entire message. While the search program reported finding more than two dozen such data fragments, its findings remained incomplete. As for the segments that had been discovered, they of course were written in some form of code, which T'Prynn was faced with attempting to translate. It had taken her in excess of six hours to decipher enough of the message that her suspicions could be confirmed: someone was reporting on the station's activities to what remained an unknown benefactor, though examination of other data fragments was leading T'Prynn to conclude that the recipient of this information either was a Klingon, or someone working for the Empire.

A logical development.

That concession was only strengthened upon her decrypting a partial reference to the *U.S.S. Sagittarius* and its current assignment to reconnoiter the Traelus system. The Klingon Empire's seemingly sudden interest in that system now made sense, as did the *Sagittarius*'s running afoul of a Klingon scout vessel while carrying out its survey mission. Other segments T'Prynn had reviewed appeared to contain references to the movements of other Starfleet and civilian vessels between Vanguard and destinations throughout the Taurus Reach. Even information collected by the station's long-range sensors with respect to Tholian ships passing through the region was mentioned. The amount of intelligence this agent was able to gather was as impressive as it was disconcerting.

Despite what she had found, T'Prynn had not yet discovered anything that might be construed as a reference to the Taurus Meta-Genome. This was encouraging, especially if the Klingons indeed were the ones benefiting from the efforts of a covert operative. Still, if the Empire succeeded in establishing footholds on worlds known to harbor samples of the complex, artificially engineered DNA strand—or, perhaps, other artifacts or evidence of the unknown race responsible for creating it—Starfleet's mission to contain the secrets surrounding Operation Vanguard would be jeopardized.

That is not your concern now, T'Prynn reminded herself. Her immediate priority was tracking down the spy and ending his or her clandestine activities before such efforts could undermine or even expose Starbase 47's mission.

And what will you do to achieve that goal?
Whatever was necessary, T'Prynn decided.

7

The door to Captain Nassir's quarters slid aside and Clark Terrell entered the cramped room to find the *Sagittarius*'s commanding officer lying on his bunk, his booted feet resting atop a folded field jacket as he held a data slate before his face. The glow of the device's compact display screen illuminated the captain's features, making him appear gaunt and pale. As Terrell stepped into the room, Nassir dropped the data slate onto his chest, but did not rise from the bunk.

"You sent for me, Skipper?" Terrell asked by way of introduction. Then, taking an extra moment to study Nassir's face, he added, "Are you okay? You look tired."

Nassir waited until his door shut before answering, "You sound like Ilucci an hour ago." Closing his eyes, he reached with both hands to rub his temples. "I was helping him with repairs to the warp engines, but then Theriault alerted me about her latest report on the sample you two retrieved." He did not have to offer any clarification for Terrell to understand that the captain was referring to the meta-genome. "According to her preliminary findings, the sample possesses several properties that are identical to what was found on Ravanar."

"Really?" Terrell asked, his curiosity piqued.

Shrugging, Nassir replied, "It also contains elements that look to be unique to Traelus II, but Theriault's report shows a definite match to other aspects. Whoever put it there also placed it on Ravanar and who knows how many other worlds, thousands of years ago."

Terrell shook his head as he moved to sit in the small, straight-backed chair situated before the equally diminutive desk that jutted out from the bulkhead next to the captain's bunk. "Any ideas on what that might mean?"

"Only that whoever was responsible," Nassir said, "their level of scientific advancement had to be extraordinary. I mean, I know we've already been theorizing along those lines for a while now, but it's still incredible to consider what we may really be talking about here. Any civilization capable of creating that meta-genome, no matter what its purpose might have been, would have about as much in common with us as we do with a colony of ants."

Nodding, Terrell chuckled. This was not the first time a discussion along these lines had been held, of course. "And I'm going to ask the same question I always ask: Where are they? What happened to them? Did they die out because of some natural disaster, or were they conquered by someone even more powerful than they were? And if *that's* the case, then where are *those* people?"

"That's the fun part, Clark," Nassir said, offering a wide grin. "Sooner or later, we're going to find something else, something more substantial that can tell us about these people. I can't wait for that day."

Terrell laughed again, unable to resist the infectious enthusiasm with which his captain approached the exploration aspects of Starfleet's charter. "You really are in the wrong line of work, you know."

Sighing, Nassir waved away the suggestion. "Except for days like today, I wouldn't trade this job for anything." Reaching for the data slate on his chest and laying it beside him on the bed, he rose from the bunk and stretched his back muscles. "Enough goofing off. I'm going back to engineering to help Ilucci."

That idea was interrupted by the telltale beep of the ship's intercom, and the voice of Bridget McLellan. *"Captain Nassir, please come to the bridge, sir."*

Without bothering to respond to the call, Nassir exited his quarters and made the transit to the bridge in seconds, with Terrell following on his heels. No sooner did the two men enter the

Sagittarius's nerve center than McLellan turned from the tactical station to face them, her expression one of concern.

"What is it, Bridy Mac?" Nassir asked.

Nodding toward the main viewscreen, which at the moment depicted the desiccated, pockmarked landscape of the desert region in which the *Sagittarius* had sought temporary refuge on the surface of Traelus II, the second officer replied, "Long-range sensors just picked up a contact, Skipper. Hard to tell unless we move out into the open, but I'm thinking we might be looking at a Klingon battle cruiser."

"Well, that was predictable," Terrell said before looking to Nassir. "What do you think? Get a better look?"

Standing with his arms crossed behind McLellan, the captain did not say anything for a moment, but Terrell could guess what the other man was thinking. As a precaution and after Ensign Theriault had provided a comprehensive sensor scan of Traelus II and its two moons, Nassir had ordered Lieutenant zh'Firro to guide the *Sagittarius* toward the largest continent of the planet's southern hemisphere. Scans of that area showed it to contain vast quantities of thallium and other minerals that were capable of disrupting sensor scans. Once there, the ship had soft-landed near one of the larger deposits of thallium, allowing the massive storehouse of untapped ore to act as a rudimentary yet still effective camouflage screen. The trade-off was that while here, the ship's own sensor array was to a large degree compromised, as well, but it had been Nassir's hope that the admittedly feeble protection might still work long enough for Master Chief Ilucci and his engineers to finish repairs to the ship's warp drive.

Our luck might be running out, Terrell mused.

"Theriault, how long do you need to get a decent reading?" Nassir asked.

Seated at the science station, Ensign Theriault replied, "Ten to fifteen seconds should be good enough for a decent snapshot, sir. About double that, if you want a full readout. Any more than that and they might be able to pinpoint our position."

Nodding in approval, Nassir said, "Get us the quick picture

and anything else you can before I pull the plug." He then turned to Lieutenant zh'Firro at the helm. "Take us up to a low orbit, Sayna. Just enough to have a look around."

"Aye, sir," said the young Andorian before glancing at McLellan and nodding as the two women began to coordinate their efforts.

Terrell felt a tremor in the deck plates beneath him and sensed similar vibrations coursing across every surface of the bridge as the ship's impulse engines came on line and zh'Firro applied just enough thrust to lift the *Sagittarius* from the ground. Despite the artificial gravity and inertial damping systems, Terrell's stomach still lurched as the ship ascended toward orbit. In short order, the barren, uneven terrain displayed on the viewscreen gave way to the black of empty space, and the first officer half expected to see the screen dominated by the massive forward hull of a Klingon battle cruiser and its ominous forward disruptor array. He failed to suppress a small sigh when such an image did not appear.

Small favors, and all that.

Within seconds, Theriault's workstation began to emit a series of almost musical indicator tones as the young science officer bent over the console's hooded sensor viewer. "Definitely a Klingon ship." She paused, and Terrell saw her frown as she studied the data being relayed to her. "It's a D5, Skipper."

"D5?" McLellan repeated. "Wow. I didn't think I'd ever see one of those."

Terrell shrugged. "The Klingons have always been big on getting the most out of proven ship designs. I guess that goes double for the ships themselves." So far as he knew, the D5 class of battle cruiser had been all but replaced by the Klingon Empire more than a decade ago in favor of the larger, faster, and more powerful D6 and D7 designs. That such older ships were still in service—or had been returned to service—might itself be an interesting clue to the present status of the Klingon military apparatus.

Doesn't make them any less nasty when the shooting starts.

"Any sign they've spotted us?" Nassir asked.

Theriault shook her head. "Not that I can tell, sir."

"Okay, then," the captain said. "Let's not press our luck. Take us back down, Sayna." As zh'Firro set about returning the *Sagittarius* to its makeshift refuge, Nassir turned to regard Terrell. "It seems the Klingons are serious about planting their flag here."

"It's a sure bet they like it for the same reasons we do," Terrell replied. "They need dilithium to feed their ships, too."

Frowning, Nassir shook his head. "Still, it's a long way from the Klingon border, and it's not as though there aren't plenty of resource-rich planets a lot closer to home. And so close to Tholian space? It's like they're hoping to provoke a reaction."

"I've never known a Klingon to turn away from a good fight," Terrell said, "but even they usually have a plan. If they're here, they've got a reason." Whether that reason had anything to do with the Taurus Meta-Genome, he could not say, though the notion of the Klingons attempting to acquire knowledge of the mysterious alien DNA and all it represented was not one that provided him comfort.

The sound of the ship's engines changing pitch made both men turn toward the viewscreen, and they were treated to another exhibition of zh'Firro's piloting skills as the *Sagittarius* settled once more on the surface of Traelus II. Dust from the ship's maneuvering thrusters billowed up from the ground, obscuring the view depicted on the screen by the vessel's array of imaging sensors. A moment later zh'Firro cut the engine power and the hum of the impulse drive faded.

"Nice driving, Sayna," Nassir said before turning back to Terrell. "We need to call home and tell them what's going on."

Terrell released a small, humorless chuckle. "Well, until our friends out there decide to go looking somewhere else for something to do, or Ilucci gets the warp drive back on line, we're not talking to anyone. Any ideas?"

Moving to sit in the command chair, Nassir replied, "Unless someone has a warp-capable carrier pigeon handy, for now we wait."

"What about when it's time to leave?" zh'Firro asked, turning

from her console. "We can't sit on top of a thallium deposit forever, after all. Sooner or later, they will find us."

Terrell started to reply, but stopped when he noted Theriault
sitting quietly at her station, a thoughtful expression on her face.
Then, her expression changed, and a mischievous grin graced her
delicate features.

"What?" Terrell asked, confused.

Without responding, the ensign turned back to her station and
began to key instructions on the array of controls before her. As a
pair of the console's display screens began to scroll data in response to her queries, her smile only broadened.

"I think I've got an idea."

8

Though Starbase 47's officers' club had been open and available
for use by the station's crew for several weeks, it was only the
second time T'Prynn had seen fit to visit the facility. Unlike her
human colleagues, she did not find the club—with music broadcast over the intercom system to accompany the numerous conversations taking place around the room—conducive to any form
of real rest or relaxation. She instead preferred the tranquillity
and solitude of her quarters. Failing that, there was the station's
gymnasium, which often was largely unoccupied during gamma
shift, midnight to 0800 hours.

The club's atmosphere two hours prior to the start of gamma
shift was anything but quiet. The overhead lighting had been ex-
tinguished in favor of rows of recessed track lighting along the
walls near the ceiling, and small lamps on each of the tables as
well as various points along the bar. A quick visual inspection
told T'Prynn that most of the seats at the bar as well as the tables
and booths scattered around the room were occupied, either by
off-duty Starfleet personnel or members of the station's civilian

contingent, who had been provided with club access privileges by Commodore Reyes until such time as the various restaurants and taverns located in Stars Landing were open for business. Moving around several tables and their patrons, T'Prynn looked for the commodore but did not see him, nor did she see any other member of the starbase's senior staff. Ambassador Jetanien was present, seated alone at a secluded booth in the room's far corner, his attention focused on whatever meal he had ordered as well as one of three data slates arrayed on the table before him. She was thankful for the ambassador's choice to dine alone rather than sharing the company of his subordinates—and one subordinate in particular: Anna Sandesjo.

None of the other chairs at the young woman's table were occupied, and T'Prynn watched Sandesjo for several moments as first a Starfleet lieutenant and then a civilian—both males—approached her table and inquired about joining her or perhaps asking her if she wanted a drink. A data slate sat on the table near Sandesjo's right hand, along with a glass filled to the halfway mark with a clear liquid. She did not drink from it during the few minutes T'Prynn observed her interactions with her would-be suitors, both of whom she rebuffed with what appeared to be practiced ease and poise. T'Prynn surmised that this was the sort of situation the ambassador's aide encountered on all too frequent occasions. It therefore prompted the question why Sandesjo would come to a place like this, knowing she would encounter unwanted attention from prospective companions.

Perhaps she simply awaits someone who conforms to specific criteria. It seemed to T'Prynn a logical notion, and she decided it was a theory worth testing.

Moving from her vantage point at the front of the room, T'Prynn maneuvered around tables and patrons, offering or returning greetings as she made eye contact with a fellow officer or a civilian she recognized, until she stood before Sandesjo's table. The other woman's attention was on the data slate before her, and from watching her expression and body language T'Prynn realized that the young human knew someone had approached her.

Sandesjo was pretending to have taken no notice, and it was another five seconds before she released a small sigh and looked up from the table. When her eyes met T'Prynn's, Sandesjo's widened in surprise.

"Commander," she said, a slight stutter accompanying the first syllable.

T'Prynn nodded. "Ms. Sandesjo. It is . . . agreeable to see you again."

Smiling, Sandesjo replied, "It's good to see you, too." She gestured to the chair closest to T'Prynn. "Please, sit down."

"You're not expecting someone?" T'Prynn asked, placing her hand on the back of the chair.

Sandesjo shook her head. "I'm afraid not, though several people have tried to get me to change my mind." As T'Prynn settled into the proffered chair, the human woman asked, "May I get you something to drink?"

"You may," T'Prynn replied, sitting up straight in the chair.

A few seconds passed with the two women eyeing each other before Sandesjo's brow knit in apparent confusion and she released a small chuckle. "Well?"

Maintaining her impassive expression, T'Prynn asked, "Yes?"

"I asked if you wanted something to drink," Sandesjo said, her eyes beginning to glance past T'Prynn.

The Vulcan shook her head. "No, you asked if you could offer me something to drink. I merely granted your request." Why was she acting this way? T'Prynn knew that her verbal wordplay might be seen by the other woman as being critical of her grammar, but at the same time she found she could not resist the gentle teasing afforded by the exercise.

Sandesjo's mouth curled into a small, hesitant smile, and her green eyes bored into T'Prynn's. "Would you like something to drink?"

"No," T'Prynn said, and when she spoke this time she arched her right eyebrow, and Sandesjo was unable to stifle a louder laugh.

"Commander," the aide said, "if I didn't know better, I'd say you were flirting with me, but I didn't think Vulcans flirted."

Pausing to consider her answer, T'Prynn replied, "Vulcans do not engage in the activity with the same proclivity as humans, but we recognize it as a desirable means of discourse with a potential companion." Having observed the behavior in her human friends over the years, she felt as though she understood how to employ the conversational tactic effectively.

Her blunt remark seemed to catch Sandesjo by surprise, and she blinked several times before offering a response. Then, leaning forward so that her elbows rested atop the table, she regarded T'Prynn with a bold, unflinching gaze. "Is that what we are? Potential companions?"

"There are always possibilities," T'Prynn said. For the first time since entering the officers' club, she reconsidered the course of action she had undertaken. Getting involved in any kind of personal relationship was something she had not done since Sten's death. Given her dead fiancé's lasting effects on her psyche thanks to their frantic mind-meld in his last moments of life, T'Prynn had long been wary of further emotional entanglements with anyone. Still, this woman fascinated her for several reasons, some of which she could not describe or even identify. This of course troubled T'Prynn, given what she now knew about the young ambassadorial aide.

Anna Sandesjo was the spy she sought.

At first unwilling to believe the conclusion to which her investigation had led her, T'Prynn had rechecked the information compiled and collated by the search algorithms she had launched into the station's main computer and communications systems. On its own, the evidence she had found was largely circumstantial, revolving around the woman's occasional presence in the Federation Embassy offices at odd hours of the night, each instance of which was followed in short order by the inclusion of the encrypted and purposely fragmented messages T'Prynn had found embedded in outgoing communications traffic. The gap of time between Sandesjo's working late hours and the inclusion of the covert messages was always less than two hours. Working backward from what she knew might still be a coincidental connection, T'Prynn had performed a thorough review of Sandesjo's background information and other personal data. The anomalies she found might be dismissed by a casual inspection as errors or oversights, but a more comprehensive analysis revealed to T'Prynn a pattern of minor, even unconnected inconsistencies, which someone skilled in counterintelligence might conclude were unavoidable gaps in an otherwise well-crafted false identity. As the recipient of the messages appeared to be someone affiliated with the Klingon Empire, T'Prynn now also had cause to wonder if Sandesjo herself might be a Klingon agent. Was she simply a traitor to the Federation, or might she be an alien—perhaps even a Klingon—surgically altered to appear human?

There may be only one way to be certain.

While it might not be enough to engage the services of the Judge Advocate General or even Starfleet Security, T'Prynn felt she had sufficient information to act on her own and determine the true nature of Anna Sandesjo's apparent clandestine activities. In order to prove her theories without alarming either Sandesjo herself or whoever might be providing her instructions and receiving her reports, T'Prynn would have to proceed with caution.

"I have to tell you," Sandesjo said, clasping her hands atop the table and looking down at her fingers as she interlaced them, "this isn't the sort of thing I do very often."

T'Prynn nodded, recognizing the attempt at erecting an emotional barrier. Sandesjo, if she was a spy, also would be leery of placing herself at risk of exposure, while at the same time endeavoring to ascertain T'Prynn's own motivations. It would require patience on T'Prynn's part if her scheme was to succeed, despite whatever personal feelings she might be experiencing toward Sandesjo.

The mission must come first. It was an unconvincing rebuke, T'Prynn decided.

"Nor is it something with which I have much familiarity," she said, sensing an opportunity to perhaps put them both at ease. "Perhaps we should 'take things slowly,' as you humans sometimes say."

Sandesjo smiled again. "Perhaps, but not *too* slowly, I hope," she said, holding T'Prynn's gaze as she spoke the words. There was no mistaking the sentiment being expressed. What T'Prynn now required was a strategy for turning this evolving situation to her advantage, and to do so without alerting Sandesjo to her true agenda. That would be a challenge, she realized, given that she could not deny her own physical attraction to this mysterious young woman, which only seemed to be amplified when considering her possible true identity and affiliations.

A challenge, indeed, but one T'Prynn welcomed.

9

Jetanien always had fancied himself rather accomplished when it came to studying and deciphering the nuances of facial expressions and body language. In particular, having lived and worked in proximity to many representatives of Earth during his long diplomatic career, he considered himself more than capable of discerning much from the way humans emoted and carried themselves.

Such proficiency was not required on this evening as he stood before Diego Reyes in the commodore's office, looking across the station commander's desk as the human rubbed his temples and offered the latest in a series of fervent wishes that he were anywhere but here on Starbase 47.

"They told me this job would be hard when they offered it to me," Reyes said, shaking his head as he reached for the cup of coffee sitting on the desk near his right hand. "But I had to be stupid and call their bluff."

Amused by his friend's penchant for self-deprecating humor,

Jetanien laughed. "On the contrary, Diego, I can think of no one offhand who I believe is as suited to this assignment. You have the perfect blend of healthy skepticism and objectivity as well as the consummate leadership skills which will be required in order to guide this mission no matter what course it ends up charting."

"Remind me to hire you if I ever need a publicist," Reyes said, pausing to sip from his coffee. "You can write all the press releases to go with the book I'll write when this is all over, assuming it ends up being a story worth telling." He reached for the computer terminal positioned at one corner of his desk and swiveled the unit so Jetanien could see its display monitor. "Take a look at this. It's a report from Starfleet Intelligence on the latest Klingon ship movements in the Taurus Reach. It seems our friends from the Empire have taken an interest in several systems besides Traelus where we've been poking around."

Studying the report displayed on the monitor, Jetanien noted that it had been coded and stamped with a top-secret Starfleet Intelligence classification, no doubt sent to Reyes under heavy encryption and intended only for his eyes as well as the small number of people who were aware of Starbase 47's true purpose in the Taurus Reach. A perusal of the systems cited in the report gave the ambassador pause.

"Typerias," he said, reading from the screen, "along with Korinar, Borzha, and Dorala." He paused before reading the last two names. "Palgrenax, and Gamma Tauri, as well?"

Reyes nodded. "I thought you'd like those."

Though the commodore had no reason to suspect as much, Jetanien in fact was not surprised to see such a list. While the first four systems were interesting with respect to their relative locations within the Taurus Reach and the possible strategic value to whoever claimed them or—in the case of the Federation—allied with any indigenous populations, the last two entries on the list were troubling for different reasons. Both the Palgrenax and Gamma Tauri systems had been surveyed first by automated reconnaissance drones, followed by more detailed examinations by the *U.S.S. Sagittarius*. Both systems harbored worlds where evidence of the Taurus Meta-Genome had been found, moving them to the top of the list for further research and exploration. However, while the planets in the Gamma Tauri system were uninhabited, one of the Palgrenax worlds was home to a preindustrial civilization. The Federation's Prime Directive was of course in full effect with respect to any Starfleet expedition to examine the planet and pursue any leads pertaining to the meta-genome. Such considerations would not be of paramount importance to the Klingon Empire should it decide to occupy the planet and press its native population into servitude.

"Do we have any reason to believe the Klingons are aware of the . . . special nature . . . of planets in the Palgrenax and Gamma Tauri systems?" Jetanien asked.

"Not yet," Reyes said, rising from his desk and taking his coffee cup with him as he made his way to the food slot at the rear of his office. He held up the empty mug for Jetanien's benefit and asked, "Care for a bowl of mud, or whatever?"

"Thank you, no," Jetanien replied, his attention still focused on the intelligence report. "Does Starfleet have any idea why the Klingons are so interested in these particular systems?"

The food slot's hatch rose to reveal the commodore's fresh cup of coffee, and Reyes retrieved it before turning back toward his desk. "So far, they seem motivated by the fact that we've shown interest in them. The problem with that theory is that no one can figure out how the Klingons even knew we were giving some of those systems a once-over. Palgrenax is pretty far off the beaten path, for example. Likewise Typerias and Korinar. Even though we think a few of those might make good anchor points as we expand colonization efforts into the region, the Klingons shouldn't know that; at least, not yet." Returning to the chair behind his desk, Reyes sipped from his coffee. "If I were a more cynical person, I'd say we've got a spy somewhere in the works." He then directed his gaze back to Jetanien. "But we all know how cheery and upbeat I am. Right?"

The ambassador laughed once again at the commodore's attempt at dry humor. "That would seem a logical deduction. Does Starfleet concur?"

"They say the same thing you just did," Reyes replied, "and they also say that while it's a nice theory, without proof that's all it is."

Unfortunately, it seems your superiors are mistaken, my friend.

Jetanien had entered Reyes's office armed with the knowledge that not only was there a spy feeding information to the Klingons about Starfleet operations and ship movements within the Taurus Reach, but that this covert agent also was working right here on the station. The ambassador's surprise at this discovery was surpassed only by shock, embarrassment, and a sensation of utter betrayal upon learning that the operative was his own assistant, Anna Sandesjo. If not for the attentiveness of one of his other trusted assistants, Jetanien knew he might still be ignorant of the woman's activities. The alert aide had, while working late one evening, become aware of an unauthorized message being transmitted from the embassy offices as part of several other communiqués being dispatched from the station. Though he had no idea what he had found, the aide had brought this to Jetanien's attention, and the ambassador himself had investigated the anomaly until he found the message's creator. That the message had contained information on the movements of Starfleet vessels in the Taurus Reach, in particular those assigned to Starbase 47, was itself disturbing. Even more appalling was its apparent recipient: someone within, or at least working for, the Klingon Empire.

How could Sandesjo work alongside him for the past several months without his having the slightest inkling as to her true nature? That she was remarkably skilled in her chosen profession went without saying, but it was small comfort for Jetanien. What had he allowed to happen from within his own offices? Had he enabled Sandesjo's efforts to pass on sensitive information to her handlers, whoever they might be? The very notion infuriated him.

And yet, you've elected to keep this information to yourself.

"So," he said, eyeing Reyes, "what do we do now?"

The commodore leaned back in his chair, holding his coffee cup in both hands as his gaze shifted to the viewscreen on his wall that displayed a series of updated status reports on the station's progress toward completed construction and full operational capability. He said nothing for a moment as he studied the schematics and the scrolls of accompanying text. Finally, Reyes said, "It's obvious the Klingons are going to be an even bigger problem than we thought going into this thing. If they've got spies running around the station or even one of the other starbases, how long before they stumble across information about why we're really out here?" Shaking his head, he placed his mug on the desk. "I'm going to have T'Prynn and Lieutenant Jackson conduct another sweep of background checks on everyone on the station, and anyone who's been here since we started accepting civilians and visitors."

Jetanien nodded. "A sound strategy. I understand Mister Jackson is a capable officer." Haniff Jackson, Starbase 47's chief of security, by all accounts was well suited to the task Reyes would soon assign him. "And there can be no doubting Commander T'Prynn's investigative abilities." If anyone could learn the truth about Anna Sandesjo without the benefit of fortunate happenstance, as the ambassador had enjoyed, it would be the station's shrewd Vulcan intelligence officer. Indeed, he had seen her and Sandesjo together in the officers' club the previous evening. Armed with the knowledge he now possessed regarding his aide, Jetanien had to wonder if T'Prynn either suspected Sandesjo's identity or else had already discovered it on her own. If it was the former, then the ambassador was certain T'Prynn would find the truth in short order, but if it was the latter, then Jetanien had to wonder why she had not yet seen fit to inform Reyes about what she had learned. Might she be hiding some agenda of her own?

Interesting, that, Jetanien conceded.

"Finding a spy, if there is one, is just one of our big problems," Reyes said. "The bigger one is what, if anything, the Klingons plan to do with the information they're getting. Do they just want to screw with us, or try to claim resource-rich or strategically valuable planets before we can get to them?"

Jetanien said, "There is another aspect to this new development which also bears consideration. Should the Klingons elect to seize worlds which already are inhabited, one could argue that the Federation holds some measure of responsibility for the affected people's fates."

"Don't think I haven't thought of that," Reyes replied, shaking his head. "But you could also argue that much is true even with respect to normal exploration efforts. We've been crossing paths and butting heads with the Klingons for more than a century. How many worlds have they conquered or claimed that they might otherwise have bypassed if not for trying to counter some move on our part?" He paused, and Jetanien saw the look of resignation in the commodore's eyes as he waved a hand as though to sweep aside the question. "Those are problems for somebody way above my pay grade. I've got enough to worry about just keeping what we're doing here secret while trying not to start a war at the same time."

Nodding in agreement, Jetanien decided a change of subject was in order. "Have you heard anything more from the *Sagittarius*?" According to the last report Reyes had shared with him, Captain Nassir and his crew had sought refuge on the surface of Traelus II while effecting repairs to their damaged propulsion systems.

Reyes said, "Nothing since their last report. They went quiet when their sensors detected Klingon ships heading their way." He released a long, slow breath, his expression turning to one of concern. "I figure if we don't hear from them by the end of the day, that's the ballgame."

10

Captain Kutal was not pleased.

"Helm," he snapped. "Assume standard orbit." Sitting in his command chair at the center of the bridge aboard the Imperial Klingon cruiser *Zin'za*, he watched and listened in silence as his crew went about their various tasks, all of them doing their part to hunt for their supposed adversary. He overheard fragments of the discussion taking place in hushed tones between his first officer, Commander BelHoQ, and the *Zin'za*'s weapons officer, Lieutenant Tonar. While he could not discern everything, what Kutal could hear he did not like.

"Where is the Starfleet ship?" he asked, the words laced with mounting irritation. Though he did not turn his chair to face the tactical station, Kutal watched in his peripheral vision as Tonar stepped away from the console and stood at attention to make his report.

"Our sensors do not detect it, Captain," the lieutenant said. "I am unable to explain it."

"We're certain it did not leave the system?" Kutal asked, reaching up to stroke his beard.

"If it did," replied BelHoQ, "then they would have had to leave before we entered sensor range. We detected no such activity, though there was that momentary reading during the previous duty shift."

Kutal nodded, remembering the fleeting sensor contact that had been visible above the surface of Traelus II for mere moments before disappearing. Could that have been the Starfleet ship? It had been nearly a day since the Klingon scout vessel assigned to survey this system had encountered the Starfleet ship. Despite its gnatlike size and the significant damage it had absorbed, the vessel had managed to hold its own during the brief skirmish that ensued. While Kutal credited that to the tenacity of the ship's captain, whoever that might be, his admiration would grant the Earther or his crew no leniency. Kutal's orders on this point were explicit, in that he was to prevent the Starfleet ship from escaping the system, capture it, and retrieve any and all useful information from its computer systems. As for the ship's crew, they were expendable.

Can it be that the Council is finally ready to face our enemies in battle? The question burned in Kutal's mind, even though he knew the answer. Though Chancellor Sturka and the Klingon High Council seemed ready and eager to engage the Federation, they also appeared concerned that the Klingon fleet was not yet ready for extended offensive action against its Starfleet adversaries. Intelligence reports indicated that Starfleet vessels, in particular the armada of heavy cruisers that were the Federation's most advanced starships, were a near match in offensive capabilities for the Empire's premier battle cruisers, the D7's. That claim had been tested in battle to varying degrees, though Kutal had yet to enjoy such an occasion. He hoped that would change now that the Federation and the Empire seemed on a collision course as each power worked to increase its influence in the Gonmog Sector. Sooner or later, he predicted, a Starfleet ship would overstep its bounds and dare to challenge the Empire's efforts in this region of space, and for that, Kutal could only hope the Federation would dearly pay.

For now, however, he would have to be content with hunting lesser prey. He did not know why the High Council held so much interest as to what the Starfleet vessel and its crew might have found here, but that was not his concern. Someone else could worry about such things. Kutal preferred the straightforward mission he had been given.

"According to the reports, they suffered damage to their warp drive," he said, rising from his chair. "They would need to effect repairs before they could leave the system with any hope of evading pursuit. So, it stands to reason that they're here, somewhere." He recalled what he knew of the compact Starfleet vessel's design. "Their ship is capable of making planetfall. Perhaps they went to the surface to make repairs."

Tonar nodded. "I had considered that, sir, and have subjected the entire planet to an intensive sensor scan. I found no trace of a vessel. However, it must be reported that we detected large deposits of minerals possessing qualities that interfere with our scanners."

"It would be like a cowardly Federation *petaQ* to seek refuge in a place such as that," BelHoQ said. The burly executive officer folded his muscled arms across his broad chest. "They run and hide like pathetic animals."

Ignoring the comment, Kutal instead asked, "But that was at long range, was it not? Now that we're closer to the planet, can you not manipulate our sensors to account for the interference? I don't need a complete target lock, Lieutenant; just proof of where they are."

"I am endeavoring to do just that, Captain," Tonar replied.

"Then endeavor with greater zeal, or I shall find a new weapons officer." Turning from his subordinate, Kutal was making his way back to his seat when his helm officer, Lieutenant Qlar, looked over his shoulder, his heavy brow creased with concern.

"Captain, our navigational sensors are detecting an odd reading."

Moving to stand behind the helm officer, Kutal glowered at the array of status readings and gauges filling Qlar's console, all of them highlighted in shades of crimson. "What kind of odd reading?"

Qlar shook his head. "I don't know, sir. It's not like anything I've seen before." His massive hands drifted across the console, calling up new status reports to the workstation's bank of display screens before he pointed to one monitor. "Do you see it? There?"

"I don't understand," Kutal said, at first perplexed by the strange sensor return. "What is this thing trying to tell us?"

"According to this," Qlar replied, "there is a very small area that is immune to our sensors. No feedback whatsoever." He shook his head. "It's like a hole in space, Captain."

"Is it a threat to the ship?" BelHoQ asked.

The helm officer said, "I am unable to determine that, Commander. I'm able to confirm that there is no gravitic pull, and I cannot detect anything that might hint at an artificial power source."

"Could it be a mine?" Kutal wondered aloud. "Like the ones the Romulans used to employ in orbit around their planets, equipped with sensor-scattering field generators."

Pausing to consider the question, Qlar finally answered, "It's possible, sir."

"Let me see it," Kutal ordered, directing his attention to the viewscreen. He waited as Qlar entered the necessary commands, and the image on the screen soon shifted from empty space to a view of Traelus II. The planet was visible in the screen's upper right corner, but that was not what drew Kutal's attention. Instead, he studied what looked like a large chunk of rock drifting free in space.

"What is that?" he asked. "It looks like an asteroid."

BelHoQ said, "Our scout vessel's survey reports indicated no asteroids present in the system, Captain."

Grunting in annoyance, Kutal waved toward the screen. "Do your eyes not work, Commander? What would you call that?" The screen showed an oblong body of jagged rock, tumbling slowly as it rolled past the edge of the viewer. Qlar adjusted the picture so that the asteroid remained centered. "What's its range?"

"Seventy thousand *qell'qams,* Captain," Tonar replied. A moment later, he added, "We are close enough now that I'm detecting an energy reading from it. It's faint, but it is unmistakable." Then he turned from his console, his eyes wide with realization. "Captain!"

Kutal had already made the same deduction. "All power to weapons and shields!"

Despite the best efforts of the ship's environmental control systems to provide a comfortable room temperature—even at their current rate of reduced power—Clark Terrell felt sweat forming beneath his tunic on his chest, between his shoulder blades, and at the small of his back. Around him, the bridge of the *Sagittarius* was cloaked in almost total darkness, the only illumination being whatever was cast off by the few workstations that remained active. On the main viewscreen, which, like every other active system, was operating at less than half efficiency, lines of static crossed the image of the Klingon D5 battle cruiser that was closing to what Terrell considered a disturbingly small distance.

Anything less than a light-year is pretty damned disturbing right about now.

"Captain," he said, his voice barely a whisper. He knew there was no logical reason to keep his voice low, as sounds would not travel across the vacuum of space separating the *Sagittarius* from the Klingon vessel, but he could not help himself. "I don't think they're buying it."

From where he sat in his command chair, Captain Nassir also spoke in a low voice when he replied, "If they suspected anything, they'd have fired by now."

That was not enough to convince Terrell, who also had been the last one to buy into the crazy scheme concocted by Vanessa Theriault to provide cover for the *Sagittarius* as it lifted away from Traelus II. Once it had become obvious that Master Chief Ilucci and his engineers would not complete repairs to the warp drive systems before the Klingon cruiser's arrival at the planet, Theriault had devised a scheme to continue using the large deposit of thallium on top of which the ship had rested while on the surface. Employing the ship's phasers, Bridget McLellan had excavated a large section of the ore from where it rested in the ground beneath the *Sagittarius*, carving away pieces and fragments until what remained was a somewhat oblong, lopsided sphere. When the time came for the ship to lift off, McLellan utilized the tractor beam to haul the oversized fragment to orbit with the *Sagittarius*, holding the hunk of ore before the ship like a makeshift shield. Dealing with the fragment's mass had posed some challenges, which Theriault had overcome by reconfiguring the tractor beam emitters.

The result was a haphazard thallium shell that—according to Theriault's theory—would act to conceal the scout vessel from all but the most intensive sensor scans. Terrell had been skeptical throughout the preparation process, his doubts lingering even as the ship ascended from the surface and made its way into space.

"I don't know if this is the craziest damned thing I've ever heard of, or if you're just a genius," he said, placing a reassuring hand on Theriault's shoulder.

"I'm only a genius if it works," the science officer countered. "If it doesn't, then it's going to be a long walk home."

Terrell shrugged. "Look on the bright side. We probably won't have to worry about that."

For this ruse to work, Theriault had explained, and for the ship to appear as nothing more than a barren asteroid trapped in orbit around Traelus II, the *Sagittarius*'s power levels had been reduced to the bare minimum. All nonessential systems had been deactivated, and several other key systems also had been taken off line or else were operating in low-energy mode. The tractor beam emitters were generating just enough power to hold the thallium shell in place. Nassir had even taken the extra risk of ordering Master Chief Ilucci to power down the impulse drive, lest its telltale energy signature be detected by a sharp-eyed Klingon sensor officer. While the warp drive also posed a similar threat, there had been no choice but to leave it on line if the *Sagittarius* was to have any hope of escape. Theriault and McLellan had tried to compensate for that by positioning additional, smaller fragments of thallium in the ship's cargo bay. It was improvisational camouflage at best, though everyone aboard knew it would not have to work for very long.

It only needs to work long enough, Terrell mused.

Tapping a control on the arm of his chair, Nassir said, "Bridge to engineering. Master Chief, what's your status?"

Michael Ilucci replied, *"I can give you warp five from the jump, Skipper, but no more than that. If somebody's planning on chasing us, it's going to be a pretty short run."*

"I should've gone to law school like my mother wanted,"

Terrell said, affecting a grim smile as he shared knowing looks with Nassir. Warp five had been an optimistic estimate from the chief engineer at the start of his repair efforts, and even though he had met that goal, it would not be enough if they were forced to flee the Klingon ship. The only option was a daring, perhaps even foolhardy plan to smack the enemy vessel across the nose before trying to make a run for it.

"Klingon ship closing to two hundred thousand kilometers," McLellan reported, studying the sensor readouts on her console. "Their posture so far doesn't seem to be aggressive. No more than normal, anyway, at least so far as I can tell. They look to be on a course for standard orbit." She frowned. "The thallium's affecting our sensors, too."

"That's the trade-off," Nassir said, his voice calm and composed. Terrell nodded in agreement, as Theriault had warned them of the mineral's effects on their own scanning systems. Anything more than short-range sensors would be all but useless, which at present did not matter, given the Klingon cruiser's proximity. "Where are we in relation to them?"

Examining a readout on her console, Theriault replied, "We're just crossing the terminator, and their orbital attitude suggests they're not changing heading to come our way."

"What do we look like to their sensors?" Nassir asked.

Theriault shook her head. "Hard to say, sir. Maybe a sensor void or dead spot. The thallium will affect their sensor returns enough to distort whatever visuals are created by their imaging processors. If they get close enough, they'll be able to cut through the interference and maybe even pick up our power emissions."

"They've got to be thinking something doesn't add up," Terrell said, shaking his head. "The question is whether they come closer to investigate, or just blow us to hell from a comfortable distance."

McLellan called out, "One hundred twenty thousand kilometers. So far as I can tell, they haven't raised their shields." Terrell saw that her left hand hovered over the controls that would activate the *Sagittarius*'s deflector shields. Doing so now would all but ensure that the Klingon ship would fire on them, but if they raised their own shields before Nassir decided to act, then this entire crazy scheme would have been for nothing.

Come on. Terrell almost shouted the words. *Just a few minutes more.*

A red indicator flared to life on McLellan's board, and the tactical officer looked over her shoulder at Terrell and Nassir. "They're changing course and heading this way."

"Damn," Terrell muttered. "I knew it was too good to last."

"Look sharp, people," Nassir said, leaning forward in his chair. "We're only going to get one shot at this, if that. Stand by."

On the viewscreen, the image of the Klingon D5 cruiser solidified and took on sharper resolution, an effect of drawing closer to the *Sagittarius* and its compromised sensors. McLellan called out, "Ninety thousand kilometers and closing. Their shields are down."

"Once they cross seventy-five thousand kilometers," Theriault said, "they might be able to spot us."

Nassir nodded. "Helm, on my mark, disengage the tractor beam and maneuver us away from that rock. Bridy Mac, fire as soon as you get a clear shot. You've got your targets picked out?"

"Forward disruptor array and starboard nacelle," McLellan replied. "That's probably all we'll have time for before they raise their shields."

"Always the optimist," Nassir said.

On the screen, the Klingon ship drew ever closer, its image growing so large that it seemed ready to punch through the forward bulkhead. How much longer would deception hold out?

"Eighty thousand kilometers," McLellan said.

Nassir slapped the arm of his chair. "Now!"

At the helm, Lieutenant zh'Firro tapped a sequence of controls. "Disengaging tractor beam." The image on the viewscreen began to clear within seconds as the *Sagittarius* backed away from the massive chunk of thallium ore.

"Targeting!" McLellan called out, her own fingers a blur as they worked her console. "Firing!"

"They're raising shields!" Theriault shouted.

McLellan punched the air with her left first. "Direct hits. I missed the disruptor array, but it still tore a chunk out of the primary hull. The starboard nacelle has massive damage. I don't think they can go to warp, but they're still maneuverable at impulse speeds."

"Raise shields," Nassir ordered, his tone sharp and direct. "Sayna, initiate evasive. Keep us out of their gun sights, and stand by to go to warp."

"They're coming about," McLellan said, her fingers continuing to work. "Phasers standing by."

Nassir replied, "Let's hold off unless they don't give us another choice." Engaging the intercom once more, he said, "Engineering, are we ready?"

"Almost there, Skipper!"

Zh'Firro said, "Captain, I'm having trouble evading them. They're still pretty maneuverable."

"Not to mention three kinds of pissed," Terrell said, realizing as he spoke that his grip on the back of Theriault's chair was so tight that he was very near tearing away the upholstered material.

"They're locking weapons!" McLellan shouted.

"Fire!" Nassir snapped, and the response was immediate as the *Sagittarius* released another barrage of phaser fire. On the tactical display at McLellan's station, Terrell could see two white streaks representing the phaser beams as they crossed space to the larger crimson circle depicting the Klingon ship. The vessel's movements, along with those of the *Sagittarius,* were such that both salvos missed their mark.

"Damn it!" McLellan hissed through gritted teeth. "They're firing!"

Even before Nassir could order evasive action, zh'Firro was reacting, guiding the ship away from danger as she used the *Sagittarius*'s smaller stature to her advantage. Terrell, his attention divided between the main viewer and McLellan's tactical display, could only watch as zh'Firro maneuvered the ship back toward its Klingon adversary.

"Whatever Ilucci's going to do," Terrell said, "he'd better do it now."

"Engineering!" Nassir snapped.

"Go!" shouted Ilucci through the intercom.

Her fingers moving in frantic fashion across her console, zh'Firro executed a final evasive maneuver, dropping the *Sagittarius* beneath the Klingon cruiser. Terrell was certain he could count rivets securing hull plates on the enemy vessel before it vanished from view an instant before those stars that were visible stretched, contorted, and extended into infinity as the ship leaped to warp.

"No sign of pursuit," McLellan said after a moment. "Looks like we're in the clear."

Feeling the tension leave his body, Terrell uttered an audible sigh of relief. "A lawyer, my mother said. Or a doctor. I could've been a doctor."

The comment had its intended effect, with everyone on the bridge laughing, smiling, or shaking their heads in disbelief.

"Hello?" Ilucci said over the still-open intercom frequency. *"Is it over?"*

Nassir leaned back in his chair, wiping sweat from his brow. "Yes, Master Chief, it's over. Well done, if a little late."

"Everyone's a critic," the engineer replied before the connection was severed.

Chuckling at that, Nassir cleared his throat and straightened in his seat. "All right, Sayna. Since it appears we haven't flown into a planet, star, or other interstellar obstacle, please plot us a course back to Vanguard."

"Already laid in, sir," the young Andorian replied.

"That was some nice flying," McLellan said, reaching over to pat the helm officer on the arm.

"Nice job all around," Terrell added. "Take the rest of the day off." Reaching over once more, he tapped Theriault on the shoulder. "That goes double for you."

The ensign smiled. "Thank you, Commander."

Turning to face Nassir, Terrell asked, "What now?"

Shrugging, the captain replied, "Reports to file, repairs to finish, miles to go before we sleep, and all that." He indicated the viewscreen and its view of warp-distorted space. "We got lucky today, but you and I both know this is only the beginning. The Klingons are in the Taurus Reach to stay. Tomorrow could be a whole other fight."

It was a sobering thought, but not an inaccurate one. If the Klingons were willing to act with aggression in order to claim Traelus II, there would be no stopping them if and when they found another planet of even greater value, and if that world happened to harbor a key to the mystery of the Taurus Meta-Genome, then the Federation's problems would only worsen.

"Tomorrow," he said, echoing Nassir's comment.

Nassir nodded. "Count on it."

11

T'Prynn waited precisely ten seconds after pressing the call button that would announce her presence to the occupant of the room behind the door she now faced. When there was no response, she reached for the small, recessed keypad set into the door frame and again tapped the control. Her acute hearing was able to detect faint sounds of movement beyond the door, as though the person inside was in the midst of making the room presentable for a visitor. T'Prynn heard footsteps moving in her direction, and a moment later the door slid aside to reveal Anna Sandesjo, dressed in a blue silk robe that left exposed her forearms and her legs below her thighs. Her red hair was dark and damp, and there were droplets of water on her exposed skin, suggesting that the woman had just emerged from her shower, or that T'Prynn perhaps had interrupted that activity.

"Good morning," Sandesjo offered, her fleeting look of uncertainty upon first seeing T'Prynn now replaced with the hint of a smile playing at the corners of her mouth. "This is a pleasant surprise. Miss me that much already?"

T'Prynn's right eyebrow arched as she regarded the other woman. "Indeed. Following our conversation last evening, and after spending the balance of the ensuing hours immersed in my work, I concluded that enough time had elapsed since our previous meeting."

Her smile broadening, Sandesjo released a small laugh. "You have a funny way of putting things. So what you're saying is that you just couldn't wait to see me again?" She stepped back from the door and gestured for T'Prynn to enter her quarters.

"I certainly could have elected to wait a longer interval before calling on you," T'Prynn replied as she entered the room. "However, I saw no reason to do so, and in fact, the thought of seeing you again this evening is pleasing to me."

In truth, since leaving Sandesjo at the officers' club the previous evening, T'Prynn had spent the ensuing hours considering her options. There was a pressing need to expose the scope of Anna Sandesjo's activities and perhaps even the identity of her superiors and anyone else who might be receiving the information she passed. An obvious secondary goal was to determine what other sensitive data Sandesjo might have disseminated before T'Prynn's investigation led her to the covert operative.

Combating that line of reasoning was the simple fact that T'Prynn could not stop thinking about Anna Sandesjo, the woman. She recalled the way her eyes gazed upon her during their time together in the officers' club, the way her mouth moved when she talked in her low voice, and how her hands caressed the glass she held. Even her scent, enhanced to the slightest degree by the perfume she had worn, seemed to linger.

T'Prynn wanted more.

She followed Sandesjo into the main room of the woman's quarters. While anyone living on Vanguard had the option of furnishing their personal living spaces with whatever items they might have brought with them from their homeworld or previous assignment, Anna Sandesjo seemed content with what T'Prynn recognized as standard-issue furnishings available from the station quartermaster for civilian billeting spaces. While some of the shelves contained books, plants, or generic sculptures of the sort one might find in a physician's waiting room, no photographs of relatives or other loved ones were visible, nor was there anything that might be construed as a personal memento. The only evidence that someone lived here was a few items of clothing strewn about—a jacket on a hook near the door, a blouse draped over the back of a desk chair, a pair of shoes near the sofa. Other, unidentified clothing lay across the bed, which was just visible through an open doorway at the rear of the room, and a slim, silver briefcase sat on the floor next to the desk positioned before the wall to T'Prynn's right. A cup and saucer sat atop the small dining table in the near corner, and the faint odor of tea drifted to her nostrils.

"Would you like something to drink?" Sandesjo said, making her way to the food slot set into the wall behind the dining table. "I made myself some tea."

T'Prynn.

The voice, Sten's, clawed once more from the depths of her mind, interrupting her before she could reply to Sandesjo's offer. It required sheer force of will for T'Prynn not to show any outward reaction to the abrupt intrusion. "Tea would be agreeable," she said, feeling the strain with each word as she labored to maintain her normal stoic façade.

Why must you torment me at every turn? Her mind hurled the question at the dark mass she could sense moving to envelop her consciousness.

I will never stop, Sten chided her. *Not until you submit. You belong to me.*

T'Prynn felt the muscles in her face twitch as she fought to retain emotional control. Sandesjo, facing the food slot, was not privy to her inner turmoil, which threatened to erupt at any moment. *I belong to no one, least of all you.*

You will never be free of me, Sten said, each word a hammer blow to the inside of her skull. *Eventually, you will relent. I have eternity on my side.*

Then you will spend eternity in the grips of frustration and defeat, T'Prynn countered, *just as you were when I killed you.*

The food slot's door slid upward, revealing a cup sitting atop a saucer and filled with a steaming beverage. Sandesjo retrieved it before turning and setting it on the table near the chair opposite the one before which her own tea sat. Seeing T'Prynn staring at her, she smiled again.

"Join me?" she asked.

Submit, Sten challenged, as he had each day for decades.

Never.

Sandesjo's smile seemed to have a calming effect, and for a moment T'Prynn thought that Sten might have returned to the darkness from which he had come. Instead, a soothing warmth seemed to be growing from deep within her, radiating outward to suffuse her entire body.

Ignoring the tea, T'Prynn stepped around the table and without another word reached for Sandesjo, drawing her close. Her hand found the back of the other woman's neck and she brought her forward until their lips crushed together and she forced her tongue into Sandesjo's mouth. Her free hand slid between the folds of Sandesjo's robe, pushing past the smooth silk to find the warm, damp skin beneath. She felt hands on her own body, searching for the closures to her uniform, and then there was the touch of fingertips against her own skin. Their kiss remained unbroken and Sandesjo uttered a low moan of desire as T'Prynn's hands pushed the robe from her shoulders before continuing their frenetic wanderings.

It was not until she sensed herself falling forward that T'Prynn realized she must have lifted Sandesjo off her feet and carried her to the bed in the other room. Sandesjo landed first, on her back, and T'Prynn allowed the weight of her own body to press down upon her. Hands roamed as if possessed of their own will, and T'Prynn sighed with unrepentant lust as Sandesjo freed her from the last remnants of her uniform. T'Prynn pushed herself to a sitting position, straddling Sandesjo's hips. She looked down at her lover, their eyes locking in mutual fervor before she felt hands on her stomach, moving lower as fingers searched, driven by ardor. T'Prynn moved her hands across Sandesjo's chest, feeling skin bristle beneath her touch. With the lightest of strokes she traced the curves of the other woman's neck and the sides of her face. In response to her touch, T'Prynn began to sense hints of images and emotions which were not her own.

T'Prynn?

Hearing Sandesjo's confused query blending with her own thoughts, T'Prynn did not press her innocuous mental probe any further. For Vulcans, initiating a mind-meld without the consent of the other involved party was considered to be among the most severe breaches of etiquette. Children learning to control their telepathic abilities were taught never to attempt such a nonconsensual bonding, and that the privacy of one's own thoughts was inviolable except in the most desperate of circumstances.

The momentary telepathic connection faded, and T'Prynn's attention returned to the body beneath her. Sandesjo pulled her down onto her, pressing their mouths together, and T'Prynn felt the other woman's tongue pushing past her lips.

T'Prynn.

She had hoped that any physical activities she pursued with Sandesjo might bring with them some fleeting psionic contact which might offer some insights into the woman's true identity. Even with that goal in mind, T'Prynn was reluctant to push such mental connection. As the unwilling recipient of a forced mind-meld, she was sensitive to the potential for damage such an act posed for the person on whom the unwanted contact was inflicted. That risk increased when the other party was nontelepathic, as T'Prynn believed Sandesjo to be.

My mind to your mind.

The words rang in T'Prynn's consciousness, and it took her an extra moment to realize that they had not come from her or Sandesjo.

No!

Without her conscious control, T'Prynn's hands moved to Sandesjo's face; to where *katra* points would be on a Vulcan. She felt the pressure of her fingers against Sandesjo's skin as the other woman's eyes widened in confusion and fear.

My mind to your mind.

Sten! No!

T'Prynn sensed Sandesjo's body jerk beneath her just as she felt her own legs wrapping around those of her would-be lover. Her body weight was pinning Sandesjo to the bed, and T'Prynn held her head between her outstretched fingers as Sten's mocking voice echoed in her mind.

Our minds are merging.

Their naked bodies were intertwined, their faces centimeters apart, and T'Prynn read the anger and betrayal in Sandesjo's eyes. From the depths of her consciousness, T'Prynn heard Sten's simple statement of victory.

Our minds are one.

The meld took hold and Sandesjo's expression went slack, and T'Prynn was gripped by the sensation of falling through darkness. That gloom just as quickly faded and she found herself standing in a small, dimly lit room. A mirror, dirty and scratched, hung on a stone wall before her, and when she looked at it she was greeted by the reflection of a Klingon female, her long dark hair flowing past her shoulders and accentuating the line of prominent ridges extending from the bridge of her nose up and over the back of her head.

I am Lurqal. I am Klingon, a servant of the Empire.

Everything disappeared in an explosion of pain, and T'Prynn could only stand and watch as her Klingon reflection morphed, her features cut, stretched, and reshaped. The ridges dominating her forehead melted, replaced with lighter, smoother skin. Her hair grew shorter and lightened in color, framing a new face, that of a beautiful young human female, which now stared at her from within the mirror.

Anna Sandesjo.

• • •

Get out of my head!

Sandesjo tumbled to the sand, feeling the weight of her opponent crashing down upon her. His breath was in her face, hot and pungent with the stench of unchecked anger. One hand clenched into a fist and he brought it down, smashing the side of her head. She lashed out, hearing his grunt of pain as the edge of her hand struck his face.

We are one, T'Prynn.

Where was she? How had she gotten here? All around her was sand, surrounded by ornate stone pillars. Somewhere out of her line of sight, someone beat drums in a rhythmic cadence, the tempo increasing with each passing moment. Sandesjo had never seen this place, and yet there was a familiarity she could not understand, just as she knew her opponent and the unrestrained desires which now guided him.

You are mine.

No!

Sandesjo struck out once more, her fists pummeling Sten's chest. He ignored her attacks, his hands reaching to grasp her head so that he might pull her to him. Placing her hands on his chest, Sandesjo pushed back from him, but she was pinned to the sand, unable to move. Sten leaned closer, his face filling her vision.

Reaching up, Sandesjo felt her hands tighten around Sten's throat. Even as her fingers dug into his skin, Sten pressed closer, his eyes burning with unrelenting need.

Submit.

The word pounded against Sandesjo's consciousness as she twisted her hands, feeling Sten's neck snap.

Never.

Unchecked emotion slammed against T'Prynn's mind, and she gasped at the ferocity of the sensations washing over her. A new heat raged within her, forcing her consciousness to retreat from the forced meld. Her fingers abandoned the contact points on Sandesjo's face, and both women cried out in simultaneous shock, their eyes opening and their gazes once more locking.

"I'm sorry," T'Prynn said, her voice low and strained. "It was not my intention to . . ."

"What . . . what was that?" Sandesjo asked, every word racked with pain as she rolled away from T'Prynn. She reached for her robe, pulling it against her body. T'Prynn said nothing, opting to sit in silence and watch as the other woman regained her composure. After a moment, Sandesjo looked up to regard her with an expression of comprehension and perhaps even acceptance. "So," she said, her breath shallow and rapid, "now you know."

T'Prynn nodded. "Yes, though it was not my intention to treat you in this manner."

"I . . . know," Sandesjo replied. "It's not your fault. It's . . . Sten. You're carrying his . . . whatever you call it?"

"His *katra*," T'Prynn said. "You would think of it as something akin to a 'living spirit.' He forced it upon me at the moment of his death. I am unable to free myself of his presence, and dealing with him can be . . . difficult." She paused, mindful of the fact that Sten's actions, unwanted and offensive though they had been, had provided her with the information she sought.

As though still aware of T'Prynn's thoughts, Sandesjo said, "Well, now you know the truth about me. What are you going to do about it?"

Pausing a moment, T'Prynn studied the other woman's face before her eyes began to wander downward across her body. "For the moment, nothing." Even as she spoke the words, she knew she could not allow this to continue. It required effort to tear her attention from the other woman and turn her head. "No, this is wrong." She moved to the edge of the bed, reaching for her discarded uniform. "I must go." She stopped as she felt Sandesjo's hand on her bare arm.

"Please stay."

Feeling shame well up within her, T'Prynn turned to see Sandesjo gazing at her, unchecked yearning in her eyes. "I don't blame you for what happened. You're even more a victim of Sten than I am." She inched closer, her hand moving from T'Prynn's arm to caress her shoulder.

T'Prynn was uncertain whether she or Sandesjo moved first, but then their mouths were once again upon each other, bodies converging in feral passion.

You are weak, T'Prynn, Sten taunted, mocking her yet again. *That is why I ultimately will triumph. Submit.*

Never.

She pushed Sten back into the depths of her mind, forcing him into the void from which she knew he soon would reemerge, driven by his unending quest to crush her consciousness with his own. T'Prynn ignored that, and him, just as she set aside the knowledge that she had found her spy. The quarry was not going anywhere, at least not right away. For now, there was only her raw, primal yearning, and the realization that her own inexplicable feelings were matched if not exceeded by what she recognized as Anna Sandesjo's unbridled adoration for her.

This would pose a problem, sooner rather than later. Of that, T'Prynn was certain.

12

Reclining in the high-backed chair that was a match for the one in his office, Reyes regarded the image of Captain Adelard Nassir displayed on the computer workstation situated in one corner of his quarters. The incoming transmission from the *Sagittarius*'s commanding officer had come at just before 2100 hours station time, well after the conclusion of his normal duty shift but not so late as to have roused him from sleep.

"Sorry to disturb you, Commodore," Nassir said, his voice sounding somewhat hollow as an effect of the data compression and encryption processes being used to push the captain's trans-

mission through however many subspace relay beacons currently separated the *Sagittarius* from Starbase 47. *"But I figured you'd want to hear from us as soon as possible."*

Reyes chuckled as he rubbed his chin, which he had last shaved nearly twenty hours previously and now once again was rough with beard stubble. "Be thankful I'm still sober and wearing pants, Captain. It's been a long day, but not so long as the last couple you've had. My compliments to your crew. That's quite a talented bunch you have working for you."

On the screen, Nassir nodded. *"For which I'm eternally grateful, Commodore."* He then offered a wry grin. *"You'll be happy to know that Ensign Theriault is insufferably pleased with herself. The way things are going, there might not be enough room aboard ship to contain her ego."*

"Let her have this one," Reyes replied. "Anybody who could pull off that stunt has to be good, or at least damned lucky, and sometimes that's all you need." He had read with fascination and no small amount of amusement the ingenious sensor tactic Theriault had employed in order to evade the *Sagittarius*'s Klingon pursuers while escaping from Traelus II. "Tell her the first round's on me once you make port."

Smiling, Nassir said, *"She'll be only too happy to collect."* The captain's expression then turned serious. *"I trust you've had time to review our other reports?"*

"Yes," Reyes replied. "They definitely make for interesting reading. The science teams here can't stop talking about them." That he found it so easy to slip into a form of code when talking even over an encrypted frequency surprised him, but as he had learned in short order upon taking command of Starbase 47, such measures were necessary in order to preserve operational security. No mention of the Taurus Meta-Genome by name was allowed in verbal communications, and any references to it in written reports were made using euphemisms, where the meta-genome was referred to as a "Type V life sign." To further cement the disinformation campaign with respect to the enigmatic alien DNA, Federation and Starfleet life sciences data repositories listed that life sign as a form of primordial mold. It was true enough, given the circumstances surrounding the meta-genome's discovery two years earlier, but no further mention of its unique properties or potential origin was to be found in those publicly accessible records.

"You know how those science types can be," Nassir said. *"Theriault can't wait to get back to Traelus for more research. She thinks she's really on to something there."*

Even without the specifics, Reyes knew to what the *Sagittarius*'s captain was referring. Ensign Theriault's theory that the meta-genome samples found on Traelus II held several stark similarities to those discovered on Ravanar IV two years ago had been confirmed by one of Operation Vanguard's dedicated science teams, lending credence to the theory that the same party was responsible for depositing the complex DNA on both worlds, and likely on a still-unknown number of additional planets. Whoever created the meta-genome, if they even still existed, appeared to possess a level of technological prowess—and by extension, far greater power—than previously believed. What would life be like on a world ruled by such beings? Had they eradicated all disease and suffering? Had they learned to traverse the stars in some manner so far unimagined by even the greatest known scientific minds?

And what of any weapons they may have fashioned? Where were they, and what would be the consequences if such ghastly creations fell into the wrong hands?

That's the sort of thing that'll keep me up nights, Reyes mused.

"I'm afraid Theriault's out of luck," he said. "According to Captain Desai, the Klingon Empire did in fact make official notification through the Federation Embassy here on the station of its intent to settle on Traelus II, well before you got there."

On the viewscreen, Nassir's brow furrowed in confusion. *"How's it possible something like that was missed?"*

"Talk to Lieutenant Ballard," Reyes replied. "You know those system glitches we've been having all over the station for weeks?

The communications array looks to be just as prone to them as everything else." Starbase 47's chief engineer had assured Reyes that he and his team felt they were close to finally having a handle on the ongoing problems plaguing the station's advance toward full operational capability, but at this point the commodore remained less than convinced.

"So, we're saying we've definitely lost Traelus?" Nassir asked.

Nodding, Reyes replied, "Looks that way. The Empire's notification was in order, and after review the Diplomatic Corps and the Federation Council have agreed that there's nothing to be done. Traelus belongs to the Klingons now."

"The Tholians won't be thrilled about that," Nassir said, *"but that would've been true even if we'd gotten there first. It's awfully close to the Tholian border, and that's before you take into account how much the Tholians like to shift their territorial boundaries on a whim."*

Reyes knew it was a notion shared by many within the halls of leadership at Starfleet Command. Whereas the Federation would have been content to colonize the Traelus system—even as a cover for exploring Traelus II for further signs of the meta-genome or its creators—and leave the Tholians well enough alone, many of Starfleet's foremost tactical minds worried about what the Klingons might do in such close proximity to Tholian territory. It would not be long before the Tholian government issued some form of protest at the Empire's perceived encroachment, but how would the situation evolve or deteriorate from there?

And what if the Klingons somehow stumbled across the meta-genome, and from there discovered Starfleet's interest in it?

"Stop trying to cheer me up, Captain," Reyes said, attempting a small, humorless smile to soften the remark. "We'll have to worry about the Tholians and the Klingons another day, and Ensign Theriault will just have to find another place to play. Anything else to report?"

Nassir shook his head. *"Only that we're tired, and that some shore leave would not go unnoticed or unappreciated."*

"Duly noted," Reyes replied, tapping his fingers on his desktop. "I'll do everything I can to get you some decent downtime once you get back, mission permitting. Safe travels, Captain, and we'll see you in a couple of weeks."

Touching his right forefinger to his temple in an informal gesture of salute, Nassir said, *"Thank you, Commodore. Nassir out."* His face disappeared in a burst of static as the subspace connection was severed, after which the screen shifted to depict a condensed version of the station's current status schematic as displayed on the larger viewscreen in Reyes's office. The commodore studied it for a moment, noting the few lines of text in red that detailed systems currently being serviced by one of Lieutenant Ballard's engineering teams.

The sound of his door chime made Reyes turn toward the entrance to his quarters, and he frowned. Who would be calling on him at this hour, and in person, no less? "Come," he called out, and was surprised to see Captain Rana Desai standing at the threshold as the door slid aside, her Starfleet captain's uniform smooth and straight as though she had just donned it. Rising from his seat, Reyes glanced toward the chronometer on his desk. "Captain," he said, his confusion mounting. "I'm sorry, did we have an appointment I've forgotten about?"

Desai stepped into the room, and Reyes noted that unlike almost every other occasion on which he had seen her since that first meeting in his office, she was not carrying the data slate that seemed to be an extension of her body. "No, sir, this isn't duty-related." She paused, looking about the room before continuing, "I'm sorry, Commodore. Are you busy?"

"Not at all," Reyes said, gesturing with his hands to indicate that he was not otherwise occupied. "What can I do for you?" He heard her clear her throat, and she glanced at her hands, which were clasped before her and held near her waist.

"I . . . I just left my office," she said, "and I was wondering if you might like to join me for a late dinner?"

Unable to keep the expression of surprise from his face, Reyes replied, "That sounds great, actually. I . . . I missed dinner. Paper-work. The life of the commanding officer, and all that."

Stop babbling, you idiot.

Their first dinner had been a quiet, unassuming affair in the officers' club, and while they had maintained a professional de-meanor throughout the evening, Reyes could not help but sense that Desai had wanted something more, just as he had. Neither party acted on those apparent feelings, and their dinner con-cluded with Reyes returning to his office to catch up on review-ing backlogged reports, while Desai continued her efforts to settle into her new assignment. What Reyes wondered was whether the captain, like him, had simply sat at her desk, ignor-ing her work and ruminating on how the evening might have gone if either or both of them had chosen a different path.

Swallowing the odd lump that had formed in his throat, Reyes asked, "So, what are you hungry for?"

Desai seemed to ponder the question for a moment, and then Reyes saw her features soften before she stepped toward him. "I've decided I don't want dinner. We can talk later about what to have for breakfast." Reaching out, she grasped his head in her hands and pulled him to her.

Well, this changes some things, was the last rational thought to pass through Reyes's mind before he surrendered it and every-thing else.

13

Ambassador Jetanien had never liked waiting, despite the knowl-edge that waiting—and being able to make others wait—was a time-honored weapon in any diplomat's arsenal. He employed it himself on frequent occasions, using it as a means of informing other parties that he was in control of a given situation, and that events would evolve and progress according to his agenda and desires.

He was rather less enamored of the practice when it was utilized against him.

Holding his hands together before him, Jetanien tapped his long fingers in rhythmic fashion as he waited for the image on his desktop computer monitor to show him something else besides a spinning crimson dodecahedron superimposed upon a black background. He had been staring at it for no less than five minutes, and was sensing his patience beginning to wane.

One has to wonder if this species' apparent obsession with punctuality is a ruse.

Jetanien was almost ready to declare this venture a wasted exercise and terminate the connection when the image on the monitor shifted from stark, unmoving black to a sea of roiling blue. At the center of the image now stood an angular, crystalline silhouette, its crimson hue all but leaping through the screen. Boring into Jetanien was a pair of triangular pink eyes, the sole features on the face of the Tholian now staring at him from across dozens of light-years of interstellar space.

"I am Sesrene," the Tholian said, *"special diplomatic envoy representing the Tholian Assembly. You are Ambassador Jetanien?"*

Jetanien nodded. "Indeed I am, Ambassador. It is an honor to finally make your acquaintance. As you no doubt are aware, the Federation has for some time now been attempting to engage your government in the interests of cooperation and peace."

"You do this even as you seek to encroach upon our territory?" Sesrene asked. *"Do not think we are unaware of your aggressive expansion into the region flanking our borders. This does not seem to us to be the acts of supposed allies."*

Well versed in Tholian xenophobia, Jetanien considered Sesrene's words before replying, "Ambassador, the Federation has always demonstrated, through word and deed, restraint and respect when attempting to expand or simply explore beyond its borders. We view the sovereign claims of any civilization to be inviolable. Our surveys into the Taurus Reach are limited to worlds which harbor no indigenous populations or which are not otherwise known to have been claimed by another power. It is not the Federation with which your government needs to be concerned, sir, but rather the Klingon Empire."

On the screen, the Tholian appeared to lean closer, as though intrigued by the statement. *"We know of some efforts by the Klingons to invade the sector of space you call the Taurus Reach, but according to our latest reports, their attempts to this point have been rather limited."*

Seeing his opening, Jetanien said, "That appears to be changing, Ambassador. Indeed, the Klingon Empire has recently laid claim to a mineral-rich world in the Traelus system, which is very close to Tholian territory. It is but one of several such systems the Klingons are planning to conquer. Unlike the Federation, they are unconcerned with the welfare of anyone who might already be living there. Such people will simply become subjects of the Empire. This may expand to include allies of the Tholian Assembly."

"We will never allow such heinous acts," Sesrene warned, though the tone of his voice even as filtered through the translation software running in parallel with the subspace communications relay still betrayed surprise at what Jetanien had reported. *"Any form of military buildup in the Traelus system would provide a point from which to launch an offensive campaign into our territory. We cannot allow that to go unchallenged."*

"I am sympathetic to your concerns, Ambassador," Jetanien replied. Sensing the Tholian's skepticism, he raised a hand and added, "A Klingon invasion of your territory presents a problem for us, as well, as the Federation wants no part of the conflict which surely would result, and in which we would likely find ourselves trapped. While it's too late for us with respect to the Traelus system, we obviously would like to avoid such an incident being repeated." What he of course did not say was that he was still angry at the fact that his failure to detect the spy working on his staff, Anna Sandesjo, had allowed her to inform her Klingon handlers about Starfleet's interests in Traelus II, if not the reasons behind wanting to subject the planet to further scrutiny. There was nothing to be done about that, Jetanien knew, though he might well be capable of turning at least part of the situation to his advantage.

"What are you suggesting?" Sesrene asked.

Adjusting himself to a more comfortable position atop his *glenget*, a backless chair constructed to support a Chelon's physique, Jetanien said, "That we work together, Ambassador, against our common adversary. Though our diplomats are locked in seemingly unending negotiations with their Klingon counterparts, anyone with any experience in interstellar politics knows that the Empire is simply using such talks to provide cover as they mobilize for their next armed confrontation. It is their way, and always has been. What you and I have is an opportunity to perhaps serve both our peoples and enable them to be ready when the Klingons finally choose to strike."

Sesrene seemed to consider that for a moment before responding, *"For this to be of any use to us, we would need access to information which currently lies beyond our grasp, such as data on Klingon ship movements and targets for conquest. Are you in a position to provide such information?"*

"Officially?" Jetanien asked. "No, but as we both know, there are occasions where diplomacy must be conducted in the shadows in order to succeed." It would not be difficult to obtain such intelligence data, he decided, particularly given his current role as one of Commodore Reyes's only on-site advisers with respect to Operation Vanguard. Getting that information to Sesrene or the ambassador's duly appointed representative might prove more challenging. Still, if the Tholians could be informed as to the location and activities of Klingon assets within the Taurus Reach—in particular when such assets posed a threat to Tholian security, as was the case with a possible Klingon base in the Traelus system—that might go a long way toward keeping their attention occupied on matters away from some of the more sensitive missions Starfleet ships would soon be undertaking elsewhere within the region. It was impossible to know how much time such a ploy might buy the Federation as it continued its own investigations into the Taurus Reach.

Likewise, Jetanien reminded himself, *you cannot predict whether what you propose might have other, costlier consequences.*

As always, there were risks to be considered, but to Jetanien, such overtures on his part might be a step toward leveling the playing field so far as the Tholians and the Klingons were concerned. His actions today could help his efforts toward eventually bringing both parties as well as the Federation to some form of negotiations, which he foresaw taking place right here on Vanguard under his own guidance. If all worked according to his plan, he might well succeed in forging a lasting agreement between the three powers.

If his plan failed, he might well be responsible for embroiling the Federation in a massive, two-front war.

So, let us not fail, then.

"Allowing our respective peoples to become mired in conflict requires no effort or risk on our part, Ambassador," Jetanien said. "However, I suspect you feel as I do and that you and I, given the roles we've chosen for ourselves, consider it our responsibility to help our leaders find a better way to resolve our differences. Surely, by working together we can present our governments with alternatives far more attractive than that of going to war with one another."

Sesrene paused, perhaps to consider Jetanien's words, before replying, *"You have given me much to consider, Ambassador. We will contact you shortly with our decision."* Before Jetanien could offer any kind of response, the Tholian's visage disappeared and was replaced by the image of the rotating polyhedron, before that too faded as the computer screen deactivated.

He sat motionless for several moments, reviewing the conversation that had just taken place. There could be no doubt that the Tholian ambassador would examine Jetanien's offer from every possible angle. This would almost certainly include how to exploit such information so that it perhaps even turned the Federation and the Klingons upon one another, leaving the Tholians to collect whatever remained. Would they even be interested, given their demonstrated lack of desire toward anything within the Taurus Reach? That remained to be seen, but it was not something with which Jetanien could be concerned, at least for the moment. Embarking on the course of action he was envisioning was fraught with its own problems, not the least of which was how Anna Sandesjo fit into the equation.

Not just Sandesjo, he reminded himself, *but T'Prynn, as well.*

Based on his own observations as well as those of a few trusted assistants, Jetanien was certain that T'Prynn must now know that Sandesjo was a spy. Unsubstantiated accounts alleged that the two women had engaged in at least one clandestine romantic liaison. If that was true, and given what Jetanien knew of Vulcan telepathic abilities, he saw no means by which T'Prynn could have avoided learning Sandesjo's true identity. Therefore, if she did know, then why had she not yet elected to inform Commodore Reyes? Was it possible that the Vulcan was pursuing some other agenda, and that Sandesjo somehow fit into that scheme? Perhaps T'Prynn was a spy herself, and was now considering a means of manipulating Sandesjo for her own ends.

Interesting.

Though he had considered taking this information to Reyes himself, Jetanien had opted against such action. Keeping Sandesjo in place and providing what she thought was valuable intelligence data to her superiors might prove useful, at least for now, as he continued with his own plans, or until such time as he could find a more overt way of turning her presence here to his advantage. Perhaps T'Prynn had similar thoughts, in which case she certainly had a head start on Jetanien. He decided he also would wait and observe that developing situation, in the hope that there might be something there for him to gain, as well.

And what of Sandesjo herself? Jetanien had of course given considerable thought as to what she might be planning. Were she to somehow gain the trust and confidence of the station's intelligence officer, it could only help to further her mission here. Would T'Prynn see through such a ploy? If she did not, what sort of damage might that cause? And if she indeed was a spy, in what way might T'Prynn use this knowledge, and who stood to benefit from her actions?

These, Jetanien decided, were problems for tomorrow, as this day already had seen its share. If even the smallest fraction of the potential represented by Operation Vanguard came to fruition, there would be all manner of new questions to answer and challenges to overcome, and much work to be done.

Much work, indeed, for all of us.

HARD NEWS

Kevin Dilmore

*For Colleen, for whom a dedication is long overdue;
and for Dan, Larry, Deborah, Jane, and Paul—Star Trek
journalists without equal.*

HISTORIAN'S NOTE

The events of this story take place in 2266, one week after the publication of Tim Pennington's accounts of the disappearance of the Jinoteur system and the actions of Commodore Diego Reyes on Gamma Tauri IV (*Star Trek Vanguard: Reap the Whirlwind*).

THE TAURUS REACH

2266

1

"Biological perversions. *That's* what they have going on down there."

Admittedly, I had been half listening to the Starfleet ensign at that particular point in our conversation, which was discourteous if nothing else given that he had paid for the round of drinks sitting before us. The young man had his urgent whisper to thank for snapping me back to attention. Evidently, he had reached the salient point toward which he had been steering for the twenty minutes or so that we had been there.

"Right, um, perversion," I said. "Now, you're not talking about unnatural monsters with a taste for human flesh or something, are you?"

The ensign's look soured a bit. "I'm not sure you're taking me very seriously, Mister Pennington."

"It's Tim, please," I said, and smiled, hoping a little familiarity might soothe his offense. "And I apologize if I'm coming across as disinterested. Remember, it's my role to be the skeptic here. I need to dig into this story, poke holes in it. As a reporter, I'm the advocate for all the Federation News Service readers who might have a harder time swallowing all of this than I."

Wrinkles smoothed from his brow as he appeared to mull my words. In a moment, he nodded affirmatively. I guess he bought it—or at least enough of it to continue talking. "Like I was saying, the word is that somewhere in the lower decks, in a place that is so secret it doesn't show up on the station's schematics, is a research laboratory that houses specimens from across the Federation and outside it, too."

"Okay, but consider it from my side, Ensiiign . . ." I drew out his rank long enough to fire whatever neurons in my brain would enable me to come up with his name. Damn me for messing it now.

"Um, Saura?"

"Of course, Saura. Sorry, mate," I said, cursing myself silently. Regardless of whether I found the young man's story credible to this point, I certainly could not rule out his offering up at least one fact or idea I'd not yet considered in this latest hunt for news. But there is no quicker way of closing up a source than to scarcely recall his identity in the middle of an interview. He appeared to shrug it aside, so I continued. "On the surface of things, it's no surprise to anyone that Vanguard has research facilities on board. It's the largest Federation presence in this sector. When you're this far out from the center of civilization, it's bound to have everything they can pack inside its hull."

And pack the hull of Starbase 47 they did. At nearly one thousand meters tall and more than eight hundred meters wide, the place was more spaceport than Starfleet facility, housing a crew larger than five starships and half again as many private citizens—including me. Vanguard came complete with civilian residences, terrestrial green space, shopping and recreation centers, restaurants and bars such as Tom Walker's, the one in which we sat. The station even housed hotel accommodations for deep-space passersby. Not that many people toured the Taurus Reach for the thrill of it all, but still, this was no mere way station for simply refueling and restocking a ship out of necessity. That said, I had been here more than a year, now, and there were plenty of places on Vanguard I certainly still had not seen. Secret research lab? I would not rule that out in the least.

"And you know as well as I do, Ensign, that the publicly available schematics of Starfleet facilities and equipment contain plenty of sensitive areas blacked out for security reasons. Even I can appreciate the boundary between the public's right to know and the security of the Federation."

"I'm a Starfleet officer, Mister Pennington," he said. "I'm not arguing that aspect of it at all."

"Fair enough," I said before taking another sip of my drink. Just then, I caught the eye of an approaching server, a young and round-faced brunette I had seen here before only recently, and waved her off from interrupting us. Had I been here alone, I might have knocked back a pair of whiskeys by now. As I had simply doubled Ensign Saura's request for some sort of foul-tasting fermented cider, a move to help instill a little camaraderie with him from the get-go, I continued to nurse the one I had rather than subject myself to more of it. And at that point, I was not going to buy us a second round, either. "So, what you're suggesting is that it's not the secrecy of the lab itself that alarms you, but what is happening inside it."

"Exactly," he said, leaning forward to me again. "From what I hear, our scientists are conducting genetic experiments on all sorts of species down there. Animals from Earth, creatures of all shapes and sizes from any number of worlds, and more."

"What do you mean by more?"

"It's not just animals that are being tested and experimented on," Saura said. "It's other races—sentient beings."

"What?"

"That's what I heard. There's even a Tholian captive down there, being held against its will and having who knows what done to it by our scientists."

The thought soured my mouth even worse than did my cider drink. In my time aboard Vanguard, there had been a number of aspects of Starfleet's mission that I had learned on my own, and others of which I had been made aware by station personnel, including by the now-former commanding officer of the station, Commodore Diego Reyes. I knew full well the lengths that Reyes would go to fulfill Starfleet's mission in the Taurus Reach, despite my not being privy to just precisely what that mission might fully involve. But I also knew Reyes well enough—at least I imagined so—that I believed he would not condone any such secretive inhumane actions on his watch. This was a man who just days before had all but given up his command, his career, his freedom itself not to hide but to reveal unflinching details about his role in Starfleet's operations in this sector. Reyes not only allowed me to report on the fate of Jinoteur IV, a planet that inexplicably blinked out of existence entirely, he authorized the release of my own video from an alien city on that planet that may have been home to the Shedai, an ancient race of super-beings unlike any we have before seen. And if that were not enough, he

chose me as his confessor for his decision to decimate the planet
of Gamma Tauri IV, sacrificing every living thing on its entire
surface in order to protect the quadrant, maybe the galaxy, from
those very beings. As someone so willing to stop himself from
being burdened by harbored knowledge, he did not seem the type
to exploit another being without mercy. A tortured soul such as
his seemed unlikely to create another, even complicitly.

"That's a very serious allegation you're making, Ensign," I
said. "It's certainly not one that would be taken lightly. Do you
have any evidence of this happening beyond your tapping into the
rumor mill?"

"No," he said. "I figured getting that was your job."

"I'm a reporter, not a human-rights investigator."

"But these aren't humans I'm talking about!"

I responded to his elevated tone by taking another sip from my
cider, hoping that my calm might encourage him to dial back any
rising sense of urgency. "What I mean, to be clear, is that I remain
on the station at the will and pleasure of Starfleet administrators.
I could attempt to investigate the kind of offense you're describing, but the number of avenues I might take to even begin such an
investigation is limited. If you're this concerned, might I direct
you to the station's consular offices of the Federation Embassy.
Ask for Ambassador Jetanien. He's the one who, well, who looks
like a turtle."

"There's that tone again, Mister Pennington," Saura said.
"The one that makes me think you aren't that interested in my tip
after all."

"It's not a matter of interest, Ensign. Your story is plenty interesting. It's a matter of credibility." As soon as the last word came
from my mouth, the young man's eyes widened and he made a
move to scoot away from our table. "The credibility of the *information,* not of you. If you would indulge me a moment, let me
play the role of my editor and tell you how she might respond
when I come to her with this tip of yours. First, she might ask
what your source might be."

"Well, I don't want to name names. Let's just say that I've heard it around and from more than one person."

"Right. We'll deem that 'unsubstantiated' then. So, at this point she might turn her attention to you. To what division are you assigned?"

"I'm a communications specialist."

"And how long have you been stationed at Vanguard?"

"Well, I've been here for the duration." Saura's tone and expression did not seem to mark his service milestone with pleasure.

"The duration being . . . that you have been assigned here since the station opened."

"And before that," he clarified. "I was attached to the station to help build its communications array."

"Excellent. Then you must be very proud of your service record and of your accomplishments here."

"You could say proud . . ." Saura's voice trailed off.

So I picked it back up. "Buuut, you're ready for a different challenge, shall we say."

"Yes, I am."

"And you've been out here a long time."

"I've made no secret about wanting to rotate off the station," Saura said. "I put in for transfer over a year ago."

"More than a year ago?" I unconsciously corrected his grammar, then sipped at my drink again. "And yet, here you remain."

"Evidently."

"So, if you've got no love left for the station, and you can't get a move on, no matter who or how you ask for it, there's always the hope that Vanguard gets put out of business."

"Pardon?" Saura narrowed his eyes. "Space stations don't get put out of business."

"But one might get repurposed should a primary mission change," I said, leaning forward. "Equipment would get changed out, crew assignments would shuffle. All of that isn't hard to imagine as a result of a turn of public sentiment against a station's purported goal. There isn't a story that would kick up disapproval and distrust of activities at Starbase 47 faster than allegations of inhumanity against sentients sanctioned by Starfleet Command. And on the heels of the Jinoteur incident, too."

Saura sat up in his seat and spoke crisply. "That's not at all what got this talk started."

"Sure would be a clean ticket home, right, Ensign? I mean, if *everyone* had to go."

"You've twisted my words completely out of context, Mister Pennington," Saura said, and stood from the table.

"I twisted no words, sir," I said. "I merely speculated one path my editor might take to substantiate your information. Or not."

Saura left, but not before saying over his shoulder, "I should have expected as much from the press."

"Cheers," I offered back, hoisting my half-full glass of the nasty brew in his direction but not following it with a quaff. Not that I was totally unappreciative of his time. It was simply that "tips" such as Ensign Saura's were becoming the norm since the day I broke the news about Jinoteur and Gamma Tauri IV and the Shedai and Reyes—and the whole bloody mess. Whether I was walking through Stars Landing and the other civilian areas of the station or between Starfleet offices within its central command tower, a great many more eyes were turned to me as I passed by these days. Not that I became some sort of instant celebrity aboard Vanguard. I had been on the station long enough that my face was recognizable to those who paid any attention to FNS newsfeeds. But this time, my reports of activities aboard Vanguard broke big, leading news reports of the day practically across the Federation. Now, many of my station mates were sure they carried the one bit of information I would need to reveal even more wrongly kept secrets or uncover the next group of corrupt Federation officials or whatever perceived injustices they might harbor. They wanted to spill, and it was my job to listen to them all. Better that than to risk pushing aside any information that might actually be newsworthy—particularly in my editors' eyes if not mine. They were as keenly interested in the next big news to come out of Vanguard as its denizens were.

So I was no longer simply a reporter. No, I was a muckraker—a lovely, little centuries-old sobriquet we get saddled with whenever one of our stories brings down someone in power, whether in politics, private enterprise, or, in this case, Starfleet. In the wake of my story, Commodore Reyes was relieved of command and arrested outside his own office—hell, the man called me ahead of time so I could come see it transpire myself. And why not? Had I delivered a phaser blast rather than a news story, I would have watched him fall just as ignobly. I owed it to him to pay witness to the results of my actions.

We might not have fully realized it back when we conversed in my emptied apartment merely a week ago, but for Reyes and me, our worlds changed forever in those moments: mine after choosing to publish and his after choosing to permit me. The question that continued to dog me from the moment he was taken into custody was . . . *why*? Why did Starfleet respond so quickly and harshly against Reyes? Why did Reyes seem not to care what happened to him as a result? Why would even a single detail of information offered by my reporting be capable of compromising any aspect of Starfleet's operations from Vanguard? Reyes let me report what I saw, knowing full well what I knew as I was writing it: no matter what I said, or showed, about my experiences on Jinoteur, no one out there would have the first clue what to make of the Shedai, their capabilities, any of it. Even I scarcely understood what the hell happened—and I lived through it.

A pair of beeps from my pocketed data device shook me loose from my thoughts. I checked the soft glow of its readout to find a text notification of a pending subspace communication from my FNS editors, and I had just enough time to rid my system of what cider it had processed and make my way to a public comm station to catch it.

So, why tell everyone, Commodore Reyes? Hell, why *not*?

2

In the shopping promenade of Stars Landing, the screen on the public subspace viewer kiosk I occupied was filled with printed words on a shaking sheet of paper. The voice coming from behind the paper was unmistakably my editor's.

" *'Fact-finding continues in the case against a Starfleet officer accused of publicly revealing his orders to destroy a planet in the Taurus Reach.'* This *is your lead,"* came the voice, which by then sounded about as unsteady as the wavering paper.

"That one's mine, yes," I said, my back pressed against one wall of the viewer kiosk while I sat on a thinly cushioned stool anchored to the floor. "The Federation News Service just paid for an awfully expensive call for you to confirm that."

The paper dropped from view within my vantage point to reveal the scowling face of a clearly disgusted Frankie Libertini, the latest in my career run of editors to oversee my work for the FNS. Assigned to the Alpha Centauri bureau, there must have been a dozen other editors closer in physical proximity to me than she was. My guess is that after Arlys Warfield dumped me, my supervision became an editorial short straw that Frankie was merely the latest to draw. Frankie was a lifer in FNS terms, having covered Starfleet before I was even born. Consequently, she kept a fairly hands-off approach to how I ran my beat here. For her to request a subspace video connection with me on Vanguard meant either she wanted to check on my general well-being or she wanted to look into my eyes while scolding me. Evidently, any good grace I had earned from my Reyes story was being exhausted more quickly than I had hoped.

"How about the fact-finding mission I just finished, Tim? Would you like to ask me about that?"

"I don't follow."

"I found no new facts in this alleged news story you filed

today." I laughed a little, but more from the sneer that tightened Frankie's mouth than her clever turn of phrase. It did not endear me to her. *"This is a recap story at best, and even that's a generous word for it. Did you even write this today?"*

"I did. At least, I wrote the lead you liked so well."

"This is not the follow-up I assigned, and it's not the follow-up that anyone who gives a damn about this story would want to read," she said. *"You might as well have come out and said that you don't know what's happened in the case for a week."*

"Well, I *don't* know what's happened in a week."

"Why the hell not?"

"As you might imagine, I am not on the best of terms with the majority of my sources right now," I said, looking over my shoulder at a pair of passing shoppers before leaning into the viewer's recessed microphone. "And, to be honest, this isn't the atmosphere most conducive to this particular conversation."

"What, are you in a public booth or something?"

"I am, actually."

"And what were you thinking when you connected with me from there?"

"Well, until you establish a Vanguard bureau office, I pretty much have to rely on my own resources."

"What happened to calling me from home?"

"I've . . . run into a bit of a situation, there," I said, not wanting to delve into the details of how my ex-wife had relieved our apartment of every single possession we once shared, including our personal communications equipment. I still had not put together the time or the resources to return the place to anything resembling actual occupancy. Had Lora chosen to rid me of my own clothing as well, I would probably still be wearing the same outfit I had on at the moment I discovered she had left and petitioned for divorce.

Several locks of Frankie's salt-and-pepper up-do had fallen into her line of sight. She brushed them off her forehead before speaking in what seemed to be a calmer tone. *"I can help you with an advance if you need passage out of there."*

"Pardon me?"

"Well, it sounds like you're traveling pretty light right now, and you are fresh out of sources. If there ever is a time to follow the story somewhere else, this sure seems like a good one."

The idea momentarily struck me dumb. She raised a point that I had not until then even considered. Leave Vanguard? Hell, I had just started to finally piece together Starfleet's interest in the Taurus Reach, let alone whatever Starfleet knew—or might hope to learn—from the remains of the Shedai civilization. Just abandoning my work here did not feel right at all.

"Thanks, Frankie, but I don't think I'm ready to pull up stakes just yet," I said. "Besides, follow what story somewhere else? If I'm going to stay on top of Starfleet activities in the Taurus Reach, where else would I do that from?"

"Maybe the story of the Taurus Reach is over," she said. *"As my uncle used to say, 'A fish always starts to stink at the head.' "*

"A fish always . . . what? What does that mean? I don't even know what the hell that means."

"You rooted out Reyes, and he hadn't been there that long. He probably didn't have time to corrupt things too far down in his command chain," she said. *"You seem to be able to win the confidence of Starfleet officers . . . before they get themselves arrested, anyway. Go someplace new and start over. There's plenty more Starfleet operations that could stand some scrutiny, and plenty of officers like Reyes."*

"But there's not." The words were out of my mouth before I could stop them.

"What?"

"Um, there's not many officers like Reyes," I said. "That's another reason worth staying."

"So," Frankie said, leaning a little closer to the pickup on her end of the conversation. *"Maybe you're a little too close to the story then?"*

Once again, she had given me pause. I did not feel any real friendship with Reyes, but something evidently had happened to change his perception of our relationship in such a way that he could allow me to work with no interference from him. He all but encouraged me to file my stories with the Federation News Service as if he decided to dare Starfleet Command to further suppress the nature of Vanguard's mission. And what was more, I trusted him—not simply his authority or his judgment, but him as a person—and that was something I had not done since, well, since T'Prynn.

"I don't think I'm too close, Frankie."

"Then figure yourself out and get back to work," she said. *"I don't want to see your face from a public booth next time. Get yourself a viewer for home. I don't want to hear any more about your sources cooling off. I'm sure you have warmed them up before. And I don't want to get any more stories that read like something you write ahead in case you wake up from a two-day drunk with a deadline on your back."*

"Understood," I said as the viewscreen went dark. Sliding off the kiosk stool, I walked among the Stars Landing shoppers as I weighed my options. Getting a home communications viewer would be simple enough. Getting a decent story sent Frankie's way would take some leg work, but I knew it could be done once I tapped a few leads. Warming up some Starfleet sources, well, that seemed the most daunting part of my task. But I had a good idea of where to start.

3

"Oh. Um, hi."

I admittedly was hoping to get a little more than a bemused expression and a few syllables from Vanessa Theriault once she had triggered open the sliding door of her temporary quarters on board the station. She stood before me barefooted, her petite frame draped in loose-fitting house clothes and her red hair disheveled enough that it appeared I had just awakened her. As she took a sip from the ceramic mug she cradled in two hands, she created an awkward silence that I wanted to fill quickly.

"Hi, Vee," I offered, hoping I did not sound overly familiar. We had spent some time together following my trip to Jinoteur and our subsequent hairbreadth escape as the planet disintegrated around us, but not enough for me to feel comfortable seeming too buddy-buddy. "Relaxing afternoon?"

"When you drop by without calling first, you kind of get what you get with me."

"I never intended that as an editorial comment. Sorry about that," I said. "I just wanted to see how your time off was going. I didn't mean to interrupt."

Vanessa looked up from her mug and smiled a little. "You didn't. I've just not been around people for a while. Do you, um, want to come in?"

Despite what struck me as a halfhearted offer, I accepted and followed her into the living area of her quarters. Aside from a few scattered pieces of clothing and a rust-colored blanket wadded up at one end of a couch, the place appeared no different than when I joined her here on the first night she had occupied it. She had accepted an offer of some time away from her duties as science officer aboard the *U.S.S. Sagittarius,* but it was not leave time in the true sense of the term as she merely deferred her requisite debriefing and medical exams to facilities on the station rather than on her starship. Given what I knew of her activities on Jinoteur, including her conversations with an actual member of the Shedai race, she certainly had a lot to talk about with her superiors.

Vanessa turned into an area adjacent to the living room that served as a kitchen. She mentioned on that first night how much she appreciated even a brief chance to prepare her own meals rather than subsist on whatever came from the food slots on board *Sagittarius,* and from the appearance of a small basket of fresh vegetables on the countertop and the open shelves stocked with what appeared to be spices and condiments, she seemed to be making use of the space as she had hoped. At the moment, however, she was stopped along a wall in front of the standard-looking synthesizer. "I'm warming up my coffee. Can I bring you something?"

"Sure, please. A tomato juice would be fine, thanks."

"Tomato juice? You're not carrying a flask of something to pour into it, are you?"

"You're confusing me with the other guy."

Vanessa smiled a little again as she shuffled through a handful of colored data cards before selecting one to slip into the device's corresponding slot. "And how is your friend, Mister Quinn?"

"Evidently well. I've not had the pleasure of his company of late. I've been a wee bit busy."

"So I gathered," Vanessa said rather flatly as she emerged from the kitchen carrying our drinks. She took a seat on the couch and set my glass on a low table in front of it. I took that as an invitation to sit down as well. "How are your ribs?"

"Better, thanks. The medic running the bone-knitting laser evidently knew what she was doing. Not a twinge left," I said, running my hand flat along my torso in some need to illustrate my words. "And how are you? You look well."

"Despite what you said at the door?"

"I did apologize."

"You did." She drew her legs up and under her as she nestled into her corner of the couch, facing me. "I'm sorry I'm not quite myself, Tim. I'm still sorting a lot of things out."

"I can appreciate that you're feeling a little detached," I said as I reached for my juice. "So how did your interviews with Starfleet go?"

She stared again into the mug she cradled in her lap. "You must know that's something I cannot discuss with you."

"Oh, of course. I wasn't meaning to pry." I took two swallows of the thick, salty liquid and set the glass back on the table, all under her silent gaze. "I wasn't."

"I believe you, in a way."

"In a way," I repeated. "But in a way that's not too trusting."

"Tim, we shared a lot on Jinoteur," she said, looking into my eyes. "You saved my life. I won't ever forget that. But I know that I may never be able to talk to you like you might want me to."

"I'm not sure where this is coming from, Vanessa. I just wanted to see how you were."

"Why?"

"Why? Because we went through a lot together. Because I like you and want to know more about you. Because we've already shared so much."

"Because you need more information about what happened to us?"

"I don't know how that would help me sort it all out, maybe ever."

"I guess I didn't mean specifically for you."

I smiled a bit as I got a better idea of her meaning. "Ah, you mean for work."

"You did write in great detail about what we did the first chance you could."

"What *I* did, not we. I held up my end of an agreement with Commodore Reyes and wrote only what I witnessed myself and what I was told on the record."

"And look where it got him."

I paused, trying to gauge the defensiveness I felt sure would creep into my voice. "Anything you shared with me has stayed between us."

"It didn't feel like that when I read your story."

"Be fair and read it again."

"I got enough out of it the first time." Vanessa set her coffee cup on the table, not having once sipped from it, and ran one hand through her red hair. "I'm sorry, Tim. I do like you. And if the circumstances were different, I might like you a lot."

"That's, um, comforting," I said, "as I sit and wait for the 'but' you're about to say."

The smile I had hoped to elicit did not surface on her soft face. "I might like you enough to wish that I could share everything with you. But I can't. And I don't want to walk around kicking myself in the ass every time I start to."

"Or every time you slip and do it, anyway," I said, getting a silent nod in response. "Because I'm too damn charming to resist? That's it, isn't it?"

Vanessa let a chuckle loose through her nose. "Something like that. And please go to hell for making me laugh."

"I get it," I said as I rose from her couch. "It's not as if you're the first woman to shoo me away like this."

"And go to hell for saying that, too."

I caught her gaze and I smiled—and most of it was even sincere. "I didn't say it had stopped stinging to hear."

"I'm sorry. Like I said, I'm still sorting this out. And I need to do it on my own, at least for a while."

"It's fine, really. The last thing I want to be to you is a nuisance." I crossed to the door. "Should you have something you want to share on the record, then, you'll think of me?"

"Of course."

"Or anyone you might know?"

"You're pushing, Tim."

"Right." I moved close enough to the door that it slid open. "So it's friends, but I reserve the right to check on you now and again."

"And I reserve the right to change my mind."

"A function of biology, as I have learned."

"Go to—"

And as the door slid shut, I muttered to the empty corridor, "Oh, I'm well on my way."

4

"How do I know that thing isn't recording?"

I talked around a bite of my battered fish with the hope that any frustration carried in my voice might be interpreted only as speech garbled by poor table manners. "You watched me turn it off," I said, scooping my recorder from the tabletop inside Tom Walker's and turning its video display toward my companion. "See? Off."

"I hope you understand, Mister Pennington," said the slightly built, balding man, "but I could lose everything by talking to you. Without permits to fly through this part of space, I'd never work as a trader again."

"And you believe that whatever you have to tell me this evening could put all of that at risk?"

"Yes, sir."

"And that's why you're choosing not even to tell me your name?"

"You can call me Donnie, if you want. But that's not my real name."

"Well, 'Donnie,' at least you aren't so paranoid as to walk in here with a bag over your head," I said, which elicited a smile from my companion. "If you were truly paranoid, you would never have agreed to meet me in an establishment you know I frequent, thus one at which I would certainly have relationships with the owners or managers—relationships I most certainly could leverage to obtain image files from the security cameras surrounding us and cross-match those images against interstellar commerce permit application records to determine your identity in a matter of seconds."

What color I had seen in the man's cheeks had drained away along with his smile. "Uh . . . heh. But you're not . . . heh, heh . . . serious," he said. "Are you?"

"Of *course* I'm not serious," I said, smiling and reaching over to clap him on the shoulder. "The confidential relationship between a reporter and his source is implicit, right?"

"Uh . . ."

"Inviolable? Sacrosanct?"

All he returned was a gap-mouthed stare with a look in his eyes that hovered between panic and bewilderment. I was starting to get the feeling that the gentleman before me might be lucky to verbally command the navigation computer on his ship, let alone manage a conversation above a basic reading level. It started to feel a little mean to toy with him like that, but not mean enough for me to want to stop.

"Donnie, a reporter would not turn a source over to the authorities. If I started doing that, I would run out of people who would want to talk to me. And then how would I get my work done?"

"Oh. That makes sense."

"So, tell me why you've met me here," I said, looking over the fish before me until I chose not to take another bite.

"Here's my idea," he said, scooting a little closer to me at the table. "I think Starfleet is not enforcing its rules against smuggling around here. I hear all the time about how shipments of one thing or another are getting through. So, I want to help you prove it."

"I'm listening."

"I figure that I can go around and just put the word out there that I'm open to moving a few things that need to be moved quietly. A few cases of Romulan ale headed one way, a few cases of Klingon disruptor rifles headed another way. I can take care of that part of it."

"Hmm. Okay, but I'm not sure where I come in."

"Well, I will keep records of all my activities in the sector, especially—here it comes—movements of Starfleet ships in the areas of my travels. Once I get caught, I can show all of the instances when Starfleet was present at the time of my transactions but chose *not* to enforce trade regulations, and then we'd have them down cold with proof positive of their being in on the situation. Or maybe then I'd get bribed by Starfleet to keep it to myself and just operate like I have been. Wouldn't that be something?"

"Oh, that would be something, all right," I said. "So, what you're proposing is a sting operation against Starfleet."

"Yeah! That's a good name for it. A *sting*."

"Now, you realize that a sting involves proposing a criminal act and trying to get someone, in this case, someone from Starfleet, to agree to break a law and not necessarily to seemingly ignore one."

"Oh."

"And it doesn't involve actually committing the crime, in this case, smuggling whatever it is you intend to smuggle."

"Oh."

"And whatever end you're attempting to justify, that would not exonerate you from the means you took to achieve it."

"Um . . ."

"Of course, 'exonerate,' " I said under my breath. "You still can go to prison for smuggling anything you smuggled while waiting to get caught."

"Oh!" Donnie bolted upright and practically launched himself from his seat. "I need to take a second look at this plan."

"You might at that."

"Just pretend that I never came by, Mister Pennington," he said before pointing to my recorder on the table. "That thing didn't record any of this, right?"

"Still off." I smiled until he turned his back on me, when I could not keep myself from rolling my eyes. As Donnie left, I noticed the same brown-haired server I had seen earlier start to make her way to my table. "Nice story tip. Thanks a lot," I said, prompting only a grin big enough to narrow her eyes.

"You can thank me in advance for the next few then, too," she said, reaching into a front pocket of the short, black apron she wore to produce several data cards. "I guess word is getting around on how to find you."

"I guess," I echoed, taking the cards. "Remind me of your name, then."

"I don't remember you asking for it in the first place."

"Right. Then allow me some grace for my lack of manners while I ask as I should have done earlier in the day."

"In the day or in the week? I've seen you in here several times."

"Now you're simply embarrassing me."

"My name's Meryl," she said, smiling again as she glanced down at the small basket of half-eaten fillets in front of me. "How was your fish?"

"Honestly? It was a little off. Did you fry it or get it from the synthesizer just like that?"

"Do you really want to know?"

"Point taken. Next time, I'll just bring you my own card. That way I can get some decent chippy sauce with it, too."

Meryl silently took the basket from my table, and I reached into my bag on the seat next to me to pluck out a section of a newsprint edition I had replicated of that day's FNS feeds. I unfolded the paper as noisily as I could, purposefully shaking out creases and holding it open wide enough for it to appear to create a black-and-white wedge in front of my face. At every opportunity, I liked reading the news as conspicuously as I could aboard Vanguard, if nothing else than to make a visual statement to whoever might be around that reporting and news are important to me—and should be important to everybody. And no, not simply because I had a job gathering it.

Just as my eyes had settled on an account of sesquicentennial celebrations for Earth's first colony on Alpha Centauri, a sharp, skin-chilling snap sounded against my newspaper. I brought the paper down quickly from my face to discover a young woman in civilian clothing—professional attire, more precisely—smirking at me from across my table. Her right hand remained poised in front of where my paper had been, its fingers splayed out following the quick flick she evidently had given it to rouse my attention.

"Print is dead, Mister Pennington."

"Sure it is, miss," I said, allowing a smile. "Just as they've been saying for more than two centuries. Yet here it is in my hand, defying all predictions of its demise."

"Just seems like a waste of resources to me," she said.

"Not sure how you even figure that. I press a button and the printed copy appears. I read it. I press a button and it disappears again. It's one more example of a completely efficient process of recycling, not too different from the way lots of other things are made around here."

"It makes you look dated, anachronistic," she said. "And we both know you're not."

"Let's settle on it making me look . . . unconventional. And what we both do *not* know is who you are. You have me at a disadvantage."

The young woman extended her dark brown–skinned hand and I took it, a bit fearful that my customary handshake might too roughly squeeze her slender fingers. The grip she returned changed my mind. "I'm Amity Price, and I've been wanting to meet you for some time now."

"Then the least I can do is offer you a seat, if you'll join me." As she sat, I said, "And what did I do to earn the privilege of your attention?"

"I want to talk about being a journalist for the Federation News Service like you are."

I laughed. "I can't say that I would recommend being like I am to anyone, Ms. Price."

"Amity."

"Amity it is. And I'm not that big on being called a journalist. I'm a reporter. I'm much more comfortable in the thick of things learning what I can, getting interviews on the fly and writing it altogether as objectively as I can without using too many big words. I save those for when I want to be rakish and charming."

"I'll consider myself forewarned and forearmed."

"So tell me about you then."

"I'm from Earth, I studied at the William Allen White School, and I've been freelancing for a couple of years now."

"A *couple*? I'm not wanting to be rude about things, but just how old are you?"

"I'm twenty-six, if it matters."

"Only to my growing sense of my spent youth. And you say you have wanted to meet me. While I appreciate the flattery, I can't imagine that you made your way from Earth in a week to talk to someone who for a fleeting moment happened to become as big as his story."

"Of course not." I must have winced visibly because her response was quick. "Don't be offended—"

"I'm not," I interrupted to say.

"Um, could have fooled me. What I meant was that the timing of your story about the Shedai and the commodore was simply circumstantial as far as I'm concerned. I've been reading your coverage of the Taurus Reach since I first found out about Vanguard Station, and I finally got myself together to see it for myself. It took me several weeks to get here."

"To talk to me?"

"Yes."

"They have this wonderful new invention called subspace radio, and you can use it to communicate with people from across the quadrant."

As I looked across at Amity, she crossed her arms in front of her and hung her mouth slightly open in one of the most impatient looks I had received in some time. Well, from someone who was not my editor at the time, at least. She narrowed her deep brown eyes into a glare that made my mouth go dry. "Are you about done playing with me, Mister Pennington?"

"I apologize."

"I'm serious about coming quite a ways, and this whole self-effacing and petulant thing of yours wears pretty thin pretty quick."

"Sincerely, I apologize," I said, taking a sip of water as I paused to regard Amity with a new seriousness. "It's been a while since I've talked to someone in the business who either wasn't gunning for my story or chewing me out for something."

"Mm-hmm," she said. "Subspace radio. Would you even have taken my call? Better yet, if you were me, would you have thought about simply making a call, even for a minute?"

I did not need to ponder that answer. "No chance."

Her broad, white smile returned. "I knew we were kindred spirits, Mister Pennington."

"Please. Just call me Tim."

"All right then. Tim." Amity held my gaze a moment before digging into a handbag slung over her shoulder. "I did drop by unannounced, so I don't want to take up more of your time tonight."

"After a trip such as yours, I can understand your enthusiasm to track me down."

She looked up from her bag. "Tim, I'm not fresh off the transport. I've been on Vanguard for nearly a month."

"And you're just finding me *now*?"

"I wasn't ready to talk until now." Amity pulled a light green data card from her bag and passed it to me. "Here are some clips—audio, video, and text—so you can get an idea of who I am and what I've been doing. I figure it's only fair, since I've been reading you for a while."

"So, once I read up on you, then we talk?"

"Something like that. I have a proposition for you."

"See? I knew it. It's the charm of the newsprint. Irresistible."

Amity dropped her chin and looked up at me with an overly pained expression that I knew I deserved. "Tim, please. A little professional courtesy."

"Certainly," I said as I accepted the card. "And how shall I contact you?"

"You're not hard to find. I'll track you down tomorrow."

"I'm looking forward to it already."

"And Tim," Amity said as she slid from the stool. "Be ready to work."

5

I had not intended to be stealthy as I crossed the metal-walled hangar bay toward the squat, discolored Mancharan starhopper that had pulled my fat out of the fire several times over, but any noise of my footsteps had been effectively neutralized by the clanging of tool on hull plating as the craft's owner and pilot, Cervantes Quinn, sat cross-legged on the ship's port wing and undertook what I could only assume was some sort of repair work near one of its warp nacelles.

"Baaah!" Quinn let out his exasperation physically as well as vocally by putting a little too much energy into tossing the tool he held toward a handled tray of other implements perched on the ship's wing behind him. The impact of the tool slid the tray just enough from its somewhat precarious perch to send it off the wing's edge and clattering to the deck.

"Quinn!" I decided to announce my arrival as soon as the din subsided so as not to startle the man. He turned, his brow and white hair showing the first signs of sweat from his labors, and on seeing me it seemed some of the tension left his face.

"No scoop here, newsboy," Quinn called out as I closed the gap between the *Rocinante* and me. "Just a rogue and a ship and they're both pretty beat to hell this morning."

"Differentiating the morning from your typical routine precisely how?" I swung my left arm to lob in his direction the small white paper bag I had been carrying. If he had been drinking the night before, something I had assumed from his remark, his reflexes showed no ill effects as he snatched the bag from the air with ease.

"What's this?" He opened the bag without waiting for a response and squinted to peer inside. "Oh, look. It's a biscuit."

"It's a proper scone, you damn savage. Thought I would bring you breakfast."

"He brings me a biscuit without any coffee," Quinn said to no one, "and I'm the savage."

"I've seen you drink coffee a grand total of once. I bought it for you, and for my trouble you punched me in the jaw and chipped two of my teeth."

"Things change." Quinn bit down on the bag and it swung from his mouth as he made his way down from the wing and onto the deck. He spoke again through clenched teeth. "Thanks for this."

"Enjoy," I said as he tugged the bag from his mouth and grabbed its contents. "How goes it?"

"You're looking at it," he said between bites. "Just getting her ready for the next run."

"What have you got lined up?"

"A couple of prospects, nothing certain." Quinn squared his shoulders against the *Rocinante*'s hull and leaned back. "You're not asking to tag along, are ya?"

"As much as I might enjoy another opportunity to nearly get killed, it's probably in my best interests to stay behind and get some work done."

"Suit yourself. That's probably the better idea, anyway. Quit resting on your laurels of fame and get back to the job of digging up stories to write."

I laughed despite myself. "I'm resting. Right."

"What's the latest with the commodore? Talked to him?"

"I should think not. Starfleet has him locked away in a cell under limited access. Even if Reyes himself said he wanted to see me, I can't imagine I would have a chance to talk to him until the court-martial proceedings conclude. And should things go bad for him, I doubt I'd get a chance at all."

"Hmm. Guess you'll be asking someone else about him then."

"That's a brilliant idea, Quinn," I said a little too sharply. "And I don't suppose you have any suggestions who."

"Damn," he said. "I hit close to the nerve?"

"Sorry. I've been getting pressure from the boss about following up my Jinoteur report as well as my Reyes report, but no one is talking to me. It's a bit of a surprise if I get even the courtesy of a hello from someone in a Starfleet uniform who just happens to pass me by."

"That's no good. I would think someone out there would be willing to at least point you in a direction for a story."

"Not that I'm aware." I paused and looked at Quinn. "But maybe you are?"

"Maybe."

Quinn simply looked at me and took another bite of the scone.

I waited what I assumed was long enough to get an answer before filling the silence. "But maybe you don't want to tell me?"

"Because that's how I do things? Dangle something out in front of you to tease you when I know you're struggling?"

"What makes you think I'm struggling?"

"Damn, this thing's dry." Quinn paused to chew and swallow. "Fine. So you're not struggling. But I haven't seen ya coming around for a while, so I figured something was up. And I hadn't seen anything big on the news about the station with your name on it, so . . ."

"Wait a minute. You look for my byline?"

"What of it?"

"No, it's just . . . I'm flattered," I said. "You look for my byline."

"And I'm not seeing it."

I paused for a moment and drew a breath. "Okay, yeah, I'm struggling."

"And maybe I can help."

"Thanks."

"Don't go thanking me until something breaks loose," Quinn said. "I know a guy who owes me a favor. I can't guarantee that I can call in my marker for you, but I don't mind asking. I've been calling in a few lately, anyway."

That gave me pause. "Something going on?"

"Simmer down, newsboy. I said there were no scoops here. Give me a little time and I'll let ya know."

"I didn't come around looking for handouts, but I'll take this one," I said. "Thanks. Sincerely."

He waved his hand at me as if to brush aside my appreciation as he got the final bite of his breakfast down. "Been to the hospital?"

"Why?"

"I figured you were keeping an eye on T'Prynn."

"Oh," I said, my mind snapping to the last time I had seen the Vulcan intelligence officer who arguably was the person most responsible for the shattered state of my career at that point. She had witnessed, as had Quinn and I, the explosive destruction of the Starfleet cargo ship *U.S.S. Malacca* while it was docked at Vanguard. But in that moment, and either as a result of the sight or merely coincidentally, T'Prynn suffered a completely debilitating psychic collapse, one that I imagined could yet prove fatal to a being with her cultural mastery of emotional control. I had even captured the entire event on my recorder, but chose not to keep it. "Well, no, I haven't been following her case. I'm a little surprised to know you thought I would be."

"I get that she's not your best friend and all, but I thought you would at least be curious."

"Curious as you are."

"Sure."

"So why not stop by and check on her yourself?"

"I've got no business poking around up there," Quinn said. "And it's not hard to guess what her reaction would be to my doing anything that might connect her to me personally. No, I won't be making a visit."

"So, is this your fee for trying to connect me with a source? Asking me to pay a visit on your behalf?"

"I won't ask you to go for me," he said. "I want you to think about going for yourself. The two of you have some unfinished business, and I don't think you would want it to end that way."

"To be truthful, I hadn't considered it. I also can't deny that part of me might have wished this on her."

"Not the part of you that deleted the vid you made," he said. "I'm just saying that you might want to wander past the hospital. When you get there, you can decide whether to go in."

"If it's any consolation, you do have my curiosity piqued about one thing."

"Okay."

"How something got into your system to reactivate your compassion program," I said. "Maybe there are more risks in being exposed to the Shedai than Starfleet is telling us."

"Well, look at the time," Quinn said. "Someone needs to be moving along."

"Evidently, I do," I said as I started back across the hangar. "You know how to find me. And for what it's worth, Quinn, you look good."

He squeezed his eyebrows together at the unexpected compliment, almost as if he did not believe me.

"Okay, maybe that's generous. You look . . . better."

I actually managed to get a smile out of the man. "Now that I'll buy, but only because I've looked a lot worse."

6

"Damn you, Quinn," I said under my breath as I passed through the main doors of Vanguard's medical center. I promised myself in that moment I would not divulge to him how I walked to the central facility directly following our conversation. I needed to maintain some sense of pride.

In my time on the station, I had made relatively few visits to the hospital, and when I did, I happened to be the one in need of care. The last time, I had come for a brief scan to follow up on the injuries I had suffered on Jinoteur, and as I walked into the main reception area, I hoped my visit had been recent enough that I might look a little less conspicuous as I breezed past the admissions desk. I was following one of the most useful pieces of advice from my days in journalism school: if you look like you belong somewhere and know what you're doing, no one will ask you any questions. I gave a sideways glance to the desk, and to a woman seated there wearing a loose-fitting nurse's uniform whose attention seemingly was on the desk-mounted viewer before her, and turned the back of my head to her just as I passed.

"Sir? Can I help you, please?"

I sighed, knowing it would be too unbelievable had I pretended not to hear her. "Oh, hello. Sorry, I didn't want to interrupt. You looked busy."

She looked up at me with her slender face framed by straight blond hair and what may have been the widest pair of hazel eyes I had ever seen. "You're very kind, but I'm fine. Now, what can I do for you?"

"I'm wanting to check on a friend. She would have come in about a week ago with what I suspect was brain trauma."

She returned to her desk monitor. "Can you tell me her name?"

"Yes, it's T'Prynn, and as you might suspect, she's a Vulcan woman."

"Ah," she said, looking back at me. "I'm sorry, but I'm afraid she is not allowed visitors at this time."

I leaned a bit onto the desktop. "I'm just trying to ease my concern, Ms. . . ."

She lowered her eyes and softened her posture a bit, almost as if she had been hoping I might ask. My hope for getting past the desk buoyed a bit, so I offered a smile as soon as she looked back up. "Braun. Jennifer Braun."

As I offered my hand, I had considered keeping my name to myself, or even giving a false one, but when she took my grasp, I could not help but play straight with her. "I'm Tim. And I assure you that I would not stay if I could only look in on her. I was with her when she fell ill, you see, and I've heard nothing about her condition."

Jennifer withdrew her hand. "And going back into the isolation wards will ease your concerns?"

"Is that where she is, Jennifer?"

"I'm not able to release any information about a patient, or even confirm that someone is a patient," she said. "But the isolation wards are where you might have ended up, had you kept going."

"I see. And I do understand. You're sticking to policy and you should, given that we've only just met."

Jennifer smiled. "But as we get to know each other, I'll certainly relax my approach to hospital policy. Is that what you're hoping, Tim?"

"Well, hospital and otherwise."

She bent her smile down into a frown and snorted as she nodded her head knowingly. "Ohhh, but you're good. So why are you trying so hard to look like you're trying so hard?"

"Damn, I knew I should have gone with the sincere approach."

"It might get you further next time."

"Further than what?"

"Well, further than a discussion of hospital policies with me," she said. "If I were to talk with someone on staff about a medical condition concerning a Vulcan, I would start with Doctor M'Benga."

"Would Doctor M'Benga be able to let me see her?"

"That is up to him," she said, allowing another smile. "But I can assure you that were your friend under his care, then once you spoke to him you would not need to see her. You would realize that she is in good hands."

"That's good to know," I said. "And maybe for now, that's all I need to know. Is there a way I can contact Doctor M'Benga?"

"You can leave a message with me and I'll make sure he gets it."

"Or I can take it back to him myself." The gravelly voice snapped my gaze from Jennifer and up to find a dark-skinned, gray-haired man wearing a white lab coat over a blue satin, low-collared version of a Starfleet uniform tunic and cradling a coffee mug. Evidently, I had been engaged enough with my bantering that I had not noticed his approach.

"Doctor Fisher!" Jennifer's voice let me know she had been equally startled.

"I'm not meaning to intrude," he said to her, "but I should be able to assist Mister Pennington here without having to interrupt Doctor M'Benga." Then he looked back at me with the expression of someone who seemed as interested in talking to me as I might be in talking to him.

"Of course, Doctor, thank you," she said as Fisher stepped away from the desk and tilted his head toward a grouping of chairs in a corner of the reception area. I took it as a suggestion to follow him.

"Thank you, Jennifer," I said as I joined him. "I hope to see you again."

"Mister Pennington," she replied, widening her eyes and raising her eyebrows a bit as if she might be warning me of the conversation to come. I winked in reply and caught up with the physician, whom I knew to be the space station's chief medical officer as well as a personal friend of Commodore Reyes.

"I appreciate your help, Doctor," I said.

"There's no guarantee how helpful I might be, but it's nice to hear your optimism."

"I'm not asking you to speak on the record about anything—"

"Then we're off to a positive start. Sit down, Tim."

I laughed a bit in midsentence as we each sat. "Well, thank you. I admit that this is a personal query, so I'm asking your indulgence. I'm curious as to the condition of Lieutenant Commander T'Prynn."

"Then allow me to be curious as to the personal nature of the discussion."

"I happened to be in the thoroughfare near the hangar observation windows when she collapsed. I witnessed the whole thing."

"I see," Fisher said. "I can imagine that would be rather unsettling for you."

"Well, yes," I said, finding myself quickly at ease with the man owing to the nature of his voice and presence. As must be the case with the most seasoned physicians, he seemed to have a way of gaining my trust and confidence in a matter of moments. "It's all a bit . . . haunting, I suppose."

"I'm told there was more to the onset of T'Prynn's condition than her simply dropping to the deck," Fisher said. "Any insight you could offer might be helpful."

When I looked up into Fisher's eyes, it was easy to sense his interest was hardly prurient. I could sense the care he had for T'Prynn, and in that moment, I grasped that her situation might be more dire than I had thought. "In the moment, she was obviously emotional. Her face was twisted . . . anguished. She was crying, I'm sure of that. It was as if she had been startled . . . well, no, it was more. She looked shocked, almost as if she had snapped under a sudden realization, or had learned something that she did not want to know."

"Yes."

"And then, her face just wiped blank. It simply . . . reset to looking no different than usual. But she just crumpled. Truthfully? I thought she was dead."

"Just as truthfully? She soon may be. It's pretty clear that she suffered some sort of trauma. From our scans, there is no physical evidence of an injury relative to a concussion. We can find no bleeding nor any blockage of blood to the brain, so she hasn't had a stroke. And yet, here we are, witnesses to the mysteries of the psychosuppressive wonders of the Vulcan mind. I'd be fascinated by it all . . . if I were a Vulcan."

It was easy for me to tell from the physician's face that his quip was more to mask his frustrations than to dismiss himself as disinterested in the neuroscientific studies of an entire race. "I'm confident you're doing all you can, Doctor."

Fisher regarded me quietly and nodded, then took a sip from his mug. "She's not my patient, she's Doctor M'Benga's. And I will be sure to tell him you stopped by with your concerns."

"Any chance that I might be able to see her?"

"Not this morning. That's his call to make, and he's not available right now to make it. Try later, and we'll see what we can do."

"Thank you, Doctor," I said. "As long as we're here, might I ask as to the condition of another of your patients?" I paused as Fisher's eyebrows rose in anticipation of my words. "Diego Reyes."

Fisher smiled slyly as he stood up from the chair. "And now you're pushing, Mister Pennington."

"No, sincerely," I said as I rose to meet his gaze. "Well, professionally, too, but sincerely. We're still off the record."

"I've always been curious how this whole on-the-record-off-the-record thing works for a reporter," Fisher said. "I would venture to guess that your real determination of what stays off the record is made *after* it's told to you."

"Well, would you prescribe a course of treatment for a patient before considering the results of your own examinations?"

Fisher nodded. "That's what I thought."

"But in this case, I'm not asking for a story. I'm, well, I'm concerned."

Fisher paused before speaking. "If I have the opportunity, I will send the commodore your regards. Fair enough?"

"Fair enough," I said, extending my hand. Fisher met it with a firm and noticeably warm shake. "I appreciate the chance to talk."

"I'm usually around," Fisher said. "I'm even usually agreeable, if I've had my coffee."

7

"You're that journalist, aren't you?"

With a bite of my eggs poised on my fork and almost in my mouth, I stopped myself before being forced to respond to the question with my mouth full. I also had to mentally revisit a few personal mantras upon which I relied in moments like those, the ones when what I would like to do is answer no and keep eating: the next story can come from anywhere and anytime, be polite, and when I don't want to be interrupted I don't eat at Tom Walker's.

"I can't be certain I am *that* journalist, but I am one, yes." I looked up to find standing next to my table a young man wearing a Starfleet uniform with a red tunic, which told me he was in some area of operational services. From the look of his chest and upper arms, I assumed he was in security. At least, I hoped someone of his size was in security.

"The one who wrote the reports about what we're doing out here. That's you, right?"

I could sense from the man's tone of voice that his intensity was rising, but I could not imagine he was there to pick a fight. I hoped that my being in a public restaurant at a time of day that one was not likely to be drunk—Quinn's example excepting—might be my saving grace. "Yes, sir, that's me."

"I thought I recognized you. Hey, I have a story for you."

"Really? Then let's hear it."

"Get the hell off the station. There's my story."

"I see," I said, noting that the scowl now on the man's face had done an effective job of checking any condescending remark that might have tumbled from my mouth in reply. Instead, I ventured to think that some civility might defuse the situation. It certainly was not the first time I had been approached by an upset reader and I doubted it would be the last. Such incidents typically worked to my advantage. "You seem anxious to talk about it. Would you like to join me?"

"No, I'm fine where I am. You must feel pretty good about what you wrote."

"Well, I feel as though I presented a fair story about activities here, yes. I won't lie about that."

"Fair," he said. "Is it fair to put a Starfleet mission at risk? People's *lives* at risk?"

I set my fork down onto my plate. "My personal observations on a planet that now no longer exists as we comprehend it should not put lives at risk, sir."

"It's more than that and you know it. The more people who know about what is happening here, the more of them will get interested in what might happen next out here, and the more of them will show up."

"Well, I do appreciate there might be some sightseeing interest out here."

"It's not just civilians. It's traders, anyone who thinks there are ancient ruins with advanced technology just waiting to be discovered and turned into credits from the highest bidder. That's just the kind of circus Starfleet doesn't need at a time like this."

"I can understand your frustration and concerns about keeping people in line, but look around you. Starfleet didn't build simply a collection of laboratories, refueling stations, and supply storerooms out here. There's a hotel, restaurants, shopping, a theater, a full-fledged terrestrial area that feels closer to being back on Earth than you can get for hundreds of light-years around. Vanguard is practically a resort at the rim of the quadrant with some of the most spectacular views of space that I've ever seen. Regardless of what I might report, word is going to get around that it's an interesting place to be and people are going to come."

"Oh, people will come, and not just people inside the Federation. The Klingons are already here, trying to figure out what's going on, and nothing good can come from that. You think they don't monitor our news reports to decide what military actions they want to take here? You keep telling everyone what there is to see here and find here, and the Klingons and everybody else will push in and we could have a war on our hands."

My adrenaline surged a little at this point, but I did my level best to keep that from creeping into my voice. "If war were to break out between the Federation and the Klingon Empire, it would be the result of a great many more circumstances than a reporter's accounting of events."

The man glared at me. "And we are in the perfect position to defend ourselves with our commanding officer in the brig."

"Ah, so that's what this is really about. You are upset about what has happened to Commodore Reyes."

"It's your fault he's in there."

"I disagree. Commodore Reyes is facing charges brought by Starfleet Command for actions he took that violated the code of conduct for an officer. I may have made people aware of his conduct, but the decisions he made to do the things he did were entirely his own."

"Part of what he's being court-martialed for is because of what you put in your story. You can't deny that."

"His charges include releasing information to me that was deemed confidential by a higher authority. I did not force the commodore to tell me what he did. And the information I reported came directly and completely from him. I did not steal classified documents and shoot them across subspace channels without a care as to how that information might put lives at risk, as you put it. I take my responsibilities as a reporter very seriously, Mister . . ."

"You don't need to know who I am. I've said what I wanted to say." The young man tugged at the hem of his red tunic, pulling it taut across his chest, almost as if he wanted to make sure I was aware of just how defined his musculature underneath it might be. "Maybe you'll think about it the next time we have a ship blow up inside a docking bay or when we watch this station rubbed right out of space like what happened to that planet."

The man left the table and I picked up my fork again to poke at my eggs. From the looks of them, I could tell without needing a taste that my breakfast had cooled beyond the point of palatability for me.

"Now that was worth getting up to see," came a voice from across the table. I looked up and into the deep brown eyes of Amity Price.

"I didn't notice you come in," I said, offering a small smile as I felt the tension start to leave my body.

"You were a little busy," she said, sliding into the chair opposite mine. "But you sure sounded convincing."

"I sure as hell ought to. It's the same discussion I've been having with myself several times a day for a week. First time I've heard it out loud, though."

Amity nodded. "My grandfather was a reporter."

"No kidding?"

"Mm-hmm. Not for the FNS directly, but I suppose his stories got picked up once in a while. He moved around a lot and just wrote for the newsfeeds about whatever colony or outpost he lived in at the time. When I told my dad that I wanted to go into the news like Papa did, he told me about when he was growing up and how he remembered very clearly seeing people stop Papa and give him hell for something he wrote. Didn't matter whether they were having lunch or shopping or just walking someplace, and he never knew when it might happen but it just happened. A lot, from what he said. And the rule was that if they got stopped, my dad had to stand perfectly still and quiet, and let whoever was talking say their piece."

"Ah, so you were just following the rule."

Amity smiled and gestured to the water glass on the table. "That one yours?"

"Yes, but I've not touched it," I said, pointing my thumb toward my half-drunk glass of tomato juice.

"Thanks," she said before taking the glass and sipping from it. "And I talked to Papa about it and he laughed and laughed. And you know what he said? 'Amity, a colony is a small place. And you can write up when someone is born and when he scores a touchdown to win the big game. You can write when he gets married and has a boy of his own. You can write about his accomplishments or his discoveries or his travels, all of it, and you won't hear a word from him. But you write about something he did wrong, even if it's little, and you're that son-of-a-bitch with the news service and you always have been and you always will be.' "

I laughed, and that appeared to satisfy her. "Your grandfather is an insightful man."

"He is . . . he is. And inspiring, too."

"I can see from your writing that you're getting inspiration from somewhere."

The bright smile I recalled from our first meeting returned to her face. "You read my work?"

"I did, and you've got good stuff. Thank you for sharing it with me. But I'm still a little puzzled why you did."

"How did you get started with the FNS?"

"Well, I do things pretty much the way you described your grandfather's work. I just happened to catch someone's attention at the FNS a few years back with a story I did about a Starfleet officer who had just gotten promoted to fleet captain. The editor said it sounded like I had a good rapport with the officers and that I knew my way around explaining missions and what they really meant for the Federation at large. So she asked me whether I had ever considered a Starfleet beat. And here I am. It was probably more luck of the draw than anything."

"You might get away with saying that to a lot of people, but not to me. You're a great fit. You're creating quite a record of this place with what you're getting that actually makes it into the feeds. I can only imagine what you've got that you're keeping for your book."

"My book."

"Absolutely! What, you haven't thought about that?"

"Frankly, no," I said. "But you're straying from the point. What's got you here and with me?"

"Things are happening out here. I want to tell a story that gets me some attention from the FNS just like you did. It sure seems like a big enough beat for the both of us."

"Big enough and dry enough," I said, taking a drink of my juice. "I hate to disappoint you, Amity, but right now even I can't squeeze a story out of this place. Nothing seems to be happening and no one is talking."

"No one is talking to *you*."

"So that's your angle? Slip in and talk to my sources while they're freezing me out?"

"Not your sources. I want to talk to the people you're not talking to—people you can't talk to, at least for a while."

"What's stopping me from talking to people?"

"You. That smiling face of yours," she said as she reached across the table and patted my left cheek several times. "Right now, people recognize you. You're part of your own story, and that's going to work against you with sources you don't really know—people like your new friend I just met. If anyone has something to say with any real merit, he's not going to come up and just offer it."

"But he might offer it to you?"

"Didn't say that, either. But he sure won't recognize me while I'm eating my eggs."

"Right," I said. "So what are you proposing?"

"I want to work together. You dig up your stories and I'll dig up mine. I'll do my own reporting and my own writing. But if I come up with something that you think is worth putting on the feed, you vouch for it with your editor and it goes with my byline."

"And you want to work totally independent of me."

"Well, it kind of defeats the purpose of my being an undercover reporter if everyone sees me just tagging along with you, right?"

"Very true. And I'm not responsible for you, and neither is the FNS. So don't go poking around into things that might get you into trouble. If you end up incarcerated, there won't be much I can do about it."

"I'd never dream of it."

"Well, fine, then. You're on. So, what is your first idea?"

"I'll tell you tonight, late, if you're up for meeting me."

"Okay, I'll bite."

"Perfect," she said, sliding from her seat and stepping over to me. "And thank you. This means more to me than you might imagine." She leaned in without warning and planted a soft, quick kiss on the same cheek she had patted earlier.

"So, where are we meeting?"

"The *Omari-Ekon,*" she said. "Heard of it?"

"Well, of course I have. Everyone on Vanguard has. Are you telling me you have a propensity to gamble?"

"We'll talk there," she said and smiled. "Maybe roll some dice, if you like."

"Amity, I believe I may be rolling the dice with this agreement already."

8

I considered the stale, regulated smell of the air in a spacecraft, a smell that typically strikes but quickly fades as nasal passages dry out, neutralizing the act of breathing to a point that wrings every bit of satisfaction from it. Then I thought of the unnatural, chaotic smell of the air in a gambling establishment, with its attempts at creating a pleasant atmosphere for patrons through timed wafts of deodorizing fragrances that ultimately mask only a portion of ambient body odors, breath vapors, and whatever else might be exuded from the individuals surrounding every table and viewscreen in the place.

And then I took another breath of the smell where I sat on the recreation deck of the *Omari-Ekon*. Too heavy to be scrubbed clean and too desperate to be ignored, the atmosphere seemed almost foggy with spiced smoke from pipes filled with narcotics, flowery perfumes used nearly to saturation point, and unsavory aromas existing in that range of human olfaction that made it impossible to distinguish whether they emanated from a steaming platter of saucy food or from the unwashed individual consuming it. I did not want to think too long about how effectively it would permeate the fibers of the jacket, shirt, and slacks I chose to wear that night.

Combining that with a lighting scheme that alternated between sporadic spotlights and bursts of strobing white light, and the pervasive thumping that seemingly set every song to the same rhythmic time, it was not an environment to which I willingly exposed myself.

Yet there I was at a side table, watching my fellow patrons with a curiosity that admittedly was high enough to overrule my nostrils' desires to relocate. If nothing else could be said about the *Omari-Ekon,* the Orion merchantman craft certainly had the ability to draw a varied crowd. Besides the requisite emerald-skinned Orions, all wearing outfits of a flashy gold lamé that accentuated the rich hue of their skin, members of a dozen or more races—some of which I could not even identify—comprised the population of the gaming area. While I waited in view of the main entrance, and a chance to see Amity enter the place, I let my gaze wander about the main floor. To one side, a Tellarite waved his arms and complained loudly about his meal to the waitstaff and then who knew what else. A pair of Edosians—or perhaps Triexians or some other tripedal race—wandered around, craning their oblong heads over the crowds at several tables before deciding to place a bet at what approximated a roulette wheel, from what I could see of it. I spotted a Zaranite walking past my table and I envied him the breathing apparatus he wore to be able to survive in these particular environs. I wondered whether it was efficient enough to filter out the airborne horrors of the place. Then again, I had no clue as to whether he might ultimately prefer the ship's relatively polluted atmosphere. Maybe for a Zaranite, this place feels like home.

From the looks of the gamblers and diners filling the place, I gathered that the majority of them were merely visitors to the station rather than personnel. From the looks of their attire—soiled jumpsuits and the like—many were laborers of some variety and had probably been aboard some of the civilian supply ships docked at the station before coming here for whatever recreation they sought. In my few times aboard the vessel, I rarely if ever spied someone I recognized from my daily dealings aboard Vanguard. And if civilians from the station were that infrequent, Starfleet personnel were even more infrequent. Evidently, even Commodore Reyes' removal from command was not enough to tempt crew members into ignoring his standing orders against paying a visit to the *Omari-Ekon*.

I let my attention become transfixed by the Edosians once again. Evidently, they had found some success at the gaming table because the pair tipped their heads up and engaged in an ululating bleat of a cheer, then began some sort of choreographed victory dance together that appeared intricate and involved, at least to someone with only four limbs, such as myself. Just as I began to sense a pattern to their movements, I heard a voice next to me rise above the din.

"Hey, can I get you something to drink?"

Recognizing the words as Amity's, I spoke while keeping my eyes on the dancers a moment longer. "Just sit down. I'm sure a server will be by here in a moment."

"Sir, can I get your order?" I felt a tug at the tail of my jacket.

Not understanding her impatience, I turned to look at Amity and saw her standing next to the table—in an outfit identical to that worn by the females working in the gaming area. I could not hold back my first response. I laughed. "Now that's an odd coincidence to show up in that outfit, of all nights."

"Shall I just bring you a beer, sir?" Amity opened her eyes wide and nodded slightly, just enough for me to catch on that she needed me to agree to the request. I nodded back and she wheeled around on a heel and walked into the crowd. While I had no clue as to why she might be impersonating a server, I could not fault her effort at successfully blending into the situation. She cut a very fine form in the outfit, from the fullness of her bikini top to the curve she added to the sarong-style short skirt that exposed a very large portion of her ebony legs. I tried to rationalize my ogling as a professional appreciation for her undercover efforts, but stopped when enough guilt had made its way to the forefront of my mind.

She returned a few moments later carrying a tray laden with a bottle and a clear, empty glass. "I'll pour this for you," she said, setting the glass onto my tabletop then scooping the bottle off the tray, which she then deftly tucked under her arm.

"Okay, I get that you've done this kind of work before. Want to join me now?"

"I'm working," she said in a softer voice as she poured.

"Wait . . . you mean you're employed here?"

"Have been for a few weeks now."

"Seriously?"

"We'll talk specifics later. I have to keep moving. Did you bring your recorder?"

"Recording devices are strictly prohibited at gaming establishments," I said. "I was searched at the door after being asked specifically whether I had any communication devices on me at all."

"I understand all of that," she said. "Did you bring your recorder?"

"Of course I did. What, do you think this is my first time here?"

"The next time I come back, have your drink finished and be ready to follow me."

Amity left before I could agree to whatever plan she might have had up her sleeve—or up her nonsleeve, in accordance with her current state of dress. I took a long swig of my drink, which tasted no different than an ale served in my faraway Scotland, and tried to imagine what Amity must have accomplished to land a job aboard the *Omari-Ekon*. I hoped she had had the where-withal to provide identity documents that did not reveal her true identity nor anything that might lead her new employers to her actual past ones. On the other hand, I imagined that many of the people working aboard the ship came to the job with some hope of escaping whatever previous lives they may have led. Perhaps the Orions had an appreciation for such situations and accounted for them. There must be some measure of honor among thieves, after all, I thought, or no criminal organization would be capable of functioning. Regardless of any level of honor or respect among the ship's employees, I at least understood that taking a job under Ganz, the Orion merchant-prince that commanded the ship, was risky business at best. I hoped Amity had a clear appreciation for that as well.

Wanting to be at the ready, I made quick work of downing my beer. Not long after, I saw Amity's figure cutting around and sometimes through the clusters of gamblers milling about the floor. When she reached me, she said loudly enough to be heard over the din, "Sir, it's easier if I just show you to the toilet facilities."

"I understand," I said, and followed her back through the crowd. She moved rather quickly on much higher heeled shoes than I had seen her wearing previously, but not so fast that I could not match her pace. With a few more zigzags around patrons, we reached a pair of doors situated in the ship's bulkhead. Amity grabbed the arm of my jacket to pull herself into me.

"He went in there. I hope he's still finishing," she said.

"Human male, about your height. Blond hair. Reddish leather coat over a light-colored shirt."

"Okay. And?"

"Record him so we can identify him. He's Starfleet."

"And that's an issue because . . . ?"

"Because he doesn't want anyone in here to know," Amity said before releasing the grip on my arm. In a louder voice, she said, "Oh, you're welcome, sir," and left my side.

I walked into the bathroom, squinting as my eyes reacted to the brighter light that shone from the doorway. I passed a grouping of wall-mounted sinks and rounded the corner into the bathroom proper, which turned out to be larger than I had expected. The Orions could not be faulted for a lack of hospitality, as it appeared from the variety of accommodations that they had accounted for a wide range of biological needs, albeit chiefly humanoid ones. Wall stations featured differently shaped basins at various heights as well as flexible hoses with connector nozzles for those in atmospheric suits. Stalls appeared to be of various sizes, with labels on each door to indicate which ones were best equipped for which races. It all struck me as very efficiently handled—not to mention that the bathroom actually smelled better than the majority of the gaming deck.

A pneumatic rush of water sounded from one of the stalls, and I turned toward the wall-mounted fixture closest to me. I fumbled around a bit not only to appear as if I had been tending to my own needs but also to position my recorder as surreptitiously as possible. Just as I thumbed the switch to begin recording, a stall door opened and out came a man fitting Amity's general description.

I spun and acknowledged him with a silent nod of my head. As we walked to the hand basins, I got far enough ahead of him to position myself where I wanted. I moved my hands near the spigot to trigger a flow of water but immersed only one hand in a way I hoped was not obvious, then turned away from the basin. Holding my hands in front of me as I turned afforded me what I hoped was the best vantage point for the recorder's lens, which was positioned between my wrist and shirt cuff.

And the man turned to me full on, smiled, and said, "Enjoy your night."

"Same to you, sir, and good luck on the games," I answered as he left. And that was that. In that moment, I was a little surprised it had gone so smoothly. Unless I had totally missed the mark on the recorder's position, I had captured more than enough to be able to determine just who the man was. And then, inspiration struck. If I could get that image so easily, I wondered whether I had a bit of good fortune operating on my side that evening.

I took off my jacket, draped it over my arm to carry it out, and left the bathroom. I paused for a moment as my eyes readjusted to the much darker gambling deck, then made my way through the crowd, spinning myself as I bobbed and weaved in an attempt to sweep my recorder's lens across as many of them as I possibly could. Not that I expected to net the images of a great number of evildoers who just happened to be aboard the ship that night, but if I chanced across something that might prove helpful, I would be glad I had taken the risk.

Rather than press my luck any further, I made my way straight for the gangway off the ship. The two Orions guarding the entrance appeared to me to be the same pair of green-skinned hulks I had passed to get into the place, so I had some hope that I might pass them quietly and quickly. The sounds of my footsteps were enough to prompt one of them to turn and look my way. As I approached, the guard turned his back to the side of the gangway, which seemed like a token gesture at best as the space he created was barely enough for me to slide through. But slide I did, with the hope of not making a scene.

"Have a good night, gentlemen. If you'll pardon me," I said, shimmying my way between them. As I made it past and bounced into my stride, I felt a tug of resistance that snatched my jacket from my grasp. I turned to see my jacket collar snagged against the handle of a dagger tucked in the guard's belt, but I could not stop my forward inertia quickly enough to provide the slack that might have loosened it. My arm was tugged straight and my jacket fell to the floor in a heap at the sandal-clad feet of the larger of the two guards.

And I realized I no longer felt the pressure of my recorder wedged into my shirtsleeve.

Hoping a look of wide-eyed shock was not more pronounced than it ought to have been, I immediately crouched down to scoop up my jacket with a burst of nervous laughter. "Och! Sorry about that, gentlemen." I grabbed the jacket and held it in a wadded ball to my chest, hoping the dislodged recorder might have been caught up in the folds of its fabric, while making sure to offer quick apologetic smiles to each of the massively muscled guards. My heart thumping in my chest loudly enough to ring in my ears, I turned and headed down the gangway once more.

"You dropped something, sir."

At the baritone sound of the voice behind me, I quelled an immediate and unbidden urge to rush headlong down the gangway. Despite my greatest hopes, my rational mind grasped I had no chance of escaping the Orions regardless of how far I may have made it into the station and, more important, into sovereign territory of the Federation.

"Oh, thank you," I said as I trembled a bit and turned back to see what he might have found.

The guard held a folded piece of paper in his meaty green fist.

"Ah," I said, exhaling a breath that until then I had not realized I had held. "Old theater program. Shows you the last time I wore this coat."

"Enjoy your night, sir," the guard said.

"I will, thanks," I said, hoping I had turned out of view before the beads of sweat I sensed were forming on my brow became visible. As nonchalantly as possible, I hugged my coat while patting down my right sleeve . . . until I found my recorder had slid down closer to my elbow.

9

"Newsboy, you look crappier than a Klingon outhouse. And that's saying something."

"Particularly coming from you."

While I had not walked myself past a mirror yet that morning, I had no reason to doubt Quinn as he stood in my apartment doorway. On my way home from the *Omari-Ekon,* I had picked up a right bottle of whisky and managed to get a good amount of it down me before settling into sleep. Okay, before passing out. I did not want to admit to anyone, least of all myself, that the close encounter with the Orion guards had put the fear of God in me in a way I had not felt in some time—Jinoteur notwithstanding. But the situation on Jinoteur was flat-out survival against the elements. Last night was a matter of trusting my wits in the face of danger, and I had looked that danger in the eye and nearly soiled myself. So, I drank it away when I got home. And if I now looked at all the way I felt, his comments likely were generous. Quinn, on the other hand, appeared to have avoided what I assumed was his usual evening bender. He was shaven, his hair was groomed back into a ponytail, and his clothing appeared clean and unwrinkled. He was everything I was not.

"I looked for you last night," Quinn said.

"And you found me this morning. Coming in?" I turned from the doorway to head into the kitchen area and heard the door slide shut without a response from Quinn, but I knew he had entered as his shoes across my floor made an echo that the empty room did not do well in absorbing. "I'll make coffee."

"You actually going to make coffee or are you just going to pull two cups from the food slot instead of one?"

"Why, Mister Quinn, I had no idea you were a man of such refined tastes. Yes, the food slot."

"That's fine. Not that I really care. I just wanted to know what I was in for."

I came from the kitchen bearing a pair of gray cups that were standard issue for the slot. "I'm sorry to disappoint."

"Truth is, you didn't," he said before taking a sip. "I happen to know how you make coffee."

"I'd offer you a seat, but . . ."

"I didn't expect one, and I'm not staying." He fished into a pocket of his coat and passed me the folded slip of paper he removed from it. "There's your name."

With no place to set down my coffee, I fumbled a bit as I unfolded the paper one-handed. "Thomas Ginther."

"He owes me a favor, and he knows you'll be the one asking for it. He's Starfleet security, and he will give you a one-time pass through the computer records and help however he can. For what it's worth, I'd get ahold of him sooner rather than later. He's a little fidgety about lending a hand."

"Because I'm not you?"

"No, because you are *you*. He's not as sweet on you these days as I am, what with the commodore and all."

"Right. This comes as a complete shock to me." I refolded the paper. "Thanks for this. I don't mean to sound unappreciative."

Quinn took another sip of his coffee and paced a couple of steps within my empty living room. "So where were you last night?"

"Depends on how I want to spin it. I could say I was with a woman, and that would pique your interest in an approving way."

Quinn looked at me with a hint of a smile. "And were you?"

"In a fashion, yes. Or I could say that I was on the trail of a possible story. Not that I even know what it is or how things might shake out, but I truly was working and not just drinking and carousing around. And that might earn your favor, too."

"Maybe. Or maybe what you need is some . . . carousing. I'm the last person to judge someone for that."

"Fair enough," I said. "Or I could tell you that I spent part of my evening aboard the *Omari-Ekon*."

"What the hell made you think *that* was a good idea?" Quinn snapped his words through an instant scowl.

"Precisely why I led my story with the woman."

"Seriously, Tim. What were you doing there?"

For the first time in what felt like quite a while, I found myself wanting a chair in my living room. As there was little I could do to remedy that situation, I chose to sit on the floor with my back against a wall. Quinn decided to sit as well, but cross-legged and facing me rather than positioning himself along the wall. "I've started working with someone, a young woman who fancies herself a reporter for the FNS. Evidently, she has been living on the station for several weeks and has struck out on her own initiative to get a story she can use to break in."

"If you're leading up to answering my question, I have a feeling I'm not going to like it."

"She asked me to meet her on the ship's recreation deck last night to discuss what she's working on."

"You're kidding me. Fishing for a story in Ganz's pond is a piss-poor way of getting a start at anything," he said. "Back her off. Today."

"I'm well aware of what problems she could be creating for herself."

"The hell you are."

"And it gets more complicated," I said. "What I didn't realize until I had arrived last night is that she is working there, aboard the ship, as a cocktail server or something."

Quinn lowered his head and pinched the bridge of his nose between his eyes. "Then it's not a matter of just backing off. She needs to get off the station, head toward wherever else she might want to try and make a name for herself, and not look back. I know you're not right in the head, newsboy, but this girl is clueless."

"She's enthusiastic," I said. "She's young."

"Yeah, no shit."

"I'll take care of it."

"You need to, and send her on her way." Quinn rose to his feet, prompting me to push myself from the floor as well. "How's T'Prynn?"

"I don't know. The impression I have is that nothing has changed. I tried to get more information for you, but I wasn't able. I apologize."

"It's fine," he said as he crossed to the door. "I'm just curious. I have to admit, she's been on my mind."

"Not to sound callous or anything, but why?"

The door slid open as Quinn approached. "Well, the timing, I suppose. She goes to whatever trouble to put things right for me, you know, to smooth everything over to reset my life. And then this happens."

"So, you're thinking this is divine retribution for doing a favor for Cervantes Quinn? In this universe, no good deed goes unpunished?"

Quinn closed his eyes and smiled as he smoothed his hand over his head of salt-and-pepper hair. "Something like that, newsboy. There's not much I can do to get right with her in return, though, is there?"

I sensed his authenticity when he posed the question, rhetorical as it may have been. I had not been gripped by any overwhelming feeling of compassion for the stricken woman, aside from the levels of concern I would for anyone whom I had witnessed suffer a great illness or injury. But Quinn was in a different place. He seemed beholden to her, while acting as if he could share that burden only with me. In that moment, I hoped I was providing the support he seemed to need.

"What can I be doing, Quinn?"

"Just keep me posted," he said. "And fix the thing with the girl."

"I hear you," I said as the door slid closed. I did hear him about Amity—but part of me was unsure whether I wanted to listen.

10

"I'm not doing this for you, you know. Just so we're clear."

"I fully understand, Lieutenant," I said to Thomas Ginther just after stepping into a small security monitoring station within Vanguard's command tower. It was a simple, flatly illuminated gray-colored room that consisted of little more than a computer access console, a workdesk, and a couple of chairs. I had contacted him quickly, as Quinn had suggested, and he seemed anxious to meet and dispose of the albatross around his neck that I evidently represented. After meeting the broad-shouldered and square-jawed man somewhat furtively, I followed him through an alternating series of corridors and turbolifts to arrive at this destination. Were I pressed to reach this place again on my own, I was certain the task would be impossible.

"I don't even know what it is you want from me," Ginther said. "And I'm not guaranteeing I can even access it. Even if I can access it, I'm not sure I'll do it for you until I understand what exactly it is you want and why you want it."

"You've extended me quite a courtesy here, and I appreciate what's at stake for you."

"It's not like I would just lose my job. This is a court-martial offense. I could end up at a prison colony."

"I am aware of that."

"And this, what we're doing, it's a one-time situation. Once we walk out of here, never again. I don't know you and you don't know me. You have never seen me and you have never seen this office, and we never talk about this to anyone ever."

"You certainly cover your bases." The stern expression on Ginther's face assured me that my previous path of being as contrite and appreciative as I could muster was the one of lesser resistance. "As well you should. I like knowing our Starfleet security guards are thorough."

"So, what do you want?"

"I need to be candid with you, Lieutenant. I'm not entirely sure."

"Oh, perfect. Quinn said you might be like this."

"He did?"

"Yes." Ginther thumbed the switch that illuminated a pedestal-mounted viewer as well as several rows of flashing bulbs and started the streams of audible ticks and clicks that seemed to characterize Starfleet computers.

"*Working*," came a digitized female voice from a speaker mounted separately on the desktop.

"Computer, disable audio responses," Ginther said. "What do you want?"

"Right . . . and forgive me, Lieutenant, but just what did Quinn say?"

Ginther sighed. "He said I shouldn't give you the keys to the candy store, but then again, maybe it wouldn't matter because you would just go in there and not even know where to start. He said that if I helped you narrow your search parameters, you would be in and out of my hair pretty quickly."

"Hmm. Well, he's not that far off," I admitted. "While I'm thinking, if I may, tell me what happened between you and him that you now find yourself with me."

"I'm not going to discuss that. Period. What else do you got?"

"Well, there is this," I said, reaching into my pocket to extract my recording device. "I have some video recorded on this and I wonder whether it might be cross-referenced against the central computer banks so I might learn the identities of the persons on it."

Ginther knit his brow. "Um, that's it? You want some IDs?"

"If it's not too much trouble."

"Pass that to me," he said, holding out his hand. I gave him the recorder and he placed it near the flashing console. "Computer, scan this device and retrieve all audio and video recorded in the past . . . twenty-four hours." He looked at me as he established the time parameters for the scan, and I nodded in agreement. In moments, the viewer displayed a still image of what appeared to be a skewed view of the bathroom in which I had started my recording.

"Well, would you look at that."

"Computer, play video and cross-reference facial characteristics of persons with all identification files on record." The image on the viewer began to move, and before long it displayed a very clear shot of the subject of Amity's attentions. "Where did you shoot this?"

"Aboard the *Omari-Ekon,* last night."

"You're kidding me," Ginther said, turning his face toward me with a look of near appreciation. "You got on and off that ship with a pocket recorder?"

"Well, I didn't necessarily keep it in my pocket, but yes."

"I don't need details," Ginther said, raising his hand as if to shield himself from any unsavory information. "But this just got a whole lot more interesting."

The viewer continued to reflect the chronicle of my path from the brightly lit bathroom into the cavernlike dimness of the recreation deck. The video image jostled and blurred almost to the point of inducing nausea, and several times I had to take my eyes from the screen. Faces swept in and out of view, some of them revealed in no more than a profile, or perhaps an eye and lock of hair that happened to catch one of the venue's swaying spotlights. The great majority of the patrons I managed to capture appeared as no more than smudges of light amid the blackness, indistinguishable from the surrounding gaming tables or background objects, let along from each other. Excepting my lone successful shot in the bathroom, the entire exercise appeared to be a wash.

When the image showed me nearing the gangplank, I spoke. "You can cut it here. There's nothing really beyond this." Given that I already felt that I had squandered my opportunity to glean a story from Quinn's proffered computer access, I was not interested in exposing myself to the humiliation of my encounter with the Orions.

"Computer, end playback. Begin cross-reference and display full and probable matches."

"I have to admit, Lieutenant, that I was hopeful my recording had contained better raw material for you to sc—"

"Got it."

"What?"

"It's done. See for yourself."

I looked back at the viewer, which displayed the following message: Identification cross-reference complete. Probable/partial matches: 14. Verified matches: 37. I was shocked, to say the least. "Thirty-seven?!"

"We do know what it is we're doing around here, you know," Ginther said with a definite air of self-satisfaction as he seemed to warm to me. "Computer, present identity information in chronological order."

The viewer displayed a small still image of the bathroom man as an inset next to a more official looking mug shot and some biographical data. I scanned for the man's name, and when I found it, I read it aloud.

"Adan Chung."

"Looks like a solid match to me."

"Says he's with matériel supply command. You know him?"

"Starfleet's a pretty big organization. It's not like we all get together on the weekends or read the company newsfeed to see who went on what mission and got what promotion."

"You don't know him."

"No, I don't know him. But he's got something to do with supply and cargo transport and storage. If you wanted something moved in or out of Vanguard without anyone noticing, he might be the guy."

"That's a conclusion an Orion might draw as well," I said.

"I'd say so," Ginther said. "So, this is the kind of thing you're hoping to dig up here? Links between Starfleet personnel and the Orions that may not be on the level?"

"It seems to be a recurring theme in my recent activities, yes."

"You certainly don't shy away from some potentially trouble-some company."

"So I've been informed."

"Well, let's call that a start. The rest you can do on your own time," Ginther said as he slipped a data card into a slot on the computer station. "Computer, prepare to transfer all relevant files to this search and cross-reference, and encrypt file as . . . 'news-boy 37.' Initiate transfer."

A whir of clicks and pulses of light followed the command, and as soon as they had ceased, Ginther slid the card from the slot and passed it to me.

"While I won't inquire as to how you decided upon your en-cryption, I thank you. And you are welcome to keep a copy of my recording, Lieutenant, if it would help you in any open investigations."

"Hmm," he said. "I could do that anyway, but I appreciate the offer. I have a feeling this might go a ways in helping us with a number of situations. There's only one problem."

"Yes?"

"I've got this personal code about stuff like this. If you help me, then I help you. So you help me with this, then I'm stuck help-ing you."

"I could let you off the hook."

"It's not that easy," he said. "You've got another pass. What else do you want?"

As I opened my mind to ideas, I found myself thinking of Quinn and, not surprisingly, T'Prynn. If I could in some way offer peace of mind to one, maybe it could help them both. "What can you tell me about the explosion of the *Malacca*? Something I don't know. It's important to a friend."

"The cargo transport? Not to disappoint you, but I won't be able to get into that investigation without raising some flags," he said. "I can give you what has been released so far, but that's about it. I'm sorry."

I nodded. "I understand. I figured it was a long shot to ask."

"We're done here, then," said the security guard, who extended his hand as a farewell. "Mind yourself, Mister Pennington. If I were offering advice, I'd say let us take a look at Mister Chung's situation from our end. And please keep me posted."

I was puzzled. "What happened to 'I don't know you and you don't know me'?"

"I told you things weren't that easy," Ginther said. "I still owe you one."

11

As pleasant as a walk through Fontana Meadow could be, there were times that I found myself caught in a pattern of journalistic scrutiny that took much of the fun and mystery out of it all.

The meadow was what we called the green space blanketing the floor of a massive terrestrial enclosure that flourished within Vanguard. To the senses—the look, feel, and smell of it all—Fontana Meadow was in all ways natural. Grass and soil gave way under my stride with no physical indication to my feet of what my mind was acutely aware—that a few meters underneath it all lay cold metal deck plates to separate me from a set of docking bays, each one big enough to house comfortably a *Constitution*-class starship. In the distance, one could see groves of trees as well as structures for living and working nestled into rolling hills. My mind, however, was yanking me from the fantasy of that stretching horizon with the reminder that it was an optical illusion created by earthen berms and architectural trickery intended to keep me from seeing the walls rimming the enclosure. More than fifty meters above me stretched the dome itself, capping the enclosure and protecting us from the vacuum of space. But I knew it was merely camouflaged by paint and holographic projections to render the illusion of an actual sky as I walked along underneath it.

Then I let myself be reminded that despite the natural

appearance of this environment, its behavior over time was anything but. Our temperature remained constant at a degree deemed most tolerable and pleasant by the majority of visitors to and residents of Earth. Weather was no real issue, as winds never blew beyond a pleasant breeze, rumbling thunderstorms never threatened, and blistering heat never baked. Ambient light in the enclosure artificially brightened during waking hours and dimmed during restful ones to account for the natural rhythm of light and darkness experienced on Earth as the planet spins on its axis. Its journey around the sun, however, was not approximated, as Fontana Meadow never experienced a seasonal change. No fall breezes swept shed leaves into small vortices to scoot down the street. No cycle turned grasses green then brown then green again as time passed. No sense of promise of what was to come ever was carried by budding trees and opening flowers.

Sometimes, the more technology accomplished to make the frontier seem like home to everyone else, the more reasons I found to make me miss it.

I was feeling a little wistful and maybe a little old as I then crossed the meadow into Stars Landing. While I was bemoaning my inability to just give up and appreciate the splendor of my sur-roundings—artificial as they may be—I also cursed my current struggle with the approach I was taking these days to my job. When I had started as a reporter, I likely would have paid little heed to anyone—friend, law enforcer, editor—who cautioned me against personal risk when it came to getting the story. Pointing a finger, righting a wrong, blowing a whistle—these felt like praiseworthy goals when I chased the news in my youth, ones worth the personal risk. Before Jinoteur, I felt as though my sto-ries were being parceled out to me by authorities who dictated what and how I wrote them. Before Reyes had cut me free from his own restraint, I had forgotten what it had been like to write something capable of upending the world even a little bit.

So as I turned the corner toward Café Romano and spotted Amity Price sitting in its "outdoor" seating area, I could not help but feel a spring to my step with a renewed rush of my youthful vigor toward collecting the news. She was onto something, and while it might not have been big, I sensed it might have been just the thing to get each of us feeling good about why we do what we do.

"How about that for a night?" Amity said and smiled.

"Yeah, how about that. When you left me a message to meet here, I didn't know whether I was going to show up to give you a hug or a beating."

"Aw, you can be a little gracious about it. Had I told you what was going on, I was afraid I couldn't count on you showing up."

"Oh, I would have showed up," I said. "But it might have been to forcibly escort you out of that place."

"And yet you didn't."

"I'll admit to a mild curiosity as to what might happen next."

"Can I be curious about whether you're going to sit down?"

"I wasn't done admonishing you," I said, letting myself smile a bit before I pulled a chair away from the table and settled into it comfortably. "Now, I'm done."

"A little better?"

"A little. It does help that you chose for us to meet at my second-favorite spot on the whole station."

"Oh, yeah?" Amity said. "Mere coincidence."

"No reason at all?"

"Well, I always have a reason for doing something. I'm just not ready to tell you yet."

I looked at Amity until she held my gaze. "I do hope you are ready to tell me a lot more than you have so far."

"I am. You have been very kind to help me out, and I'm not trying to be secretive about anything."

"That part I understand. You want to do this yourself."

"Yeah."

"But, Amity, I need to tell you that more than one person has cautioned me against trying to pull a fast one on Ganz and his people. He is a resourceful and dangerous man, and he will let nothing get in the way of his business and his plans for controlling trade in the Taurus Reach."

"Are you telling me to quit?"

"I, well, I don't know." I paused as a server stopped at our table to deliver a pair of iced teas that Amity evidently ordered. "I was told to wave you off, yes."

"And?"

"I want to know what you know and what you're planning."

Amity took a drink from her glass. "You know I am pretty new to Vanguard, but it didn't take long for me to get the sense that whatever is happening between this station and that ship just isn't right."

"I can't fault you for your observations, but amicable relationships between Starfleet and fringe elements in frontier territories is nothing new. It's a necessary evil that can reduce friction among locals and maintain the established ways of doing things until Starfleet gets in a position to truly control a territory."

"Tim, I'm all about going along to get along. But this is a lot more than our guys occasionally looking the other way while their guys run past with a few cases of contraband. What I'm seeing is profiteering and exploitation of the situation by Starfleet personnel."

"What you're seeing, or what you're expecting you'll see? You've been here for all of, what, three weeks?"

"What of it? I certainly think you're smart enough to come into a new situation and assess what's right and what's wrong pretty quickly."

"So you have proof of Starfleet officers violating their duties, Starfleet regulations, or Federation law through their activities with the Orions?"

She paused. "No, but I think I'm close."

"Well, the truth is that you may very well be close."

Amity's eyes widened and she rocked forward in her chair. "What do *you* know, Tim Pennington?"

I laughed a bit at her intensity. "With the help of station security, I did a little cross-checking on the man to whom you introduced me last night. And you were right about him being in

Starfleet. He is in a position that would greatly benefit Ganz were he to be compromised."

"Compromised? Let me tell you, he is plenty compromised," she said. "He has regular meetings, um, 'behind closed doors' meetings if you follow me, with a woman who works with me. Their meetings are like clockwork."

"How did you land that job, anyway?"

"I applied."

"No, seriously."

"I am being serious! I spent some time over there, made friends with a few of the ladies, got them to vouch for me, and the bar manager gave me a uniform."

"Some uniform."

Amity smiled and narrowed her eyes at me. "You liked seeing me in that uniform, didn't you?"

"I'm not answering that."

"What part did you like most, Mister Pennington?"

"That's enough," I said, hoping that my tone of frustration might have couched the likelihood of my uncontrollably blushing were she to continue. "What about your credentials?"

"I provided them," she said. "Not legitimate ones, but they're airtight. I know a guy who set me up."

"The catch, though, is that Ganz knows a lot of guys. Ganz *owns* a lot of guys."

"I wouldn't do this if I wasn't careful."

"I trust you. But I have to tell you, Amity. In a story such as this, as exciting as it can be—and I need to admit that I'm a little caught up in it myself—there's just not a lot to be gained by working it from our end."

"So whose end works it? Starfleet? Tim, they are *involved*."

"Well, one or more individuals may be involved. But don't go into this thinking you're going to tug on one string and unravel an entire conspiracy with the Orions. I think we are better off delivering what we know to Starfleet security as an internal matter and moving on to another story."

"What *we* know? This is my story."

I sensed an understandable edge of defensiveness creeping into her voice. "Of course it is. I get that."

"And as you have pointed out, we don't really know anything. So let me make you a deal."

"You're all about this deal-making."

She smiled. "Let me see this through long enough to get some real evidence on this guy. Let me do my reporting my way and then we take it to the authorities."

I weighed the option Amity proposed, but not against my concerns for her continued involvement on board the *Omari-Ekon,* which were bolstered by Quinn's reactions as well as Ginther's apprehension. I weighed it against my agreeing with her choice and her continuing to inform me of her activities versus my refusal and her going ahead with her investigation but leaving me totally in the dark. In the end, I simply did not want her in this by herself. "Okay. So what's your next step?"

"Hmm," she said. "The next step is for me to tell you why I picked this location in the first place."

"I'm listening."

Amity answered not with her voice but with a subtle nod of her head toward my right. I waited a moment, then shifted in my chair so a sideward glance might be a little less noticeable. I looked just in time to see an impassioned and lingering kiss between a strikingly beautiful and totally bald woman and the subject of last night's surreptitious recording, Adan Chung. It was simultaneously uncomfortable to watch and impossible to turn away from.

"Now I see what you mean by totally compromised."

"See? Just like clockwork," she said. "That's Aurelie, and she's Deltan."

"And you're suggesting Aurelie is a woman who isn't adhering to her people's oath of celibacy in regard to humans in Starfleet?"

Amity simply looked at me. "*Please.*"

"So they come here for dinner? Breakfast?"

"If they come here for food, I've never seen it. They kiss,

sometimes they're even more involved than they were today, make their swap, chat a bit, and leave."

"Make their swap? What? I didn't see them swap anything. Well, a few germs, perhaps."

"That's exactly it," Amity said. "You watched the kiss. Everyone watches the kiss. I watched her palm something he slipped into her hand."

"I sure as hell missed that."

"Mm-hmm. So, who are we following?"

"Pardon?"

"Who are we following? I've never figured out where they go when they leave."

"Right. Well, his activities would likely be traced through records on Starfleet computers, and hers might not be recorded anywhere. If she really did take something from him, my guess is that she's heading directly back to the *Omari-Ekon,* but I'm all for tailing her if for nothing else than to satisfy our curiosity."

Amity scooted back from the table and practically leapt from her chair to dash toward the patio doorway into the café. "We'll cut through the— *Watch out!*"

My body tensed with adrenaline at Amity's shriek as she roughly collided with a server carrying a tray filled with plates of food. Amity screamed again as it became clear that the server would not be able to recover the teetering tray, which showered its contents loudly onto the brick patio. Metal plate covers, china serving dishes and the various meals they contained, all of it smashed and clattered to the ground amid cries of alarm from several nearby diners.

I looked to Amity as she lay on the ground spattered with bits of food, then I snapped my head up toward the Deltan—only to discover her staring right into my eyes. I felt time expand uncomfortably in that moment, each of us caught searching the face of the other in what certainly was a mere moment but felt like an eternity. I regained my presence of mind as soon as I saw Amity start to rise from the ground.

"Stay down!" I implored in a stage whisper that must have

struck anyone overhearing it as very odd in the moment. Amity began to reposition herself but thankfully did not rise from the ground right away. I looked up again to see the Deltan woman had disappeared. "Okay, it's okay now. Are you all right?"

"Yeah, I'm fine. Humiliated, but that's not new." As she rose, she turned to share a sour look of embarrassment with me before reaching out to the server she had toppled. "I am so, so sorry. Please tell me what I can do."

The server, who by this time was joined by several other members of the café staff, responded with grace and told us all would be set to rights shortly. Amity turned to me, her clothing soiled to the point of ruin, smiling seemingly in the hope of making a joke out of the situation to defuse her anxiety over causing a scene. I took her hand and led her away from the clamor.

"Your friend, Aurelie."

"I know. I don't even know what to say about that."

"No, listen," I said. "She saw me, and I mean she took a really hard look at me while all that was happening."

"Do you think she saw you or she saw Tim Pennington?"

I shrugged. "There's no way of knowing. It may be nothing. Maybe it was just the kind of look you give to a passerby when you share a strange moment. I'm sure I'm simply reading too much into this. Are you sure you're okay?"

"You're just being cautious, and it's cute. I'm fine." Amity leaned into me, completely unconscious of a smudge of some sort of sauce on her face, and softly kissed me on the cheek. "But I need to go home and get ready for work."

"Is that really such a good idea?"

"How about this? I go tonight. I get a feel for my own comfort level while I'm there and we talk about it again tomorrow."

"I can live with that."

"Good," she said, and smiled. "I'll give you a call then. Oh, and one more thing."

"What's that?"

"Be a dear and pick up our tab, would you?"

12

Either the stench was less oppressive than I had experienced the night before, or I had been spending way too much time on the *Omari-Ekon*.

However, in all fairness, I should have accounted for all of the differences that separated that particular moment on the Orion ship from my visit the previous night. First, it was a different time of day for me to be there. Upon my arrival home from the café, I had showered, had recorded a number of notes from the day before they slipped my mind, and had laid myself down for a nap. Thus, while I previously had met Amity near the beginning of her shift, tonight I arrived near what I assumed might be the conclusion of it. Yes, she had offered to contact me following her shift as a cocktail server, but I found myself not wanting to wait. I wanted to speak with her as soon as possible.

And what a difference my timing made not only in the breathable atmosphere of the ship but in the overall mood of the place as well. While there were noticeably fewer patrons at the gaming tables, the overall noise and raucousness about the place seemed even greater, owing to the relative per capita intake of alcoholic beverages, no doubt. Wins seemed less frequent at this time of night, but they were celebrated with even more fervor.

Something else that seemed to come on with a little more fervor was the waitstaff. Not only did they seem more enthusiastic about plying the patrons with alcohol, I began to wonder whether the servers—males and females alike—were offering themselves for the taking. If that happened to be the typical situation among workers of the late shift, or something of an expectation placed on them by managers or even Ganz himself, it was a detail that Amity spared me. More likely, at least in my mind, was the possibility that management turned a blind eye to ambitious or entrepreneurial employees who chose to seize an opportunity to turn a profit from an inebriated or winning gambler.

I had been on board awhile at that point, but not long enough for Amity to have traded sections of responsibility for the bar area. Besides, she had not been keeping a lookout for me among the patrons, as she had no way of expecting my arrival. I had hoped that would be the case, as it afforded me a better chance to observe her without being seen. I must admit that my first glimpses of her in the skimpy costume worn by all the female servers did flatter her body to the point that I found myself paying much closer attention than I had intended. But that night's visit was much more to put my mind at ease rather than get it spinning with ideas. I needed to see for myself how she managed this undercover gig of hers. From the look of things, she could manage just fine.

I noticed her fending off drunken advances and juggling a myriad of drink orders. I saw her working behind the bar as well as on the floor in the manner of a seasoned professional. And I watched as she engaged people in conversation—all sorts of them, from gamblers to servers to the hulking Orion guards. Amity immersed herself in the environment of the *Omari-Ekon* to a point that made me feel at least a little more secure in her decision to keep fishing for leads on stories that might get her noticed by the major news outlets.

I was caught up in the rhythm of the electronically driven music, absently staring beyond a series of multicolored spotlights and into the void, when a sharp rap shook my tabletop. I glanced down to see a full glass tumbler grasped by a slender-fingered hand. My gaze quickly followed that hand up an arm and into the eyes of the Deltan woman, Aurelie. I felt myself flinch just a little, and I hoped it was something I could easily dismiss as being startled by her arrival more so than her identity.

"Whoa! I'm sorry, I wasn't quite here when you arrived."

"I understand, and I take no offense, sir," said the lithe, baldheaded woman I knew as Aurelie. I had to remind myself, however, that she had no inkling that I knew her at all.

"And I'm sorry, but I didn't order this. It's some kind of mistake."

"Oh, not at all. I noticed you were dry and so I had the bartender make this for you," she said. "It might take the edge off your bad afternoon."

I decided to play dumb. "Bad afternoon? I'm not sure I understand you."

"Today, at the outdoor café? I saw a man get caught in an awful accident with a dropped tray of food. I could have sworn it was you."

"Right! Of course! You were there, too?"

"Oh, I was passing by when it happened but it would have been impossible not to notice," she said, and smiled coyly. "I remember it was you because you looked right at me."

I laughed in a way that I hoped did not sound too forced. "Oh, I'm sure I did. The whole thing happened so fast that all I can really remember was the noise."

"I may never forget that crash," she said. "So, relax. Have a drink. It's nothing heavy but it's very relaxing."

I played along and raised my glass as a toast and took a drink. She was right about its being of light flavor and consistency. The only place I even tasted its potency was on the tip of my tongue and, oddly enough, my gums. "Thank you. This isn't something I've had before."

Aurelie laughed softly, at least relative to the ambient noise of the place. "I'm sure it's not. It's an Orion infusion, something you don't find just anywhere. So, you're here at Vanguard on business?"

"Sure," I said, figuring it was just as easy to feed off of her cues as it was to try and fabricate a story on the fly, especially considering that I had now started to feel the action of the day begin to weigh on me. "I'm helping to install an upgraded communications array for the station. It's a job that will keep me here awhile."

"There's nothing wrong with that," she said, seeming to look at me a little more closely in that moment.

I took a second sip from my drink and felt an unnatural spin begin to swirl in my head. I looked at the drink in my hand and tried in vain to decipher its contents.

"What's in this, anyway?" I managed to ask.

"It's special for you, sir. A house blend."

"Well, I hope you're ready. By the time I'm finished with this, I'm going to be incredibly charming."

She chuckled a bit. "You're already very charming," she said, darting her tongue tip into one corner of her mouth. "I can see why Amity likes you."

My blood chilled and my stomach churned as I tried to clear my head. "Pardon me?"

Aurelie's eyes narrowed into slits yet still carried the power to make me feel as if they were boring into me and cause a wave of dread that momentarily superseded my disorientation. "Get up, Mister Pennington."

I was able to quell at least one flash of panic in my brain. In that moment, I appreciated my decision to leave my recorder at my apartment.

I went to push against the table so my chair would scoot away from it, but I evidently misjudged my strength as the whole table toppled, its metal top ringing as it struck the floor. I tried to stand but felt the floor turn to thick mud as my knees gave way under my own weight. Just when I thought I would fall to the floor, I felt a rough grip under one arm and then the other before I was hoisted into the air. I tried walking, but it felt as though only the tips of my toes were brushing the floor. I turned my head to see one of the massive green-skinned guards on my left side, then I spun my head to confirm my suspicion that a second one was on my right.

"Sorry, friends," one of the guards spoke loudly, practically yelling into my ear as I was carried. "Got one who's had a little too much fun tonight. Pardon us. Coming through."

Above the din, I heard a shriek and recognized it as coming from Amity. I looked to see her rushing from one end of the gaming deck toward me, but I just kept shaking my head no and trying to wave her off. By then, my tongue felt too thick to attempt to speak, but I had no other way of warning her that Ganz and his men had connected her to me. And obviously, they knew precisely who I was.

I locked on to her rich, brown eyes, attempting to apologize and to soothe and to assure her this could be straightened out—at least those were my intentions. But just as quickly, I was carried past her, off the gaming deck and into a darkness I could not distinguish from sleep.

13

Light returned, or at least it had to one of my eyes. And that was followed by pain.

As best I could tell, I was back in the terrestrial enclosure of Vanguard. Judging from the level of light from the artificial sunrise, I guessed it was early morning. And from the cool, scratchy surface upon which the side of my face rested, I was probably lying on a paved walkway near a drinking establishment in Stars Landing. To any early risers, I simply would have appeared as a drunkard who had attempted to stumble home only to find rest and respite from his condition in the street.

I pushed myself to a sitting position and surveyed my location. I was correct in that the front door of Tom Walker's place was a few meters behind me. I then managed to bring myself to my feet and take a look at my overall condition. My clothing was soiled and bloodied, ostensibly the result of the Orion guards dragging me about as I unconsciously endured whatever indignities they felt fit to serve me. I then looked at my hands, which for whatever reason had been spared from injury beyond a few cuts and knuckle abrasions I hoped were the results of my getting in a few wild punches rather than mere dragging. And—something for which I was equally thankful—I seemed to have suffered no joint injuries. My knees did not overly pain me to move, nor did my elbows. I felt a few twinges as I rotated my shoulders and wind-milled my arms, but those were not new to my experience since regaining consciousness, anyway.

I then mustered the courage to shuffle to a storefront window and use the reflection in an attempt to ascertain the injuries to my face. Once I got a look, I wished I had waited until I had returned home. As I suspected, my right eye was swollen shut from what I assumed was repeated pummeling. My brow above the eye had been split, and blood from the wound had created a dried trickle of crimson around my eye and down my cheek, appearing almost as if the gore had been cried out rather than spilled. My swollen lower lip appeared to bear two splits, and each cheek sported abrasions I remember my mother calling strawberries when they occurred on my kneecaps. My left ear had been boxed pretty effectively as well.

"You should see the other guy," I slurred to myself through my wounded lips, and when I did so, my attention was held by some-thing I saw in my mouth—or did not see, to be more accurate. I pushed my lower lip down despite its throbbing protests to the contrary and spied a hole where one tooth had been.

"Well, shit."

I made my way back to my apartment without further inci-dent, managing to startle only a handful of fellow pedestrians along the way, and spent a portion of my morning in gingerly at-tempts to clean and dress my wounds. As pain can be a clarifier of thinking as well as a duller, I managed to have my wits about me at a level I frankly did not expect, considering the potency of the drink I had been served. Then again, maybe the Orion intoxi-cant was created to be as quickly purged from a system as assimi-lated into it. In either event, I was not suffering exaggerated symptoms of a traditional hangover, as I had initially suspected.

Once I was back in order, the equally pressing matter at hand was to determine the whereabouts of Amity and hope she had not been equally brutalized. My recording device, which also served as a communicator, registered no contact from Amity, and my repeated calls to her device, which I began making as soon as I had reached my apartment, went unanswered. A hurdle I had not anticipated until that moment, however, was my ignorance of where she lived during her time on Vanguard. She had not divulged that information, and none of our few meetings had ever occurred in her quarters. In a typical situation, I would have relied on myself to do the footwork and determine the whereabouts of her living quarters. At that moment, I chose to call in some assistance and contacted Lieutenant Ginther from my recording device. He answered the audiovisual connection almost immediately.

"Security. Ginther." He paused as the look of my visage registered in his mind. *"Pennington? What the hell happened to you?"*

"An altercation, Lieutenant, but that's not the reason behind my contacting you. I need your help, and it's urgent."

"Well, this may be the one I owe ya. What can I do?"

"You may remember my mentioning a friend who got mixed up with Ganz and the crew of the Orion ship."

"I do. I hoped you might have impressed upon her what I said, that she should get untangled from him as soon as humanly possible."

"I'm afraid that she may not have gotten untangled soon enough. I wonder whether you might be able to locate her living quarters for me, so I might check on her."

"Absolutely. What's her name?"

"Amity Price."

Ginther's end of the connection went silent momentarily as, I assume, he worked his computer database. *"Amity Price? A-M-I-T-Y?"*

"That's correct, sir."

"I'm sorry, but we don't have a record of any lodging for someone with that name."

"I don't understand."

"I'm not trying to be confusing. What I'm telling you is that according to the station directory of residency, she is not listed.

Just a moment. Computer, broaden the name search to encompass all records including ship manifests and temporary accommodations."

"I appreciate your efforts, Lieutenant."

"Well, thanks, but this search isn't going to make you any happier. According to this, an Amity Price did arrive on Vanguard about a month ago."

"Yes! That's the one."

"Yeah, but then she left the station as a passenger on the same transport ship two days later."

"What? That's not possible."

"Well, it's possible if the person you're dealing with isn't being entirely straight with you. Maybe Amity Price *is an alias. Do you have any identification information on her at all? A photo or a signature?"*

"I'm afraid I don't, sir," I said. "I have a data card filled with samples of her journalistic writing."

"I'm not sure what we might be able to pull from a card like yours that would prove helpful."

"I see."

"I am sorry, Tim. I wish I could help more. There's just nothing at all here. If something breaks loose that I can help with, find me."

"Indeed I will. Oh, and thanks." I surprised myself by remembering to add my thanks before terminating the connection, as I felt stupefied almost beyond my ability to speak. I could not rule out that Amity had duped me into believing she was someone other than who she truly was, but doing so made no sense and gained her no advantage. I could discern no reason that she herself or some larger organization, including Starfleet itself, would gain anything from a play like this one. She was not an imposter, and she was not a plant. I knew this. Amity Price was real.

As real as the icy yet polite voice that just then echoed in my apartment.

"It's all pretty simple, Mister Pennington. She's gone."

I wheeled around to my now open doorway to see a tall man

in a finely tailored business suit leaning against the jamb. His deep black skin almost glistened in the light, as if he had been formed from a pool of crude oil.

"I beg your pardon," I snapped loudly. "Who the hell are you and what are you doing in my apartment?"

"I'm a little disappointed you can't place me. I'm certain we have been introduced before now."

My eyes scanned his form again, not terribly eager to play his game but hungry for answers. "Zett," came the answer, as if summoned unwillingly. "You work for Ganz."

"I do," he said. "And I came to offer you information I think you will want and I hope you will take to heart."

"What did you do with Amity Price?"

"I merely aided her in her request to be gone from the station."

"She wouldn't have made such a request."

"Ah, but she did," Zett said as he strode into my living room. "If I recall correctly, she said she wished she never had stayed on Vanguard, and that she had stayed on the ship that brought her here. So, I did what I could to accommodate her request."

"How could you rub someone's existence from every data bank on Vanguard?"

"She wanted to be gone, so I helped all that I could."

"You killed her."

"She is gone, and she will not be missed."

"That part is absolutely not true," I said. "She has friends all over your boss's ship."

"As you can imagine, we have a high, let us say, turnover rate of employees. Our workers are used to comings and goings, many of which occur on very short notice. Consequently, they find such matters . . . uninteresting to discuss."

"Someone will look for her."

"And they will find, as did you, that Miss Price's arrival and departure went by largely unnoticed," Zett said. "I would venture to say, Mister Pennington, were you someone who also would not be missed, you would have . . . left with her."

"But I do have a bit of an exposure issue these days," I said, "and that might work to my advantage should I continue to make visits to the *Omari-Ekon*."

"However, it would not work to the advantage of your known associates. I would be disappointed to see . . . Mister Quinn, for example, follow Miss Price away from the station. Wait, I should correct myself, if I may. I would not be disappointed at all."

If Zett was going to push a button with me, he had just pushed it. Putting myself at risk for my job is acceptable for me—but never at the expense of someone else's health and safety. I did not have to respond to Zett for him to recognize he had made his point. My bruised, fallen face and aching, slumped shoulders likely communicated that for me.

"I believe we have reached an understanding, then," Zett said, "and I thank you for your time and attention." And the door slid shut.

I stood in my silent, empty apartment that morning for I have no idea how long, wishing that Amity Price merely had been sent away so intently that I almost had myself convinced of the possibility. I imagined her walking down the boarding ramp onto the first shuttle away from Vanguard to pursue every big story she ever hoped to write during a big career elsewhere on the frontier—a place where a reporter and a story can make a difference without getting people arrested or hurt or killed.

It was a place where I had not been for a long, long time. And maybe it was time to go.

14

"You look like hell, son. I don't mind tellin' ya."

"Doctor Fisher," I said, "should I ever need a refresher course in candor, I trust you will be available to teach it."

As the chief medical officer was leaning in so close that I thought our foreheads would touch, I more felt him laugh than heard him. When I had arrived, he happened to be milling about the reception area of Vanguard's medical center cradling a mug of coffee in his large hands—practically in the same place that I had left him after my attempt to see T'Prynn. As soon as he spotted me, he ushered me back into an exam room personally rather than have me wait on an available medic.

I sat on an edge of the room's only biobed as Fisher tended to my wounds while demonstrating his apparent habit of talking his way through procedures. I had to wonder whether he did this to steady himself as much as to soothe me; regardless, it seemed to work. I humored myself by trying to predict where he would choose to pause in a given sentence.

"This autosuture I'm . . . using here . . . runs a little slower than a dermal regenerator," he said as he passed the device over my right eyebrow. The ice-blue glow of its emitter shone through my eyelid, and I could feel my skin tingle in response. "But I . . . use it on places like this because . . . it's more precise. Newer isn't always . . . better."

"Not always," I echoed.

He clicked off the autosuture. "You can open your eyes now. I know your lip is still pretty sore, but hold it down a minute while I recheck the root of that tooth I replaced."

I complied despite the jolt of pain my action delivered, then I looked down my nose into his eyes as he peered into my mouth.

"Mm-hmm. Now, how did you lose this again?"

"I'm not able to tell you. I woke up this morning and it was gone."

"Woke up or regained consciousness?"

"Little of both?"

Fisher raised the tip of a bone-knitting laser to my gumline, and I watched a hair-thin beam lance from the device and onto me. The sensation was different from the autosuture, but equally soothing.

"Got someone you can talk to about . . . all this?"

"Not really," I said, still holding my lip down so he could work.

"Care to talk to me?"

"Not really."

"Okay, then. You can let go now." I saw the beam snap off. "I can give you something that will take the edge off your pain. This may not be what you want to hear, but for facial wounds such as yours, sometimes it's best to let the swelling subside naturally before we rush right in and fix anything."

"That makes sense," I said.

"I'm glad you concur." Fisher did not look up from putting away his surgical instruments, but that did not silence him. "Did you ever track down Doctor M'Benga?"

"Actually, no, I didn't. I'm certainly still interested in T'Prynn's condition. It's just that, well, I've had a few matters to attend to."

"Kind of figured," the physician said. "Typically, I would not circumvent Doctor M'Benga in matters of his patients. But being that you are here and all, I can make an exception in this instance, if you would like to see her."

"You would do that?" I was genuinely surprised by the offer and had not even considered asking Fisher, given our last conversation. But I was not about to turn him down now, regardless of the fact that, physically and emotionally, I was as close to being a candidate for the biobed next to T'Prynn's as I had ever been. "Please, I'm happy to go."

Fisher led the way out of the exam room and down a corridor to an area marked with a simple sign: Isolation Ward 4. He pushed open the door and we entered silently. Fisher did not break stride as he approached T'Prynn lying on the diagnostic bed, whereas I found myself unconsciously slowing my pace. "Come ahead, Mister Pennington," Fisher said, "I assure you that you're not going to wake her."

The Vulcan's features were stoic yet soft as she reclined motionless, while tones from the biobed indicating her heart rate, respiration, and brainwave activity combined to create a rhythmic accompaniment to her apparent restfulness. On occasion, a nurse would come by to read a monitor or check a connection or even just to pause and place a hand on T'Prynn's. There was no way of knowing whether such gestures made a difference in her treatment or whether the unconscious woman even noticed them, but the routine seemed to comfort everyone involved in her care.

After a few moments of being in T'Prynn's presence— moments during which my thoughts did not wander outside what was happening right there—Doctor Fisher motioned me out of the ward. I followed him, noticing as we went back into the corridor that a breeze somehow had brought a chill to my cheeks. Then the physician reached over to pass me a disposable handkerchief.

I raised it to my cheeks and wiped away rivulets of tears. Evidently, without even realizing it, I had wept while standing with T'Prynn.

I felt a hand on my shoulder, and it was Doctor Fisher's. "Tim, let's take a walk."

I followed him to a small staff lounge with a door that he closed for privacy's sake. I sat in an armless upholstered chair and he took a seat in an identical one opposite mine. "I apologize, Doctor," I said. "I'm not really sure what came over me in there."

"You're not the first to have that experience, and you won't be the last."

"Experience? I'm not sure what you mean."

"It's not easy to see someone in her condition, and an emotional response isn't uncommon. Your reaction could stem from a number of things. It's pretty obvious you have a lot of things going on in your world. I'm certainly aware of the history you share with T'Prynn, of the personal pain and loss she brought about for you. Doctor M'Benga even has this theory that T'Prynn or any other Vulcan in severe psychotic distress might be able to project a shadow of what they are feeling while in a comatose state. Think of it as a distress beacon from one psychic to another. And he suggests that in rare instances, the signal from the beacon is strong enough to be picked up by anyone around it."

"Is that possible?"

"With those people, who the hell knows," Fisher said. "But

M'Benga hasn't offered that theory yet to anyone but me, so treat that one as off the record."

I laughed a little. "Right."

"So, am I close?"

I mulled my words a bit before speaking. "My mind keeps returning to her breakdown. The pain I saw on her face. I thought seeing her in a state of calm and peace would help me rationalize that her pain is over, and push that image out of my mind."

"Maybe you can push that image out of your mind by helping in some way," he said, "if not her then definitely yourself. If you have been hanging on to your anger at her, if you have been feeling spiteful or hoping for retribution, what might be anchoring her pain in your mind is a good dose of guilt."

"Oh, there's plenty of that to go around, believe me," I said. "With Reyes in the brig, T'Prynn in a coma, Quinn caught in the crossfire of an Orion mad as hell at me, and an entire Federation frightened about the return of ancient, wrathful aliens, hell, I'm the life of every party in the whole damn quadrant."

"Oh, so you did all that by yourself."

"Didn't I? I got in this job—hell, I *stay* in this job—because I want to help put things right, not to be the architect of doom for everyone I know. But I'm not putting many things right these days."

"Then consider this, Tim," Fisher said. "Maybe you don't try to engineer positive change one quadrant at a time or one planet at a time or one station at a time. Consider doing what's right by one individual at a time. When you change one life for the better, you can get to feeling pretty damn good about the world. Why the hell else do I stay in medicine?"

"It's not for the free coffee?"

Fisher smiled and nodded at me, then gave me a clap on the shoulder while rising from his seat. As we walked back toward the reception area, I could not help but look back toward Isolation Ward 4, where I knew staff members were checking readouts, holding hands, and changing the world one life at a time.

But the only life I wanted to change in that moment was my own.

15

It should have come as no surprise to me that two days of drinking at Tom Walker's place would do little to change my life. Well, little to change it beyond the fact that by that time, even the most indulgent of the establishment's servers had lost a measure of patience with me.

Not that I had become an unruly, unwashed sot as I occupied my usual table. I had done my best to bide by the establishment's regular business hours as well as to maintain my professional demeanor, despite my carrying myself in a manner that I assumed made me seem more unapproachable than usual. Yes, I knew my next story could have come from the next person passing by my table, and that my appearing open and interested might well have been the key to unlocking that person's secrets. But in that moment, I would not have wanted a good lead even if a source had poured it over ice and served it to me in a glass. What was more, while I had the air about me of someone who had come to the place to drink, even that was a façade. Rather than knocking back whisky after whisky on a growing tab of expenses, I simply stared into the glass before me, swirling its contents frequently to appear as though I had been consuming it. In all likelihood, I was losing as much of the alcohol to evaporation as I was to ingestion.

"Freshen that for you, Tim?"

I snapped my head up to look at the source of the question, almost expecting to see Amity in her skimpy barmaid's outfit from aboard the *Omari-Ekon*. Rather, it was Meryl, the young brunette who seemed to be the only server with any remaining interest in checking on me. "I'm sorry," she said. "I didn't know you were asleep."

"I wasn't. And I don't."

"Don't?" she repeated. "Don't sleep?"

"Do sleep. Don't want whatever it is you asked me."

"Okay," she said, setting a tall tumbler of ice water on the table. "But I brought this for you anyway."

"Fine." I reached for the glass and brought it to my mouth, the coolness of the water delivering a bit of a sting to my healing lower lip as well as a burst of clearer consciousness to my mind. A bead of water dripped down my chin, and as I brushed it away with the side of my finger, the sensation of the scruff on my unshaven face reminded me that I likely looked much like I felt inside: disengaged and unmotivated. Considering that I had not returned any of my editor's messages, nor Quinn's for that matter, since Amity's disappearance, Meryl here was likely the only person even aware of where I was.

"Tim?"

"Yes?" I set the glass down and looked at her.

"I know I haven't known you long, but I don't think this is very like you," she said. "I don't know whether I should ask if you want to talk or if I should just leave you alone."

"What are you wanting to do?"

"Ask."

"Leave me alone." Her eyes dropped to the tabletop as my words seemed to sting her at least a little. "Meryl? Sorry. That was my idea of a joke."

"Then this is my idea of a laugh," she said stone-faced.

"I deserved that. And I'm just a little wrapped up in myself, it seems. My responses to the contrary, I do appreciate your asking."

"Then I'll ask again," she said, offering a small smile. "If nothing else, just to make sure you haven't died."

"If I need to move along, just let me know."

"I could," Meryl said over her shoulder as she walked from the table, "but it would be more fun just to call Security."

I returned my gaze to the tabletop, choosing to chase my sip of water with a nip from my whisky glass. I swallowed, knitting my eyes shut as I did to savor the burn of the single-malt spirit, thankful for the familiar sensations that helped to cover my memory of whatever it was I had been served on the Orion ship that led to my disorientation and my inability to keep any harm from befalling Amity.

"Mister Pennington?"

The low voice prompted me to open my eyes, and as they focused, all I could discern before me was a field of red that began to coalesce into the outline of a man in a Starfleet tunic.

"Wait," I spoke quickly to the red shape, "the woman's remark about calling Security was merely a joke, I assure you."

"I wasn't called to take you away," the man said. "At least not yet."

My eyes unblurred enough to see the face of who addressed me. "Lieutenant Ginther."

"I have some information for you, but we're not talking in here," he said. "Follow me out."

I complied, but not before settling what small bill I had with Meryl. Ginther left Tom Walker's place and strode ahead of me, eventually turning into an alleyway between buildings in Stars Landing. I stepped in as if it were a natural path to take rather than hesitating and looking around to determine whether I had been observed. I simply took it on trust that Ginther had a good idea of the area's discretion.

The broad-shouldered man seemed to examine my current state of appearance, but extended the grace of not making a verbal comment. "I did some follow-up on your report and I wanted to tell you what I found," he said, "but what I tell you doesn't leave this alley. Are we clear?"

"Of course," I said. "But what report?"

"Your missing-persons report on Amity Price."

"What? You filed a report?"

"No, I didn't file a report. But I did some checking, and I found something. Well, someone."

"You found Amity? You're kidding?" I felt a wave of relief and joy start to wash over me.

"Calm yourself, Pennington," he said. "It's not what you think. The scrubbing of Vanguard's computer records was not as untraceable as the responsible party had hoped. We detected evidence just fast enough to lead us to the perpetrator and it was a Starfleet computer engineer, someone who had a high clearance for a great amount of information."

"Who was it?"

"I can't tell you that. Just know that we were able to plug a sizable security breach as a result of your call, so I thank you."

"That's fine," I said, my joy giving way to some confusion. "And that led you to Amity?"

"Not directly," Ginther said. "We have reason to suspect foul play, but that investigation has been sealed."

"What? Why?"

"It has become a matter of Starfleet Intelligence."

"Wait," I said, trying to sort these new facts. "You're telling me Amity was in Starfleet Intelligence?"

"No," he said. "Slow down and listen. The perpetrator of the computer work revealed himself as employed by someone outside the Federation as an intelligence gatherer. In return for leniency in prosecution from the Judge Advocate General's office, he has agreed to offer information about his employer's operations and all details on what Federation secrets have been leaked to this point."

"Leaked to who?" I had asked the question out of reflex, but I knew full well who lurked behind it all without being told. That did not stop Ginther from revealing the information as my disgust at the situation mounted.

"The Orions," he said.

"Damn it," I spat. "So now you get to hear who has been whispering what to whom, and who has been secretly moving whatever piece in any number of the political games everyone plays on board this goddamned station. Meanwhile, a young woman is dead—or worse—and the bastards responsible get away clean. That's bleeding brilliant!"

"Pennington, I'm no less frustrated than you are," he said, "but I understand how this plays into the greater benefit to operations in the Taurus Reach and, yes, regardless of how far-fetched it sounds to you right now, the entire Federation."

I was livid. "If you quote that 'needs of the many' shit to me right now, I'm going to gobsmack you."

In a flash, Ginther snatched my wrist in his grip and held it firm. "You don't want to be hitting anyone, and you don't want to be raising your voice to me. Are we clear?"

I glowered at the security officer. Despite my rage at learning how Amity's fate would go undetermined and unpunished, I knew that moment was not the one to seize in the name of justice. "We are," I said as my deep breathing began to slow. "We're clear."

"And I offer this information to you with my appreciation for your help," he said. "It will not be acknowledged officially, and should any hint of it appear in a news report, any further cooperation in your work from Starfleet officials will be greatly discouraged. And I will be greatly disappointed. Is that also understood?"

"Yes, Lieutenant," I said as he released my wrist.

"Quinn says you're one of the good guys, Tim," Ginther said in a calm voice. "Believe it or not, after seeing your response to this, I agree."

"One of the good guys," I said, rubbing my wrist a little. "Then tell me how one of the good guys just leaves someone's story unfinished when I can't report it and I bloody damn well can't go vigilante against the Orion Syndicate."

Ginther looked at me and paused a moment. "When I'm where you are, and I'm there more than you might think," he said, "I find someone I *can* help. Maybe the opportunity just pops up, or maybe I look up someone who my business isn't finished with, as you say. When I get someone back on track or settle an account that I've left open too long, it goes a lot farther toward filling that hole you're feeling than a grudge or a bottle ever will."

I let go a somewhat cynical laugh that part of me immediately regretted. Ginther shrugged his shoulders and extended his hand. I took it. "I appreciate your letting me know. And your advice."

"Let me know how it turns out, if you like. I'd offer the same, but, well, I can't."

"Right."

As I turned to leave, he spoke my name to get my attention. "Tim, you may do it with your words or your actions, but whatever it might be, I suggest you do it. We all have unfinished business. You'll know yours when you see it."

My mind replayed Ginther's words. I'll know it when I see it? As I walked back to my apartment, and back into the reporter's life I once again felt fated to lead, I hoped to hell the guy was right.

THE RUINS OF NOBLE MEN

Marco Palmieri

For Jem and Ben:
Dream big, my sons.

HISTORIAN'S NOTE

This story is set primarily in early January 2368, in the days following the final chapter of *Star Trek Vanguard: Precipice*.

1

2268

Vanguard groaned as another piece of its hull tore free and fell into the void.

The creak of rending metal vibrated through the bulkheads as if the station were in agony, but Rana Desai took little notice. Even the sight of Starbase 47's open wound was lost on her. Less than two hundred meters above the viewport at which she stood, EV-suited engineers dotted the curved underside of the station's immense saucer, surrounding the hideous gash in the enormous doors of Docking Bay 4—damage inflicted just days ago by a being of incomprehensible power.

The new hunk of wreckage tumbled silently through space until a work bee moved in to capture the bent and blackened metal plate. Once secured in the tiny craft's manipulators, the huge fragment was guided safely downstation to a designated cargo bay where debris from the attack was being gathered for analysis.

None of it registered. Desai's gaze fell instead on the bloated vessel moored to one of the primary spokes of the station's external docking wheel. The Orion merchantman *Omari-Ekon*, den of iniquity and illicit trade, and inviolable domain of the crimelord Ganz, had recently returned from months of exile, now sanctuary to the most unlikely refugee imaginable: Desai's former lover, Diego Reyes.

He's alive.

Desai tried to wrap her mind around the thought, to come to grips with how so much had changed. Two years ago, Diego had been a decorated Starfleet flag officer—a commodore and the commander of Starbase 47, overseeing a massive colonization effort that had been initiated in order to mask the real reason for the Federation's rapid expansion into the Taurus Reach. But the cost of maintaining the secrecy of that mission, both in rising casualties and ever-escalating tensions with the Tholians and the Klingons—to say nothing of the lethal power Starfleet had inadvertently awakened in this region of space—had eroded Diego's certainty about the Federation's imperative to decode the transformative potential of the Taurus Meta-Genome.

Shadows moved at the edge of her awareness. Outside, shuttlecraft-sized utility ships shifted position, redirecting high-intensity spotlights toward another compromised section of the bay doors.

Having come to believe he'd been following unjust orders, Diego enabled the public disclosure of classified information related to Vanguard's mission, an act that brought down the full wrath of Starfleet Command, against which Desai, as his defense counsel, had been unable to protect him. Relieved of his command, court-martialed, and convicted, Diego's disgrace had been the end of his career, as well as the end of their relationship.

And still there was worse to come. The ship transporting Reyes to his imprisonment on Earth was destroyed en route, and for months Diego was believed to be dead.

How can he be alive?

She was dimly aware of distant thunder shaking the deck, passing through the soles of her boots as the engineers cut away another section of Vanguard's armor, this one even bigger than the last.

After she was nearly consumed by her grief, Desai somehow found the will to move on with her life. For a time she'd even taken a new lover; nothing serious, at least for her—an unsought dalliance to fill the void of physical intimacy, companionship she'd permitted herself to dull the ache of Diego's absence. After all . . . he was dead.

And then he turned up alive. What am I supposed to do with that?

And how did it change anything, really? Diego remained a convicted criminal and a fugitive from Starfleet justice—and for all she knew, he was complicit in recent acts of theft and sabotage aboard Vanguard. There was nowhere in the Federation he could set foot without being placed under arrest. Desai could see no way to alter any of that, or envision a future that allowed them to be together.

More hull metal sailed past. The breach in the station grew wider, exposing the deeper wounds that had been inflicted upon its core.

What the hell am I doing here?

The bosun's whistle of the station's comm system cut through her contemplations. *"Ops to Captain Desai."*

She sighed, as much in relief as in annoyance. She had come to this unused observation lounge hoping to figure out certain things in quiet and solitude. But with anything remotely resembling clarity remaining stubbornly elusive, Desai actually welcomed the interruption. Without taking her eyes off the *Omari-Ekon,* she thumbed the wall-mounted intercom next to the viewing window. "Desai here."

"Rana, it's Cooper," answered Vanguard's first officer. *"The admiral wants to see you in his office immediately."*

Of course he does. Diego's replacement as base commander had been none too happy about being maneuvered into allowing Ganz back inside Vanguard's protective shadow, but the Shedai artifact the merchant prince had offered in exchange for safe harbor had made it impossible for the admiral to refuse. The fact that Diego had done the actual maneuvering only made it worse, especially since he was shielded from extradition by the Orions' thorny relationship with the Federation. Desai's romance with Reyes was no secret, and she knew it was only a matter of time before Heihachiro Nogura would demand to have words with her. *The wonder is that it took him this long to get around to it.*

"On my way," Desai said, and signed off. She thumbed the channel closed, but her gaze lingered on the *Omari-Ekon.*

He's over there somewhere, she imagined, searching the lighted dots along the ship's upper half. *Maybe he's even looking up at the station for some sign of me.* She considered the distance between her and Diego. It wasn't far. It felt like light-years.

"Sorry I haven't been around," said Ezekiel Fisher. "I've been meaning to visit more often, but it hasn't been an easy time around here. Seems like this place is always attracting the wrong sort of attention. Tholians one day, Klingons the next, and now the Shedai have ripped into us like—" Fisher stopped, raising his hand. "I didn't come here to make excuses. I don't visit enough, that's the bottom line. I'm going to work on that. But I'm here now, because something's happened that I knew you'd want to hear about. Our old friend has beaten the odds again, Hallie. Diego's alive."

The flowering dogwood made no reply, but not once in the past two years of ever-less-frequent visits to Fontana Meadow had Fisher expected one. His one-sided conversations with Hallie Gannon, here at the tree Reyes had planted to memorialize the captain and crew of the *Starship Bombay,* always went unheard; Fisher had no illusions about that. Such rituals were for the living, not the dead.

Fisher took a moment to appreciate the breeze that wafted across the meadow. The convincing illusion of an open blue sky and sunlight was no small miracle, of course, nor the expansive plain of genuine green grass or the groves of trees that disguised the false horizon. Vanguard's groundskeepers did a masterful job tending the station's terrestrial enclosure, but as far as Fisher was concerned, the real magic of this place was the breeze— randomized gusts of cool wind that caught you by surprise and made the place seem real in a way that nothing else did.

Fisher smiled. "Had a hunch you'd like hearing that," he told the breeze. "It's not exactly the sort of news most people around here are celebrating, but I'll take it. I'm a little worried about Rana. Ever since Diego resurfaced, she's been finding excuses to avoid me. I know better than to take it personally, but still . . ."

Fisher's gaze shifted to the brushed metal plaque set into a rough slab of stone beside the tree. The polished silver inscription stood out against textured gray:

IN PROUD MEMORY
U.S.S. BOMBAY, NCC-1926
"OUR DEATHS ARE NOT OURS; THEY ARE YOURS;
THEY WILL MEAN WHAT YOU MAKE THEM."

Many of the two hundred twenty-four names listed below had been little more than strangers to Fisher. Some he'd met in the normal routine of his duties as Starbase 47's chief medical officer, but the *Bombay*'s infrequent and always-too-brief returns to base had made it difficult to know most of them socially, and that failure weighed upon Fisher now, deepening the hole in his chest.

"I've missed you, Hallie. I know Diego misses you too—now more than ever, I suspect. God knows there were times in the last couple of years when he would have valued your good advice. Sometimes I think things would have turned out differently for all of us . . . if only you had been here."

"Doctor Fisher?"

Fisher turned, startled. Standing at parade rest a respectful distance away was Haniff Jackson, Vanguard's chief of security. "Lieutenant. Something I can do for you?"

"I apologize for the intrusion, Doctor, but Admiral Nogura requires your presence in his office immediately."

Fisher's eyebrows went up. "And he needed to send you to deliver the message? How'd you even know where to find me?"

Jackson shrugged. "I volunteered. This is the only place on the station out of earshot from the nearest intercom . . . and it's the only place you go without your communicator."

"Should I be worried about how you would even know that?"

"Just doing my job, sir."

"And a helluva job it is," Fisher said, casting a wistful glance back at the dogwood tree before returning his full attention to Jackson. "Lead on, Lieutenant."

Fisher knew better than to try to cajole Jackson into telling him the reason for Nogura's summons; if the young man were at liberty to divulge that information, he would have offered it back on the meadow. That Jackson hadn't required him to pick up his medkit on the way ruled out a medical emergency, but the normally talkative Haniff had little of anything to say on the turbolift ride up to the command tower, and that in itself troubled Fisher . . . as did the dour faces that greeted him in the operations center. *This is not good.*

As Jackson escorted him into Nogura's office, it surprised Fisher to learn it wasn't the admiral waiting inside, but Rana, looking as if she had just risen from one of the guest chairs. Her pale brown face, framed in shimmering, straight black hair, reflected Fisher's own growing uncertainty.

Jackson exchanged a cordial nod with Desai, which Fisher pretended not to notice. "The admiral should be along shortly," the security chief said. Then he added, "I'll be right outside the door if you need anything."

Fisher murmured thanks and waited for the door to close before he turned to Desai. "Did he just warn us not to try leaving?"

Desai's brow furrowed as she sank back into her seat. "It's probably best if we don't jump to any conclusions. I take it you're as much in the dark as I am?"

"Without a candle," Fisher said, smiling as he took the unoccupied guest chair next to Desai's. "Though I will say it's nice to see you, stranger."

He watched Desai carefully for her reaction. The smile she volleyed back seemed genuine enough, but it failed to reach her big brown eyes. "Oh, come on, Fish," she said. "It's not like I've been AWOL."

Was that an acknowledgment that she had put some distance between them? Fisher supposed it must be, but he wouldn't probe deeper . . . just as he never pressed her about what had transpired between her and Jackson last year, around the time the first rumors of Diego's survival had begun to spread. Rana would open up to him in her own time, or she wouldn't. All he could do was be there for her if and when she needed him.

The office door opened. "Stay seated," Admiral Nogura said

as he entered the room, stopping Fisher and Desai halfway out of their chairs. "Sorry to keep you waiting," he added as he strode briskly toward his desk. Not for the first time, Fisher envied the shorter man's vigor. Despite being nearly the same age as the octogenarian doctor, Nogura showed few signs of it. The admiral's deeply lined face and silver-streaked hair belied the energy with which he always moved.

"What I'm about to tell you will be made known to the rest of the crew shortly, but I wanted you two to hear it from me first," Nogura began as he lowered himself into the high-backed chair behind his desk. He paused as if considering how he should proceed before he finally told them, "There isn't an easy way to say this, so I'll come right to the point. It's my sad duty to inform you both that Commander Aole Miller is dead."

The words were a kick in the gut. Rana froze in disbelief. Fisher looked away, shaking his head.

God, not Aole . . .

Miller had been among the first arrivals at Starbase 47, on the same transport as Fisher. The doctor had been instantly taken with the younger man's upbeat and gregarious nature, and the two became fast friends before either of them had set foot on the station. But Aole had that effect on everyone, Fisher quickly learned, his apparently inexhaustible optimism and indiscriminate affability quickly making him one of the most well-liked members of the crew—the proverbial ray of sunshine even during Vanguard's darkest days.

Such a loss for all of us . . .

"How did he die?" Rana asked, her voice cracking.

"Commander Miller was on assignment to the New Anglesey colony on Kadru," Nogura said. "This morning I was informed by the colony's governor that Miller accidentally drowned when he ventured too far outside the settlement without an escort or authorization."

Fisher swore under his breath. He knew from experience that young colony worlds were dangerous places, each with its own unique set of hazards, which had to be learned over time by the settlers. But there was always the danger of visitors forgetting that a planet had not been "tamed" the moment colony ships touched down, and in those rare instances the consequences were too often tragic, even for experienced Starfleet personnel.

The hell of it was, if anyone knew landing party protocols, it was Aole Miller. He might not have written the book on the subject, but as Starfleet's colonial liaison for the entire Taurus Reach, he had probably contributed more than a chapter or two. The idea that he could have made a mistake that cost him his life—

"Has anyone told Ahmed?" Desai asked.

Nogura nodded. "That's the reason I was late getting here. I gave Mister Farahani the news myself."

Fisher wanted to kick himself. On top of everything else, Miller was a newlywed of four months. That it had taken him this long before he gave a thought to Aole's widower shamed him. Fisher imagined Ahmed alone, overcome with anguish, and it was more than he could endure. Rising from his chair, he said, "Admiral, if you'll excuse me—"

"As you were, Doctor," Nogura said without force, but in a manner that had the effect of nailing Fisher's boots to the deck. "Lieutenant Goldrosen went with me to see Mister Farahani, and I left him in her expert care. I'm sure you'll agree he's in good hands."

Fisher opened his mouth to protest, but quickly tamped down the impulse. Nogura was right. Tziporah Goldrosen was an experienced grief counselor. For Fisher to show up now would probably be more disruptive than helpful. But that raised another question, and once again, Rana was half a step ahead of him.

"Admiral . . . may I ask why you elected to inform the two of us personally, and ahead of the rest of the crew?"

Nogura rose and stepped around his desk. He leaned back against the forward edge and folded his arms. "I'm tasking the two of you with completing Commander Miller's assignment."

Fisher blinked.

"Which was what, specifically?" Rana asked.

"To convince the colonists to evacuate Kadru."

Fisher and Desai exchanged looks before the doctor asked, "What are we looking at? More territorial challenges from the Klingons? Or has someone detected the presence of the meta-genome?"

"Nothing so dramatic—at least, not yet," Nogura said. He picked up a remote control resting on his desk and pointed it at the office viewscreen, calling up a map of the Federation's colonial holdings in the Taurus Reach. Blue dots denoted the settlements. A number of arcing yellow lines radiated from the spot that symbolized Vanguard, weaving among the colonies, and Fisher knew these represented starship patrol routes.

"Starfleet Command is increasingly concerned about its ability to adequately safeguard Federation colonies in the Taurus Reach," the admiral said. "Some of them are simply too remote for the resources available to Operation Vanguard."

"It was my understanding the recent increase in dedicated starship support was supposed to have addressed that," Desai said.

"Unfortunately, the rising frequency of military engagements in the region has effectively negated the benefits of our enlarged fleet. Simply stated, the Taurus Reach is too hot, and we're spread too thin, for the number of colonies we need to protect." Nogura tapped his remote, and several of the outermost colonies shifted from blue to red. "The Federation Council agrees with Command's assessment, and has determined these four settlements are in areas where continuing to provide Starfleet support would be contrary to Federation interests at this time." Another touch on the remote, and the patrol routes shrank, leaving the red dots well outside their arcs.

"A strategic withdrawal," Rana interpreted.

"A temporary one, we hope," Nogura said.

"The Klingons won't see it that way," Fisher warned. "They'll see it as a sign of weakness, and they won't hesitate to exploit it. Admiral, we're essentially relinquishing our claim on those systems."

"I don't disagree with you, Doctor," Nogura said. "I'm against this course of action for those very reasons, but the decision has been made. One month from now, all four of these colonies will be outside our regular patrol routes. We need to get those settlers relocated ASAP."

"And New Anglesey?" Desai prompted.

"The one holdout." Nogura keyed the screen to zoom in on one of the red systems, displaying a cloud-heavy Class-M planet, second out from a G0 main sequence star, HD-24040. "Kadru was colonized three years ago. It's a scientific research settlement that went independent after just six months. Since then relations between New Anglesey and the Federation—Starfleet in particular—have deteriorated to the point where they've been denying our people permission to set foot on the planet. We notified them of the Federation Council's decision, but they're refusing to cooperate. They've dug in and have no intention of leaving Kadru."

Desai frowned. "If they're not allowing Starfleet visitors, how is it Miller was able to go there?"

"He sweet-talked his way in," Fisher guessed.

"You're not far off," Nogura confirmed. "A few weeks ago Miller started building a rapport with Governor Ying Mei-Hua over subspace, and he finally persuaded her to give him permission to make his case in person. He was four days into his visit when the colony contacted us with news of his death. And judging by the conversation I had with Ying, the New Anglese haven't changed their position on being evacuated. That's where you two come in."

"Begging the admiral's pardon," Desai said, "but this sounds like an assignment better suited to someone on Commander Miller's staff, or perhaps Ambassador Jetanien—"

"Under ordinary circumstances, that would be true. But as I said, there are other colonies besides New Anglesey affected by this decision, and Miller's department is fully occupied with the logistics of relocating those settlements. Ambassador Jetanien's office is likewise engaged in ongoing diplomatic talks with the Tholians, the Klingons, the Romulans, and more recently, with the Orions."

The slight emphasis the admiral placed on the word *Orions* was not lost on Fisher, and he was certain Rana hadn't missed it either, though she gave no sign she had noticed it. Fisher wondered how Jetanien, who considered Diego a friend, was handling his assignment to somehow negotiate Reyes's extradition.

"All that aside," Nogura went on, "you're far too modest about your own qualifications for the mission, Captain. You frequently coordinated with Commander Miller's department in matters of Federation law and Starfleet regulations as they pertained to TR colonies. You're also no stranger to dealing with the colonial mindset, and that's exactly what's needed here.

"More to the point, however—and this should matter to both of you—the circumstances of Commander Miller's death are far from clear. Governor Ying offered to have the body returned to Starbase 47 in a colony transport, but I insisted that a team from Vanguard be allowed to recover Miller's remains personally. Ying agreed to allow two more officers to visit the colony for that purpose, but she did so grudgingly. That makes me suspicious. If there's more to Miller's death than she's saying, I want to know what it is."

Nogura returned to his chair and continued, "The *Endeavour* is set to depart within the hour for its next assignment, which will take her to within shuttlecraft range of Kadru. She'll be back in the vicinity in a week's time. You two have that long to perform an autopsy, verify the cause of death, and complete an investigation into what transpired when the commander lost his life.

"But whatever you find, I expect you to persuade those colonists to evacuate before their sector is removed from Starfleet patrol routes. They need to understand the consequences of remaining on the planet: if they run into trouble, help may be too far away to make a difference."

When Desai didn't answer, Fisher cleared his throat and said, "We understand, Admiral. Any other instructions?"

Nogura shook his head and picked up a data slate awaiting his attention, which Fisher took as their cue to leave. He rose and started for the door, stopping when he realized Desai hadn't budged. "Rana?"

The admiral looked up and frowned when he saw Desai staring at him. "Is there something else, Captain?"

"I was just wondering, Admiral," she began in a quiet voice, "if it's even remotely possible that the real reason Doctor Fisher and I were selected for this assignment is because we're the two people on Vanguard closest to Diego Reyes, and you wanted us both off the station while you contemplated some ill-advised plan to get him back into custody—the nature of which might compel the filing of formal protests by the station's chief medical officer and its senior representative of the Starfleet Judge Advocate General?

"That's not possible, is it, sir?"

Rana, what in the world are you doing? Fisher's eyes went to Nogura, who regarded Desai as if trying to decide, from among several options, which form of disciplinary action would be the most appropriate response to her insubordination.

Instead, the admiral leaned back in his chair. "In light of recent events, Captain, I'm going to do you a favor and forget the last thirty seconds." To Fisher's disbelief, Rana started to respond, but Nogura silenced her with a raised finger. "Don't push your luck, Desai. Just be glad I'm in a forgiving mood. The *Endeavour* departs in forty minutes. I suggest you start packing."

Far too slowly, Desai released her grip on the arms of her chair and stood. "Admiral," she said by way of acknowledgment, then turned and vacated the office. She didn't even look at Fisher as she passed him.

Fisher's brow creased with worry as he followed her out, and his thoughts returned unbidden to dogwood trees and the void left behind by absent friends.

2

2259

Rechecking the settings on his medical tricorder, Zeke Fisher realized it was the third time in the last ten minutes he'd done so and abruptly snapped the device closed. The tension in the room, he decided, was contagious.

From his seat on the steps of the energizer stage, Fisher glanced around at the score of khaki-shirted engineers and blue-shirted medical personnel crowding the emergency transporter, and tried to take the room's emotional temperature. Lots of fidgeting, very little talking, the frequent snaps and clicks of field equipment being adjusted—all spoke volumes about the group's growing impatience. At any moment, *Dauntless* would drop out of warp and the "go" word would come down from the bridge, sending all twenty-two members of the crisis response team scrambling for the pads. The waiting had them all on edge.

Even the ship's new XO wasn't immune; she paced the deck in front of the transporter console, the other members of the landing party giving her a wide berth. Tall, blond, and athletic, Commander Hallie Gannon was an imposing physical presence, but still an unknown quantity to many of the crew, having joined *Dauntless* just nine weeks earlier when the ship's extensive repairs had been completed at Starbase 7. Lean and long of limb, Gannon moved like a dancer.

"Something I can help you with, Doctor?"

The question made Fisher blink, and he sheepishly realized Gannon had caught him staring. She'd stopped pacing directly in front of him, her piercing green eyes daring him to say something unrelated to ship's business. "Martial arts," he ventured to say.

Gannon frowned. "Excuse me?"

"Your extracurricular fitness training. I'm guessing it was some form of martial arts. Am I right?"

Her eyes narrowed. "This is that thing the captain warned me about, isn't it?"

"Oh, he *warned* you about me, did he?"

Gannon smirked. "Well, not you per se . . . just your odd little preoccupation."

"Is that what he called it? My, my. I never realized the practice of guessing a crewperson's Academy sport was something anyone would find particularly odd."

"It is when you consider you could find out easily enough by checking my personnel file," Gannon said. "Or, I dunno, just *asking* me."

Fisher smiled. "Where's the fun in that?"

Before Gannon could offer a rejoinder, the room's starboard doors parted to admit the last member of the crisis response team. Everyone not already on their feet, including Fisher, rose as Chief Engineer Shey made a beeline for the XO. The Andorian held out a data slate.

"It's about time," Gannon said as she accepted the slate and started to scroll through it. "The ARA certainly cut it close."

Shey's antennae dipped toward Gannon in agreement. "At least they came through, though I'm not sure how much the new data will help."

"We'll take what we can get," Gannon answered. She raised her voice to be heard by the rest of the team. "All right, people, listen up. We still don't know what exactly we're beaming into, but Commander Shey has our update from the Arkenite Resources Administration, so pay close attention. Commander?"

Shey's antennae were taut as she addressed the room. "By now, the ARA's most current schematics of the Azha-R7a asteroid mining complex have been uploaded to your tricorders." She gave the team a moment to call up the files, but Fisher opted to peer over the shoulder of Soledad Valdez, one of the other doctors, who already had her tricorder open. "Please note they show that the mine has sixteen levels, not the twelve indicated in our library computer database," Shey continued. "Also, the tunnels are spread over a much wider area than we were led to believe. You have a question, Mister Okano?"

Kunimitsu Okano, a structural engineering specialist, lowered his upraised hand. "How recent are these files?"

"The update is eighteen months old," Shey answered.

"The schematics in our library computer were four years old," Okano said over the murmurs rising among the other engineers. "If the complex expanded this much in thirty months, the actual number of levels and the area they cover must be even greater by now."

"Correct," said Gannon. "But as we've still had no success in contacting the colony directly since the initial distress call, this is the best we have to work with."

Shey said, "We do know that in addition to mining topaline, copper, and zinc, the Arkenites have begun tapping deposits of uridium. These sections are marked in orange on your maps. If it becomes necessary to enter these areas, you'll be required to rely on hand tools. Medical team, this means absolutely no use of laser scalpels or defibrillators."

"Why not?" asked Doctor Valdez.

"Raw uridium is unstable," Okano offered. "It reacts explosively if exposed to an electrical charge or a particle beam."

"That's right," said Shey. "Injured personnel requiring treatment with powered equipment will have to be moved out of those areas before the procedures may be carried out. No exceptions."

"The mission hasn't changed," Gannon said. "We still don't know what precipitated the distress call, the exact nature of the emergency, which areas of the settlement may be affected by it, or even what the Arkenites' needs may be. Supplemental crisis response teams are standing by in Emergency Transporter Rooms 2, 3, and 4, and will await deployment as needed. If it becomes necessary to transfer colonists to *Dauntless,* we'll be following Evacuation Protocol Alpha, unless otherwise dictated by conditions within the mining complex. Hopefully we'll get a clearer picture once *Dauntless* is able to scan the asteroid."

Gannon didn't bother stating the obvious. The distress call from Azha-R7a had reached *Dauntless* thirty-two hours ago. Because it had broken up in mid-transmission and all attempts to reestablish contact with the colony had failed, there was a very real possibility they would arrive too late to do any—

The alarm Klaxon wailed, derailing Fisher's train of thought. *"Red alert,"* came the announcement over the comm system. *"All hands to battle stations. This is not a drill."*

As if a switch had been thrown, the assembled CR team started streaming toward the exits. Fisher hesitated, watching as Gannon moved behind the transporter console and toggled its gooseneck intercom. "Gannon to bridge. What's going on?"

"Ensign Kendrick here, Commander. We've come out of warp two thousand klicks from the asteroid, and there's a Klingon battle cruiser keeping station directly above the settlement. It's the Chech'Iw."

Fisher winced. *Gorkon's ship. Of all the Klingons, why him?*

"Do we know the status of the Arkenites?"

"Is that Gannon?" came another voice over the comm. *"What the hell is she waiting for, an engraved invitation? Tell her to get her ass up here, pronto."*

"Commander, the captain—"

"I heard him, Lloyd. I'm on my way. Gannon out."

Fisher followed Gannon out the door. "Mind if I tag along?"

She spared him a glance without slowing her brisk march to the turbolift. "Don't you need to prep sickbay?"

"My people know the drill," Fisher said as they entered the lift. He held up his hand to block Doctor Valdez, who ran to catch up before the doors closed. "Nonstop to the bridge, Soledad. Take the next one." As the doors hissed shut, Gannon called out their destination to the lift's voice interface. Fisher felt the elevator car rotate on its vertical axis and then glide forward. "Besides," the doctor continued, "sickbay was already on high alert for the rescue mission. There's little else to do unless we start getting wounded."

Gannon let out a long breath. "Let's hope your department has a slow day."

"Amen to that, Commander," Fisher said. The lift's forward motion slowed to a stop, then it started to ascend.

"This'll be the first time the captain's faced Gorkon since Xarant," Gannon said.

Fisher kept his eyes facing the doors. "That's true," he said neutrally, uncomfortably certain he knew where Gannon was headed with this. The engagement at Xarant five months ago had torn up *Dauntless* pretty badly, and cost the lives of eighteen members of the crew, including Gannon's predecessor, Commander Rajiv Mehta. For all the survivors, memories of Xarant were still raw, but especially so for *Dauntless*'s captain.

"Is he past it, do you think?" Gannon asked.

Fisher didn't offer an answer, and to his relief, the commander didn't wait for one when the lift stopped again and opened onto the bridge. Gannon stepped out ahead of him and headed straight for the command well. Fisher hung back, stopping at the portside aft railing. At starboard aft stood Lieutenant Terence Sadler, ship's chief of security, whose intense blue-gray eyes regarded the doctor's presence on the bridge with only slight disapproval before he turned his attention back to the situation at hand.

Privileges of seniority, Terry, Fisher thought. *That, and being the captain's close personal friend for close to fifteen years.*

In the center of the bridge, Captain Diego Reyes leaned forward in the command chair, his gaze fixed on the viewscreen where the dark, vaguely liver-shaped rock of Azha-R7a was partially eclipsed by the distinctive droop-winged silhouette of a Klingon warship. "Any change in their energy readings?" Reyes asked.

At sciences, Anya Brzezinski stared into the hooded viewer that fed her sensor telemetry. "No spikes. Weapons remain cold. Shields are still down." She turned to face the captain. "Sir, they may not know we're here."

"They know," Reyes said with certainty. "We came in too hard and fast for them to miss our entrance." He looked up at Gannon, who stood just to the right of the center seat. "Nice of you to join us, Commander."

"Sorry for the delay, sir," Gannon said. "It won't happen again."

"See that it doesn't," Reyes advised her. "When I call for battle stations, I expect my XO's first response to be to head for the bridge, not second-guess the alert. Are we clear?"

Ouch. That bad already, Diego?

"Aye, sir," Gannon answered, her pale cheeks flushing against the public rebuke. "Readings from the colony?" she called out to Brzezinski.

"Evidence of a recent explosion in one of the subsurface sectors," the science officer said. "A number of the aboveground structures have been compromised."

"Life signs?"

"I'm reading approximately seven hundred humanoids, mostly Arkenites. Eighty-five of them are Klingons."

"An occupation force," Sadler said.

"They damn well aren't there for the coffee," Reyes agreed. "Talk to me, Mister Kendrick."

Seated to Fisher's right, Lloyd Kendrick swiveled away from his console while making an adjustment to his earpiece. "No response from the colony to our hails, Captain. I'm unable to pick up any internal comm traffic. The *Chech'Iw* is dark to us as well."

Reyes pushed out of his chair and crossed his arms as he stood watching the Klingon ship. "Tactical assessment, Lieutenant Sadler?" he said over his shoulder.

"We collected considerable intel on the D7-class battle cruiser during our last encounter with the *Chech'Iw,* sir," Sadler said confidently, his Oxford enunciation always making an interesting contrast to the unique lilt of Reyes's own voice, which was at times tinged with both Castellano and a subtle Texas twang. "Commander Shey and I put that knowledge to good use during the repairs and in subsequent combat drills. There's no doubt in my mind that we have the advantage."

"Captain, the Klingons learn from experience too," Gannon said. "You can be certain General Gorkon and his crew have an equally improved understanding of how to fight a *Pyotr*

Velikiy–class starship. And given *Dauntless*'s history with the *Chech'Iw,* provoking a hasty resumption of hostilities may be exactly what Gorkon—"

"You don't get to lecture me on this ship's history with Gorkon, Commander," Reyes said coldly. "This crew has shed blood every time we've tangled with him, and I don't recall *you* being there on any of those occasions."

Sadler frowned. Kendrick and Brzezinski looked toward Reyes in surprise. *So it isn't just me,* Fisher thought.

"Sir," Gannon said, "with all due respect, this sort of situation is exactly why Starfleet Command recommended me for this assignment. My specialized training in Klingon culture—"

"—was part of a program specifically designed to produce officers who could advise starship captains during Klingon encounters," Reyes finished for her. "All right, Gannon. What's your recommendation?"

"Talk to them."

Reyes stared at her. "I must have misheard you, Commander. Could you repeat that? For a second it sounded as if you suggested I open a dialogue with the ship that attacked a Federation colony."

Instead of rising to the bait, Gannon called out, "Lieutenant Commander Brzezinski, is there any evidence to suggest the damage to the settlement was the result of Klingon ordnance?"

Brzezinski consulted her instruments before reporting, "Negative. Scans reveal no Klingon weapons signatures of any kind."

"Is the *Chech'Iw* still maintaining a nonaggressive posture?"

"Affirmative."

Gannon turned back to Reyes. "Like you said, sir, the Klingons know we're here. And that has to mean they know what we're picking up on our scanners. They're counting on this crew's hostility toward them, especially after our . . . *your* last engagement, to make us rush to judgment. So, yes, Captain, I'm recommending we challenge the Klingons to explain their presence in Federation territory before we start shooting each other."

Reyes's eyes narrowed. He held her gaze while he spoke.

"Ensign Jordan, are we maintaining a target lock on the *Chech'Iw*?"

"Aye, sir," said the helmsman. "All banks locked on."

"Arm photon torpedoes and target their command pod." After Jordan acknowledged the order, Reyes said, "All right, Gannon. We'll try it your way. But make no mistake. If Gorkon so much as twitches, I'm gonna blow him straight back to Qo'noS."

"Mister Kendrick," Gannon said. "Hail the Klingons. Send this message: *I.K.S. Chech'Iw, this is the U.S.S. Dauntless. We are responding to a Federation distress call. You are instructed to withdraw all personnel from Azha-R7a and leave the area immediately.*"

Kendrick tapped his board for several seconds, then lifted a hand to his earpiece. "Message received. They're opening a channel."

Fisher let out a long breath. He hadn't even realized he'd been holding it.

"On screen," Reyes said as he returned to the center seat.

As the view of the *Chech'Iw* dissolved into a shot of its bridge, it surprised Fisher to see Gorkon was not the man sitting in its command chair. Whereas Gorkon was tall and lean and kept his upper lip shorn above an otherwise full beard, the robust Klingon facing the *Dauntless* bridge crew sported a long goatee braided with a silver chain. *"Captain Reyes. How unexpected. It seems not so long ago we watched your vessel limp away like a wounded Ha'DIbaH."*

"I'm surprised you noticed through all the charged plasma you were bleeding after we perforated your starboard nacelle, Mazhtog," Reyes said, and Fisher recognized the name as belonging to Gorkon's executive. "But as nice as it is to reminisce, I don't have time to waste on pissants. I want to speak to your boss."

Mazhtog bared his teeth, and Fisher wondered how the translators had handled the insult. *"General Gorkon is unavailable, Earther. And you will show proper respect to a soldier of the Empire."*

"Fine," Reyes said. "The day I meet a Klingon worthy of the

title, I'll be sure to salute him. Until then, you're trespassing in Federation territory and interfering with a rescue operation. You've got fifteen minutes to pull your people out of our colony and back the hell off. Failure to comply will be considered a hostile act and met with force."

Mazhtog's rictus widened into a grin. *"So like a human. So arrogant."* He leaned forward, his face growing larger on the screen. *"You come here prepared to attack, blind to the obvious fact that the crisis on the Arkenites' asteroid is already under control; that Dauntless's assistance, so late in coming, is no longer required; and that it is you who are trespassing here. And you dare to threaten us!"*

Reyes stood up. "So that's what this is? A land grab for your territory-hungry chancellor? Is Gorkon really stupid enough to believe I'm just going to sit back while he carries out the illegal seizure of a Federation settlement and the capture of its citizens?"

Mazhtog slowly leaned back into his chair, nodding to someone offscreen before turning his jagged smile back to Reyes. *"You still fail to grasp what has happened here, Earther. We have stolen nothing. These Arkenites have given their asteroid and their allegiance to the Klingon Empire of their own free will."*

"Captain," Brzezinski said, "the *Chech'Iw*'s tactical systems are coming on line! Shields up, weapons arming—"

"And we are prepared to defend them."

3

2268

"I don't know what went wrong," Captain Hallie Gannon said from her log. *"If I did, maybe I could have fixed it. But they aren't even interested in talking anymore. They've denied permission to*

let anyone beam down to Kadru, and they've declined Commodore Reyes's invitation to discuss their issues aboard Vanguard. Bottom line: the New Anglese told us to take a hike, and then they turned their backs to us.

"The worst thing is, there isn't a damn thing I can do about it. Every decision they've made is totally within their rights. It's their planet. They opted to go independent, and if they want as little contact with Starfleet as possible without even explaining why, we just have to live with it."

"Computer, pause playback," Desai ordered, making a notation on her data slate. She set down her stylus and rubbed her weary eyes, thinking she really should have allowed herself more than six hours of sleep last night.

She had wasted little time getting to work after she and Fisher boarded the *Endeavour.* First Officer Katherine Stano, a youthful lieutenant commander, met them as they came through the airlock, just seconds before the shipwide command came down from the bridge to seal all external hatches in final preparation for the vessel's departure. Stano went through the standard formalities of welcoming them aboard, reviewing the facilities and services available to them during the two-day voyage to the Kadru system, and then proceeded to escort them to their individual quarters on Deck 7 of the *Constitution*-class starship.

Desai didn't even bother to unpack. She settled immediately at the cabin's workstation, accessed the ship's secure network, and found her mission file waiting in her temporary database. She spent most of the next thirty hours immersed in reports on Kadru, the colony, and its population; Starfleet Command's recommendation to redraw its patrol routes in the Taurus Reach; a transcript of the Federation Council's deliberation of the matter as well as the resolution to uproot the colonies named in Command's recommendation; historical precedents for colonial relocation; recordings of Miller's communications with Governor Ying; and the relevant logs of the starship that, three years ago, had assisted in establishing the New Anglesey colony: the *U.S.S. Bombay.*

Her cabin's buzzer sounded. She called out, "Come in," and Fisher entered carrying an oversized tray with several covered plates, a teapot, and a small vase of flowers.

"What's this?" Desai asked.

"Afternoon tea," Fisher answered, as if the question surprised him. He set the tray down on top of her desk, and she barely got her data cards out from under it in time.

"Not that I don't appreciate the gesture, Fish, but I'm really too busy to—"

"Who said it was for you?"

She tilted her head to one side. "Right. What are you doing here, then?"

"I was temporarily evicted from my quarters," Fisher said, starting to uncover the plates. "Glitch in the climate control. I've got fog. Mm, these look good." On one plate were stacks of small sandwiches: some salmon, some cucumber; on another, scones with strawberry jam and clotted cream.

"Fog?" Desai asked, trying to ignore the fact that her mouth was suddenly watering.

"Yeah, can you believe it? The chief engineer said half the compartments in my corridor are affected. They just need a couple of hours to sort it out."

Hours. Wonderful. "Fish, I've got a ton of prep I need to finish—"

"So do it. You won't even know I'm here," he said, pushing the tray deeper into her workspace. "Does that slate need to be there?"

Sighing, Desai moved the device safely out of the way.

Fisher took the lid off the teapot, releasing a cloud of aromatic steam. He leaned into it, breathing deeply. "Ahh . . . Darjeeling. It's too bad you're so busy, this is almost more than I can—"

"Shut up and pour me a cup, already."

The doctor smiled. "Happy to. Mugs?"

"Behind you."

"Help yourself to a sandwich or three," Fisher said as he went to retrieve a pair of mugs from a shelf in the back wall. While he poured, Desai filled plates for both of them.

"Where'd you get all this?" Desai asked. "And don't tell me it came from a food slot."

Fisher pulled the cabin's lounge chair closer to the desk. "While you've been barricaded in here, I've been making friends. Happened to mention to a nice fellow in the galley how much I used to enjoy afternoon tea and . . . *voilà!*" With a playful flourish, Zeke produced a shot glass candle from somewhere, gave the bottom a sharp tap to ignite it, and set it between them.

Desai smiled in spite of herself. "Nice touch."

"My wife always thought so," Fisher said as he sat down.

"Afternoon tea was a tradition for you two?" Desai brought her mug to her lips, inhaling the steam through her nose before sipping. It was exquisite.

Fisher smiled and picked up a sandwich. "You could call it a tradition, I suppose. It's what I always did when I needed to apologize for something."

Desai laughed, then stopped as she realized the subtext of Fisher's answer. "Wait. You think you need to apologize to me?"

"Do I?" he asked.

She set down her mug and sighed. "If I've given you reason to wonder, Zeke, maybe I'm the one who ought to apologize. I know I've been—"

"Rana, stop," Fisher said. "Don't you dare say another word. I didn't mean to guilt you into unburdening yourself. I just wanted to spend some time with a friend I've seen far too little of the last few months. I won't pretend to understand what you're going through right now. This thing with Diego . . ." He paused and then continued with a chuckle, "Hell, I'll just say it: *any* damn thing with Diego is enough to drive a person crazy, even someone who's known him as long as I have."

Desai had the absurd impulse to laugh even as she wiped at the tears forming in her eyes. Fisher's kind brown face, all crow's feet and silver whiskers, radiated a tenderness that was unconditional and free of judgment.

"But if the time comes when you need a friend to lean on, you know I'll be here for you, right?"

She reached out and placed her hand atop his. "Right." Her voice sounded hoarse in her ears. "Thank you, Fish."

He waved away her gratitude. "Drink your tea. You'll feel better."

Desai arched a black eyebrow at him over the brim of her mug. "There's no fog in your quarters, is there?"

"I'm invoking the Seventh Guarantee."

"That's what I thought."

They ate in companionable silence for a while, then started swapping memories of Aole. Zeke had several funny stories to relate, as did Desai, and for the next hour the two kept each other laughing to the point of breathlessness.

"Well," Fisher said at last, rising to his feet. "I know you have work to do, so I'm just gonna gather up these things and clear out." Licking the tips of his thumb and forefinger, Fisher snuffed out the candle.

"This was nice, Zeke," Desai said sincerely. "I didn't realize just how much I needed the break. Thank you."

Fisher finished loading up the tray and lifted it off her desk. "It was my pleasure. So I guess I'll see you tonight?"

"Tonight?"

Fisher froze in place. "I forgot to mention Captain Khatami's dinner invitation, didn't I?" At the look she gave him, he hurriedly added, "It's just a small thing with the captain and a few of her officers."

"You're telling me this now?" She cast an exasperated glance at the time displayed on her slate. "It's sixteen-thirty! When are we expected?"

"Nineteen hundred, in the captain's mess."

"And where's the captain's— Wait, never mind. I'll look it up. Get out of here now so I can get some work done before I have to start getting ready."

"I'm gone."

As Fisher started for the door, Desai took up her slate and found where she had left off. "Computer, resume playback."

"What saddens me most is the way Mei-Hua threw it all

away, as if the friendship we'd built over the last six months meant noth—"

A crash startled Desai, and she spun around to see Fisher struggling to keep his grip on the tray. A couple of plates had toppled to the deck. She rushed to his side, reaching to steady him. "Zeke, are you okay? What happened?"

"I'm fine, it's just . . . Is that Hallie?"

Oh, God, I forgot he knew Captain Gannon! What was I thinking? "Computer, pause playback! Zeke, sit down." She tried to relieve him of the tray, but he refused to let go of it.

"Rana, please. I'm okay," he assured her. "She's been on my mind lately, and it just caught me off guard to hear her voice all of a sudden. Was that an old log entry from the mission file?"

Desai nodded, recovering the fallen plates and setting them gently back onto the tray. "Gannon's ship helped set up the colony on Kadru."

"Is that a fact? How about that. . . ."

"I can authorize your access, if you'd like to—"

"No, that's okay," Fisher said. "I appreciate the offer, but . . . I'm not sure that's a good idea."

Desai frowned. *What in the world does that mean?* "Zeke, are you sure you're okay?"

"Who's the doctor here?" Fisher asked. "I'll just be on my way. Sorry I startled you. See you at nineteen?"

Desai nodded. "Nineteen."

She watched him go, and as he did, it occurred to Desai that Zeke's life was all about looking after people. And not just his patients; she had long suspected he had delayed his overdue and well-deserved retirement just so he could be there for Diego, and when that was no longer possible, he had honored the obligation he'd felt he owed his oldest friend by staying on to look after the woman Diego loved.

But who looked after Fisher?

"To absent friends," said Atish Khatami as she raised her water glass. The other five officers at the table, their own small glasses filled with a ruby port, mirrored the captain's gesture as they echoed her toast. The sweet after-dinner wine proved to be a delightful follow-up to the baked pears *Endeavour*'s master chef served up for dessert, the hot caramelized fruit steaming from crystal bowls. Desai found it easier to lose herself in the dish than to take part in the current topic of conversation.

The captain's mess was impressive. Desai had expected to dine in a repurposed briefing room or something similar. This was nothing so austere, with soft recessed lighting, warm colors, real wooden furniture, and art on the walls. Apparently every *Constitution*-class starship had a small percentage of discretionary space, subject to the preferences of the commanding officer. Khatami's immediate predecessor, the late Captain Zhao Sheng—whose portrait hung on the wall behind Khatami next to that of *Endeavour*'s first commander, Captain Mary-Anne Rice—had ripped out the tennis court that had been here when he first took command and replaced it with one for racquetball. In the process, Zhao had converted the leftover space into a formal dining room. Bersh glov Mog, Khatami's Tellarite chief engineer, claimed to have it on good authority that at least one of *Endeavour*'s sister ships had a bowling alley, but CMO Anthony Leone refused to believe it.

From there, the evening went downhill as far as Desai was concerned. It was impossible for the group not to talk about the recently resurfaced Reyes, and Desai patiently endured speculations from First Officer Stano about the likelihood of Reyes's eventual return to Federation custody.

The conversation eventually moved on to the sad subject of Aole Miller, and then more generally to the challenge of safeguarding planetary colonies, which everyone agreed was difficult even in the best of circumstances.

At length, Khatami said, "May I ask how your research into New Anglesey is progressing, Captain Desai?"

Desai took a sip of her port while she considered how to answer. "It's all a little strange," she finally admitted. "I've been wading through more background material than I know what to do with, yet nowhere is there any explanation for why things went south between New Anglesey and the Federation. Nobody seems to understand why they became so inflexibly isolationist."

"Aole never figured that out?" Fisher asked.

"If he did, it isn't in the files. Maybe he hoped to find out by going there in person, effect a reconciliation even while he tried to persuade them of the need to evacuate."

Fisher chuckled. "I wouldn't put it past him."

"Nor would I. I've seen the man work. He wasn't always successful at solving every problem, but he never encountered one he didn't feel he could talk his way through."

"What is it about this planet that these people are clinging to?" Doctor Leone asked.

"My understanding," Khatami said, "is that the scientists who founded New Anglesey were granted their colonial charter primarily in order to conduct research on the planet's ecosystem."

"That's it?" Leone scoffed and consumed the last of his port.

"Then why are they being so obstinate?" Stano asked.

"That's hard to say," Desai replied. "But in my experience, there are essentially two kinds of colonists: those who believe they can find greater prosperity in the service of Federation expansion, and those who believe they can find prosperity living independently, free from what they consider the too restrictive core worlds of the UFP, so they can build a world better than the ones they left behind. The former expects Federation support and Starfleet protection. The latter expects the same thing—they just want it on their terms.

"New Anglesey falls into the latter camp. It's almost a case study in a growing trend among the outer colonies, more and more of which believe that the Federation has too much control over their lives."

Leone shook his head. "Yeah, until the Klingons decide they want the planet. Then suddenly the Federation can't do enough."

"That's a rather ungenerous position, don't you think?" Mog said.

"It may have escaped your notice, Mog, but I don't have a lot of sympathy for ingrates who think they can have it both ways."

"Imagine my shock," Mog said.

Leone pressed on. "It's all well and good to think you have better answers than the prevailing authority. But that's what elections are for. Chucking reason out the airlock and then taking pride in the act is just a stupid way to make a point."

"To some colonists," Desai said, "what you call 'chucking reason' is actually a narrowing of focus on fundamental issues that they feel aren't getting enough attention."

"In other words, provincial thinking," Leone countered. "They're so caught up in their own interests, they don't see the big picture."

"And they would probably argue that they are too frequently overlooked in the big picture," Desai said.

"Respectfully, Captain," Leone said, "if that were true, you and Doctor Fisher wouldn't be on your way to New Anglesey, and Commander Miller would still be safely back on Vanguard. Instead, he gave his life trying to help those people. And still they don't trust us!"

"Why is that, Captain?" Stano asked Desai. "Clearly the New Anglesey settlers once trusted Starfleet enough to help get their colony up and running. What went wrong?"

Desai sighed. "That's a puzzle I've been trying to solve for the last thirty-six hours, Commander."

"Are you at liberty to share your suspicions?"

And there it is: the opening. "To be honest . . . with so little time until Zeke and I make planetfall, it might be helpful if I could discuss them," Desai admitted. "I'm just not sure it would be prudent."

"Why would it be imprudent?" Khatami asked, her brow furrowing.

"Because you all were there when everything changed," Desai said. "This isn't something isolated to New Anglesey. What's happening on Kadru is symptomatic of something bigger: a chasm of suspicion and mistrust that's grown only deeper in the last couple of years, because of events right here in the Taurus Reach."

Her listeners stared at her, their startled faces hardening into masks of anger and disbelief. Desai wasn't surprised; this was a sensitive subject to broach with this group. Two years after the fact, the disaster at Gamma Tauri IV had left livid scars on every Starfleet officer assigned to the Taurus Reach. But for the captain and crew of *Endeavour,* the incident remained an open wound. This was, after all, the ship charged with implementing, at Diego Reyes's command, General Order 24: the legally sanctioned destruction of that colony world in an attempt to contain the threat of the Shedai, who were in the process of slaughtering every sentient being on the planet.

"Who the hell do you think you are?" Stano whispered into the shocked silence. "Do you have any idea what we—"

"As you were, Kate," Khatami said. "Captain Desai has an unenviable task to accomplish in a very short time, the nature of which makes it hardly surprising she would need to consider uncomfortable questions."

"Thank you for understanding, Captain," Desai began.

"However," Khatami continued, her voice sharpening, "while I have no doubt the New Anglese may have concerns about the impossible choices Starfleet officers must sometimes face, and act upon, the service has done a great deal to protect and assist the Federation's colonies over the last hundred years, and that good work continues."

Khatami wasn't speaking in the abstract, Desai knew. She'd nearly lost her civilian husband and daughter last year, when the planet Deneva was overrun by neural parasites. Fortunately, a Starfleet crew had been able to end the threat and save the majority of the colonists. And that was hardly the only example of Khatami's point: Desai was fully cognizant of Starfleet's extensive record of assisting colony worlds in crisis.

"I don't dispute anything you're saying, Captain," Desai said. "But let me ask you: How much comfort would you take from your knowledge of Starfleet's good work, if the captain of the *Enterprise* had been compelled to implement General Order 24 in order to contain the parasite threat on Deneva?"

Khatami's mouth dropped open, as much in disbelief as in her own futile attempt to form an answer. She recovered quickly, her lips closing into a hard line. "Perhaps," she said, rising from her chair, "we should all call it a night."

"Are you out of your damn mind?" Fisher demanded when he accosted Desai in her quarters a short time later.

"Let's not do this, Fish." Desai kept her back to him while she removed her earrings and set them down on the dresser. She avoided looking at his reflection in the mirror.

The doctor wasn't dissuaded. "First Nogura, now Khatami? Are you that determined to commit career suicide?"

"Look, I appreciate your concern, Zeke. I do. But I promise you I'm not going off the deep end."

"Then what is it? Can you give me a good reason why you've been acting the way you have, and why I shouldn't be worried about you?"

"It wasn't my intention to offend Captain Khatami, but I'm not sorry I rattled her. The question needed to be asked."

"For God's sake, *why*?"

Desai finally turned to face him. "Because I fully expect that when we meet Governor Ying and I tell her she and her people can trust Starfleet to act in their best interests, Ying is going to ask me the same question, or one very like it . . . and I honestly have no more idea how to answer it than Khatami did."

2259

"Hold fire, Mister Jordan!" Reyes shouted.

"Sir?" the helmsman said.

"That was an order, Ensign." Ignoring Mazhtog's sneer from the viewscreen, Reyes turned to sciences. "Brzezinski, status of the *Chech'Iw*?"

"Unchanged, sir. Maintaining combat readiness. They're just mirroring us."

Reyes's gaze panned back to the Klingon. "Well . . . that's certainly interesting. Looks like you were right, Gannon. They're trying to provoke us into attacking first." Reyes took a step forward, stopping at the foot of the helm console. "Give Gorkon this message, Mazhtog. I'm hereby demanding that my officers and I be allowed to visit Azha-R7a so that we can assess the condition of the colony and ascertain whether or not your ridiculous claim has any merit. Reyes out." Putting his back to the screen, Reyes made a throat-cutting gesture to Kendrick, and the comm officer quickly closed the channel.

Reyes suddenly noticed for the first time that Fisher was on the bridge. "The hell are you doing here, Zeke?" As Fisher opened his mouth to lie, Reyes cut him off. "Never mind. It's just as well. You're joining me in the landing party."

Oh, great, Fisher thought. *This is exactly what I needed. Why didn't I just go to sickbay?*

"Captain," Sadler said. "You aren't truly considering going down there yourself while there are Klingons still occupying the colony?"

"That wouldn't be my first choice," Reyes granted, "but I have no real expectation they're going to leave anytime soon. The fact is, we aren't going to find out what's really going on from up here. Talking to the Arkenites is our best bet."

"Assuming the Klingons allow it, you mean."

"They'll allow it," Gannon said.

"How can you be sure of that?" Sadler asked.

"Denying the captain's request would be the same as admitting they have something to hide. The fact that they were trying to goad us into firing the first shot means they're concerned about justifying their actions here."

Sadler folded his arms, his skepticism palpable. "Since when do Klingons have to justify anything beyond the need to expand their empire? It seems as if everything they do falls rather conveniently under that aegis."

Gannon shook her head. "They're governed by a code of honor, Lieutenant, even if we may not always recognize it as such. It's complex and faceted, but make no mistake: there isn't any action they take that isn't guided by it."

Fisher saw Reyes watching Gannon intently.

"Message from the *Chech'Iw,* sir," Kendrick said. "They say our request has been granted, and they've provided transporter coordinates. But we have to limit the landing party to three individuals."

Sadler spread his hands. "Sir . . ."

"Mister Kendrick," Reyes said, "kindly acknowledge our receipt of the *Chech'Iw*'s message, and inform them our people will be beaming down shortly. Also, I want a coded report of what we know of the situation so far sent to Starfleet Command, including the Klingons' claim regarding the Arkenites, and a request for instructions. Gannon, Zeke, you're with me. Mister Sadler, you have the conn."

"Captain, I want to go on record as advising against your leading this landing party," said Sadler.

"Your objection is duly noted, Lieutenant. But I'm not passing on this opportunity, especially when we have the advantage."

"What advantage?"

"We agree to the Klingons' terms, and they're more likely to think they have things under control. They'll have their guard down. I intend to use that."

Sadler remained skeptical. "Fine. Have it your way. But with the captain's permission, I have a few suggestions. . . ."

As the transporter effect dissipated, Fisher found himself surrounded by Klingons.

Four of them were at the beam-down coordinates, a fairly antiquated-looking transporter room on Sublevel 1 of the colony, ten meters below the surface of the asteroid. To no one's surprise, the Klingons met the landing party with weapons drawn. Their leader, a scowling lieutenant who identified himself as Dravak, required them to surrender their hand lasers before he would let them any farther into the settlement. He also scanned the team's communicators and Fisher's medical kit for explosives, and only when he was thoroughly satisfied with the results did Dravak authorize two of his subordinates, a male and a female, to escort the *Dauntless* officers inside.

No one was sure what to make of what they saw when they went through the door.

In dim corridors that had obviously suffered recent and extensive structural damage, Arkenites and Klingons worked side by side to effect repairs, shoring up load-bearing walls and compromised support columns. The Klingons were all military, but they wore bulky utility vests over their uniforms. Kits and crates containing tools too big to fit in the vests sat on the floor.

"This isn't an occupation force," Fisher heard Gannon say. "These are engineers." Reyes could only nod mutely, frowning as he took it all in.

Fisher watched the Arkenites. The ones they passed all seemed healthy and in good spirits. None of them appeared to be in distress. This wasn't forced labor. It was willing cooperation.

The *Dauntless* officers were eventually led to a door marked with a sign in both Arkenzu and Federation Standard: ADMINISTRATOR DUVADI. The Klingons ushered them through the door, then followed them inside.

The office was more spacious than Fisher expected for a mining colony, but he quickly saw why: it doubled as a conference room. The center was dominated by a table big enough to seat ten, with a desk at the far end of the room.

From behind the desk came a shout: "My God, you're Starfleet!" To Fisher's surprise, the speaker was not an Arkenite, but a human—an auburn-headed man of average height, though to Fisher's eyes he seemed pale and a little gaunt. As the Klingons took watchful positions in adjacent corners at the opposite end of the room, the man came out from behind the desk, unmistakably overjoyed. "They told me they wanted me to meet with someone, but they didn't say who it would be. I can't tell you how glad I am to see you!"

Reyes moved toward him and shook his hand, clearly wanting to keep their conversation as far from the guards as possible. "We're glad to see you, too, Mister . . . ?"

"Doctor Philippe Latour," the man said. "I'm the deputy administrator of Azha-R7a."

"Captain Reyes of the *Starship Dauntless*. My first officer, Commander Gannon, and my chief medical officer, Doctor Fisher. We came in answer to your distress call."

"Better late than never, I suppose," Latour said with a nervous laugh as he glanced at the guards across the room. "Dare I hope you're here to relieve our current benefactors?"

"We're working on it," Reyes said, and then gestured toward the conference table. "All right if we sit down? There's a lot we don't understand about what's going on here, and it was our hope you could shed some light on it."

"Please," Latour said, taking the seat at the head of the table while Reyes sat down on his left. Gannon remained standing, situating herself where she could watch them as well as the Klingons.

Fisher set down his medkit and opened his tricorder. "Mind if I run a scan on you while you chat with the captain, Doctor?"

"I guess not. So, uh, where would you like me to start, Captain?"

"What prompted the distress call?"

"There was an explosion near our energy reactor, at one of the power distribution nodes. A majority of the colonists were trapped in a sealed sector of the facility with a toxic coolant leak. Our transporter was out, and we had only hours before the coolant would reach lethal levels. The Klingons arrived just in time, but they offered their assistance on the condition that the colonists swear loyalty to the Empire."

Fisher glanced at Gannon. The commander frowned, not in anger but in confusion.

"The Klingons gave assurances that we'd be well treated and see little change in our day-to-day lives," Latour went on. "Doctor Duvadi—she's our chief administrator—she didn't take long to agree to the Klingons' terms on behalf of the entire colony. There were children at risk during the crisis, entire families, and there was no way Duvadi would let them die. The Klingons sent work crews in, sealed the leak, freed the people who were trapped, and coordinated with our miners and engineers to repair the damaged areas. So far, they've been true to their word."

Reyes's eyes smoldered as he listened. "True to their word or not, Doctor, I can assure you that no agreement your people made under duress will be allowed to stand. I'm not about to permit Federation citizens to be blackmailed into becoming subjects of the Empire."

"Captain, I can't tell you how relieved I am to hear you say that," Latour said, "but I have to warn you, it isn't going to be that simple."

"Doctor Latour, are you aware you're anemic?" Fisher asked as he closed his tricorder.

"What? I am?"

Fisher *tsked* and opened his medkit to prepare a hypospray. "I can just imagine what the dietary deficiencies are in a place like this. I'm going to give you an iron supplement, if you have no objection."

Latour shrugged and nodded his assent.

"Doctor Latour," Reyes said, "what exactly did you mean when you said it wouldn't be that simple?"

As Fisher's hypo hissed against the deputy administrator's shoulder, Latour said, "I don't know how much experience you have with Arkenites, Captain, but they have very strict ideas about the repayment of debt. It's a cultural thing, deeply ingrained. None of them wanted to leave the Federation or cooperate with the Klingons, but their code of ethics doesn't permit them to do otherwise. Every Arkenite here feels an obligation to repay the Klingons for their assistance, in spite of the way it was offered. I'm sorry to say it, but your biggest problem in this mess may not be the Klingons."

Fisher reopened his tricorder and ran another scan of Latour.

"Where is Doctor Duvadi?" asked Reyes.

Latour shrugged. "I haven't seen her since she was summoned to the laboratory wing thirty hours ago. The Klingons set up their command post there and locked it off right after Duvadi agreed to their terms. That's when they put me in her office."

"The lab wing," Reyes said. "Where is it, exactly?"

"On this level. Not that far. I could show you, but it wouldn't do any good. It's off limits."

Reyes nodded to Fisher, who touched a specific control on his tricorder—one that Lieutenant Sadler had reprogrammed before they'd beamed down. A prolonged hiss from Fisher's Sadler-modified medkit was the only obvious sign that anything had changed. The Klingon guards reacted to the sound, drawing their distruptors as they started toward the humans, but both fell unconscious before they could go three steps.

While Gannon moved to recover the guards' weapons, Reyes stood and flipped open his communicator. "Reyes to *Dauntless*."

"Sadler here," came the response. *"Orders, Captain?"*

"Send in the troops, Mister Sadler. Mine level sixteen, zone yellow."

"Acknowledged. . . . Troops away. Shall I beam you up?"

"Negative. Restore shields and stand by for further instructions. Reyes out."

Gannon returned and handed a disruptor to Reyes, then offered one to Fisher.

"Don't you need one?" the doctor asked.

She held up her other hand, revealing a third disruptor. "One of the guards had a spare."

"Swell," Fisher said as he reluctantly took the Klingon weapon, hoping he'd be able to find its stun setting.

Latour looked at the *Dauntless* officers in abject confusion. "I don't understand. What's going on? Why did the guards—?"

"Anesthetic gas," Fisher explained quickly. "Packed in liquid form among the medicinal vials of my medkit, and triggered from my tricorder to be released as an aerosol."

"But why weren't we—?"

"The three of us were immunized before we left the ship," said Fisher, and then gave Latour a friendly pat on the shoulder where he'd applied the hypo. "You were immunized a few minutes ago."

"But what good is that going to do?" Latour asked as he turned to Reyes. "This level is still full of Klingons, and you had your ship send troops to a level that's currently empty of—"

"Shhh," said Reyes, his eyes scanning the ceiling. "Wait for it."

Moments later, an alert Klaxon blared over the colony's comm system. Klingon shouts and rapid footfalls began to sound outside the office.

Reyes moved immediately to a position near the door. Gannon took the opposite side. Fisher grabbed Latour's arm and led him against the wall next to Gannon.

Then they heard the bleat of a Klingon communicator. It was coming from one of the unconscious guards.

"Damn," Reyes whispered.

Gannon blurred past him, skidding to a crouch next to the female Klingon. She found the device and raised it to her mouth. *"nuq DaneH?"* she barked. *". . . HISlaH. net Sov! . . . jIyaj. latlh De' wIloSneS."* She closed the connection and hurried back to her place at the door. "They think we're secure," she told Reyes. "I bought us a few extra minutes."

"You're full of surprises today, Commander."

"Just doing my job, sir."

"And then some," Reyes acknowledged. "Keep it up, Hallie." The noise outside the door had lessened considerably, reduced to the deep drone of the Klaxon. "Zeke, can you give me a reading?"

Fisher handed his disruptor to Latour and ran a new scan with his medical tricorder, setting the biosign range to maximum. "Corridor's clear. No Klingons within a hundred meters."

"What about the civilians?"

"Looks like they went for cover." He looked up at Reyes as he closed the device. "I think this is our window, Diego."

"All right," Reyes said, his hand hovering over the door's manual control. "On my mark."

Fisher looked at Latour and nodded at the disruptor. "You want to hang on to that?" he asked hopefully.

Latour looked horrified. "I don't know how to use one!"

"Terrific," Fisher said, and unstrapped his tricorder. "Switch with me. Keep an eye on the screen for Klingon life signs."

"And . . . *now*," Reyes said, slapping the button. The captain went out first, verified the absence of enemy combatants, and gave the others the all-clear. "Doctor Latour, you're with me. Which way?"

Latour pointed.

"Stay behind me," Reyes told the civilian. "Gannon, watch our stern." He sprinted down to the end of the corridor and peered around it as the others caught up. Once again, no one stood in their way.

The next few corridors were as deserted as the first two, albeit riddled with abandoned tools and cases. Unfinished repair jobs marred the walls and ceiling.

"Talk to me, Latour," Reyes whispered as they approached another bend. "Are we clear?"

Latour swallowed as he panned the tricorder. "Um . . ."

"Don't wave it around so fast," Fisher advised. "Give it a chance to work."

"I think we're—"

"bIH vISam!"

—*so screwed,* Fisher thought as he pulled Latour into cover behind a support column. Disruptor fire burned the air. A few steps ahead of them, Reyes found shelter behind a tool crate, while several meters behind, Gannon returned fire from a recessed doorway along the corridor, shooting past her fellow officers.

Their attackers, firing rifles from behind a thick cross brace at the next T-junction, were two of the biggest Klingons Fisher had ever seen.

"What are you doing?" Latour yelled as Fisher fumbled to reset the disruptor. "Start firing back!"

"Son," Fisher grated as enemy fire seared the wall between them, "I've gotten this far in my Starfleet career without taking another sentient life, and I'll be damned if I'm gonna start now."

"Are you crazy?" cried Latour. "They're going to kill us!"

"Zeke!" Reyes shouted, trying to get off a shot from behind the crate and failing. The Klingons kept him pinned. He nodded in their direction. "The ceiling!"

Fisher looked, saw what Reyes meant, and stared back at his friend in disbelief. "Are you out of your mind?"

"I can't make the shot!" Reyes snarled. "Gannon's at the wrong angle! It's gotta be you!"

Another blast tore into the column. Fragments flew. "I'm getting too old for this!" Fisher yelled at Reyes, blinking sweat from his eyes as he tried to take aim.

"Oh, really?" Reyes. yelled back, ducking lower to escape more suppression fire. "I seem to recall you saying the same thing ten years ago back on the *Artemis*! Exactly when the hell were you young enough for this, Zeke?"

"Will you just shut up?!" Fisher shouted, and pressed the trigger.

The beam struck true, blasting through a severely compromised section of the rock ceiling supported by the cross brace. Chunks of rock broke free, descending on the Klingons in a cloud of dust. Fisher waited for the inevitable cave-in, or for the burly Klingons to shrug off the debris, madder than ever. But after nearly a minute of silence and slowly dissipating cloud, neither of his expectations was met.

Reyes, covered in fine gray dust, cautiously picked himself up off the floor. Fisher squinted down the corridor. The brace was still there, as was the thick rock roof that protected them from hard vacuum. The Klingons could be heard groaning under the pile of rubble.

Reyes nodded in approval. "That was nice work."

"I want a transfer," Fisher said.

Reyes scoffed. "No, you don't."

"You're gonna get me killed!"

"You're too ornery to die."

"Are you gentlemen finished?" Gannon asked as she made her way past them. "We haven't reached our objective yet."

"Fine, you take point this time," Reyes said. "I'll bring up the rear."

Fisher sighed and went to coax Doctor Latour to his feet. The poor fellow had gone fetal at some point during the firefight, and needed reassurance that the immediate danger was past.

They picked their way past the fallen Klingons and finally reached the entrance to the facility's laboratory wing, but the door was sealed. Gannon pried open a nearby maintenance panel, started making adjustments to the hardware within, and was just about to force the door when it suddenly opened.

Standing just beyond the threshold was Gorkon.

Tall and imposing as ever, the Klingon looked as if he were cut from stone. His elaborate baldric was emblazoned with the symbols of his rank and House, and his personal dagger—his *d'k tagh*, Fisher remembered—showed prominently at his hip. A pair of armed guards stood just behind each of his broad shoulders, and an all too familiar hint of derision tugged at the corners of his mouth.

"'Once more unto the breach' . . . ?" the general asked softly. "And yet you still wage war like a child, Reyes, resorting to trickery and subterfuge in order to escape confrontation."

"I'm here now," Reyes pointed out. "And I'm not the one hiding in a hole."

"No, you're simply the one covered in its dust, like a *targ* rooting through ash," said Gorkon. "How does it feel to know you could get this far only by taking the coward's way—beaming biosign decoys into the mines to trick my warriors into believing *Dauntless* had deployed assault teams?"

Reyes smirked. "That really pissed you off, didn't it?"

"I always suspected you had no true stomach for battle." Gorkon's eyes moved to consider the rest of the landing party. "Doctor Fisher, is it not? And you must be Commander Gannon. May you die as well as your predecessor."

That was when Reyes lost it, raising his captured disruptor with surprising speed and pointing it at Gorkon's face. The general's guards quickly raised their weapons toward Reyes, even as Fisher and Gannon took aim at the guards. Standoff.

There was dark amusement in Gorkon's eyes.

Fisher knew Diego wanted nothing more than to pull the trigger on the man he held personally responsible for last year's deaths aboard *Dauntless,* especially that of Rajiv Mehta. The pain of those losses had not abated, and Fisher worried it might yet blind Reyes to the consequences of indulging his need to avenge his fallen friends.

The moment passed. Reyes slowly lowered his disruptor and surrendered it butt-first to Gorkon. One by one, the other weapons all went down.

Reyes's eyes never left the Klingon's. "I demand to speak with Doctor Duvadi."

"You're in no position to demand anything, Captain. This asteroid is no longer Federation territory, and its inhabitants have chosen freely to join the Klingon Empire."

"You mean they were coerced."

Gorkon shrugged. "Semantics. They made a choice. Had they chosen instead to wait for *Dauntless* to answer their distress call, they would be dead now. They chose life." The derisive smile returned. "Is that not what the Federation advocates?"

Reyes nodded toward the *d'k tahg* hanging from Gorkon's belt and said in a quiet voice, "You allow me to speak to Doctor Duvadi now, or I'm going to take that dagger you're so fond of and feed it to you. How's that for a choice?"

"That's enough!"

Fisher looked past the Klingons, startled. Even Gorkon seemed surprised. An Arkenite woman, possessing the elongated, backswept, and hairless head that made her species so easily recognizable, strode toward them from the inner laboratory complex. Shouldering her way past the general's guards, she interposed herself between the two ship captains. Looking up at Gorkon, she said, "General, I would like a few minutes to converse privately with these officers."

Gorkon stared at her. "Of course, Doctor Duvadi," he said after an awkward moment, and with that blessing, the administrator of Azha-R7a led Latour and the landing party down the corridor, away from the Klingons.

"Let me get right to the point, Captain," Duvadi began, her eyes becoming highly reflective in the subdued light. "I know what you're doing here, but it needs to stop. I'm honoring my pact with Gorkon, and I don't want you interfering."

"Forgive me, Doctor," Reyes said, "but how can you possibly believe I'll allow this to continue?"

Duvadi looked at her human deputy. "Did you explain it to him?"

Latour nodded. "I did. But there's a cultural divide here, Doctor. And frankly, this is a difficult thing for any human to grasp."

"But you honor your debts," Duvadi insisted, turning back to Reyes. "I know that you do."

"Yes, of course," Reyes agreed. "But under conditions when the parties involved are both acting in good faith."

"This is good faith."

"The Klingons took advantage of your people during a crisis, and exploited your vulnerability! How is that good faith?"

"The Klingons were being true to their nature, and we are being true to ours."

Reyes shook his head as if unable to process what he had just heard. "Look, Doctor, even if I were to let this go—something I have no intention of doing—do you really think the Federation will honor a deal you made while the Klingons held a gun to your head?"

Duvadi fixed him with a harsh gaze. "We did not agree to stop being Arkenites when we joined the Federation, Captain.

Or am I to understand that only your human value system is relevant here?"

"Of course not. But—"

"If the Klingons can be persuaded to release my people from our agreement, we'll have no objection, Captain," Duvadi assured him. "But let me be clear that there is no military alternative to this course that any Arkenite would support. We will not compromise who we are simply because you cannot comprehend our moral choices."

"You're putting me in a very difficult position, Doctor," Reyes said.

"I realize that," said Duvadi. "That's why you need to leave, Captain."

Reyes nodded toward Latour. "What about the people here who aren't Arkenites?"

"My deputy is the only one."

"I'll have to insist that he be allowed to depart with me."

"I would not object to that. Philippe is bound by a different set of ethics. He doesn't share our obligation. Besides, he would likely face a harsh punishment from the Klingons for his role in your recent mischief, and I have no desire to see that happen." Duvadi turned and walked back toward the lab complex.

Reyes exchanged a look with Gannon. "Recommendation?"

Gannon shook her head, at a loss. Reyes glanced at Fisher, and the utter frustration behind the captain's eyes looked as if it was about to explode.

Finally Reyes turned back to face the Klingons. "We're going," he told Gorkon. "All four of us. You have a problem with that?"

Gorkon looked at Duvadi, his eyes narrowing, and it was becoming clear to Fisher that however the general might have wanted to respond, he wished to avoid antagonizing the Arkenite administrator more.

"'Stand not upon the order of your going, but go at once,'" he told Reyes, who then flipped open his communicator and called *Dauntless* for beam-out.

"This isn't over," he promised Gorkon, just before the transporter beam took them.

5

2268

Turbulence shook the *Guo Shoujing* as the shuttlecraft arrowed through the dense clouds that shrouded Kadru. Working the helm, Desai fought to compensate, but whatever she tried seemed only to make things worse. "Fish, where's that beacon?"

Fisher looked as if he was trying very hard not to be sick as he struggled to read the navigation console. "I had it a moment ago. . . . Hang on. . . ."

A rough jolt nearly bounced Desai out of her seat. "I need it now!"

"I can't— Wait, there it is! Eighteen degrees to starboard! Can you get a lock?"

"Trying . . ." Desai applied thrust, angling the shuttle to the right and dipping its nose in slow increments as the wind crashed against the hull. On her board, directional targeting icons started to intersect, and as they finally became one, Desai keyed the autopilot.

The *Guo Shoujing* shook again, and for one terrifying instant Desai thought the shuttle would go into a roll and drop from the sky like the brick it really was. But then the turbulence abated and the ship leveled off, letting its occupants catch their breath as the shuttle eased into a much gentler descent.

"That was some chop," Fisher said. "Is that normal?"

"Did you even *try* reading the mission file?" Desai scolded.

"I'm a doctor, not a lawyer."

Desai shook her head. "The upper atmosphere's highly active

and heavily ionized. Plays hell with sensors, too. I knew it would be a rough entry, but that was even worse than I expected."

"How about if, next time, we ask for a pilot? No offense."

"None taken," Desai assured him.

The air on Kadru was soup. Fog rolled everywhere, just dense enough to reduce the one- and two-story buildings of the New Anglesey settlement to gray silhouettes, a kilometer west of where the *Guo Shoujing* had set down. Beads of moisture started collecting on Desai's skin as soon as she stepped out of the shuttlecraft.

"This landing field doesn't get much use," Fisher said. Desai followed his gaze and saw immediately what had prompted the comment: coarse green shoots broke through the tarmac all around them.

From somewhere far away came a trumpeting sound, like an elephant in agony. A startled flock of cranelike avians took to the air from a line of trees south of the landing field, and for the first time Desai noticed the densely forested ridge rising above the tree line. Then she remembered: New Anglesey had been built at the foot of that ridge in order to take advantage of the immense river that flowed on the other side of it. The river led down to the ocean, fifteen kilometers east.

"Company," Fisher said.

Desai squinted into the distance. From the direction of town, two skimmers sped toward them. One of them towed a cargo sled, its oblong burden draped in a plastic tarp and held down by thick elastic cords. As the vehicles hovered to a stop, three humans got out, all wearing the two-toned civilian jumpsuits that were ubiquitous on frontier worlds. From the first skimmer emerged two middle-aged women, one with long black hair tied back, the other with a blond buzz cut. The second skimmer, the one towing the sled, let out a thin-faced, bearded man shouldering a Starfleet duffel bag and carrying a data slate. Desai recognized all three of them from the mission file . . . and all three, she noted, wore sidearms.

"Welcome to the independent colony of New Anglesey," said the woman with the black hair. "I'm Ying Mei-Hua, governor of this settlement. This is Helena Sgouros, head of security, and Anatoly Dolnikov, our senior physician."

"Captain Rana Desai, Judge Advocate General's office, Starbase 47," Desai said, extending her hand to Ying as she stepped down off the shuttle's ramp. "This is Doctor Ezekiel Fisher, our chief medical officer. Thank you for coming out to meet us, Governor, and for granting us permission to visit your planet."

"It seemed the decent thing to do," Ying said. "I can appreciate your admiral's desire to have Commander Miller's remains handled according to Starfleet custom. And on behalf of my people, I want you to know that we share your grief. Aole was an exceptional individual."

"Thank you," Desai said. "I'll be sure to convey your sentiments to his friends and family."

"I know you must be eager to return to your base, and we have no wish to delay you," Ying continued. She nodded at Doctor Dolnikov, who stepped forward and offered his slate to Desai.

"My autopsy report," the doctor explained, "as well as the release transferring custody of the body and Miller's personal effects. If you'll sign it, we can assist you in loading his stasis chamber onto your shuttlecraft."

Desai made no move to take the slate. "I think there's been a misunderstanding. We won't be leaving until Doctor Fisher has conducted his own autopsy and confirmed the cause of death to his satisfaction, and my own."

Dolnikov tensed. "That's hardly necessary. A tricorder scan will confirm my findings."

"I have no doubt they will," Fisher said diplomatically. "This isn't intended to impugn your forensic skills, Doctor. It's a matter of regulations. Autopsies on Starfleet personnel have to be carried out by authorized Starfleet medical officers."

"Surely you can do that back at your base," Sgouros said.

"We'd prefer to remain within easy access of the place Miller died," Desai said. She turned back to Ying. "If any questions arose, I'm sure you'd prefer we addressed them sooner rather than later, especially if it meant we'd have to return here to get the answers."

"That isn't what we agreed to—" Sgouros began.

"That seems entirely reasonable, Captain," Ying said, speaking over her head of security. "Anatoly, why don't you take Doctor Fisher and the body back to your lab so he can carry out his duty. Please extend to him every courtesy."

"You're welcome to leave Commander Miller's duffel bag here in the shuttle," Desai offered.

"Thanks," Dolnikov said, tossing the bag through the open hatch before leading Fisher back to his skimmer.

"I imagine they're going to be a while," Ying told Desai. "Can I interest you in a late lunch, Captain?"

"That's very gracious of you, Governor," Desai said. "I'd welcome an opportunity to speak with you."

Until Fisher had stepped off the *Guo Shoujing*, he had managed to avoid thinking too much about his role in the Kadru assignment. It was easier to focus on worrying about Rana, or trying to cheer her up, or doing damage control with the senior officers of the *Endeavour*. Not that he didn't take this saddest of his duties seriously; of all his responsibilities during his fifty years as a Starfleet physician, performing an autopsy paradoxically required the greatest level of sensitivity as well as the highest degree of detachment.

But it was different when the one on the slab was somebody he knew.

Dolnikov wasn't one for small talk, despite Fisher's attempts to engage him on the ride into town. At first Fisher thought he was just irritated about another doctor waltzing in to redo a procedure he'd already performed. But it was more than that, Fisher realized. Dolnikov didn't seem resentful so much as worried.

It was too bad, really; stripped of his obvious unease, Dolnikov seemed like he might be a decent enough fellow . . . the heavy stun pistol strapped to his hip notwithstanding.

With a population still barely over three hundred, New Anglesey was too small to warrant its own medical examiner, much less dedicated facilities for one. It therefore came as no surprise to Fisher that the room Dolnikov used for autopsies was in the building that housed the colony's infirmary as well as laboratories for the study of biological samples.

Just after the two doctors had finished changing into surgical scrubs, a striking young woman entered the lab from outside, carrying a small sample case. She couldn't have been much over twenty, if Fisher was any judge—about Rana's height, and with the same caramel complexion. There the similarities ended. The young woman's hazel-eyed face had sharper angles than Rana's, and her light brown hair was streaked with gold.

She froze upon seeing Fisher, and her initial surprise changed very quickly to suspicion.

"Who's the Herbert?" she asked Dolnikov.

Fisher raised his eyebrows.

"Tavia, what are you doing here?" Dolnikov said. "I'm in the middle of something! Come back later!"

She glared at him. "Relax, Doc. I'm just dropping off some new samples. I didn't know you'd be—" She broke off as she noticed the exam table, atop which lay the draped body of Aole Miller.

"What the hell is this?" she grated. "This was done, Anatoly!"

"Tavia, calm down!" Dolnikov urged.

"Why are you cutting him open again? Can't you leave him in peace?"

"Maybe I should explain," Fisher began.

Her eyes blazed with open hostility. "Maybe you should go to hell."

"That's enough!" Dolnikov shouted. He grabbed her by the arm and started ushering her forcefully toward a set of double doors leading to an inner room. "He's Doctor Fisher, from Aole's base. Mei signed off on this. So put your samples away and go cool off!" To Fisher's surprise, the young woman didn't resist. Her anger had already burned out, leaving only anguish.

"Were you Aole's friend?" Fisher asked.

She looked back at him, suspicious again. "I dunno if I knew him long enough to say, but . . . yeah. Yeah, I was his friend."

"Aole was my friend, too," Fisher said, and he smiled at her. "And the thing is, this is the last thing I'll ever do for him. So you can believe me when I tell you I'm going to treat him with the utmost respect."

Her expression softened, but only slightly. Still, it was enough.

"You'd better," she warned him, and disappeared through the double doors, leaving the men to their grim work.

As Sgouros drove them through town, Desai absorbed as much as she could of New Anglesey. It had clearly started out like most Federation settlements, with a well-organized core grid of standard one- and two-story prefab structures, giving way to more individualistic buildings that combined imported construction elements with materials that had been obtained locally. Dull white prefab walls had been painted in dramatic colors, varying from building to building according to the user's taste. An enormous geodesic dome—the colony's greenhouse—dominated the southern end. In the center of the settlement was a paved town square surrounded by a handful of commercial establishments, including an open-air café. Governor Ying's home was one of the more modest structures on the northern end of town, and doubled as her office.

Lunch was a salad of fresh greens, sliced tomatoes, chopped celery, and carrot shavings, tossed with a raspberry vinaigrette and prepared by Ying herself. Sgouros disappeared for a few minutes, returning with pitchers of real lemonade and freshly brewed iced tea she brought over from her own house down the road.

"I hope this isn't too rustic for you, Captain," Ying said as the three women sat down to their meal.

"On the contrary, Governor," Desai said. "This is just what I needed."

"Good. But I prefer 'Doctor Ying,' actually," the colony leader corrected as Sgouros poured Desai some iced tea. "We're a scientific community, and my role is administrative, not political. Titles like 'governor' only remind us what we're trying to get away from."

Desai saw the opening and wasted no time stepping through. "If you don't mind my asking, Doctor . . . what *are* you trying to get away from?" she asked.

Ying shrugged as she took up her fork and started eating. "Too little freedom, too much compromise, too many broken promises . . . take your pick, Captain. We aren't short on reasons for being here."

"I guess not," Desai said.

"Were you and Aole close?" Ying asked.

"Somewhat. Our jobs intersected a great deal. That's how we became friends."

"I envy you that. I wish I could have known him better. He had this way about him . . ."

Desai smiled. "I know. Everybody who spent enough time talking to him says the same thing."

"That's quite a legacy. I'm glad to know my experience with him wasn't unique."

"I take it his powers of persuasion weren't enough to convince you of the need to evacuate this planet."

Ying exchanged a look with Sgouros. "No, they weren't."

Desai set down her fork. "Doctor, help me to understand. Why are you fighting this? What sense does it make to remain out here, on your own, so far from Starfleet protection?"

"We long ago accepted that New Anglesey and the Federation have grown apart," Ying said. "Maybe you should do the same, Captain."

Desai noticed Sgouros watching her, and she decided to try a different tack. "I couldn't help but notice as we traveled through town that everyone in New Anglesey walks around armed. Is that one of the freedoms you believe you have too little of?"

"Newly colonized planets are dangerous, Captain," Sgouros answered. "Surely *that's* something Starfleet needs no help understanding? Especially given the events of this week."

"Because Commander Miller left the safety of the settlement by himself?"

"Yes, but let's be clear about this," Sgouros said. "We don't carry weapons to make a political statement. We have no shortage of dangerous predators on Kadru, and we've had to adjust our everyday behavior to fit that reality. We can't even use communicators safely outside the town perimeter, because for some reason the sound of electronically filtered voices attracts the predators."

"The bottom line," Ying said, "is that we're playing the hand we've been dealt. We're big believers in self-reliance."

"I actually have no trouble believing that, Doctor," Desai said, "given New Anglesey's abrupt shift toward isolationism."

"As I mentioned earlier," Ying said, reaching for her lemonade, "there's a great deal we wanted to get away from."

"It didn't start out that way, though, did it? Back when the *Bombay* assisted you and your people in establishing this settlement, you weren't motivated by the desire to get away, but by a passion to explore a new and biologically diverse world. Then, for no reason you were willing to explain, you started keeping Starfleet at a distance. Captain Gannon was quite distraught about it. She thought you were her friend." Ying seemed taken by surprise at the mention of Gannon, and suddenly seemed uncomfortable. "So what changed?"

"Maybe you should ask the colonists on Gamma Tauri Four," said Sgouros.

Desai nodded. "I did consider that the destruction of the New Boulder colony might be the reason for your sudden withdrawal, but the chronology doesn't line up. New Anglesey went independent six months before the incident at Gamma Tauri."

Ying set down her glass and leaned forward. "Then call it validation of our decision—the most recent in a long history of so-called 'incidents' where Starfleet failed the colonies it was supposed to be protecting—Tarsus Four, Azha-R7a, Ingraham B, Deneva, Omicron Ceti Three, Cestus Three, Janus Six, New Paris—do I really need to go on, Captain? Oh, yes, I know: some of those settlements were actually *saved* by Starfleet intervention, but you couldn't actually *protect* any of them, could you?"

Desai said nothing. Everything she feared Ying might say had been heaped at her feet.

And still Ying wasn't done. "Twenty years ago on Tarsus Four, the system failed spectacularly. When famine threatened the colony, Starfleet sent ships to help, but they didn't get there before the colony's warped leadership exterminated half the population in order to save the other half. Our entire colonial system has been paying for that crime ever since. Each new crisis has led to stricter laws, tougher regulations, tighter controls, forced relocations, and less freedom to live as the colonists choose—which is the reason many of them became colonists in the first place!

"So let me say it as plainly as I can, Captain. If Starfleet abandons this sector, New Anglesey is prepared to stand on its own. My people won't be pressured into leaving Kadru by *anyone.*"

"Is that why Aole Miller died?" Desai asked.

Sgouros frowned. "Exactly what are you implying, Captain?"

Desai looked at her. "I'm on Kadru to investigate the death of a Starfleet officer. By the governor's own statements, her feelings toward Starfleet represent those of her constituents. I need to know if some of them would resent Miller's presence here—and his purpose—enough to do something about it."

Ying rose slowly to her feet. "You want to know if one of my people was capable of murdering Aole?"

"That's exactly what I want to know."

"Then this is my answer: you and your doctor have twenty-four hours to complete your investigation and get the hell off this planet."

6

2259

"... *Unfortunately, Captain Reyes, this matter is beyond your authority,*" Admiral Telles Vindeilin said from the briefing room monitor, the Denobulan's usually genial manner taking a back seat to her grim news. "*You're to take no action while the Federation Council tries to resolve the situation diplomatically.* Dauntless *is ordered to withdraw to the edge of the Azha system, escorted by the* Chech'Iw. *I know that adds insult to injury, Diego, but it was the only way the Klingon ambassador would even consider meeting with the Federation Council about this. Starfleet Command wants you to remain in the vicinity and to continue monitoring the situation as best you can. Keep me updated, and I'll advise you of any changes on this end. Vindeilin out.*"

Reyes, Fisher knew, had already sat through the recording once. He spent the replay watching the faces of his gathered senior officers, as well as that of their guest, Philippe Latour, for their reactions. No one looked happy.

As silence settled over the circular room, Reyes tapped the comm on the tabletop's computer interface. "Reyes to bridge."

"*Jordan here, sir.*"

"Mister Jordan, I believe the *Chech'Iw* is waiting to hear from us. Please inform them we'll be ready to get under way at one-quarter impulse in ten minutes. You may then proceed at your discretion to a position thirty astronomical units from Azha."

"*Understood, sir.*"

"Reyes out."

"That's it, then," Brzezinski said.

"The hell it is," said the captain.

"Sir, Starfleet Command—"

"We may not be able to engage the Klingons directly," Reyes said, "but I'm not about to simply do nothing. Think, people! Let's break it down: an explosion of indeterminate origin on Azha-R7a forces the Arkenites to send out an SOS, just when the *Chech'Iw* was close enough to be the first responder. Does that strike anyone else here as even remotely suspicious?"

"It can't be a coincidence," Sadler agreed. "And since when do the Klingons come to the aid of Federation citizens in distress?"

"It's unlike them," Gannon admitted, "but not unprecedented, as long as it suited their purposes. The real question is, what have they achieved by answering the Arkenites' call for help?"

"It's a diplomatic knife between the ribs," Shey said. "Think about it, the Klingons have acquired new territory and absorbed its population without firing a shot, essentially beating us at our own game. When word of this gets out, and it will, the Federation will be humiliated. Its ability to protect its members and holdings will be cast into doubt. If Gorkon did engineer all this, he knew exactly how to hit us."

"Commander Gannon," Reyes said, "what's your read on Gorkon?"

"Current leader of the House of Makok and a thirty-year veteran of the Klingon Defense Force," Gannon recited. "Thought to be a favorite of Chancellor Sturka, who is rumored to be grooming him for the High Council. Widely regarded as a brilliant strategist and one of the foremost military minds in the Empire. As commander of his current ship, the *Chech'Iw,* he's been directly involved in sixteen skirmishes with Federation forces. Five of those involved the *Dauntless.* His wife and three of his sons are deceased. He has two surviving children, a twenty-one-year-old son in the KDF, and a daughter, six. As a grand master of *klin zha*—"

"That's enough background," the captain interrupted. "I'm more interested in how you'd assess his behavior inside the colony."

Gannon hesitated. "I think that whatever is going on, Gorkon is worried about something," she said at last. "He held all the cards, yet he twice acceded to Doctor Duvadi, as if he felt he had no choice."

Reyes turned to Fisher. "Doctor, do you agree with Commander Gannon's assessment?"

"I do, Captain," Fisher said. "I got the same impression."

"So did I," Reyes agreed. "So what does that tell us?"

"That Duvadi is the one pulling the strings," Brzezinski said.

"I wouldn't go that far," said Reyes, raising a finger toward the science officer, "but he definitely didn't want to do or say anything to piss her off. That suggests to me he needs her for some purpose, and he's willing to take atypical steps to ensure her continued cooperation."

"*Atypical* is exactly the word for it," Gannon said. "Nothing about this reflects usual Klingon behavior. Azha-R7a has little value strategically. Its mineral resources have some worth, but they represent neither a crippling loss to the Federation nor a significant gain for the Empire. No offense, Doctor Latour."

"None taken," Latour said.

"Arkenites, as a species, have never been of particular interest to the Klingons before, so it's unlikely this has anything to do with them," Gannon went on. "And with all due respect to Shey's valid analysis of the astropolitical fallout of this crisis, the tactics employed simply don't track with Klingon psychology. They favor direct confrontation to subtlety and lateral thinking. It's hard to see what they've really gained from this."

"The science labs," Reyes mused, suddenly turning his full attention to Latour. "Why is it that, of all the locations to set up as their command post, the Klingons chose the laboratory wing?"

"Honestly, Captain, I have no idea," Latour said.

"But what are the labs *for*?" Brzezinski asked. "I thought Azha-R7a was strictly a mining complex?"

"We started branching out last year," Latour explained, "after a survey of a high-impact region revealed the presence of a subsurface frost layer teeming with exotic microbial fossils and unusual organic compounds, which we've determined were deposited by past cometary strikes. The Federation Science Council granted us a full array of state-of-the-art analysis-and-research equipment to study what we found. We've been at it ever since. But before you draw any hasty conclusions about that, we've made a thorough study of the frost and its contents, and I can assure you there's nothing dangerous about our discoveries."

"Let's say you're correct," Sadler said. "What about the lab equipment itself? Is there anything about it that might be cause for concern if it fell into the wrong hands?"

Latour started to reply, but his confidence in whatever answer he was about to give faded quickly. "I'm not sure."

"Shey," Reyes said. "Take Doctor Latour with you to engineering. I want you to work together on compiling an inventory of everything the FSC sent to the colony. Check the library computer for their specs and review them for all possible applications."

"Aye, sir," said the Andorian engineer, nodding to the deputy administrator as the two of them got up from the meeting table and exited the briefing room.

Reyes turned to his chief of security. "Terry, I want you to start developing contingency plans to storm the colony. If we find out that diplomacy has failed, Starfleet Command might want us to take direct action to liberate the Arkenites, regardless of the political consequences."

"Will do. But you need to know this, Captain . . . I've already made a thorough study of the mining complex, and in my current estimation, there's no scenario that won't involve civilian casualties."

"Find one," Reyes said. "Brzezinski, please assist Mister Sadler."

That left only Gannon and Fisher in the room with Reyes. "Captain, I understand the necessity of preparing for worst-case scenarios," the XO said, "but you must realize that if we do resort to force, we'll be giving Gorkon exactly what he wants: an even stronger claim on Azha-R7a."

Reyes looked close to losing his patience. "Commander, I respect the fresh perspective you bring to the table, but I know this man in ways that transcend what you can memorize from a computer file. And despite any pretense of honor, Gorkon is a ruthless, cunning bastard who won't hesitate to space those people down there if and when he decides he doesn't need to perpetuate this farce any longer. Once he has whatever he came here for, they're as good as dead. My job is to make sure that moment never comes. Now, is there anything relevant you have to contribute to that objective?"

"There is one thing," Gannon said evenly, "but I don't think you're going to like hearing it."

Reyes's eyebrows shot up. He cast a glance Fisher's way, then leaned back in his chair. "Speak freely, Gannon."

Gannon laced her hands atop the wood-stained oval table. "Gorkon takes great satisfaction in pushing your buttons, Captain. And frankly, that's something he shouldn't know how to do. This has gotten personal. You can't seem to respond to him any way other than viscerally, and Gorkon knows it. He's using your hatred of him to keep you off balance, to throw you off your game, to interfere with your judgment. And from what I've observed so far, he's succeeding."

Wow, Fisher thought. *Go, Hallie!*

Reyes's eyes blazed. "Observation noted," he answered curtly, abruptly vacating his chair and moving toward the exit.

"Gorkon was paying Commander Mehta a compliment, by the way," Gannon called after him, and Reyes stopped in the doorway. "Before you threatened to blow his head off, when he told me to die as well as my predecessor? He wasn't threatening me, or spitting on Mehta's memory. He was acknowledging the honorable death of someone he considered a warrior. Among Klingons, it's high praise."

"What's your point?"

"Only this, sir: The only way you're going to beat Gorkon is by understanding what's driving him, not by judging him according to human values. He's never going to fit into the box you keep trying to put him in."

• • •

As he strode down the curved corridor two hours later, Fisher told himself he'd waited long enough. When he reached his destination, he stopped at the door and thumbed the buzzer. It was answered in a distinct tone of resignation: "Come in, Zeke."

The door slid open, and Fisher stepped inside the captain's cabin to see Reyes working at his desk. "How'd you know it was me?"

Reyes's eyes rolled toward him. "Everyone else aboard has the good sense not to bother the captain when he's in a bad mood."

"That's a relief. I was afraid you were gonna make some smart-ass crack about hearing my joints creaking from down the corridor."

Reyes rose and moved to his food slot. "Look, Zeke, if you came here to say something, just say it and go. Or you can shut up and join me for some bad coffee. Either way, I'm too busy to put up with the usual crap."

"I'll take the coffee," Fisher said agreeably as he strolled toward the desk, where the screen displayed Reyes's after-action report on the incident at Xarant. The doctor ignored it, reaching instead for the slate that Reyes had placed facedown on the desk when Fisher walked in. He turned it over and saw Gannon's personnel file.

"Archery," Fisher noted. "Who would have thought?"

"Hey, do you mind?" Reyes said irritably, grabbing the slate and handing Fisher a steaming cup. "What if this had been a top secret file?"

Fisher waved dismissively and went to sit in the chair opposite Reyes's desk. "So what? You hate keeping secrets."

Reyes sighed and returned to his own chair. "So what do you want, really? If you came here to talk to me about Gannon—"

"Actually, I came here to talk about you."

"What about me?"

Fisher smiled. "Are you going to keep Hallie as your XO?"

Reyes scoffed and leaned back. "That's none of your damn business, Doctor," he said without heat.

"Well, now, that's where you're wrong, *Captain*. But we'll let that one go. Here's a better question: do you think she's right?"

Reyes didn't answer, and after a moment, he picked up the slate again and handed it to Fisher. "That special training she received about the Klingons . . . Look who she studied under."

"Doctor Emanuel Tagore," Fisher read. "The former ambassador?"

"The same. He's been on the lecture circuit since his retirement. Felt he owed it to the Federation to share what he'd learned from living on the Klingon homeworld for four years. Somebody at Command finally realized Starfleet had something to gain from his knowledge and experience. The thinking was that starship captains would benefit from having officers with specialized training in the Klingons' language, culture, history."

"Let me guess: somewhere in this file is a glowing recommendation from the ambassador."

"Glowing? It's radioactive. She was one of his star pupils."

Fisher shrugged and handed back the slate. "So she's got a black belt in Klingon and she's not afraid to use it. That doesn't really tell you anything you didn't already know."

"No . . . but it does make me wonder if I really am making this personal." Reyes stared into his coffee. "This thing with Gorkon . . . I'm letting it affect me exactly the way she described, aren't I? And if Hallie is right about that . . . What if the reason *Dauntless* got the tar beaten out of it last year—the real reason Rajiv died—is because I'm not able to understand what really drives the Klingons?"

Fisher set down his cup. "Diego, listen to me. You have to stop blaming yourself for Rajiv, and everyone else who dies on your watch. We all knew the score when we signed on. Tomorrow it could be someone else. Maybe me. And if it happens, I hope you'll feel the loss. But the last thing I'd want is for you to be crushed under the weight of it, or for it to compromise your ability to function as captain of this ship. It's the last thing Rajiv would want, too."

Reyes remained silent, his eyes filled with doubt.

The bosun's whistle sounded from his desk's intercom. *"Bridge to Captain Reyes."*

Reyes switched it on, and Gannon's face appeared on its tiny screen. "Reyes here. Talk to me, Commander."

"Sir, we have a situation," she told him. *"All hell is breaking loose aboard the* Chech'Iw.*"*

"Kendrick managed to tap into their intraship communications," Gannon explained once Reyes and Fisher were on the bridge. "The *Chech'Iw* has suffered some sort of disaster in the surgeon's bay. They've lost containment of something toxic, and whatever it is, it's spreading quickly throughout the ship. They don't seem to have the medical personnel on hand to deal with the crisis."

"Captain, if I might make a suggestion?" Sadler said. "This could be an opportunity."

Fisher didn't like the way that sounded. "An opportunity to do what?"

The security chief continued speaking directly to Reyes. "We can offer them the same sort of deal they gave the colonists—help in exchange for their agreeing to relinquish their claim on Azha-R7a."

"Or what?" Fisher challenged. "We're going to let them die?"

"That's exactly the choice they gave the Arkenites," Sadler said.

"Since when do we take our cues from the Klingons?" Fisher asked.

Reyes stared at the viewscreen. The *Chech'Iw* hung above them, astern and to port, offering no outward sign that anything was wrong. "I agree with Mister Sadler—this *is* an opportunity."

Fisher couldn't believe it. *Well, if that's the way it's gonna be, I sure as hell don't need to stick around here to watch.* Fuming, he started for the elevator.

"As you were, Doctor."

Dammit. Fisher stopped and slowly turned back around, folding his arms. "Aye, sir."

"Hail the *Chech'Iw*," Reyes told Kendrick as he strode toward the center seat.

"Hailing frequencies open, sir."

"*I.K.S. Chech'Iw*, this is the *U.S.S. Dauntless*. Do you require assistance?" When no answer came, he looked over his shoulder. "Are they receiving us?"

Kendrick nodded.

"*I.K.S. Chech'Iw*, we have crisis response personnel standing by to assist you. Please respond."

"Reply coming in, Captain," Kendrick said.

The screen warbled and dissolved to show Mazhtog, sweat beading on his forehead, his breathing labored. "*What are . . . what are your . . . terms?*" he rasped.

"No terms," said Reyes, and Sadler's mouth dropped open. "We're offering our assistance without condition. Do you accept?"

"*We . . . accept.*"

"Fine. My chief medical officer will be beaming over shortly." Reyes looked as if he were about to sign off, but then added, "After the first few minutes, you'll probably want to shoot him. Please don't. Reyes out."

The captain spun his chair around and faced his officers.

Fisher smiled. "You surprise me sometimes, Diego."

"Don't be too impressed," Reyes cautioned him. "I have ulterior motives. This is our best chance of obtaining first-hand intel about what the Klingons are really up to." He looked at Sadler. "There's more than one kind of opportunity, Lieutenant."

Sadler nodded. "Understood, sir."

"Gannon, go with Doctor Fisher. Do what you can to help the Klingons, but be careful over there. And keep your eyes open."

As the Klingon ship solidified around him, Fisher's thought from the previous day came back to him: *That boy is gonna get me killed one of these days.*

Suited up in biohazard gear, he and Gannon had once again

beamed into a phalanx of armed Klingon guards, all wearing breathing masks. A strident alert Klaxon bleated from unseen speakers, forcing Gannon to shout over it as she spat at the guards in their own language.

One of the guards spat back, and then he and another Klingon took Fisher and Gannon by the arm, ushering them out of the transporter room and into bedlam.

The Klingons who could still walk stumbled through corridors strewn with the twitching bodies of those more gravely stricken. Some of the fallen bled from their noses, or ears, or eyes.

Fisher opened his tricorder, and the readings he took confirmed his fears.

The *Chech'Iw* was dying.

7

2268

"Dammit, Desai, what the hell were you thinking? I sent you to Kadru to fix things, not make them worse!"

Cringing as Nogura responded to her mission update, Desai sat back in the navigator's seat of the *Guo Shoujing,* holding her head with one hand. She'd never been more grateful for the lack of viewscreens on Class-F shuttlecraft. "I haven't given up, sir."

"Is that meant to reassure me?" the admiral asked as the shuttlecraft's tripartite hatch opened, letting in a cloud of cool, humid air. Desai looked up to see Fisher emerging from Kadru's foggy night, carrying a bulky parcel under one arm. *"You've been there less than twelve hours, and in that time, you've managed not only to undo whatever goodwill Commander Miller achieved with the colonists, you've actually set back the Federation's broken relationship with these people even further. Is that a fair summation?"*

"More or less, Admiral."

Fisher winced.

After a prolonged silence, Nogura said, *"I want the situation on Kadru resolved, I don't care how. Are we clear on that, Captain?"*

"Yes, Admiral."

"Where do we stand on the investigation into Commander Miller's death?"

Fisher raised a hand to Rana, signaling her to stall. "I'm still waiting for Doctor Fisher to make his report, sir," she answered truthfully.

"Keep me informed. Nogura out."

Desai closed the link. "Don't say it," she warned Fisher.

"I wouldn't know what to tell you," Fisher laughed as she settled into the helmsman's chair. "I'm starting to think no matter what I say, you'll just end up doing the opposite."

Desai sighed. "I really don't want to ask you about the autopsy."

Fisher held up the tricorder slung across his chest. "It's right here. You can read it in the morning, if you like."

"I'll do that, but bottom-line it for me now."

"COD: inconclusive."

"You're kidding."

"I wish," Fisher said. "The condition of Miller's body is consistent with drowning, but he was thoroughly cleaned after the first autopsy. That's standard procedure, but it conveniently removed any trace evidence that would have confirmed his whereabouts at the time of death, or if he was really alone. There was nonfatal blunt-force trauma to the head, but if he fell and lost consciousness, then accidental drowning sounds more and more plausible."

"Unless someone knocked him out deliberately," Desai countered.

"I can't rule it out, but there's no definitive way to know, either way."

"What've you got there?" she asked, nodding toward Fisher's parcel.

"Aole's uniform . . . also conspicuously lacking in trace evidence."

"His uniform," Desai repeated. "His uniform . . ." She abruptly left her chair and raced into the aft compartment.

"What's the matter?"

Desai came out with Miller's duffel bag and spilled its contents onto the deck. There was a personal hygiene kit, several sets of undergarments and socks, a hard-copy book, a deck of cards, and his communicator. "I inventoried Aole's personal effects after I got back to the shuttle. What's missing from this picture?"

"His uniform?"

"His *spare* uniform," Desai corrected. "Aole expected to spend at least a week at New Anglesey, without access to a Starfleet quartermaster. Any officer would have brought extras on an assignment like this. I brought three. What about you?"

"Two," Fisher said.

"He didn't bring any civvies, either. But let's assume he expected to have access to the local laundry facilities. A reasonable minimum is one spare uniform for a weeklong assignment, wouldn't you agree?"

Fisher nodded. "Makes sense."

"Something's not right here," Desai said. walking back to the navigation console and deftly reopening a channel to Vanguard.

"You're contacting Nogura about this?" Fisher asked with concern.

Desai shook her head. "Quartermaster's office." It took a few minutes to reestablish the connection with the station's comm center, and only seconds for the call to be relayed to the QM. Under the authority of the JAG office, Desai requested an immediate audit of Aole Miller's uniform consumption, checked against the contents of his quarters. As requisitions and recycles were closely monitored, it wouldn't take long to confirm how many of Miller's uniforms were missing from the station. Desai kept the channel open while the officer on duty went to work.

"I know I don't need to tell you that even if they turn up a discrepancy, it doesn't mean Aole was murdered," Fisher said.

"Granted," said Desai. "But at a minimum, it would suggest one or more people on this colony are conspiring to cover up *something*. I hate to admit it, but I'm starting to think Nogura's suspicions about these people may not be unwarranted."

"Rana, are you listening to yourself? Is this a search for the truth, or a witch hunt?"

The comm system chimed. Vanguard's quartermaster confirmed that two of Miller's uniforms were unaccounted for.

Desai thanked the officer and signed off. "Tell me you don't think these people are hiding something," she said to Fisher.

"I never doubted they were," Fisher said. "I'm just not ready to believe it's a crime."

"I don't have that luxury, Fish. And since I'm ranking officer . . ."

Fisher sighed. "Fine. What do you want me to do?"

"Nothing until morning. But then I want you to talk to the locals. Nose around. Do that 'kindly old grandfather' thing you're so good at. Somebody who knows what really happened to Aole must be willing to talk about it. Find them."

Fisher nodded. "I can do that. What about you?"

Desai looked around at the cramped shuttlecraft cabin. "I'm going to finally figure out how anyone manages to get any sleep in one of these things, and then tomorrow I'm going to find Doctor Ying and try to persuade her we're the good guys."

"Are we?" Fisher asked.

Desai didn't answer.

The sun rose over New Anglesey as a hazy patch of light behind the planet's gray veil of clouds. Fisher found Tavia alone, shooting hoops at a crude basketball court. He spent a good half hour watching her play from a bench across the street. Her form was good, her balance and agility excellent, but her short stature would, in Fisher's judgment, severely limit her ability to dominate the court against a taller opponent, unless she could improve her jump shot.

"You're waiting too long to shoot," Fisher called out as he crossed the street.

She stopped mid-dribble, looking irritated as she met him at the edge of the court. "Were you talking to me?"

He nodded at the hoop. "Your jump shot. You've been making it on your way down. You've got strong legs, but you need to shoot a little earlier, right when you're reaching the apex of your jump. Give it a try."

Despite her obvious annoyance at the intrusion, she started dribbling again, then broke into a run toward the hoop, leaped, and launched the ball with both hands.

It rebounded off the backboard and went into a spin on the rim of the hoop before falling through.

Fisher applauded. Tavia walked back to him wearing a grin. "You play?" she asked.

"Me? Oh, no. I'm a professional spectator." He held out his hand. "I'm Ezekiel."

"Doctor Fisher, yeah, I remember." She took his hand and shook it. "Octavia Dawes. But you can call me Tavia."

And just like that, the ice is broken.

"Zeke," Fisher said. "But if you'd rather keep calling me Herbert . . ."

Tavia gritted her teeth in embarrassment. "Oh, hey, I'm sorry about that. I can be a little rough around the edges sometimes."

Fisher smiled. "Hadn't noticed. What do you do here, Tavia?"

"Xenobiologist. And please, no cracks about my age."

Fisher gestured toward his silver hair. "I won't if you won't."

Tavia laughed. "All right. We reach."

"Good! Any friend of Aole's . . ."

Her grin didn't disappear, but it lost much of its mirth. "He's the reason you came to see me, isn't he?"

Fisher nodded.

"I heard your friend used a real hard lip on Doctor Ying."

"I heard the same thing," Fisher said. "But if it makes you feel any better, she's going to apologize. She was a friend of Aole's, too. She's just having a hard time understanding why you all would want to stay out here after Starfleet leaves."

"What about you?" Tavia asked. "You having a hard time with it, too?"

"I'd be lying if I told you I didn't have my concerns. I had a friend, you see—Terry Sadler. Sometime back he joined the colony on Ingraham B. Then a couple of years ago, Terry and everyone else there died because the settlement was too far from help when they needed it. Part of me still wonders if we sometimes push into the galaxy too far, too quickly."

"So because your friend died on the frontier, now you're bleeding for us?" Tavia asked.

"Aole Miller bled for you."

Tavia looked away. "Why are you still here? Can't you and your friend just take him and go?"

"Not until we understand the reason he died. Do you know, Tavia?"

"Maybe."

"Were you there when it happened?"

Tavia dribbled her basketball a few times. "No. But I was the one who found his body."

Kadru's star was past its zenith when Desai met with Ying. She found the governor exactly where she said she'd be: the open-air café that looked out on the town square. Coffee for two was already set out on the table, and she sat alone. Ying gestured for her to sit, and Desai eased gratefully into the empty chair. "Thank you for agreeing to meet with me."

Ying reached for the carafe and filled Desai's cup. "Whatever you have to say, Captain, I hope you'll make it quick. I have work to do."

"I wanted to apologize for being so confrontational with you yesterday," Desai began. "I'm a trial lawyer, accustomed to adversarial relationships, and lately I've had trouble remembering that not everyone facing me across a table is my enemy."

Ying studied her face. "Apology accepted," she said finally. "But I get the sense that isn't really why we're here."

"I came to Kadru for two reasons, Doctor Ying: to understand why Aole Miller died, but also to finish what he started. Now I realize the question I should have been asking is, *Why did Aole come here?*"

"I'm not sure I follow."

Desai groped for words before she finally admitted, "You're right about Starfleet: it can't be everywhere to stop bad things from happening. There are times when it's compelled to make terrible decisions, and also times when it simply fails. But every so often it remembers that it has limitations. That's why the Federation decided these evacuations were necessary, and why Aole came here in person: it was an act of desperation, because he believed convincing you of the need to leave Kadru was too important not to make every conceivable effort. The Taurus Reach is incendiary, and Starfleet doesn't want any more Gamma Tauri Fours. When we discontinue regular patrols in this sector, Kadru won't be safe anymore."

In the silence that followed, a profound sadness enveloped Ying's face until finally the governor said, "That's why we have to stay."

Fisher and Tavia crept uphill through the fog-shrouded rain forest kilometers south of New Anglesey. The heat and humidity were intense, and Fisher saw worry in his guide's eyes when she looked at him. "Maybe this was a bad idea," she said.

"I must be quite the sight," he chuckled. "Is it much farther?"

"No, but—"

"Then I'd rather not turn back now, if it's all the same to you."

He didn't argue when she insisted they take a break, and while the two of them spent a few minutes resting and rehydrating, another terrifying animal cry rang out, not unlike the ones Fisher had heard since he and Desai first arrived on Kadru. But this time it sounded much louder and close by.

Before Fisher could ask about it, Tavia urged him to be silent and follow her. They took a well-worn path to the top of a rise, keeping low as they peered over the top. At the bottom of the slope on the other side, a carpet of fog obscured the surface of a great river, which Fisher recognized by the muffled roar of rushing water. Two hundred meters out from the hidden shore, a great rock jutted up from the fog, and perched atop it, searching the mist for easy prey, was a large reptilian predator.

The raptorlike creature was breathtaking, at least three times the height of a man, built for speed and violence. Its dramatic colors mesmerized Fisher, as did the batwing membranes that occasionally flexed open from its flanks while its four eyes attempted to pierce the fog.

Fisher started to ask about the creature, only to find Tavia's hand over his mouth. "Keep still," she whispered. "It's about to feed."

Fisher continued to watch when, quite suddenly, a huge burst of water rose behind the raptor, followed by a snakelike head at least four meters wide with massive jaws that snapped shut around the creature's body. The raptor thrashed in futility as the leviathan dragged it off the rock and down into the shrouded water.

"My God," Fisher said softly. "What was that?"

"The reason Aole died," Tavia said.

Desai didn't understand what Ying was trying to tell her, but seeing the tears streaming from the governor's eyes, she felt certain she was close to something important.

Before she could ask, both women noticed a number of colonists running south through the town square. They looked almost frantic.

"What's going on?" Desai asked.

"I'm not sure," Ying said, quickly wiping her eyes and pushing away from the table when she saw Helena Sgouros running toward them.

"Fisher's missing," she told Ying. "So is Dawes."

"You're sure?" Ying asked.

Sgouros nodded. "Witnesses placed them by the hoops a few hours ago. No one's seen them since."

Desai flipped open her communicator. "Desai to Fisher. Desai to Fisher, please respond." Nothing.

"Dawes isn't answering, either," Sgouros said. "If they've turned off their comms, they must be in the rain forest."

Ying cursed. "It's Aole Miller all over again." To Sgouros, she said, "We need to start organizing search parties."

"My people are already rounding up volunteers," answered New Anglesey's head of security. "They're meeting at the dome."

"Good," Ying said. "Take Desai into custody and confine her."

"What?" Desai said, as Sgouros drew her sidearm.

"It's for your own good, Captain," Ying said.

"The hell it is. You can't—"

"I can and I will," Ying snapped. "This is our world, and Starfleet people with no understanding of Kadru have no business venturing into places they don't belong, and where they aren't welcome. If that wasn't clear to you before, I trust it is now." She showed her comm device to Sgouros. "Home in on my transponder signal and catch up to me after she's been secured."

"Understood." Ying took off at a run, and Sgouros gestured with her stun pistol. "Start moving, Captain."

Led away at gunpoint, Desai endured the humiliation of being marched through town as Sgouros's prisoner. "Where are we going?"

"Just keep walking," Sgouros advised, eventually directing Desai through a side street near the edge of town, to a lot filled with several windowless sheds and construction equipment. They stopped at a structure bearing a sign that read, THERMOCONCRETE.

With her pistol leveled at Desai, Sgouros used her free hand to unlock the shed. She yanked on the metal door, and it swung outward with a loud creak. The shed was half empty, the walls on either side stacked with sacks of powdered building material, each one looking as if it weighed at least fifty kilos—nothing Desai could use to break out once she was locked in.

"Inside," Sgouros ordered.

So don't get locked in, Desai told herself as she crossed the threshold.

She waited until she heard the creak of the door starting to close. Then she spun around, pivoted on one leg, and kicked out sideways with the other. With a loud crack the door swung back outward, slamming into Sgouros's face.

Desai charged out, tackling the dazed head of security. She pressed her advantage, seizing hold of Sgouros's wrist and banging her hand repeatedly against the pavement until she released her grip on the weapon.

But Sgouros was already regaining her wits, shifting as if she were preparing to roll Desai off. Desai thrust the heel of her palm sharply against the taller woman's temple, and Sgouros's head lolled to one side as she lost consciousness.

Desai moved into a crouch and relieved Sgouros of her comm unit. She scrolled through the personnel list, searching the more than three hundred names until she saw the one she wanted: DAWES, OCTAVIA.

She tried opening a channel. Nothing. She selected the tracking function, and the unit's display gave her a map of the local terrain, with a blinking arrowhead in the center. Rising numbers in one corner of the display ticked off the increasing distance. Dawes was on the move.

And as Sgouros had predicted, the arrowhead pointed straight into the rain forest.

Desai recovered Sgouros's weapon and set off at a run.

Hang on, Fish. I'm coming.

8

2259

"It's theragen," Fisher confirmed, once Reyes, Sadler, and Shey had joined him in *Dauntless*'s sickbay, where the biobeds were filled with unconscious Klingons requiring intensive care. At the foot of each bed, Sadler had stationed a security guard.

"Theragen?" Reyes repeated. "That nerve gas of theirs? What happened?"

"Some containers that were stored in the surgeon's bay ruptured, not that anyone would even admit that was the problem. None of them are talking. The only reason I have any hope for these poor souls is that Hallie was able to access the Klingons' medical database, which included some very superficial molecular analyses of the agent and woefully inadequate treatment recommendations. But it gave me a place to start, and I'm happy to say I've been able to improve the treatment considerably."

"Theragen," Reyes said again, shaking his head. "I knew Gorkon could be one cold son of a bitch, but I never imagined he was vicious enough to— My God, could that be what he's doing on the asteroid? Turning it into a chemical weapons factory?"

"No," Shey said, "certainly not with the equipment in the science labs. I've finished looking into their capabilities, and they don't have the capacity to be used as you're suggesting, Captain. They're designed for research and analysis of organic compounds, and not in any way suited for the large-scale production and storage of chemical weapons."

"Maybe they don't need to be," Sadler said. "What if the Klingons' true objective was to refine the formula for the nerve agent, develop small samples of something even nastier, and then use the Arkenites as guinea pigs?"

Reyes looked at Shey. "Is that possible?"

Shey's antennae drooped slightly. "Theoretically, yes."

Reyes's hands curled into fists. The sickbay doors opened to admit Gannon, but before she could speak, the captain turned to Sadler. "Lieutenant, within the hour, I want a briefing with your recommendations for retaking Azha-R7a, with the objective of neutralizing any biohazardous materials, even if it means we have to put innocent lives in jeopardy."

Sadler nodded and started for the door, but Gannon stopped him with a hand against his shoulder. "Terry, wait. Captain, I don't think this is what it seems."

Reyes looked at her. "And how did you happen to come to that conclusion, Commander?"

Gannon held up a data card. "These are the files from the surgeon's bay database on the *Chech'Iw*. I've been reviewing them since Doctor Fisher and I got back, along with General Gorkon's Starfleet Intelligence file. And I'm now convinced that Gorkon is actually trying to develop a counteragent to theragen."

"Kintazh, son of Gorkon," Gannon said, naming the young Klingon whose image looked out from the monitor at the end of the briefing room table. "Until recently, he was a weapons officer for Captain Kavau of the *I.K.S. Qul qemwI'*. He's the reason all of this is happening."

Reyes had decided to remain standing during the briefing, and his officers followed his lead, much to Fisher's annoyance. For the sake of his old bones, he hoped it wouldn't be the start of a trend.

"Kavau was a singular captain in the Klingon Defense Force," Gannon continued. "He used theragen to quell uprisings on Klingon subject planets."

"He used theragen *within* the Empire?" Sadler asked, and Fisher shared his surprise. From everything he'd ever heard, theragen had been used exclusively as a conquest weapon, back before the Klingons abandoned it around the turn of the century.

"That's what made him so singular," Gannon said. "Officially, the use of theragen is strictly against imperial policy, chemical and biological warfare being considered dishonorable by most Klingons. That was what led to the ban in 2207. But Kavau had the backing of several powerful members of the High Council who were pushing for the use of unconventional weapons against the Federation. The councillors thought that by reintroducing theragen domestically, they'd demonstrate the effectiveness of such weapons and build more support for them on the High Council.

"That seemed to be the direction things were going until one of the theragen tests backfired, killing three-quarters of the *Qul qemwI'* crew. They were the lucky ones. The survivors were all terminal, including Captain Kavau and Kintazh. Upon learning what had happened, Chancellor Sturka ordered the program shut down and sent Gorkon to mop up. To provide cover for the High Council, this newest use of theragen was officially disavowed, the captain and crew of the *Qul qemwI'* branded renegades and criminals. Gorkon's job was to execute Kavau and the other survivors, and to destroy the ship along with any remaining stockpiles of theragen it carried."

"I think I see where this is going," Reyes muttered.

Gannon nodded. "Based on my findings, I think Gorkon couldn't bring himself to let his son die dishonorably. But Kintazh's status as a criminal meant that he was ineligible even for ritual death by *Mauk-to'Vor,* which would restore his honor in the afterlife. His only chance to die with honor was to live long enough to redeem himself. So after executing the other survivors and setting the *Qul qemwI'* to destruct, Gorkon took Kintazh and several containers of theragen aboard the *Chech'Iw*—without advising his superiors. Then he put his scientists to work on curing his son.

"But as we've now learned, the effects of theragen are beyond the ability of Klingon medicine to cope with, especially if left untreated too long. Faced with that knowledge, Gorkon must have realized Kintazh's best chance was with Federation medical technology. The problem was, he couldn't seek it openly; the

Klingons have a long-standing distrust of alien bioscience. Gorkon would be risking dishonor for himself and, by extension, for his crew and his entire House—not to mention the wrath of the High Council—by asking the Federation for help."

"What does that mean for the patients in my sickbay?" Fisher asked. "Not to mention all the people I treated on their ship?"

"It depends on whether or not Gorkon can keep the incident buried," Gannon said. "What I believe happened next is that Gorkon hatched a scheme to save his son under the pretense of capturing enemy territory and assets—assets that included a state-of-the-art bioresearch laboratory, and a population whose customs he could turn to his advantage. My guess is that he hired a third party to infiltrate the asteroid and perform an act of sabotage that would threaten the colony sufficiently to warrant issuing a distress call, which the *Chech'Iw* would be in position to answer first. To throw off the High Council to his true intentions, Gorkon made the Arkenites an offer he knew they couldn't refuse."

"Unbelievable," Reyes said.

"Now we know why the *Chech'Iw* didn't have adequate medical personnel to deal with the theragen poisoning," Fisher said.

"They're with Gorkon on the asteroid," Reyes realized, "trying to treat Kintazh."

"It also explains why Duvadi was being kept in the lab wing," Fisher added, "and why Gorkon was going out of his way to keep her happy."

Gannon nodded. "He needed her help to make sure the unfamiliar lab equipment was being used to its best effect. Her sense of obligation, the thing that ensured her cooperation, depended on his continued goodwill. Kintazh's *life* depended on it."

"All this is about saving his son," Reyes said, shaking his head. "Why the hell didn't he just tell me?"

"Sir, Gorkon was already violating custom and law, and disobeying the orders of his chancellor. If what he was really up to became known, it wasn't just *his* honor that would be forfeit.

He's a Klingon general. Every man and woman under his command, and every member of his House, would share his dishonor, irredeemable even in death. Even if he wanted to divulge the truth, he couldn't risk it."

"I think I get the picture now, Commander."

"So what are we going to do?" Sadler asked.

Reyes looked pensive. "I think, Mister Sadler . . . I see another opportunity."

After learning what had befallen his ship, Gorkon was quick enough to agree to Reyes's demand for a meeting. And while he stoically endured the dishonor of *Dauntless* towing the *Chech'Iw* back to Azha-R7a while his crew recovered from theragen poisoning, much of the wind seemed to have left his sails.

With Fisher and Gannon at his side, Reyes faced Gorkon across the conference table in Duvadi's office, and for once, the general wore no trace of his derisive smile. Nor were his guards shadowing him this time. Whatever transpired here, Gorkon clearly did not want witnesses from among his own people.

"I know about your son," Reyes began without preamble. "Doctor Fisher can cure his condition. I'm offering you that assistance, and also my assurance that I'll back up any story you come up with to give you and your people cover with the High Council. In return, you're going to give up your claim to Azha-R7a and its inhabitants."

If Gorkon was surprised by the depth of Reyes's knowledge, his stony face revealed nothing. After a time he asked, "And if I refuse? What then? Would you withhold the cure that would save my son?"

"No," Reyes said. "I'm not going to play that game. I'm here because thanks in no small part to my first officer, I think I finally understand what led to this moment, and what's really at stake for you and your boy. I'll simply remind you that I just came from saving your ship. Your crew is mostly alive and well because of *me*. So I suggest you consider carefully what your honor demands at this juncture."

Gorkon leaned back in his chair. "So . . . you would use my own honor as a weapon against me," he said. "Coercion."

Reyes shrugged. "Let's call it a choice."

Shortly thereafter, Fisher was given leave to enter the asteroid's laboratory wing, where Gorkon's bioscientists struggled to keep a bedridden Kintazh alive. Initially, Fisher's arrival was met with open hostility. But a few stern words from Gorkon in *tlhIngan'Hol* cleared the way for Fisher to gain their cooperation, assess the patient's condition, and tailor his theragen treatment to optimize the young Klingon's chances for recovery. It wasn't long before Kintazh started showing clear signs of improvement.

As agreed, Gorkon informed Duvadi that she and her people would be released from their debt as soon as his son was well enough to leave.

Duvadi thanked Reyes for all he'd done, and for respecting the Arkenites' customs. "I know it couldn't have been easy for you, Captain."

"No, it wasn't," Reyes conceded. "But maybe it should've been."

Days later, Kintazh was back on his feet, and the *Dauntless* trio returned to observe the Klingon withdrawal from the asteroid. Gorkon, his personal guards, and his son were the last to depart. The Klingons carried themselves proudly as they marched toward the transporter room, barely acknowledging the Starfleet officers watching their approach.

What followed happened very quickly, but each instant was frozen indelibly in Fisher's memory.

As the Klingons entered the transporter room, Kintazh's gaze found Reyes, and all pretense at equanimity vanished.

Without warning, the young Klingon drew his *d'k tagh,* growled something in his native tongue, and lunged.

Reyes, without even a glimmer of surprise in his eyes, easily blocked the initial attack.

Kintazh recovered, then swiped again and slashed the captain's shoulder, drawing blood.

Gannon, shouting, drew her hand laser.

And suddenly, there was Gorkon. He stepped in quickly, blocking Gannon's aim, and snapped his son's neck with his hands.

Fisher started forward, already reaching for his medkit, but one of Gorkon's guards blocked his path.

Kintazh fell on his back, and as his last breath escaped him, Gorkon knelt down, forced open his son's eyes and roared at the ceiling.

Into the shocked silence that followed, Fisher moved to tend to Reyes, whose injuries were, fortunately, superficial.

Gannon stood there aghast, unable to believe what she had just witnessed. "I could have stopped him without killing him!" she shouted. "After all you did, after everything we've all gone through to save Kintazh . . . why slay your own son?"

"Why?" Gorkon repeated. "You are supposed to be intelligent, Gannon. How can you know us so well, and still ask the question?" He regarded her with disdain, clearly disappointed by her lack of comprehension. "Turn to your captain for answers if they elude you, Commander. He understands . . . finally."

Gorkon recovered Kintazh's *d'k tagh,* stained with Reyes's blood. He handled it almost reverently. " 'I have thee not, and yet I see thee still,' " he whispered.

Then he and his guards mounted the energizer stage, and the general called his ship for transport.

Before the beam took him, his eyes met those of *Dauntless*'s captain. "Die well, Reyes."

"Go to hell."

Gorkon and his guards vanished, leaving the apparently unimportant corpse of his son behind.

Fisher moved to check the body, and after verifying that Kintazh was dead, he gently closed the young Klingon's eyes. The doctor shook his head. "It's insane."

Gannon was still visibly shaken. "Sir, I—"

"This was never about saving Kintazh's life, Hallie," Reyes said, his eyes fixed on Gorkon's son. "You said it yourself: it was about prolonging it long enough to give him the chance to redeem himself—so he could die with honor. Kintazh died trying to kill an enemy of the Empire. That's how he'll be remembered. And Gorkon performed his duty by executing a member of his House who was about to commit an act of war. Honor is served."

"I thought I understood them," Gannon said. "But nothing in my training prepared me for this. Maybe you're right to hate Gorkon, Captain. Maybe there really is no bridging the gulf between our peoples."

Reyes met her eyes, and the sadness Fisher saw in his face gave way to a look of grim determination. "Dare to hope, Hallie."

9

2268

It was twilight when Desai found the leviathan.

Her trek up the southern ridge had been slow and arduous. She followed some well-worn trails when she could, but caution had forced her off the beaten path whenever she felt she was in danger of being discovered. She had to assume the other colonists had quickly learned about her escape from Sgouros's custody, and Desai wished to avoid any of the search parties that were undoubtedly now looking for her as well as Fisher. Fortunately, she had succeeded in disabling the transponder in Sgouros's comm unit, so they had no easy way to track her movements.

From the top of the ridge she'd seen the river. Or rather, she'd seen the blanket of fog that clung to it and followed its serpentine course as far as her eyes could penetrate. From somewhere below, the signal she followed called to her.

It took her another hour to reach the muddy, fog-shrouded bank, and it was there that she saw the beached form of what looked like a gigantic aquatic serpent, the full extent of its unbelievably long body lost in the mist. The transponder signal she'd been chasing momentarily forgotten, Desai stood in the mud, marveling at the size and alienness of the life-form—at its dark blue body streaked in pale green, at its toothy mouth that was big enough to close over an elephant, at its strange multiplicity of eyes that seemed to notice her presence, but which regarded her with an unfocused quality. Desai realized then that the creature was dying.

Its body swelled suddenly, as if with a great intake of breath, and with a thunderous trumpeting that rattled Desai's teeth and caused winged creatures all around to take flight, a great tear formed in the leviathan's side, releasing thousands of smaller serpents that spilled into the mud and slowly slithered toward the river, following the current as the leviathan expired.

"Sad and beautiful, isn't it?"

She turned to see Fisher emerging from the fog along the river's edge, followed by a young woman Desai assumed was Octavia Dawes. Behind them came Doctor Ying and several other New Anglese. "The colonists named them *nagai*," Fisher went on. "They travel upriver from the deep ocean to spawn, but they can't survive the experience. Their young have to struggle their way back home, because if they stay here, they'll die too. This is the secret the New Anglese have been guarding."

Desai's stare returned to the dead mother. "What's going on here, Fish? What does any of this have to do with Aole?"

"This is why he died," Ying said. "After he came here to convince us we needed to abandon Kadru, we decided to trust him with our knowledge of the *nagai*. We showed him our data, the holos we'd taken. He understood immediately, and wanted to help us. But he wanted to see the *nagai* for himself. We were reluctant, but he insisted New Anglesey was running out of time. So while we met to debate his request, Aole took matters into his own hands and went out alone to experience the *nagai* firsthand. He came across a beached mother, just as you did. But something went wrong. He must have slipped or fallen in the river, struck his head on a rock below the surface of the water. Dawes found him not long after, but it was already too late.

"We panicked. We were afraid of more outsiders finding the *nagai*, so we went to work eradicating any trace of where Aole had been, or any *nagai* DNA he'd come in contact with. We even burned his uniform. We had to make sure Starfleet wouldn't be able to retrace his steps back here. But it was all for nothing."

"Why?" Desai asked. "Why did it need to be kept secret?"

Fisher exchanged a look with Dawes and said, "The way it's been explained to me—and the data I've been shown backs this up—the blood of the *nagai* has a very complex and unusual composition. It contains a unique combination of biochemical constituents that Doctor Dawes here has identified as a potential panacea to most of the known humanoid species, and probably many others. Imagine it, Rana: a wonder drug for whatever may ail us. A revolution in medicine throughout every world we know about.

"But it's their *blood*. And there's mounting evidence to suggest that the *nagai* are sapient, or on the cusp of it at least. When the colonists made that discovery, they began to worry about what would happen if word got out about the possibilities surrounding *nagai* blood. What might the Klingons do? Or the Orions?"

"Or even the Federation," Desai said quietly. It was a fair question: *How could anyone be trusted to treat the* nagai *with respect under those circumstances?*

"In the deep ocean they're relatively safe, and can defend themselves if necessary, but the spawning season is when they're their most vulnerable," Dawes said, gesturing toward the newborns. "The young feed on their mother's blood until they're ready to be born. Whatever's left behind lacks any of the medicinal potential we've detected, so we can't simply harvest the dead mothers. Even if we could, we still have no idea how they would feel about such a thing. We're trying to learn as much as we can while we're here, but we need time. The gulf between the *nagai* and us is unimaginably wide, and it could be lifetimes before we can bridge it."

"That's the real reason we've demanded to be left alone, Captain," Ying said, "and why we can't allow ourselves to be evacuated, even if Starfleet abandons this sector. Someone has to make sure the *nagai* aren't exploited."

"So that speech you gave me about our broken colonial system," said Desai, "that was all misdirection?"

"I didn't say anything that isn't a matter of record, Captain," Ying pointed out, "but we never wanted to turn our backs on Starfleet and the Federation, and especially not on Captain Gannon, who was as staunch a friend as I've ever had. If it wasn't for what we've found here, we'd be trying to work out our grievances, not bury our heads in the sand." Her gaze traveled back toward the moving tangle of newborn *nagai*. "But now that you know the truth, I need to ask: what are you going to do?"

That's the big question, isn't it? Desai thought. She looked at Fisher, and in his eyes she saw her own uncertainty reflected back at her. Somehow the future of much more than just this one colony had been placed on her shoulders, and whatever choice she made now, someone would have to pay a price for it.

"This isn't the outcome I sent you to achieve, Captain," Nogura said. "In fact, in most every way I can measure, it's the exact opposite."

Desai stood at parade rest, facing the admiral across his desk. He plowed on before she could formulate a response, gesturing with one hand at the slate he held in the other. "According to your report, the New Anglesey colonists have filed a formal petition to have the planet Kadru reclassified as a nature preserve and wildlife refuge, a process that will require, at minimum, months or even years while the petition awaits a proper review in the Federation Council. But just the act of filing it means Starfleet can't discontinue its oversight of that sector until the Council has reached a decision about Kadru's status." He looked up at her. "Can you explain to me how a colony of isolationist scientists obtained the legal advice to draft such a well-crafted and airtight document?"

Staring straight ahead, Desai answered, "They must have found a good lawyer. Sir."

Nogura scoffed. "I'll bet. This will *not* go over well with Starfleet Command, but that's a headache for another time. I'm pleased to note you and Doctor Fisher did manage to confirm that Aole Miller wasn't the victim of foul play . . . which means, I suppose, that the matter is effectively closed." He cleared the screen on the slate and set it aside. "There'll be a memorial service honoring Commander Miller three days from now. Would you care to be a speaker?"

"Yes, sir, I would. Thank you, sir."

Nogura nodded. "My yeoman will be in contact with you about the details. Dismissed."

"Admiral," Desai said, making no move to leave, and instead offering him the slate she'd been holding behind her back. "There's one more piece of business we need to discuss."

The memorial service was held on Fontana Meadow. Many beautiful things were said by many people, and when Desai's turn came, she kept her statements brief but spoke from her heart.

Afterward, many of those in attendance migrated to Stars Landing, the crescent of civilian commercial and residential structures that bordered the meadow. Manón's Cabaret was crowded to overflowing with Vanguard personnel in dress uniforms celebrating the life of Aole Miller. Drinks flowed freely, and the lively atmosphere was full of stories and songs.

Desai found a seat at the bar, ordered a glass of '51 Brunello Riserva for old times' sake, and was halfway through it when Fisher eased onto the empty stool next to her. "You're making a mistake," he told her over the noise. He held up three stacked fingers to the bartender and silently mouthed the words, *Saurian, neat.*

"If I am, it wouldn't be the first," Desai answered.

"But a transfer off the base? To an Earthside posting?" Fisher shook his head. "I won't even ask how you convinced the admiral to pull those strings."

"Actually, Nogura was very supportive," Desai said, taking a sip of wine. "My guess is, he thinks it'll make whatever he ends up doing about Diego less complicated for him."

The bartender returned with Fisher's brandy. "That sounds like a good reason to stay, not to leave."

Desai said nothing. Instead, she reached into her sleeve and drew out a data card, holding it out to Fisher between two fingers.

Fisher accepted it, a puzzled look forming on his face. "What's this?"

"Hallie's voice," Desai said. "All her official logs below top secret, from her days on the *Dauntless* to her captaincy of the *Bombay*, declassified for your exclusive access."

For a moment Fisher was speechless. Then his expression hardened. He set the card down on the bar between them and slid it toward her. "Take it back."

"Don't worry, there's nothing from her personal logs; I wouldn't violate her privacy."

"Even so."

"Why?" When Fisher failed to form an answer, Desai said, "Zeke, she was your friend. You miss her."

"I've lived a long time, Rana. I miss a lot of people. And I carry them with me. But this . . . I spend too much time as it is talking to ghosts. If I start listening to them—"

"Fish," Desai said, "that's not what this is."

"What is it, then?"

"Maybe I haven't lived as long as you, but I do know what it's like to lose people I love . . . and what it is to be haunted by them, to feel at times like there's nothing I wouldn't give to have one more day with them. I can't give you one more day with Hallie, Zeke. But what I can give you is a slightly bigger perspective on who she was, in her own words." Desai put her fingers on the data card and pushed it back under Fisher's hand. "You can get to know her all over again."

Fisher's hand slowly closed around the card, gratitude and sadness streaming from his eyes. "Why are you leaving, Rana?"

She turned back to her wineglass, took another sip. "It's time."

"Is this about Diego?"

"Of course it is," she admitted, seeing no point to evading or equivocating. "I love him, Zeke. But when he needed me most, I was powerless to help him. Every time he needed me, I was powerless. And just when I finally accepted it and began to move forward, he came back. He's so close at this very moment that I should be able to walk the distance separating us. But I can't. I'm still powerless . . . and I no longer have it in me to stay here just so I can be a witness to whatever happens next."

Fisher's kind eyes were devoid of judgment, as always. It made things easier. But only a little.

"You know," he said at length, "I once heard Diego offer someone advice about bridging impossible divides. You want to hear it?"

"No," Desai said. Then she set down her unfinished drink, kissed Fisher tenderly on the cheek, and walked away without a backward glance.

Diego Reyes thought he had long ago gotten over just how big Vanguard truly was, but seeing it now, from a narrow window angled up toward the primary hull, the station seemed more immense than ever. He had to hand it to Ganz: the fat bastard had made it seem as if he'd selected this stateroom at random, but there was little doubt in Reyes's mind that the self-styled merchant prince had intended for Reyes to always have a spectacular view of everything and everyone he had lost.

Reyes watched as the work to clear out the compromised sections of Starbase 47's starship bay continued, but if his armchair assessment was right, Isaiah Farber and his engineers were nearing the limits of what they could achieve on their own. They would need to call in help soon, if it wasn't already on its way.

The door chimed. Reyes tried to ignore it, but on his visitor's third attempt, he got so sick of hearing the insipidly ethereal tones all he could think about was making them stop. "What is it?" he snapped.

One of Ganz's women entered, carrying a tray of food and drink. Not another Orion, but even in the low lighting he could tell she was as shapely and diaphanously attired as all the others, and she moved with a similar sensuality. *The pheromones are just as bad, too.* Reyes didn't spare her more than a glance. "Compliments of Mister Ganz, sir," she purred.

Yeah, I'll bet. "Leave it and get out."

He heard her take her time setting down the tray, obviously in no hurry to leave. "Are you sure there's nothing else I can offer you this evening, Mister Reyes?"

Irritated, Reyes looked at her again . . . and this time he saw what Ganz had wanted him to see. The height, the caramel complexion, the shimmering black hair, and the big brown eyes that were half closed in invitation.

You son of a bitch.

With deliberate effort he turned back to his view of Vanguard, fixing his eyes on the lighted rectangles just below the saucer. "I said get the hell out."

This time she departed, her task accomplished.

Diego Reyes continued staring up at the station long into the ship's night. He could almost imagine Rana standing at one of those viewports, searching the *Omari-Ekon* for some sign of him. The distance between them wasn't far. It felt like light-years.

THE STARS
LOOK DOWN

David Mack

For Ripley,
my beloved feline companion of eighteen years:
requiescat in pace.

". . . Me miserable! which way shall I fly
Infinite wrath and infinite despair?
Which way I fly is Hell; myself am Hell;
And, in the lowest deep, a lower deep
Still threat'ning to devour me opens wide,
To which the Hell I suffer seems a Heaven."

—John Milton, *Paradise Lost*

HISTORIAN'S NOTE

The events of this story take place in early 2268, approximately two months after the end of the novel *Star Trek Vanguard: Precipice* and shortly before the events of the original-series episode "The Tholian Web."

FEBRUARY 2268

1

"Dammit, Bridy," Cervantes Quinn pleaded via the communicator, *"don't do nothin' stupid."*

Bridget McLellan—Bridy Mac to her friends—ignored her partner's advice. She drew her phaser, aimed at the master control panel for the Klingon research facility's main generator, and fired. Her weapon's scathing blue beam sliced through the array of buttons, levers, and displays. The slagged console spat sparks and belched smoke. An alarm blared over the compound's PA system and was followed by a guttural male voice barking orders in Klingon. She lifted her communicator and smiled. "Too late."

"Goddammit, lady, you love to make my life difficult."

"It's a living. Be at the gate in ninety seconds."

"Already on my way, darlin'."

Bridy sprinted past a spreading wall of fire that had been ignited by her forced entry moments earlier, winced as flames licked at her face, and bashed open the door ahead of her with her shoulder. Disruptor blasts sliced past her close enough to singe her hair. She tumbled to cover behind the low retaining wall of the landing outside the operations shack's entrance, at the top of a short flight of stairs. She snapped off a shot without aiming, firing down the stairs and stunning a Klingon soldier who had been standing between Bridy and her escape route. She scrambled past him as he collapsed to the ground.

Energy pulses crisscrossed the Klingon research compound, but most of them weren't aimed at Bridy—they were converging on the biomechanoid alien artifact around which the base had been constructed. The massive device, which to Bridy resembled a terrifying, four-fingered hand whose talons were plunged into a slab of obsidian, crackled with blue lightning as the shimmering energy being trapped within it struggled for freedom.

Bridy had no idea how or when the Klingons had captured one of the ancient aliens known as the Shedai, but her orders from

Starfleet Command had been clear: terminate the Klingons' research program on Zeta Aurigae IV immediately and with prejudice. At first it had seemed a tall order for two undercover agents such as herself and Quinn. Then she had realized that all she'd needed to do was disrupt the power to the artifact. The Klingons' captive Shedai would do the rest.

The entity was more than living up to her expectations. Massive ribbons of energy lashed out from within the artifact, cutting down entire squads of Klingons with each stroke and filling the air with terrifying cracks, as if from a giant bullwhip. Blood and viscera sprayed from dismembered Klingon bodies, clouding the air around the artifact with a grotesque fuchsia mist.

Counting off the seconds in her head, Bridy sprinted for the compound's gate, dozens of meters from the operations shack. Behind her, the screeching of disruptors tapered off and was replaced by the agonized groans of the dying. Her shadow stretched away ahead of her, preceding her to the gate. Then another shadow arced toward hers. She dodged left and dove for the ground.

A javelin-tipped tentacle of shimmering fluid shot past her, close enough for her to feel its rush of displaced air. The Shedai's pointed appendage tore a long, ugly divot into the ground ahead of her.

I set it free and this is the thanks I get? She rolled away while firing her phaser back at the wildly flailing creature. *Talk about ungrateful.*

Quinn's ship, the *Dulcinea,* appeared from behind a nearby ridge and sped toward the compound's main gate. Bridy pushed herself up from the ground and ran flat out toward the gate while using her thumb to increase her phaser's power setting to maximum. The droning of *Dulcinea*'s engines was drowned out by the Shedai's roar, an unearthly noise like a thousand rusty horns. The din overwhelmed Bridy, who felt it like needles being stabbed through her skull. Her stride faltered. She fell to her knees and instinctively covered her ears. Then the shrieking was replaced by thunderous impacts that shook the ground.

Bridy looked back. The Shedai was free of the Conduit and pummeling the structures inside the Klingons' compound into rubble and dust.

She forced herself back into motion and staggered toward the gate. Her gait was sloppy, like that of a drunkard, and as she lifted her arm to aim her phaser, she could barely keep it pointed in the gate's general direction. Pressing the trigger, she hoped she wouldn't hit Quinn's ship by mistake.

A blinding flash of phaser energy vaporized more than half the metal gate and a significant chunk of the reinforced thermocrete wall to its right, creating a gap more than wide enough for Bridy's escape. She stumbled through, careful not to touch the glowing-hot metal or stone with her bare hands. As she cleared the phaser-cut passageway, the *Dulcinea* touched down directly ahead of her. Its starboard-side hatchway was open, and its ramp had been lowered.

Through a pane of the cockpit's windshield, Bridy saw Quinn beckoning urgently, and she heard his voice over the open communicator in her hand: *"C'mon, sweetheart! We gotta go!"*

Bridy all but threw herself onto the ramp and used its railings to pull herself inside the ship, a state-of-the-art Nalori argosy that Quinn had "inherited" from his late rival, Zett Nilric, after killing the assassin in self-defense a few months earlier. The ramp lifted shut behind her, pushing her the rest of the way into the vessel's main living compartment. The deck and bulkheads thrummed with vibrations from the ship's engines as she moved forward to the cockpit. Its door slid open ahead of her, revealing a slowly rolling view of the distant horizon.

"We're clear," Quinn said. The lean and weathered former soldier of fortune had one hand on the ship's flight controls and one on its sensor panel. A small display on the center console between the pilot's and copilot's stations showed the Shedai laying waste to the few Klingon structures still half-standing and slaying the remainder of the base's personnel. Quinn nodded at the image of the berserk Shedai. "Any idea which one it is?"

"The Warden, I think."

"Not a friend of ours, then."

The Conduit on the surface crackled with violent energy, and the Shedai transmuted into a serpent of black smoke. Intense white light flashed in the Conduit's center, and when it faded the black smoke had dissipated, leaving no trace of the homicidal alien hegemon. Quinn shook his head. "Great. Now that thing could be anywhere in the Taurus Reach. God help whoever finds it next."

Bridy laid a reassuring hand on Quinn's shoulder. "Let's just hope it's not us. The Shedai tend to hold grudges."

"No kidding." He glanced toward the planet's surface as he guided the *Dulcinea* through a steep, banking turn. Except for the Shedai Conduit itself, nothing remained of the Klingon research base except debris and ashes. "Looks like our work here is done," he said. "Let's call in the cavalry and have dinner."

2

Ganz curled his hand into a fist as he stared at the comm display. "Where is he?"

Kajek, a Nausicaan bounty hunter, shrugged. *"I don't know."*

"You said you'd found him."

"No, I said I found his ship." Kajek uploaded a series of images to Ganz's screen via the subspace comm link. *"It was on Zeta Aurigae IV two days ago."*

The Orion gangster studied the photographs and paid close attention to their details. The markings on Zett's vessel were unmistakable, as was the unique bit of battle damage visible on its dorsal hull, just behind the cockpit canopy. "That's his ship," Ganz said. Then the image switched to one showing the vessel's registry. "Those aren't Nalori markings. Those are human symbols."

"It says 'Dulcinea' in Federation Standard. I have no idea what it means."

"It means someone stole Zett's ship. Who has it?"

More images appeared on Ganz's screen, narrated by Kajek. *"Two humans. A man and a woman. I suspect he is the pilot and she a passenger."*

"You're half right." Ganz massaged his left temple to stave off a nascent headache induced by the bass-heavy music resounding from the gaming floor outside his office. "The man is Cervantes Quinn, and he's almost certainly the pilot. But that woman is no mere passenger—she's a Starfleet agent. I suspect they've been working together for some time now."

It had been over a year since someone—Ganz had never been entirely certain who—had cleared all of Quinn's debts with Ganz's operation. All his attempts to trace the money to its source had proved futile. The only fruit of that labor had been a stern warning, delivered through intermediaries, that Quinn was to be left alone unless Ganz wanted to awaken one day with his throat cut.

Since taking that advice to heart, Ganz had suspected Quinn was working with Starfleet Intelligence, but until he had seen evidence of Zett's stolen starship, he would not have believed Quinn bold enough to risk inviting Ganz's wrath.

The Nausicaan interrupted Ganz's somber reflection with a loud grunt. *"Am I finished, then? Or do you have a new commission for me?"*

"Hang on, I'm thinking." He put the comm on standby and looked past its display toward his lover, Neera. She reclined in a seductive pose on the sofa, her raven mane spilling wildly over her jade-hued shoulders and concealing the choicest bits of her bare torso. "What do you think?"

She fixed him with a cold stare. "You *know* what I think."

"The situation has changed."

"No, it hasn't." She finger-combed a thick fall of hair from her eyes. "Quinn still has powerful friends. The only difference is that now he also has Zett's ship."

"Which means he just spat in our eye."

"Your eye, maybe. I never liked Zett. He was a disaster waiting to happen." She shot a diabolical smirk at Ganz. "Mister Quinn might have done us a favor."

Ganz suppressed an angry sigh. Though he played the part of the boss aboard the merchantman *Omari-Ekon,* he was merely a figurehead for Neera, the organization's true mistress. At times such as this, he had to remember not to let his role go to his head lest Neera decide to recast it with someone more pliable. "I agree that Zett's knack for bloodshed was a liability at times, but he was a loyal employee and a good earner."

"So what?"

"It'll set a bad example if we let him get killed and do nothing about it."

Neera regarded him with faint amusement. "You're afraid our hired guns will start to feel expendable?"

"They aren't loyal just because we pay them well. They stick with us because they think we'll back them up when times get tough—and avenge them when things go wrong. Zett was my right-hand man. If we don't settle this score, nobody worth having will ever be willing to watch our backs again."

His lithe mistress got up and walked toward him in slow, elegant strides. "And if Starfleet should decide to avenge Mister Quinn's death in return?"

"That's why I'm farming it out to the Nausicaan."

She stopped beside him and traced his jutting chin with one exquisitely manicured fingernail. "If this comes back at us, you'll take the hit. Understood?"

"Yes, mistress."

Walking away, she threw a dark look over her shoulder. "Good."

He waited until she had left the room through her private portal, and then he reactivated the comm channel to Kajek. "Kill Quinn, but don't hurt the woman."

"What if she defends him?"

"Not even then, so pick your moment well."

"As you wish. The price is fifty thousand."

"Thirty."

"Fifty. Half in advance."

"Thirty-five."

"Do you want this human dead or not?"

Ganz half sighed, half growled. "Fine. I'll transfer the retainer now. The Bank of Bolarus should confirm the transaction within the hour."

Kajek nodded. *"A pleasure doing business with you. I will let you know when the human is dead."* He ended the transmission, and the screen went dark.

Sitting alone in the dimly lit office, Ganz wondered whether he'd ordered the assassination of Cervantes Quinn as a substitute for a different murder that he wished for but which Neera had refused to sanction.

He got up and stepped outside to a small balcony that overlooked the gaming floor of the *Omari-Ekon*. Below him, beautiful escorts of various species and genders mingled with his patrons, most of whom were Federation civilians passing through Starbase 47, also known as Vanguard, on their way to new lives on colony planets throughout the Taurus Reach. Cheers from players with winning hands infrequently rose above the steady beat of synthetic music.

Ganz looked up. Through the transparent-aluminum dome that served as the casino's roof, he saw the towering majesty of the Federation starbase looming over his ship, simultaneously providing it with protection from Ganz and Neera's rivals while posing the most immediate threat to its continued free exercise of commerce.

Standing on another balcony at the opposite end of the gaming room was the root of Ganz's anxiety, the cause of his broken sleep patterns, the irritant he had been forbidden to remove: Diego Reyes, the former commanding officer of Vanguard, now a fugitive from Starfleet justice who resided on the *Omari-Ekon* thanks to a grant of political asylum and the technicalities of Orion extradition law.

The tall, weathered-looking human flashed an insincere smile at Ganz.

The burly, muscular Orion returned the empty gesture. *Keep smiling, you clever bastard*, Ganz fumed. *Sooner or later, you'll stop being useful. And when that day comes, I'll be waiting to toss you out an airlock.*

3

Lieutenant Ming Xiong leaned forward and looked with a stunned expression across the conference room table at Bridy Mac. "You let it get away?"

"It's not as if I had a choice," Bridy said. "Once the containment system failed, the entire op went pear-shaped. We were lucky to get out alive."

The other officers attending the classified debriefing aboard the *U.S.S. Endeavour* didn't try to mask their disapproval. Captain Atish Khatami, the ship's commanding officer, showed the greatest discretion, limiting her reaction to a thin frown. Her first officer, Lieutenant Commander Katherine Stano, let slip a barely audible sigh. The ship's chief science officer, Lieutenant Stephen Klisiewicz, registered his opinion with a deep grimace and a slow swiveling of his head.

Xiong picked up a data slate and glanced back and forth between it and Bridy Mac as he continued. "According to your report, the containment system failed after you fired your phaser into the control panel for its main generator."

Bridy's face warmed with embarrassment and anger. "That's right."

Stano asked, "Did you forget that capturing the Conduit with the Shedai still inside it was one of the mission objectives?"

"No, Commander, I didn't. But that wasn't possible, so I—"

"Why wasn't it possible?"

It had been Bridy's experience that answering such a question truthfully and in detail would likely come back to haunt her the next time her name came up for promotion. Had she been the sort of officer who gave a damn about such things, she might have censored herself. Instead, she clenched her jaw and drew a deep breath. "The mission profile was flawed, sir. Whoever wrote it underestimated the number of Klingon troops by a factor of four. The map of the compound was labeled incorrectly, and the intel on its security grid was out of date. As a result, Mister Quinn and I lacked the appropriate resources to carry out the nonviolent capture of the Klingon personnel and the Shedai entity. It should also be noted that the Klingons have broken the encryption on cipher Seven-Tango-Red, which is how I wound up being ambushed shortly after I breached the base's perimeter wall." She paused, flashed a hostile smile at Stano, and added, "Sir."

A tense, awkward silence followed Bridy's critique. Then Captain Khatami cleared her throat. "Let's move on, shall we?" She pushed a data slate across the table to Bridy. "You and Mister Quinn have new orders from Starfleet Command."

Bridy reached for the tablet. "Another monster hunt?"

"Not this time," Khatami said. "A black bag operation."

Stano nodded to Klisiewicz, who used a small keypad on the table in front of him to activate one of the room's wall displays. He nodded up at the screen, which showed a montage of star charts, log excerpts, and transcripts of signal intercepts. "Thirty-four hours ago, the *Treana,* an Orion freighter, was crippled by an unknown gravitational anomaly on the edge of Gorn territory. The *Treana* sent out an SOS and was rescued by a Gorn cruiser, which took the freighter into 'protective custody' on Seudath, one of its border worlds."

Stano glanced at Bridy. "The Gorn say they're repairing the freighter as a courtesy, but it's obvious they want it for military analysis."

Xiong entered a command on the keypad in front of his seat and activated the three-screen monitor in the middle of the conference table. The device displayed a series of waveforms. "*Endeavour*'s long-range sensors picked up these fragmentary energy readings from the *Treana*'s coordinates at the time of the incident." He shot her a wan, knowing smile. "Look familiar, Bridy?"

She nodded. "The Jinoteur Pattern. Last time I saw it, I was with you on the *Sagittarius*. All traces of the pattern vanished after the Jinoteur system was swallowed by an artificial wrinkle in space-time."

Khatami arched her brow. "Well, it's back."

Klisiewicz added, "And we don't know how or why."

Xiong met Bridy's stare. "Whatever produced these readings is of major importance. We need to track them back to their source, but there are too many gaps in our data to triangulate the coordinates."

Grim anticipation made Bridy crack a thin smile. "You want me and Quinn to sneak aboard the Orion freighter and steal its sensor logs."

"Precisely," Khatami said.

Stano added, "The good news is that the Gorn don't seem to be aware of the Shedai or the significance of this energy pattern, and we'd like to keep it that way. The bad news is that we have reason to believe the Klingons have already sent someone to retrieve the Orions' data. It's imperative you get to it first."

"And that you make sure the Klingons never do," Khatami added.

"How sure do you want to be? Should I destroy the *Treana*?"

Xiong winced. "Not exactly what we had in mind."

Klisiewicz held up two data cards. "The yellow one is blank. Use it to download the sensor data. The red one contains a worm that'll erase the data from the *Treana*'s memory banks and then erase itself." He handed the cards to Bridy.

"Got it." She tucked the cards into a pocket and looked at Khatami. "What about *Endeavour*? Will you be close enough to provide operational support?"

Khatami shook her head. "We can't risk approaching Gorn territory. The cease-fire negotiated by Captain Kirk is barely holding, and we don't want to tip off the Klingons about our intentions toward the *Treana*."

"Knowing the Gorn," Stano said, "the *Treana*'s probably docked in the segregated 'alien quarter' of Tzoryp, Seudath's principal port of call. The Gorn patrol that part of the city, but they tend to be hands-off when it comes to policing aliens. Keep the collateral damage to a minimum and they should ignore you."

The captain held up one hand in a cautioning gesture. "Move fast and keep a low profile. If this goes according to plan, no one should know you were there."

Bridy chuckled. "Since when does anything ever go according to plan?"

"Good hunting," Khatami said. "Meeting adjourned."

Cervantes Quinn stood beneath an open panel on the fuselage of the *Dulcinea* and listened. Behind the rich purr of the ship's primary power coupler lurked a high-frequency warbling. It was elusive to Quinn's ear. Each time he thought he had a bead on its source it faded, leaving him staring into the guts of his ship with no idea which component to tear apart first.

No one else had ever confirmed hearing the noise, no matter how many times Quinn had tried to point it out to people. Bridy had dismissed it as "transient tinnitus," despite Quinn's assertion that the sound was not imaginary. None of the technicians on Vanguard or the *Endeavour* who had inspected *Dulcinea*'s internal systems had reported hearing anything unusual. Quinn didn't care what they said. It was his ship, and he was certain the warble was in there, waiting to be found.

In the months since he had taken possession of the ship, he had come to know many of its idiosyncratic details. Its meal slot always clicked three times before serving solid food but only once before vending a beverage. Its air purification system had a curious rattle in the filter above the main corridor, just outside the cockpit entrance. One of the otherwise pristine metal deck plates in the main compartment was marred by a single, deep gouge; judging from the brightness of the exposed metal, Quinn suspected the damage was fairly recent, probably having occurred within the past couple of years.

Each day brought him a new discovery about *Dulcinea*. Every time he dared to think it had run out of surprises, some new imperfection revealed itself.

He heard a door swish open behind him. Looking over his shoulder, he saw Bridy crossing the shuttlebay. She waved. "How's it going?"

He shrugged. "Same as always."

"I'm sorry." She joined him beneath the ship and looked up at the exposed section of its underbelly. "Still looking for that pesky noise?"

"I think I might flush out the plasma conduits."

"Will that fix it?"

"Couldn't hurt." He wondered why Bridy had taken a sudden interest in the repair of a problem she didn't believe existed, and he surmised she was avoiding discussion of something else. "How'd your debriefing go?"

She ambled toward *Dulcinea*'s bow. "Fine."

"Were they pissed about the casualties?"

"More than somewhat." Bridy stroked her hand along the ship's ventral hull.

Quinn wondered what she was thinking. "What'd they say about the Shedai that got away from us?"

"Not much."

"So, no court-martial?"

"Not yet."

"Good." He followed her. "Any chance we're free for a while? I heard about some easy-money jobs hauling gray-market cargo to Pacifica—which, as it turns out, is a mighty fine place to kick back on a tropical vacation."

"Sounds great." She mustered a sad smile. "But we have new orders."

"I was afraid you'd say that." Tired and disgruntled, he breathed a heavy sigh. "What is it this time? More monkey-wrenching? Or another monster hunt?"

"A classic heist job—just your style." She smiled. "You'll love it."

Her appraisal of the op was far too upbeat for Quinn's comfort. He had learned to be suspicious whenever Bridy sounded optimistic. She followed him as he paced around the port side of the *Dulcinea,* inspecting the hull. "Are we expecting competition on this job?"

"Some, probably from the Klingons."

"Great." He used his arm to buff a dark scuff off the ship's hull. "Do I even want to know where we're being asked to commit this 'classic heist'?"

"In a port called Tzoryp on a planet named Seudath."

"Never heard of it." Passing under the wing, he realigned an off-center aileron with a light upward jab of his fist. "Where is it?"

"The Gorn-Klingon border."

Quinn stopped, turned, and regarded his partner with a mirthless smile. "I admire the casual way you just said that—as if it weren't an omen of doom. Pray tell, *which side* of that border is it on?"

"The Gorn side."

He shook his head. "Days like this make me sorry I gave up drinking."

"Could be worse. At least we aren't dealing with the Tholians."

"The Gorn aren't much better." He led her up the ramp and inside the ship. "Remember that guy we met in the cantina on Deskereb? He'd just come back from Gorn space—said they're the most cold-blooded bastards he ever met."

"Well, they *are* reptiles."

"Dammit, you know what I mean." He took off his tool belt and draped it by its buckle from a hook inside the open equipment locker, then continued on his way toward the cockpit. "The Gorn see the law as something for themselves only. They let their border worlds run wild because they think aliens are little better than animals. As long as no Gorn get hurt, they'll gladly stand by and do nothing while offworlders shoot each other all to hell."

He sidled into the cockpit and slumped into his seat to start the preflight check. Bridy leaned over his shoulder and fixed him with a dubious stare. "Don't you think you might be exaggerating just a bit?"

"Like hell I am. If this goes south, we could wind up in the middle of a goddamned free-for-all down there."

Bridy smiled. "That's what you have me for, honey." She kissed his cheek, patted his shoulder, and added, "Let me know when we're ready to take off."

"You'll be the second to know," Quinn said, powering up the navigation computer. Bridy turned and left the cockpit while Quinn continued prepping the *Dulcinea* for its next journey.

Looking up, he caught his worried reflection in the cockpit's canopy. *How do I get myself into these messes? Why can't I master the fine art of saying "no" to beautiful women?* He reclined his chair and palmed a sheen of sweat off his forehead and over his gray crewcut. *Because I'm an idiot, that's why.*

4

Kajek found the rhythm of his own breathing hypnotic in the deathly silence that permeated his ship, a compact Andorian outrider he had never bothered to name. Outside his capsule-shaped cockpit's wraparound canopy yawned the blackness of eternity, an endless void peppered with stars to mask its hideous emptiness.

The lean, wiry Nausicaan lounged in the broad, enveloping pilot's seat. Most of his ship's primary systems were in a low-power standby mode. Even the life-support system had been set to minimal levels, and the spacecraft's artificial gravity had been deactivated. If not for the safety restraints crisscrossing his torso, Kajek would have long since floated out of his seat.

Zero gravity didn't bother Kajek, but the bitter cold did. Several hours in the dark had dropped temperatures inside his ship to near-freezing. His exhalations spawned great gray plumes that dissipated ever more gradually. In the past hour, vapor condensed from his breath had started to fog part of the forward canopy. More troubling to him was the slow loss of sensation in his fingers and toes. He disliked wearing gloves in the cockpit because any that were thick enough to keep his hands warm interfered with his ability to operate the ship's secondary control panels, which controlled such systems as sensors and access to the memory banks.

Only the passive optical sensors remained fully on line. Kajek had set them to monitor the Starfleet vessel *Endeavour,* which was twenty light-minutes away orbiting Zeta Aurigae IV, the same world to which Kajek had tracked Zett Nilric's stolen argosy, *Dulcinea.* A magnetic disturbance above the southern pole of Zeta Aurigae III concealed Kajek and his ship from the *Endeavour*'s sensors, enabling him to spy on it at relatively close range while hiding in plain sight. His only concern was that if the *Dulcinea* launched while the *Endeavour* was on the far side of the fourth planet, he might not notice its departure until it was too late to track its escape vector.

It had been several hours since the Nalori ship had landed inside one of *Endeavour*'s shuttlebays. Kajek grew concerned that perhaps he had missed the *Dulcinea*'s exit—and then the bulkheads parted at the aft end of the Starfleet vessel's lower hull. He spread his outer fangs in a broad grin. *There you are.* He permitted himself a low chortle, which clouded the air with a spectre of his breath.

As the Nalori vessel exited the shuttlebay and maneuvered to break orbit, Kajek clicked his outer fangs against one another. It was a nervous habit, one he had struggled to overcome but so far had failed to suppress, an unwelcome tic caused by his tendency to engage in obsessive-compulsive behavior. In many ways he had channeled that psychological trait into useful habits. His attention to detail and ability to plan ahead had made him a very effective bounty hunter. He always knew his current equipment inventory and the status of his ship's fuel and provisions. His personal logs and files on bounty targets were alphabetized, meta-tagged, and thoroughly cross-referenced by more than a hundred criteria.

I am not crazy, just organized.

He leaned forward to observe the sensor data. *Where are you going? Show me your destination.* His quarry maneuvered clear of the *Endeavour* and broke from orbit. *Not heading back to Vanguard, apparently.* The small vessel came about on a bearing that would take it toward the Klingon Empire. *A bold move.* Seconds later, the *Dulcinea* jumped to warp speed and moved beyond the range of Kajek's passive sensors. Kajek kept his attention on the *Endeavour*.

Patience, he reminded himself. *Don't let your lust for the hunt make you careless.* He watched and waited as the *Endeavour*'s standard orbital pattern took it beyond the curve of Zeta Aurigae IV. As soon as the Starfleet ship vanished from his sensor readout, Kajek pulled off his gloves, switched all his ship's systems to full power, and engaged his active sensors to confirm the *Dulcinea*'s heading.

Still on course, he noted. He pulled his gloves back on and briskly rubbed his hands together. He called up a star chart and looked ahead along the *Dulcinea*'s trajectory, curious as to what populated systems lay along that heading. *They seem to be treading a fine path between Gorn space and Klingon territory. Are they en route to one of the border worlds, perhaps?* He ruled out Chirlow—it was a mostly automated mining operation on a volcanic greenhouse planet inhospitable to organic life. Likewise, he doubted they would be bound for Mazur Prime, a desolate ball of sand that the Klingons used as a toxic-waste dumping ground.

Ruling out those worlds brought him to Seudath: a major port under Gorn control, it received a fair number of alien visitors and had a sizable population of aliens, as well. Checking its position against a more precise analysis of the *Dulcinea*'s heading convinced Kajek that Seudath was the humans' destination. He engaged his ship's impulse engine, maneuvered clear of Zeta Aurigae III's magnetic field, and set his navigation computer to begin calculating a warp-speed course that would enable him to reach Seudath ahead of the ever-elusive Mister Quinn.

The course coordinates appeared on his helm.

Engaging the warp drive, Kajek watched the stars melt into bright streaks blurring past his ship, and he felt a surge of excitement. There was nothing he loved so much as the hunt, and never so much as when the prey could fight back.

The chase begins.

Quinn lay in bed, half asleep, listening to the steady thrumming of the *Dulcinea*'s warp engines. Despite his grave misgivings about his and Bridy's new orders from Starfleet Intelligence, the ship was cruising on autopilot toward Seudath.

It's not like I could've talked her out of it, he mused. *Lord knows I would if I could.* He turned onto his left side, trying his best not to wake Bridy, who lay beside him, wrapped around a body cushion like a shipwreck survivor clinging to flotsam. Her wavy dark brown hair spilled across the sage-colored pillows. As Quinn tugged on the sheets to try and cover his chest, Bridy stirred, blinked once, and squinted at him. He whispered, "Sorry. Go back to sleep, darlin'."

"In a minute." She sounded groggy. "Trouble sleeping?"

"A bit. At least I can enjoy the view." That made her smile. It had been a few months since they had escaped a bloodbath on Golmira with their lives. Since then they had shared a bed—a fact that Bridy had stressed needed to be concealed from her superiors at SI. Quinn understood her need for discretion, but he hated having to hide the true nature of their relationship even from their friends. He adored Bridy and still found it hard to believe she was his lover. Not only was she smart and beautiful, she was more than twenty years his junior.

He reached out and stroked a stray lock of her hair. It felt like silk beneath his fingertips. *Can I really be this lucky? Does any man deserve a woman as perfect as her?* When he was with Bridy, he could almost forget his own checkered romantic history. The death of his first wife, Denise, had stunned him, driven him to seek relief at the bottom of a bottle and look for escape in the ranks of a mercenary company. Since then he had been married three more times, each one a triumph of hope over experience. *But I was a drunk then,* he reminded himself. *A broken man. This is different.* Gazing at Bridy, he felt peaceful. *She's different.*

She opened her eyes. "I felt you staring at me."

"I wasn't staring, just admiring." She furrowed her brow, coaxing him to confess, "Okay, maybe I was staring, just a bit."

"Who could blame you?" She laid one hand on top of his. "You seem like you have something on your mind. Is everything okay?"

"Yeah. I guess. I just . . ." He let the sentence trail off and fade away.

The silence seemed to worry Bridy. "What? What're you thinking?"

He had rehearsed and rehashed this conversation in his imagination so many times that he no longer knew how to begin. "Do you ever think we could . . . you know . . ." His eyes scanned the bulkheads while his brain searched for words. "Is there any chance that we could ever just walk away from all this?"

More awake now, Bridy propped herself up on one elbow. "And do what?"

"I don't know. Just live, I guess."

"Wow, I can tell you've given this a lot of thought."

Quinn shook his head. "I'm serious. In between gettin' our asses half shot off, we've made some good money these last few months. We've got enough rare junk and hard currency stashed in our hold to go anywhere we want and be set up for life." He reached over and gently stroked her perfect chin with his callused thumb. "We could buy a piece of beachfront property on some perfect, blue world and just 'live large,' as my pappy used to say."

"It's a pretty notion," Bridy said, "but that's only 'cause it's far away. If we cashed in and settled down, you'd be bored out of your mind inside a week."

The accusation stung. "The old me." He clasped her hand.

"But I've changed—you've seen it. I let a lot of my life slip away while I wasn't looking, and I ain't gettin' any younger, that's for damned sure. I don't know how much time I got left, but whatever I got coming, I want to spend it with you."

Bridy sat up and tucked her knees to her chest. "I have to give you credit—you never fail to surprise me." She hugged her knees with one arm and used her free hand to finger-comb her tousled hair from her eyes. "I wouldn't have pegged you as a domestic breed. You've always struck me as a rover."

"No. Just a guy runnin' from his past." He pressed his hands over his face and tried to massage away a lifetime of accumulated stress and fatigue. "Fact is, I'm tired. Can't do it anymore. Time to stop runnin' and start livin'."

"You make it sound so easy." She pushed aside the sheet and got up to pace beside the bed. "I spent half my life working to get *into* Starfleet and the other half working *for* Starfleet. How am I supposed to turn my back on that?"

"Think about what you just said. You've given them your whole life so far—don't you think maybe that's enough? Shouldn't some of your life be yours?"

She shook her head. "I took an oath."

"For life? Are you saying you'll never hang up the uniform?"

"Never's a long time." She threw a nervous glance his way. "What are *you* saying? That if I stay in Starfleet, you'll leave without me?"

He looked away to hide his frustration at having his bluff called. "No. If you say we stay, then we stay." He put on a crooked smile. "I'd rather be in hell with you than in heaven by myself."

Bridy circled the bed and sat down beside him. "Seriously? In hell? Is our life out here that bad? I know it gets hairy now and then, but we've had some good times, haven't we?"

"Maybe a few," he admitted with reluctance. "But I've had my share of rotten luck, and I know the longer we keep goin', the better the odds one or both of us'll wind up dead."

"So, what's the alternative? How would this play out, if you had your way?"

"In a perfect world? You'd resign from Starfleet by subspace radio, and then we'd get the hell out of the Taurus Reach as fast as this ship'll go. Find a place to settle down, sell the ship, and make a few munchkins. Just be regular folks."

She looked amused, and that made him nervous. Planting a hand on her hip, she said, "Hypothetically speaking, what if I wanted to finish this mission before we go and start pricing beach houses? Would that seem like a reasonable request?"

Quinn shrugged. "Sure, I guess."

"And I'd need to be in charge of naming any munchkins."

"Now hang on just a—"

"Take it or leave it."

"*Hrmph.* Okay. Sold."

Bridy planted a quick kiss on Quinn's mouth. "In the interests of starting our new life as soon as possible, do you think you could squeeze a few extra tenths of a warp factor out of this heap?"

His knees creaked, his back ached, and his stomach gurgled loudly as he stood. Plodding out of their cabin, he mumbled, "I'll see what I can do."

5

Descending the *Dulcinea*'s ramp, Bridy tugged at the neck of the wheat-colored garment Quinn had insisted she don before leaving the ship. "Why are we wearing cloaks with hoods? What, are we joining Robin Hood's merry men?"

Quinn pulled up his cloak's hood. "You'll thank me once we get outside."

A hot, foul wind greeted them as they disembarked. She followed him away from the *Dulcinea* and across the dingy, open-air starport hangar. True to his word, he had shaved nearly an hour off their travel time to Seudath, and he had overloaded only one plasma relay to do it. Compared to the wear and tear he had routinely inflicted on his previous ship, the *Rocinante,* the sacrifice of a single plasma relay seemed like nothing. With muted amusement, she wondered whether Quinn was getting cautious in his old age.

"Nice place." She eyed their run-down environs, which in searing midday sunlight resembled a deep and heavily rusted iron pit, and waved away a cloud of noxious smoke wafting over them. "Really first-rate."

"You get what you pay for." Quinn squinted against the harsh daylight and nodded at the four-person ground crew, which was busy attaching umbilicals to the *Dulcinea*'s underside to provide it with local comms, waste extraction, fuel, and the replenishment of its air and water reserves. "At least the basics are covered. If you'd wanted luxury, Starfleet should've given us a better cover."

She scowled at him. "They had to work with what you gave them."

They paused at the entrance while Quinn programmed in their standard temporary security code. Once he confirmed the code, the door lifted open, revealing a street busy with vehicular and pedestrian traffic. The air was heavy with the scents of exotic spices, the savory aroma of cooked meat, and the acrid bite of smoke and combustion-engine exhaust fumes. He stepped over the threshold and led Bridy outside. "Away we go."

They moved in careful steps through a dense crowd of aliens, most of them humanoids, all of them being observed by armed Gorn soldiers moving in pairs or squads of four. Right away, Bridy noticed strangers glaring in her and Quinn's direction. "I get the impression humans aren't very popular around here."

"Not just humans—anybody from the Federation. We're about as welcome here as a shit stain on a wedding dress."

"Thanks for the visual."

"Pull your hood up. You'll draw less attention."

As they rounded a corner into an intersection, they could see the city of Tzoryp sprawled around them. Built on and between six low hills, it was uneven and incomplete. Its main starport had been erected atop its broadest and highest elevation, affording Quinn and Bridy a commanding view of the cityscape. Squat industrial structures stood flanked by mid-sized residential towers and hotels, and entire blocks were filled with half-constructed buildings, steel skeletons gleaming beneath the brutal white glow of a Class F star.

Quinn stopped and seemed to listen for something. All Bridy heard was the rumbling of traffic, the scuffling of hundreds of feet, and the rasping growls of Gorn conversation. Staying close to Quinn, she said in a low voice, "If you're a Gorn, I guess this planet looks like paradise."

"Well, I ain't, and I think it looks like an overbaked turd." He nodded toward a nondescript, unmarked doorway in a building across the street. "Over there." Then he gently nudged Bridy into step beside him as he hurried toward it.

Dodging oncoming vehicles, Bridy asked, "Where are we going?"

"Fact-finding mission." They scrambled off the street, slipped through the open doorway, and descended a short staircase to a dim basement cantina thumping with aggressive music. The air inside the bar was cool and thick with several fragrances of smoke, some that Bridy found pleasant and a few that made her want to retch. Quinn sucked in a deep breath and grinned. "My kind of place."

Bridy gave the joint a quick looking-over and noted two possible alternative exits. She also counted thirty-nine patrons and four employees and concluded that every single one of them was likely to be armed. "This doesn't bode well."

"It'll be fine. We're just here to do business."

"I thought you said people on this planet hate Federation citizens."

"Sure they do. But they still like our money. Call it Quinn's Law." He bladed through the knot of people crowding the room and reached the bar with Bridy close behind him. Then he waved over the bartender. "Two waters, please."

The bartender—a burly, three-eyed, three-armed chap—said, "What kind?"

"Pardon?"

"We sell nine varieties of water."

"Got one with just carbon dioxide in it?" The bartender nodded; so did Quinn. "Great. Two of those. With ice."

"Which is it?"

"Sorry?"

Impatience put an edge on the bartender's deep voice. "Ice is one of the varieties we offer. Do you want carbon water or frozen water?"

Bridy rolled her eyes at the simple transaction gone wrong.

Quinn made a fist behind his back, ostensibly in a bid to rein in his temper. "Can you break the ice into chunks and pour carbon water over it?"

"You're not from around here, are you?"

"What gave you that idea?" He drew a fistful of Gorn currency crystals from inside his cloak and dropped them on the bartop. "Two carbon waters with ice."

"Coming up." Wearing a put-upon expression, the barkeep stepped away and mixed the drinks. He returned, set them in front of Quinn, and plucked two small crystals from the pile Quinn had dropped on the bar. "That'll be six *szeket*."

Quinn maintained eye contact with the alien as he pushed a few more crystals across the bartop. "Here's thirty."

The bartender regarded Quinn and Bridy with suspicion, and he made no move to pick up the proffered crystals. "Was there something else you wanted?"

"An introduction," Quinn said. "We need to meet someone who knows how to find things. For instance, ships in Gorn military custody."

Dropping his dishrag over the crystals, the bartender leaned forward and said in a confidential tone, "Sorry. Can't help you."

"I understand," Quinn said. He discreetly placed four more crystals on the bartop. "Thanks, anyway."

Wiping up the bar—and sweeping the additional currency under his rag—the bartender replied, "You're welcome." Then he made a subtle tilt of his head toward one of the cantina's corner booths. Then he walked away, cash in hand.

Quinn picked up the glasses of sparkling water and handed one to Bridy. "Let's go say hello." They navigated a weaving path through the crowd to the corner booth, where three people sat observing their approach. The two hairy brutes seated on the outer ends of the booth looked to Bridy like the bodyguards for the slender, dapper one secluded in the back corner, just beyond the pool of light from the shaded lamp hanging by a wire above the table.

The voice that emanated from the shadows was feminine—dark, smoky, and mysterious. "Are you two lost, perchance?"

"Don't think so. The name's Cervantes Quinn. And you are . . . ?"

"Not in the habit of introducing myself to strangers."

"Then how do you ever meet anyone?" Quinn's irreverent question seemed to befuddle the mystery woman, but her bodyguards wasted no time in standing up and moving to lay hands on their employer's uninvited guests.

Just before the situation turned ugly, the woman spoke with a voice sharp enough to carve diamonds. "Geeter, Kresh—sit down." The bodyguards froze, maintained threatening eye contact for a moment with Quinn, then slowly retreated and eased back into their seats. The woman continued in a milder tone, "Forgive their exuberance. Anticans are loyal to a fault, but they can be rather excitable."

"No worries," Quinn said. "This is my associate, Bridy Mac."

"Hi," Bridy said with a small wave.

The woman in the corner leaned forward. Her dark-bronze face was framed by long curls of sable hair. She looked human, but Bridy knew that looks could often be deceiving. "A pleasure. My name is Chathani. Now, if you will forgive me for speaking directly: what do you want?"

"I hoped we might drink together," Quinn said.

Chathani dipped her chin and gave Quinn the skunk eye. "Unlikely."

"And if, while we're enjoying our drinks together, you should happen to let slip some bit of information that proves useful to me—"

"I fear you have been misinformed, Mister Quinn. I do not think I will be sharing a beverage—or anything else—with you today."

"You sure?"

"Very."

"That's a shame." He scattered another fistful of Gorn currency across the table. "Because I was buying."

In the light of the hanging lamp, the crystals burned with inner fires.

Chathani's eyes widened with avarice. She whispered in the ear of the Antican on her right. He calmly swept the crystals into one massive palm and pocketed them, and then Chathani smiled. "How gauche of me," she said. "Please, join us"—her smile became a grin—"*friends.*"

6

"That sure looks like the Orion ship," Quinn said, studying the vessel through his miniature binoculars. He and Bridy were across a wide avenue from a starport hangar even more decrepit than the one in which they'd landed. Its structure was mostly open, a series of heavy girders wrapped in barbed-wire mesh. The hangar had a few entrances, each blocked by a metal gate and armed guards.

Bridy peeked over the edge of the roof's low safety barrier. "If the Gorn were looking to secure this ship, why park it in plain sight?"

"For starters, these are the biggest hangars in the city, and probably the only ones large enough for a ship that size. For another, keeping it in plain sight makes it harder for someone to break into it without being seen." Quinn surveyed the street-level security. Traffic on their side of the avenue was heavy, but the other side was empty, having been cordoned off by Gorn infantry.

Beside him, Bridy made a clicking noise with her tongue. "The Gorn have big hangars on the other side of the planet, don't they?"

"Sure." Quinn lowered the binoculars. "But those areas are for Gorn only. Can't have the Orion crew wandering around out there. And if they drop the crew here and take the ship there, it'd be too obvious they're punking the Orions."

"Fair point." She glanced at the hangar. "Man, the Gorn are all over that thing, aren't they?" She held out her hand. "Can I have the binoculars?" Quinn handed them to her, and she used them to study the Orion ship as she continued. "The ground crew looks like it's mixed species. Some Tiburonians, a few humanoids I don't recognize, a couple of Saurians. Think we can use that?"

Quinn nodded. "Probably. Impersonating ground crew is our best bet."

She lowered the binoculars. "Swiping some maintenance uniforms might get us inside the hangar, but none of them have access to the ship's interior. And I don't think either of us can pass for a Gorn."

"No, but we could pass as Orions. You did it before, on Amonash."

"And nearly got my ass shot off—thanks for reminding me." She handed the binoculars back to Quinn. "What're you thinking? Posing as the ship's officers?"

He shrugged. "It's worth a shot. Judging by the uniform markings on the troops closest to the ship, sentry duty's been left to the grunts. Talk fast enough and rough enough, and we might be able to get aboard."

"Sounds like a long shot to me. For starters, we don't know the names of any of the ship's officers or crew, and the Gorn probably have a complete manifest."

"Okay, then that's our first objective: get a copy of the manifest."

Bridy shook her head. "Forget it, that could take all week." She pursed her lips. "We're overthinking this. How about a simple distraction?"

"Such as . . . ?"

She pointed out details of the hangar. "Exposed coolant tubing—snipe that and the entire hangar fills with smoke and toxic vapor in fifteen seconds, tops."

"Making it the last place I'd want to be."

"It would only be dangerous for people on the ground." She pointed at the top of the ship. "One of us could use the leak as cover to rappel down from above and enter the ship through its dorsal maintenance hatch."

"And get shot by the sentries posted outside the hangar, who'd have a perfect angle to see over the commotion."

Bridy folded her arms. "Good catch." Then her mood brightened. "What if we cut the power at the same time? Plant a charge on the underground relay from the city's mains, and set it off at the same time we snipe the coolant line?"

"Yeah, that wouldn't be suspicious at all."

"Who cares if it is? Once I'm in, I can hack the memory banks from the engine room and be out in under two minutes."

Quinn conveyed his doubts with an arched eyebrow. "Let's say you're right. What's your exit strategy? You'll be inside a ship teeming with Gorn military, above a hangar filled with poison gas, in the dark."

"If I sabotage the transporter scrambler mounted at the top of the hangar, I can use my rubindium transponder to activate the *Dulcinea*'s remote transporter recall. As long as the merchant-man's shields stay down, I can beam out before anyone knows I was there."

He gently slapped his forehead with his palm. "Right, the *transporter*. I keep forgetting we have it. I got so used to living without one on the *Rocinante*." Lifting his chin toward the hangar, he said, "Now all we need to do is wait eight hours until nightfall, find a way to put you on top of that hangar, and make our play."

"First, we'll have to get you a silenced projectile weapon," Bridy said. "One you can use to snipe the coolant line without giving away your position."

"I have one on the ship. What else?"

"Just a deck of cards to help us pass—"

An explosion tore through the hangar, a radiant orange fireball rending metal and scattering bodies. The shock front lifted the Gorn troops off the street below and hurled them across the avenue into traffic, which was halted half a second later by the blast wave rolling vehicles like dice. Searing heat slammed against the building beneath Quinn and Bridy as they flattened themselves on the roof, letting the brunt of the blast roar past overhead. The thunder of detonation faded, leaving behind the groaning of metal and the moaning of the wounded.

Quinn peeked over the crumbling edge of the roof at the devastation beyond while Bridy fished out her tricorder and powered it up. Inside the hangar, the Orion ship was ablaze, its hull fractured and collapsing. Beyond the crackling of flames, Quinn heard disruptor shots echo from the hangar's far side. "We've been aced."

Bridy adjusted the tricorder's settings. "One Klingon life sign, male and hauling ass, leaving the hangar's rear entrance and moving east."

"Give you three guesses who has the intel we came for."

She drew her phaser. "Time for Plan B."

Bridy threw herself flat against one of the alley's rough limestone walls and went from a full run to a dead stop without turning the corner. Half a second later, Quinn slammed into her and nearly knocked her into the street.

He disentangled himself from her. "Why the hell're we stopping?"

She thrust her elbow backward and knocked him free. "Our Klingon pal's less than twenty meters away." She tilted her head to her right. "We need to catch him before he spots us." She pulled her hood forward to better hide her face, stepped into the street, and beckoned Quinn to follow. "C'mon. Stay close to me."

They merged into the thick, fast-moving crowd. Bridy slipped and dodged her way forward, edging through narrow gaps in the river of bodies, closing the distance to the fleeing Klingon with each step. She used the folds of her cloak to hide her hands: she held her phaser in one and her tricorder in the other. Every few seconds she glanced at the tricorder, which was still locked onto the Klingon's bio-signature. "He's crossing the street," she said, lifting her chin toward the target. Leaning slightly to her left, she got her first clear look at their quarry.

The Klingon seemed short for his species—Bridy estimated his height was no more than 170 centimeters—and he was slight of build. He wore drab civilian clothes and carried a disruptor in a hip holster. His swarthy, sinewy arms were bare, and a peculiar, metallic-looking wraparound sunshade concealed his eyes. He had close-cropped black hair with matching sideburns and a goatee.

Quinn nudged Bridy's arm. "We should split up and cut him off."

"Good idea. You go left and cut through that alley. I'll stay on his six."

"Copy that." Quinn fell back a stride, stepped into the street, and darted through a break in the traffic. A few vehicles blared their horns at him, but no one—including their target—seemed to pay the commotion any mind. Then Quinn slipped into an alley that ran behind a row of buildings on the next block.

Bridy waited for the next break in traffic. The sun beat down like a hammer of fire, and she sleeved sweat from her brow. At last, she crossed and continued closing the distance to the Klingon agent. Street vendors made aggressive efforts to waylay Bridy with samples of their wares, which ranged from fruit and vegetables to exotic textiles and bizarre gadgets whose purposes she couldn't begin to imagine. She sidestepped the overzealous hawkers or shoved them aside and sustained her pace until she was within a dozen strides of the Klingon.

Twenty meters ahead, Quinn emerged from an alleyway and set himself in position to intercept the target. The intersection was an ideal spot for them to take down the Klingon, because he had only one obvious escape route, and Bridy knew it would lead him down a dead end. They had him.

She quickened her pace and nodded at Quinn, who drew his stun pistol.

A pulse of charged plasma streaked overhead with a piercing screech and blasted away a chunk of the alley wall above Quinn's head.

He cursed as he leaped to cover behind some empty barrels, trailed every step of the way by a furious volley of plasma bolts.

The crowd in the street scattered in multiple directions, all of them moving away from Quinn, the apparent target of a crazed sniper. A dozen panicked aliens collided with Bridy, the only person other than Quinn who didn't seem to be running for her life. She was too busy trying not to get run over while scanning the fleeing throng simultaneously with her eyes and her tricorder for the escaping Klingon. As she feared, he was retreating in the midst of a dozen other bystanders—and as he looked back, he saw Bridy staring directly at him. She tried to hide the tricorder, but it was too late. Her cover had been blown.

Crap.

Quinn leaned out from behind cover just long enough to return fire in the general direction of his attacker, and then he ducked to avoid another barrage.

Bridy turned and followed the incoming fire back to its source: a Nausicaan on a rooftop with a scope-enhanced rifle. She lifted her phaser and fired at him, but struck the front of the building half a meter beneath his perch. The sniper recoiled momentarily, then trained his sights on her. Bridy ducked into a doorway just in time to avoid having her head shot off.

Gray smoke that stank of scorched metal filled the air. Bridy slung her tricorder at her hip and flipped open her communicator. "Quinn! Do you read me?"

His anxious voice crackled with static. *"Bridy, get outta here!"*

"I can't leave you here."

"Every second you're yapping, the Klingon's running! I know this shooter—he's here for me. You get the Klingon. I'll handle this."

"You're sure?"

"On three! Ready?"

She holstered her phaser and checked her tricorder. The Klingon's bio-readings were continuing to move away at a brisk pace. "Ready."

"One. Two. Three!"

Quinn popped up from cover, firing wildly at the Nausicaan while letting out a whooping battle cry. Bridy sprinted from the doorway, down the street, and around a corner in pursuit of the Klingon. She struggled to hold her communicator steady while she ran. "I'm clear! Meet me at the ship!"

"Roger!" The next sound over the comm channel was a shrill whine of weapons fire, followed by a string of Quinn's most colorful curses. Then the channel clicked off. Bridy closed her communicator, tucked it away, and drew her phaser as she pressed on, desperate to make up lost ground.

The street behind her echoed with weapons fire and the whine of approaching sirens, and for a moment she suffered a fleeting pang of guilt at leaving Quinn to fend for himself. Then she shook off her doubts. *He'll be fine,* she assured herself as she broke into a full run. *I'm sure Quinn knows what he's doing.*

7

Quinn yelped in pain as a bolt of supercharged plasma grazed his left shoulder and burned a streak through his jacket, shirt, and flesh. He zigzagged and ducked without slowing down, while wondering, *What the hell am I doing?*

Fiery streaks of orange blazed above his head as he turned a corner. He stumbled and slid half a meter on the gritty pavement. He tried to break his fall by extending his left arm and was rewarded with searing pain in his wounded shoulder. Muttering curses, Quinn pushed through his pain and kept moving.

His footfalls crunched on bits of gravel and echoed off bare walls of sun-baked stone. Overlapping them were those of Quinn's pursuer, a Nausicaan bounty hunter he had seen haunting the dom-jot tables aboard the *Omari-Ekon* more than a year earlier. The lanky humanoid was much faster than Quinn had expected, and he seemed to be closing the distance between them at an alarming rate.

Desperate to get a few steps ahead of the bounty hunter and lose him in the maze of intersecting alleyways—some of which were nothing more than short passages that dipped under buildings and connected to other alleys—Quinn caromed off walls and crashed through loose mounds of garbage while trying to make turns at a full-on sprint.

Bounding up a short flight of stairs, he saw a door ajar directly ahead. He charged through it into a sweltering kitchen and slammed the door shut behind him. Clouds of scalding vapor billowed around him as he twisted and dodged past the cooking staff, most of whom looked like Saurians or Kaferians, an antlike species that had always given Quinn the creeps. One of the Saurians stepped into Quinn's path holding a saucepan from which blue-and-orange flames danced. A frantic chorus of chittering and hissing filled the air, but Quinn blocked it out and kept on moving lest the Nausicaan follow him through the back door.

He hurried down a narrow corridor toward the dining room, hopeful that he had found a place to hide. *All I have to do is pay off the maître d' and get a table in the back,* he told himself. *Once the Nausicaan moves on, I can go back to the ship.*

Quinn's hopes of hunkering down in a safe haven vanished as he stepped into the dining room. Every patron in the restaurant was a Gorn. Two dozen archosaurs looked up at him and, in unison, hissed their disapproval. Two massive Gorn standing on either side of Quinn lunged at him.

Just my luck, he realized. *I pick the one joint in the alien quarter that's reserved for Gorn only.*

The Gorn bouncers seized him with scaly hands and lifted him several centimeters off the floor. Quinn flailed his hands to get their attention. "Hey, guys, c'mon. I can see the door, right? I can let myself out, really. There's no need to—"

They hurled him through a green-tinted window.

He struck the glass-strewn pavement first with his elbows, then with his chin. Pedestrians recoiled and gave him a wide berth. Jagged shards of shattered glass cut his palms as he forced himself up. He glared at the widening circle of spooked aliens that were staring at him. *Thanks for making yourselves into a target with me as the goddamned bull's-eye,* he fumed. He lurched back into motion as a plasma bolt ripped into the street behind his foot, turning asphalt into slag.

Shouldering and shoving, he made his own path through the crowd. People raced in all directions at once, all whipped into a panic by the screeching of the Nausicaan's rifle and the wild ricochets of hot plasma deflected off metal surfaces.

A fiery flash kissed Quinn's face with heat as it ripped past and slammed into the back of an alien woman half a stride ahead of him. She collapsed face-first, dead before her limp body struck the sidewalk.

Quinn ducked and detoured right, down a wide alley. As soon as he did so, he realized it was a mistake. Less than fifteen meters away, the alley came to an abrupt end more than twenty meters above the next street, which had been built at a lower elevation on the hill. There were no doors in the alley and no sign of a ladder or staircase ahead. Screams resounded from the street behind him: turning back was not an option. There was nothing to do but run faster and try to leap over the street ahead to a window of the building on the other side.

His breaths were ragged and short and his heart slammed inside his chest as he ran for his life. At the last moment he fixed his sights on a closed window just below the roof of the building, kicked hard off the last edge of ground beneath his feet, and launched himself over the gap.

For a fraction of a second stretched by his fear, he felt himself rise . . . and then gravity took over. Free fall made his guts feel as if they were about to erupt from his mouth. Arms windmilling, he screamed with primal fear as his body traced an ever steeper arc across the void.

Bolts of energy raged past him, each one closer than the last.

The building's façade raced forward to meet him.

He shielded his face with his crossed forearms as he struck the window. It shattered into millions of granular bits as he made impact. Then he struck the heavy, burgundy-colored curtain on the other side and pulled it with him as he fell to the floor. He tucked and rolled, only to become half-cocooned in the drapery. Shouts of anger and alarm went up from the next room while Quinn thrashed and kicked and pulled himself free of the smothering fabric.

Another barrage of plasma fire surged through the bashed-open window. Quinn ducked for cover, then blind-fired a return salvo. He kept firing out the window as he backed out of the room and pushed past a furious Selay, whose cobra-like hood was fully spread in an impressive threat display.

"Sorry," Quinn said to the irked reptilian as he made a break for the door.

The portal slid open ahead of him, and he retreated into the corridor. He looked around for a lift, only to see it crisscrossed with a strip of green tape printed with alien symbols that he was fairly certain meant "out of service."

There was one central stairwell. Its design was open and airy, which to Quinn meant *vulnerable as hell*. He pondered his options: try to descend seven floors before being intercepted, or climb one floor to the roof.

From the apartment he'd vacated came the crash of another window breaking and the heavy thud of a body landing on the floor.

Quinn bounded up the stairs to the first switchback, drew his stun pistol, and shot the lock off the door to the roof. The door swung open ahead of him.

And away we go.

Kajek rolled onto his back, ignored the hissed threats of the Selay standing over him, and roared as he plucked a thick shard of broken glass from his left forearm. He had remembered Cervantes Quinn from their fleeting acquaintance on the *Omari-Ekon* as a paunchy, middle-aged human given to sloth and alcoholism—not as someone with the stamina or *guramba* to make a leap such as this.

He tossed aside the jagged hunk of glass and stood. *Either Quinn has changed or I'm chasing the wrong person.*

As Kajek moved toward the door, the Selay stepped into his path, intent upon voicing his outrage despite the fact that Kajek couldn't understand a word the reptilian said. Kajek backhanded the scaly pest, launching him up and back against a wall. The Selay collapsed to the floor, stunned but clinging to consciousness.

Footfalls echoed from the corridor outside, followed by weapons fire. Kajek drew his plasma rifle from its sheath on his back and followed the sound of his fleeing bounty. He pivoted into the hallway, his rifle level and steady. The reek of human sweat and fear pheromones lingered in the muggy air. Following the scent, he arrived at the building's central staircase and glanced down. The open layout of the building's interior made it all but impossible for Quinn to have escaped by descending. Then Kajek looked up and saw it was only one flight to the door ajar at the top of the staircase. *He's on the roof.*

Kajek charged his weapon to full power and ran up the stairs. He paused at the roof-access doorway and listened, but heard nothing, and then he opened it. Bright sunlight half-blinded him for a moment, and he tensed in anticipation of an ambush. None came. Wind buffeted his ears, and sirens wailed in the distance.

The roof was peppered with squat blocks, housings for climate-control turbines, but none were large enough to provide cover for Quinn. Kajek turned in a slow circle, looking for any clue as to the human's path, but the roof's surface was pristine white concrete. The building was flanked on two sides by much taller buildings, and its front offered nothing but a sheer drop to the street thirty meters below—leaving only the rear of the building as a possible escape path.

Drawing near its edge, he spied a pair of handholds for a ladder. *It's a long way down, human,* he gloated. *Can you climb faster than I can shoot?* He poked the muzzle of his rifle over the roof's edge and fired a few blind shots, just in case Quinn was lurking on the ladder, hoping to snipe Kajek when he showed his face. The sharp whine of plasma fire echoed and faded away, met only by silence. Curious and concerned, Kajek slowly leaned forward and looked down.

There was no one on the ladder, on any of the escape platforms, or in the alley far below. Each platform had a single, featureless portal marked "no reentry" in Gorn Standard, meaning Quinn could not have used one to sneak back inside the building. The bounty hunter furrowed his brow, baffled.

He froze as he felt the icy kiss of metal on the nape of his neck.

Quinn's voice was low and steady. "Don't move or you're dead."

• • •

Quinn strained to stop his bloodied hand from trembling as he kept the muzzle of his pistol against the Nausicaan's neck. His arms, back, and chest were aching and cramped after hanging upside down for nearly two minutes from a narrow beam on the underside of a mid-flight landing in the building's main staircase. He had dangled like a bat twenty meters above the atrium floor while waiting for the bounty hunter to pass him on his way up the stairs.

"Back up slowly," Quinn said. He backpedaled two steps and let the bounty hunter retreat from the edge. "Throw your weapon off the roof."

The Nausicaan turned his head ever so slightly to peek back at Quinn. He sounded amused. "That's a *stun* pistol, isn't it?"

"Yeah, at *point-blank* range." He steadied his aim. "That means you'll live—but with mud for brains. Now toss the rifle, crab-face."

The command elicited a growl from the bounty hunter, but then he hurled his rifle away, into the alley behind the building. Seconds later, Quinn heard the clatter of the weapon striking pavement far below. "Nicely done," he said.

He lowered his aim and shot the Nausicaan twice, once in the back of each knee. The hulking alien howled and collapsed in a heap. Quinn planted one booted foot on his foe's neck and relieved him of a disruptor pistol, two combat knives, and a bandolier of miniature grenades.

Quinn nodded to himself. "That's better." He shackled the bounty hunter's wrists with his own magnetic manacles. "I set these to release automatically in four hours. By then you might get the feeling back in your legs, if you're lucky." He rolled the ugly bastard onto his back. "What's your name?"

"Kajek."

"Ganz sent you?"

"Yes."

He crouched above Kajek and pointed his pistol at the bounty hunter's face. "So, what's this about? Zett? Or something else?"

"Zett."

"Sonofabitch." Quinn frowned and shook his head. "I *knew* dusting that little prick would come back to haunt me."

"Killing me will not save you," Kajek said. "Ganz will send others."

"I'm not gonna kill you." He poked Kajek's chest. "You're gonna take a message to Ganz. Tell him Zett went out of his way to come after me. The little thug made it personal, and he got what he deserved."

"Is that your story?"

"It's the truth." Quinn stood. "Zett had it coming."

"We all have it coming, human."

"Some of us sooner than others." He backed away from Kajek and made a threatening gesture with his pistol. "Do *not* come after me again. Because I promise: next time, I *will* kill you."

The Nausicaan spread his fangs and grinned. "You will try."

8

Bridy had no trouble following the Klingon spy's path through the crowded streets of Tzoryp. All she had to do was look for pedestrians who had been knocked down or shoved aside, or for vehicles that had slammed into walls, barricades, or each other while trying to avoid hitting the lunatic sprinting through traffic.

She had shoulder-checked and trampled more than a few people herself in the past few minutes, and the angry choir of sirens and horns swelling in her wake made it clear she also had inconvenienced a fair number of drivers.

Rounding a corner, she spotted a commotion on a footbridge above a busy road. In the middle of the kerfuffle was the spy, still running flat out and firing his disruptor wildly, generating panic and casualties to cover his escape. Bridy sprinted after him, and her body protested with every running step. Her legs ached, and she felt as if her heart were pumping acid. The city's thick, polluted air stabbed her with knifing pains between her ribs after every labored breath.

The footbridge was littered with fallen bystanders. Bridy vaulted over some and sidestepped others, and she only narrowly avoided a wild, random blast from the fleeing Klingon. She leaped over the stairs at the end of the bridge and was less than thirty meters behind her quarry.

The Klingon headed for a starship construction yard, fired his disruptor to vaporize a force-field generator along its perimeter, and raced headlong through the massive eruption of white-hot sparks. Deep warning klaxons clamored across the sprawling industrial park and resounded off the metal scaffolds that surrounded a small starship's skeletal frame, most of which lay below ground level in a yawning pit full of robotic welding arms.

Workers in powered full-body load-lifter exoskeletons lumbered awkwardly out of the Klingon's path as he dashed through the work site and over a ramp into the starship frame, unleashing a flurry of disruptor fire every step of the way. As the last worker plodded clear of Bridy's path, she raised her phaser and opened fire on the Klingon. Her weapon's electric-blue beam sliced through a chunk of the starship frame but missed the enemy agent.

She followed him across the bridge and inside the guts of the half-built ship just in time to see his feet leave the top step of a ladder at the end of a narrow passageway. Determined not to let him increase his lead or lose her inside the maze of the spaceframe, she pushed herself to keep up a breakneck pace. Three steps short of the top of the ladder she caught sight of the spy and fired. The Klingon dodged around a corner, and Bridy's phaser beam missed him and struck a small hydrogen pod at the far end of the passageway.

Bridy saw the flash and felt the explosion's impact but heard nothing. The next thing she knew, she was on her back, lying on the deck at the bottom of the ladder, her vision purpled and swimming with crimson spots, her ears ringing, and her body feeling as if it had just been crushed in a vise.

That could've gone better, she chastised herself. Overcoming her body's desire to succumb to inertia, she forced herself to stand, only to find her balance less than reliable. Her head swam, and a sick feeling churned in her stomach. She struggled up the ladder. *Can't quit now. Have to keep going.*

She staggered down the corridor, which was peppered with fire, and turned right to follow the path the Klingon had taken. It was a dead-end corridor ending at a ladder, which led to an open hatchway on the ship's dorsal hull. Bridy lurched awkwardly toward the ladder, holstered her phaser, and climbed. As she neared the top, she ducked a disruptor pulse that ricocheted off the hull near her head. She drew her phaser and fired a few blind shots in the Klingon's general direction, then pulled herself up and over the edge.

He was twenty meters away, scrambling between gaps in the ship's patchwork of a dorsal hull, heading for its bow.

Got him, Bridy gloated as she aimed at his back.

An explosion rocked the starship frame, which groaned like a wounded giant and listed sharply to port. A huge reddish plume of fire rose from its bow.

Bridy and the Klingon spy slid across the hull as it rolled toward the wall of the pit. Flailing for purchase, Bridy made a split-second decision to let her phaser fall so she wouldn't. Clinging to the edge of a hull plate, she watched her weapon bounce off the ship and vanish into the dust cloud rising from the pit below. Her only solace was seeing the Klingon's disruptor follow it into oblivion.

The spaceframe began to warp and buckle. Large swaths of hull plating crumpled, broke off, and tumbled away as the ship collided with the pit wall.

Something exploded in the bottom of the pit, and a large section of the skeletal ship's midsection buckled inward. Within seconds, Bridy found herself dangling by one sweaty hand from a crack in a hull plate as her communicator tumbled from her belt and vanished into a roiling dust cloud that was rising to engulf her. Then the ship began a moaning nose-dive into its construction quarry.

A few dozen meters ahead of Bridy, the Klingon spy slid wildly down the dorsal hull toward the ship's bow, which struck the far wall of the pit, launching him up and over the point of impact. He rolled through his hard landing on the gritty concrete and came up running.

At the same moment, Bridy was going down with the ship.

The imploding spaceframe collapsed under its own weight into a jumble of bent wreckage. Bridy scuttled clear of one crushing impact as the ship's exterior scaffolding crashed down on top of it and followed it into its fiery grave. Then she realized she was lying atop an installed escape pod. Struggling back to her feet as the ship tilted aft, she fought her way across the disintegrating hull until she found a gap and dropped through it, into a half-walled corridor choked with gray smoke and dust that stung her eyes.

She tumbled and lurched back the way she had come, taking half her strides on the deck and half across the bulkheads, until she found the escape pod. The ship had no power but she hoped that, like the emergency systems on Starfleet ships, the pod would have its own self-contained ejection system. She scrambled inside, and frantically pulled its hatch shut behind her. Then, with her hand poised on its launch handle, she looked out its tiny exterior viewport, waiting for a glimpse of sky so that she wouldn't simply launch herself at high speed into a concrete wall. Through the flames and sooty smoke she caught the faintest hint of pale blue, and she pulled the ejection lever.

The pod shot away from the spaceframe with a deafening bang, and the sudden acceleration slammed Bridy against its hatch. Everything seemed to move in slow motion—Bridy tumbled, the pod rolled, the viewport showed open air and dusty land—and then its systems powered up, and the sensation of free fall vanished. Its thrusters snapped on with a gravelly roar as it initiated its landing protocol—but then the pod crashed nose-first to the ground, and all its internal displays flickered and went dark. The inertial dampers failed, and Bridy covered her head with her arms as the pod bounced, rolled, and ricocheted across the starship-construction yard. Each collision rang the pod's hull like a hammer on a church bell. Even after the pod finally skidded to a halt, the ringing continued inside Bridy's aching skull.

More than slightly dazed, Bridy triggered the pod's hatch release. The heavy metal portal blasted away, leaving its aft portion completely exposed. She staggered out, blood-spattered and slightly charred, then lifted her tricorder only to find it smashed beyond repair. *Well, that's just great,* she fumed.

A variety of humanoids scrambled in her direction. Some looked as if they were coming to render aid. A pair of armed and armored Gorn looked intent on arresting her. She didn't have time to deal with any of them. Pushing her way through a gauntlet of concerned humanoids chattering at her in languages she didn't understand, she looked around, straining to pierce the bright haze and catch any sign of her target. She was just in time to see the Klingon hobbling out the far end of the industrial yard onto a busy main boulevard.

Gotta give him credit, Bridy decided as she ran after him, *he's got stamina.*

The cries of sirens split the air behind her, and the next thing she heard were disruptor shots tearing past her. She didn't bother to look back. It would only have slowed her down, and she had bigger problems to worry about than Gorn police.

Ahead of her, the Klingon ducked and bobbed at a brisk pace through dense tangles of pedestrian traffic. He was no longer running, which suggested to Bridy that he didn't think he was still being followed. *He probably thinks I'm buried alive by now,* she reasoned, slowing her pace and taking care to keep the Klingon in sight while keeping herself concealed. She exercised caution at each corner, searching for the Klingon's reflection in storefronts before poking her head into the open to confirm his position.

Within minutes he had led her into a sector of Tzoryp dominated by broad industrial buildings with offices stacked atop street-level warehouses. The sidewalks remained well populated with food vendors' carts, queues of job-seekers outside several businesses, and doorways inhabited by members of the city's pungently indigent underclass.

On the far side of a narrow avenue, the Klingon ducked through a wide-open warehouse entrance and vanished inside its shadowy interior. Bridy tugged her hood forward to hide her face as she sidled into a sliver-thin alley between two buildings directly opposite the warehouse, whose signage consisted of symbols from a variety of alien languages. The only set of characters she even remotely understood were those written in *tlhIngan'Hol*. Her translation skills were far from perfect, but she was fairly certain the sign advertised a pest control service. She smiled. *What a perfect cover,* she realized. *It gets them access to just about every place in the city and lets them have a license to store chemicals and low-grade explosives, and they even get to kill things from time to time.*

Shifting her gaze upward to the offices above the warehouse, Bridy saw movement in the window on the left corner. An older, gray-bearded Klingon stood up and beckoned someone. A moment later, the Klingon spy appeared, and the two clasped each other's forearms in a fierce greeting. Then the older Klingon reached back toward his desk, and the window swiftly fogged gray and turned opaque.

Not much time, Bridy realized. *I need to get in there before they transmit that data off-world.* She squinted into the shadowy warehouse. It was stacked high with crates, barrels, and bundles, and there was a large land vehicle with thick front tires and wide rear tracks. She counted four burly Klingons, all wearing civilian clothes but openly brandishing sidearms. *Too many to ambush.*

Bridy dug into her pockets and made a quick inventory of her assets. Her phaser and communicator were gone, and her tricorder was smashed. All she had was a small pouch of local currency.

Money in hand, she made a beeline to a massive, muscular alien lying half-awake in an open doorway nearby. She didn't recognize his species but could tell by the lacerations on his knuckles and the empty bottle in his hand that he belonged to the great galactic fraternity of angry drunks. As she approached

him, the bruiser looked up and growled at her through bared
fangs.

Undaunted, Bridy spoke softly in Federation Standard and
prayed the lummox at her feet understood her. "Want to make
some fast money?"

The thug narrowed its eyes. "How much?"

"Five hundred *szeket*. Cash."

Fangs bared as a threat transformed into a grin of avarice.
"Who do you want me to kill?"

"No one." She dropped her pouch of Gorn crystal currency
into the alien's soiled lap and smiled. "I just want you to put on a
show."

Ninety seconds later, none of the four Klingons from the
warehouse seemed to care which alien had started the fight in
front of their place of work. Apparently, all that mattered to them
was that the two hulking brutes were pummeling each other with
wild abandon, each pile-driver punch launching sprays of blood
and broken teeth while the Klingons cheered and shouted
encouragements.

In fact, they were so thoroughly engrossed by the impromptu
brawl that they didn't pay the slightest attention to Bridy Mac as
she slinked behind their backs and dashed through the dimly lit
warehouse behind them. To her relief, the door to the rear
stairwell was unlocked. She cracked it open, slipped through the
gap, and eased it shut behind her. Then she took the stairs two at
a time to the upper floor.

Pausing at the top of the stairs, Bridy listened for voices or
footfalls in the hallway beyond. All quiet. A quick peek confirmed
the path to the corner office was clear. She stole out of the
stairwell and skulked to the office's door, which was open. Two
voices from within, low and guttural, speaking in *tlhIngan'Hol*.
She could translate only a handful of words and phrases from
memory. *Orions. Sensor data. Spy. Human. Secure.* Beneath
their conversation, she heard the distinctive feedback tones of a
Klingon computer terminal.

She barged through the doorway and moved in a straight line for the spy. He was standing between her and the desk, where the older Klingon, who Bridy presumed was the spy's Imperial Intelligence handler, sat facing a display that showed the contents of the data card inserted into his desktop reader.

The spy grabbed a Klingon dagger off the desk and thrust it at Bridy. She dodged the attack, seized the man's forearm, and twisted it until it broke. The handler bolted from his chair, drew a disruptor from his belt, and lunged toward an alert button on the far end of his desk. Using the spy's trapped broken arm as an anchor, Bridy pivoted and caught the handler with a spinning kick that slammed him against the wall. Then she planted her feet, flipped the spy over her shoulder, and stomped on his solar plexus, taking the wind out of him.

Confident the spy was down, Bridy charged the handler as he tried to aim his disruptor at her. She sidestepped the weapon's muzzle, spun, and seized the handler's arm. He shifted his weight in an unsuccessful bid to free his arm, and Bridy jabbed her elbow into his nose, which broke with a wet snap.

The handler lurched forward, pulling Bridy with him. She grabbed the disruptor's long barrel and wrenched the weapon from his grasp. He kicked her behind her left knee, and she stumbled backward. In the half second it took her to regain her balance, the handler slammed his fist down onto his desk's alert button.

A booming alarm reverberated throughout the warehouse.

Bridy leapt at the handler, locked one arm around his throat, and pressed the disruptor's muzzle to his temple. "One word out of you," she said in broken, ungrammatical *tlhIngan'Hol,* "and you'll have a cinder for a head."

Despite Bridy's limited command of Klingon vocabulary and syntax, the handler seemed to get her point. He didn't resist as she plucked the data card from his desk reader and tucked it into her pants pocket.

Tremors of heavy machinery shook the floor and filled the office with a muted hum. The handler glared at Bridy from the corner of his eye. "The warehouse door is closed, and my men are coming. You're trapped."

"Not likely." She pistol-whipped the handler, let him fall to the floor, and then she pressed the transporter-recall button on her wrist.

Nothing happened.

Sprawled at her feet and clutching the bloodied back of his skull, the handler chortled. "Intruder alert . . . activates transport scrambler." He bared his teeth at her. "As I said, human, you're trapped."

From the hallway, Bridy heard the irregular percussion of running, booted feet. Even with two hostages, she knew that one disruptor against four would be very bad odds. She eyed the handler's desk and considered turning it on its side to use as a barrier—and then she noticed a second button, right beside the one he had pressed. The markings above it were familiar, but their translation eluded her. She aimed at the handler. "What does '*lon*' mean?" He glowered and said nothing. Bridy was about to threaten him when she remembered that the warehouse was full of toxic chemicals and low-grade explosives. Then her Klingon-language training kicked in, and she remembered why the word *lon* was important.

She pressed the second button, and a different, higher-pitched alarm wailed from the building's PA system. Then she flipped over the director's desk, fired a short fusillade through the open doorway to slow down the approaching goons, and then crouched beside the handler. Teasing him with a smirk, she said, "It means 'evacuate.' And according to Klingon standard operating procedure, an evacuation alarm drops all shields and transport scramblers." She punched the handler in the face, then keyed her transporter recall. Almost immediately, she felt the pull of a transporter's annular confinement beam. "Adios," she said, flipping the handler a one-finger salute just before she started to dematerialize. "It's been fun."

She vanished just in time to avoid the barrage of disruptor fire that blasted the handler's desk into smoldering splinters, and materialized in a golden swirl of energy inside the transporter pod aboard the *Dulcinea*, grateful that the rubindium-transponder transporter recall bracelet issued to her by Starfleet Intelligence had, for once, worked as promised.

She dashed out of the cocoonlike alcove as Quinn—scuffed, tattered, bruised, and bloody—scrambled into the ship's main compartment via the starboard ramp. They collided, locked eyes, and declared in unison, "Time to go!"

9

Ganz narrowed his eyes at the viewscreen image of Kajek, whose Nausicaan visage he found inscrutable. "He got the drop on you?" The Orion furrowed his green brow in confusion. "You're sure it was Quinn?"

"Absolutely certain." A hint of amusement crept into his tone. *"He wants me to give you a message. He says Zett came after him on a personal vendetta and got what he deserved. My life was spared to prove Zett's death wasn't personal."*

A grim chuckle rumbled deep inside Ganz's chest. He shook his head and muttered, "Dead or alive, that human never ceases to surprise me." He picked up a decanter of green Orion rum, removed the stopper, and refilled his glass.

Kajek half suppressed a low growl. *"So, what now? Shall I pursue Quinn and his woman? Or wait for you to send someone after me?"*

"Neither." Ganz sipped his drink, which was in equal measures sweet and tart. "His story has the ring of truth to it. I know Quinn; he's not the vengeful type, but Zett was. If Zett forced a showdown and lost, it was his own fault."

"What about his ship?"

"Spoils of war. Let Quinn have it."

"And the second half of my fee?"

"Was payable upon Quinn's death, which you failed to accomplish." Sensing the bounty hunter's rising temper, Ganz held up one hand to cut off Kajek's protest. "However, as I've canceled the contract, I offer you one half your remaining fee as compensation for your invested time and effort."

The Nausicaan dipped his chin in acknowledgment. *"I accept."*

"Good. Now forget about Quinn. I need you back here."

"I will return as soon as possible." Kajek terminated his transmission without wasting time on such pointless niceties as saying good-bye. The viewscreen on Ganz's desktop went dark, and he switched it off.

On the other side of Ganz's office, Neera lounged in an alluring pose across the long sofa. She teased him with a smirk. "Such restraint. Are you actually learning to cut your losses?"

"I'm learning to adjust my priorities." Ganz stood and walked to the open doorway of his balcony that overlooked the *Omari-Ekon*'s gaming floor. The thumping bass of primal rhythms pulsed from the traveling casino, and the air was sweet with fruit-scented smoke. He breathed it all in . . . and then frowned at the scene's sole discordant note, its one foul odor, its singular blemish: Diego Reyes, who paused in his nonchalant stroll past the dom-jot tables to look up over his shoulder at Ganz and crack a cold, mirthless smile. "We have bigger problems," Ganz said as he turned back toward Neera.

"Be patient. Reyes is only a temporary annoyance."

"He challenges my authority daily."

Neera shrugged. "So? Your authority is just an illusion, anyway."

Ganz absorbed the blow to his ego and continued. "Regardless, that illusion is vital to our control over those we employ. Every time Reyes defies me and you forbid me to react, you undermine my power aboard this ship."

"A small sacrifice." The sable-haired mistress of the *Omari-Ekon* made a show of studying her immaculately manicured fingernails. "Until we have enough wealth and power to shift our operations off these traveling circuses and onto worlds across the Federation and Klingon Empire, we need to court the goodwill of the powers that be. For now, that means we can't risk giving Starfleet any reason to revoke our docking privileges here at Vanguard."

It took all of Ganz's limited self-control not to point out that while Neera was the power behind the throne aboard the *Omari-Ekon*, most of his underlings were not aware of their arrangement. Which meant, if he was so inclined, he could order his men to do away with Neera whenever the mood might strike him. Of course, there would be grave consequences when the syndicate captains to whom Neera answered learned of her disappearance, but Ganz was fairly certain a generous payoff would be sufficient to assuage their desire for retribution.

"At the very least, let's ban him from the gaming floor."

The suggestion seemed to amuse Neera. "Why?"

"Because he keeps on *winning*."

Neera smirked. "It's your own fault for offering him a line of credit. At any rate, banning him now would make no sense: he's up. The odds favor the house. So, let him keep playing until he loses."

"I'm not sure he knows how."

Neera got up and walked over to the doorway. "No one draws winning hands forever." She draped herself over Ganz's right arm. "Sooner or later, everyone loses. The trick is to keep your customers playing until it's their turn."

"And if our turn comes first?"

"That's why we rig the games, darling."

Down below, Reyes bladed through the crowd on his way toward the exit. Much as Ganz tried to ignore the human, he couldn't stop staring daggers at the man's back. His hands curled into fists. "We can't be rid of him soon enough."

"All in good time, love. I know you resent him for pushing you around when we first came here, but you need to take a lesson

from Zett's fate: don't let it become personal. Right now, having
Reyes on board is good business. When it becomes bad business,
we'll put an end to it. I *promise*."

10

Quinn's voice echoed from the PA system inside the *Dulcinea*'s
cargo hold. *"Ask and ye shall receive: I've got the* Endeavour *on
the secure channel."*

Bridy stepped to a nearby comm panel and thumbed the reply
button. "Patch it down here, would you?" Because her security
clearance was several levels higher than Quinn's, her superiors at
SI insisted she exclude him from classified briefings. She took
Quinn at his word when he promised not to eavesdrop on her.

"You're on, and I'm out."

There was a soft click as Quinn left the channel, followed
immediately by a woman's voice. *"Commander McLellan, this is
Captain Khatami."*

"Go ahead, Captain."

*"There's some pretty angry chatter coming out of Seudath on
the Klingons' diplomatic frequency. What the hell happened
down there?"*

"Nothing major." Bridy looked away sheepishly. "No fatali-
ties, anyway."

*"We usually set the bar for success a bit higher than that,
Commander."*

"I have to play the ball as it lies, sir."

Khatami sighed. *"Did you get the Orions' sensor logs?"*

"Yes, sir, but we haven't had a chance to review them yet."

"What's the delay?"

"The Klingons got to the data first, and they're using a new
encryption protocol. Quinn's working on cracking it, but it might
take a while."

"Are you sure that's wise?"

Bridy made no attempt to mask her annoyance. "Why? Because of his security clearance?"

"It's a concern, yes."

"That's absurd. Do you have any idea how many times he's put his life on the line for us? We need to start trusting him."

There was a short pause before Khatami said, *"We'll take that under advisement. For now, however, operational security is our first priority."*

"If you're that worried, feel free to come pick up the data card and crack its code yourselves."

"We would if we could, but we're a bit busy at the moment." The captain softened her tone. *"I know you two are more than professionally linked, so I'll take your word for it and cut him some slack, especially since we need you to follow up on this once you break the code. Which brings me to my next bit of news: Before you left the* Endeavour *a few days ago, we hid a package for you in the cargo bay."*

Looking around at the stacks of cargo containers, Bridy asked, "Where?"

"Against the aft bulkhead, behind the gray cases."

She walked over to the stack of containers and looked behind them. Tucked into the corner behind them was a small gray backpack. "I see it. What is it?"

"A compact ordnance package. It's experimental, very high yield."

"You mean a *bomb*." She returned to the comm panel. "What's it for?"

"If you find the source of the phenomenon the Orions detected, and it turns out to be what we think it is, we can't let it fall into Klingon hands. That package is our insurance policy, and we're counting on you to use it if necessary."

She cast a nervous look in the package's direction. "What's the yield?"

"At least five megatons, but SI won't give us precise figures."

"Please tell me its detonator has a timer, at least."

"Of course it does. The instructions are inside the pack with the device." Khatami's tenor turned grave. *"One more thing, Commander."*

"I know what you're going to say: Quinn and I are expendable." She heaved a bitter sigh. "Not exactly news, Captain."

"Let's just hope it doesn't come to that."

"Do I need to keep Quinn in the dark about this, too?"

"No. If something happens to you, he'll need to trigger the device."

"Oh, he's gonna love that."

"We aim to please. As I said, this is just a contingency plan."

"Right. Like seppuku is a contingency plan."

"Desperate times, Commander. As soon as we can join you, we will. Until then, keep us apprised of your progress and coordinates."

"Acknowledged."

"Endeavour out."

The subspace channel went silent, and Bridy turned off the comm. She looked over her shoulder toward the bomb. *They have got to be kidding me.*

Quinn stood next to Bridy in the *Dulcinea*'s cargo bay and stared at the bomb. "You've got to be kidding me."

"I wish I was. The good news is that it's just a backup plan."

He folded his arms. "No, hiding a knife in your boot is a backup plan. This is a suicide plan dressed up as a scorched-earth policy." He shook his head in disgust. "I don't know what pisses me off more—the fact that Starfleet hid a bomb on my ship or that they think I'm crazy enough to blow myself up with it."

"Would this be a bad time to ask how you're doing with the code-breaking?"

"A few more hours," Quinn said. He left the cargo hold through the forward hatch, and Bridy followed him on the short walk through the main cabin and back to the cockpit. "It'd go a lot faster if we had some of those big Starfleet computer cores. You sure we can't just send this to *Endeavour* and be done with it?"

"We can't risk transmitting it, not even on a coded channel."

"Pain in my ass." Quinn flopped into his pilot's seat, which still felt too new and firm for his liking. Despite having seized the ship months earlier, he still hadn't become comfortable with its small quirks. His last vessel, the *Rocinante,* had been a beat-up clattertrap of a starship, nowhere near as advanced as the *Dulcinea,* but it also had been his home for more than a decade, and he missed it. A quick look at the helm console confirmed that the *Dulcinea* remained on course at warp five, cruising through the unclaimed space of the Taurus Reach toward the ill-fated Orion merchantman's last-known coordinates.

Bridy settled into the copilot's chair beside his and checked the progress of their brute-force code-breaking program. She made a small frown, apparently less than satisfied with their progress. "I have to give the Klingons credit," she said. "A storage card that encrypts data as it's written is damned clever. SI should use this."

"After we finish hacking it, let's 'invent' it and sell it to Starfleet," Quinn said. "I mean, what're the Klingons gonna do? Sue us for patent infringement?"

His brilliant idea was rewarded with a dubious glare from Bridy. "One crazy scheme at a time, dear. One at a time."

11

Hegron hated visiting the Tzoryp safe house's basement. Windowless and dank, it was little more than a way station for the wounded on their way to Sto-Vo-Kor. The head of Imperial Intelligence on Qo'noS had not even seen fit to assign a fully trained surgeon to the Seudath mission, having reasoned it could make do with a field medic. Even that concession had proved to be a cruel jest, in Hegron's opinion. The medic, Ragh, spent more time self-medicating with bloodwine than he did tending to the sick or injured.

An odor of must and urine lingered in the air. Passing the single row of empty, unmade beds draped with soiled sheets, Hegron grimaced at the squalor and tried to mitigate the stench's effect by taking shallow breaths. He failed and winced in disgust. His bootsteps, which had snapped crisply in the pristine corridors outside his office, were muted by the patina of filth and dried blood that caked the basement's floor.

He reached the last bed and stood at its foot. Its occupant, an Imperial Intelligence agent named Goloth, stirred. The lean, young operative opened his eyes slowly and regarded Hegron with contempt. "What do you want?"

"I'll settle for your head."

Goloth grinned. "She got away from you, yeah?"

"You won't act so smug as part of a chain gang on Rura Penthe."

The spy folded his hands behind his head. "That will never happen."

"Do you have any idea how much trouble you've caused us?"

Another insolent grin. "Enlighten me."

"You were seen leaving the *Treana*'s hangar just before it exploded."

"So?"

"Do the words 'interstellar incident' mean anything to you? The *Treana* was in Gorn military custody. Their ambassador to Qo'noS is calling your little stunt 'an act of war.' If the High Council can't placate the Gorn imperator in the next forty-eight hours, a state of war will be declared."

"*Qapla'!* More glory for the Empire!"

Hegron grabbed Goloth by his collar and hefted him half out of bed. "You stupid *petaQ*! The last thing we need is *another* enemy in the Gonmog Sector. Bad enough we already face the Federation and the Tholians."

Goloth seized Hegron's hand and wrested it from his shirt with a powerful twist. He held the section chief hostage as he rasped into his ear. "Your fears are not my problem." He released Hegron with a hard shove and crossed his arms.

"Brave talk." Hegron smoothed his rumpled tunic. "What do you think the director will say when I tell him you led an enemy agent directly to us?"

"He'll ask why your security forces let her in the building."

"Really? I think he'll ask how you let a human—a woman, no less—best you in hand-to-hand combat."

"Spoken like a man who lives behind a desk. Never judge your foes by anything other than their actions. There is no shame in losing to a worthy adversary." The spy's grin returned. "Being taken hostage, on the other hand. . . ."

Hegron quaked with rage. "Don't think you can deflect the blame for this travesty onto me, you filthy *yIntagh*! It was your job to steal the Orions' sensor data and bring it back, not mine. That means you'll pay for the consequences of your botched operation, not me."

"What makes you think my operation was botched?"

"How else would you evaluate its outcome? You led the enemy here, she beat you unconscious, and she escaped with the Orions' sensor data."

Goloth's grin tightened to a smirk. "Correction." He uncrossed his arms with the grace of a mesmerist performing a sleight-of-hand trick. Then he produced, as if from nowhere, a gray data card in his right hand. "The human woman escaped with *one copy* of the Orions' data." He extended his arm and offered the card to Hegron.

The director seized the card with a quick grab. "Should I even ask why you made *two* copies of this?"

"Insurance. In case of mishaps like the one we had today."

"A wise precaution." Hegron pocketed the card.

"Am I still to be condemned in your report to Imperial Intelligence?"

"That depends. Will *your* report mention the human woman's invasion of our safe house?"

"It doesn't have to."

"Then I suspect your destruction of the *Treana* will be presented as an entirely justified tactic, undertaken to preserve operational security."

"We understand each other, then."

"What I understand is that you might live to see your next sunrise." Hegron walked away from the bedridden spy and raised his voice so that it filled the infirmary. "And if I were you, Goloth, I'd arrange to see that sunrise on a world very, very far from here."

12

Quinn sat in the *Dulcinea*'s pilot's seat, sipped from his mug of reconstituted orange juice, and watched Bridy backpedal into the cockpit. She was paying out the ship's last few meters of backup optronic cable from a spindle. "That ought to do it," she said, holding the cable in one hand and casting aside the empty spool.

"Do I even want to know what system you've hijacked now?"

Bridy picked up a data slate and reviewed a schematic of the ship's internal command-and-control network. "The escape pod, I think."

"Good thinking. Can't imagine why we'd ever need to use *that*."

She tossed the data slate into his lap. "Just walk me through the patch-in."

He set down his orange juice, picked up the tablet, and enlarged a section of the schematic. "I thought you could do this stuff in your sleep."

"On systems I know, sure. But these Nalori circuit relays make no sense to me." Still clutching the cable, she lay down on her back and shimmied through an opening beneath the cockpit's operations console. "Help me find the transporter controls' second auxiliary data port."

"The transporter? Why the hell are we patching into that?"

"We're just borrowing its logic processor. Now, where's the port?"

He tapped at the interactive schematic. "Look for the second row of chips perpendicular to the aft end of the panel. There's a sequence of three red chips, five green chips, and four white chips."

"I see it."

"Directly forward of the center green chip."

"Got it. Patching in now."

His inner pessimist expected something to short out, catch fire, or explode. At the very least, he expected the lights to flicker and the consoles to go dark. To his relief and surprise, nothing seemed to change as Bridy connected the cable.

She wriggled back out from under the console and stood up. "So far, so good." She keyed some commands into the operations console. "Five-by-five."

"All right. Now what?"

"We analyze the data you recovered on that Klingon memory card." She smiled. "Nicely done, by the way."

"Don't thank me. I'm sending Starfleet a bill as soon as we get back."

"Trust me, they'll call it money well spent." She tapped a key on the sensor console. "Let's see what we have."

Numbers, mathematical formulas, and bizarre alien symbols Quinn didn't recognize flooded across several display screens inside the cockpit. The data blurred past, a torrent of information too fast for him to comprehend.

"Whatever we've got," Bridy said, "there's a lot of it." She entered more commands on the sensor console. "Let's apply a few filters. See if we can break this into pieces small enough to study." Seconds later, the tempest of digits on the screen thinned and slowed. Bridy nodded. "There we go." Then she scowled. "That's weird. These are gravimetric waves accelerated by subspatial lensing, but there's a subspace signal embedded in one of their harmonic subfrequencies."

"You lost me right after 'weird.' Can you tell me in simple English what any of that actually means?"

Bridy looked perplexed. "Um . . . no, I can't."

"So, where does that leave us?"

"We could wait for *Endeavour* to get here and then hand it over to them."

"And give the Klingons a chance to track us down? No, thanks."

She sighed. "Good point. The sooner we unravel this, the better."

He got up and shouldered past her to get a better look at the display. "Can you freeze it a second?" Bridy halted the steady scroll, and Quinn studied the digits and symbols. There was a pattern to it, and it felt familiar to him, though he wasn't immediately sure why. Several seconds passed while he gazed at the screen, mesmerized by its blizzard of raw intel and lost in his own thoughts.

Then it became clear.

"These are coordinates." He pointed out strings of numbers. "Look. See how close these sets are? Every eighteen digits, three sets of six." Entering commands on the console, he continued. "This ain't meant to be read like a book. This is more of a paint-by-numbers kind of thing." Keying in the final series of commands, he added, "Your hidden message is software for drawing a starmap."

The *Dulcinea*'s astrocartographic matrix engaged and parsed the data in seconds. Quinn reconfigured it to present a graphical representation on the cockpit's main status monitor. A funnel-like shape appeared on the screen, its throat narrowing rapidly beyond the mouth's event horizon and then spiraling in tight coils around its central axis as it vanished into an apparent singularity.

Bridy cocked her head at an angle. "A black hole?"

"Don't think so. Not strong enough, and it's givin' off the wrong kinds of radiation. But it's a gravity well, for damn sure."

Her eyes widened. "A wormhole!"

"That'd be my guess."

"Stable?"

"No idea."

"What's its position?"

"Don't know that, either. But I think I know how to find out." Quinn keyed new search factors into the *Dulcinea*'s sensor matrix. "A wormhole that big's gonna bend space-time for at least half a light-year. If we search for small, deep-space objects with known trajectories in the sector where the *Treana* got damaged, we can scan for any that aren't where they ought to be."

"And then triangulate the cause of their deviations."

"You got it, darlin'." The results of the sensor sweep took shape on his display. He superimposed a number of computer animations detailing the altered vectors of a handful of rogue planetoids, junked satellites, and other small objects that had been previously charted by Starfleet. Seconds later, the computer animation finished plotting the sources of the distorted paths, and more than half a dozen lines intersected at a single coordinate.

Quinn settled into his pilot's chair and folded his hands behind his head as he reclined. "X marks the spot."

Bridy shot him a mild glare of teasing reproach. "Show-off."

"It's why you keep me around, sweetheart."

She smiled, took his hand, and led him out of the cockpit. "It's *one* reason."

13

Atish Khatami winced at the sound of Ming Xiong's voice calling out from several meters behind her in the corridor: "Captain! A moment, please!"

The svelte commanding officer of the *Endeavour* halted and forced herself to exorcise any intimation of irritation from her face. Then she turned to confront her high-strung guest. "Yes, Lieutenant?"

He caught up to her and stood a bit too close for her comfort. "Why wasn't I told your crew loaded trilithium ordnance onto the *Dulcinea*?"

She grabbed Xiong's arm and pulled him toward the door of a nearby maintenance bay. It slid open ahead of them and she shoved him through the doorway. On the other side, a pair of enlisted mechanics looked up from their precision welding. Khatami's voice was sharp and cold: "Give us the room." Tools clattered across the compartment's workbenches, dropped without question by the mechanics, who were out the door before Khatami had to ask them again.

As the door hushed closed, Khatami poked a finger against Xiong's chest. "First, *never* take that tone with me on board *my* ship. Next, *never* discuss classified ops in the middle of a passageway. Last but not least, you weren't told because there was *no reason* you needed to know."

"No reason? In case you've forgotten, Captain, I'm in charge of all field missions directly related to Operation Vanguard."

"Unless I've missed a memo from Starfleet Command stating that you've been promoted to the admiralty, I don't give a damn what your billet is. My orders are to provide you with facilities, communications, and regular updates, and to offer tactical and material support to SI's operatives in the field."

Xiong paced angrily and pushed a hand through his black, brush-cut hair. "We're *so close*, Captain. So close to unlocking all these mysteries, all these technologies, all this pure knowledge. The last thing we ought to do is risk blowing it all to hell because some fool with more brass than brains tells us to."

"I don't see why you're getting all worked up over this. It's no different than the self-destruct package Starfleet builds into every starship and starbase."

Arms raised and fingers curled with suppressed rage, Xiong looked ready to explode. "It's completely different! Sacrificing a ship or a starbase only means losing matériel, fuel, and personnel."

Khatami was aghast. "Oh, is *that* all?"

"Listen to what I'm saying. Starships can be replaced.

Starbases can be rebuilt. Lost lives are a tragedy, but others will continue what they've begun." Once more he stepped too deep into Khatami's personal space. "But if we destroy unique artifacts of the Shedai, there's no guarantee we'll ever see their ilk again."

She pressed her palm to his shoulder and nudged him back half a step. "And what if the Klingons capture one of those *unique artifacts*? What do you think *they'll* do with that kind of knowledge, Ming? Develop it in peace for the good of the galaxy at large, or turn it into a weapon that'll wipe us off the map?"

"I'm well aware of the destructive potential of Shedai technology, sir."

"Then you ought to know why we can't ever let the Klingons have it."

He shook his head. "I can't condone the destruction of antiquities. Not even for national security. These are pieces of history we're talking about, Captain."

It was Khatami's turn to shake her head. "Wrong, Lieutenant." She shouldered past him, and the maintenance bay's door opened ahead of her as she made her exit. "What we're talking about is *cultural survival*."

Bridy stood behind Quinn's chair, looked through the *Dulcinea*'s cockpit canopy, and saw nothing but a placid starscape. She glanced at Quinn. "Where is it?"

"Trust me, darlin', it's out there." He tapped a few instructions into the forward console, and a holographic wireframe appeared as if conjured outside the ship. It depicted the profound curvature of local space-time into a funnel shape. "The Orions' sensor data says it's right there—larger than life and twice as ugly."

She threw a confused look at Quinn. "What does that even mean?"

"Just a cute way of sayin' it's really big."

"Mm-hm." She turned her attention back to the stars. "There's supposed to be a wormhole less than a quarter million kilometers away, but we aren't seeing any distortion in our view of the stars. Does that mean it collapsed?"

Quinn shrugged. "It might. Or maybe it only opens once in a blue moon."

"Or when something crosses its event horizon."

Bridy settled into the copilot's seat and accessed the subspace comm. "Start plotting a course. I'll send our coordinates to *Endeavour* on a coded channel."

"Hang on, whoa, stop. Are you out of your mind?"

Continuing to prep her message to the *Endeavour,* Bridy said, "We need to know if the wormhole's still there, and if it is, we need to be sure it's stable."

"By flying into it? Sorry, no." He leaned back from the helm and crossed his arms. "I think we oughta just hang tight and wait to see if it reopens on its own."

She shook her head. "Not good enough. For all we know, this thing's on a cycle measured in centuries, or even longer."

"Then it's a good thing I'm a patient man."

"One, I know that to be a lie. Two, even if you've learned to be patient, the Klingons haven't. We need to confirm this find and plant our flag *right now.*"

"Screw that. Our orders were to steal the data and crack the code. We did that. We're done now. Job over. It's time to go home and start our new lives as boring, happy civilians nobody shoots at."

Bridy sent her message to the *Endeavour,* then turned to face Quinn. "I don't have time to argue with you. It's the bottom of the ninth, we're on the ropes, and I'm not gonna drop the ball when I have a shot at the goal. Do you get me?"

Quinn heaved an exasperated sigh. "Honey, if you want to keep using sports metaphors, you *really* need to learn something about sports."

"Don't change the subject. Just set the course and punch it."

"And if I don't?"

"It might shock you, dear, to learn that I know how to fly the ship." She punctuated her point with a teasing smile. "So, what's it gonna be?"

He frowned and laid in the course. "Lady, you're a pain in my ass."

"You know you love it."

The deck shivered under Bridy's feet as the *Dulcinea*'s impulse drive kicked in. Then a burst of light flooded the cockpit. As it faded, she saw the majestic, blue-and-white whorl of a wormhole's mouth spiraling open all around them. The ship's hull rumbled ominously. "Gravitational flux," Quinn said over the noise. Flipping switches, he added, "Compensating." A momentary fluctuation in the inertial dampers made Bridy's stomach jump into her chest for half a heartbeat. She swallowed hard and shook it off.

Quinn shot her a pleading look. "Last chance to change your mind."

She gripped her chair's armrests. "Take us in."

"I hope you're right about this," Quinn said.

Then he guided the ship forward and plunged it through the wormhole's mouth into the brilliant, twisting abyss that lay beyond.

Stephen Klisiewicz looked up from the sensor hood and turned toward the center seat of the *Endeavour*'s bridge. "Captain? Our listening posts on the Klingon border are picking up major activity."

"Main viewer," Khatami said. Klisiewicz routed his sensor feed to the forward viewscreen, making it available to all the other bridge officers. The captain looked left, toward the ship's first officer. "Number One? Analysis?"

Stano stood with her hands folded behind her back and her dark hair swept back in a neat bob, a portrait of composure. "Looks like an expeditionary force from the Klingons' Fifth Fleet, out of Q'Tahl." She fixed her blue eyes on Klisiewicz. "How many ships, Lieutenant?"

"Hard to say, sir. At least three, all fast movers. They just hit warp eight."

The captain nodded. "All right, so we know they're in a hurry. Lieutenant McCormack, chart their heading and give me some idea where they're going."

"Aye, sir," said the fresh-faced young navigator.

A soft chirp from the communications console heralded an incoming signal. Lieutenant Hector Estrada swiveled his chair toward the bridge's command well. "Captain, we're receiving a coded message from the *Dulcinea*. It's marked 'Priority Victor-Alpha.'"

Khatami rose from her chair. "Route it to Science Two," she said, climbing the steps to the bridge's upper ring. The captain and first officer converged on the backup science station and keyed in their security clearance codes. Tense seconds passed as the two women huddled over the console and conferred in whispers. Klisiewicz couldn't hear what they were discussing, but he held a sufficiently high security clearance to know that Victor-Alpha was the current designation for matters related to Operation Vanguard.

Stano and Khatami turned toward the main viewscreen. "McCormack, report," Khatami said.

"No populated systems on the Klingons' current bearing." The navigator added a projection of the Klingon ships' course to the image on the forward screen. "They seem to be heading into deep space."

The captain and first officer exchanged grim and knowing looks, then descended together into the command well. "Mister Estrada," Stano said, "what was the time stamp on that message from the *Dulcinea*?"

"Nine minutes ago, sir."

"Raise them on subspace, Lieutenant, priority one."

"Aye, sir."

Khatami sat down in her chair, and Stano stood ready on her right. The captain's mien was serious, her voice stern. "Helm, set course, bearing one-six-one mark one-zero-four, maximum warp, and stand by to engage on my order."

Lieutenant Neelakanta, an energetic young Arcturian, entered the new heading with speed and precision. "Course laid in, Captain. Standing by."

The captain looked back at Estrada. "Report."

"No reply, Captain. Repeating the hail."

Anticipating the captain's next request, Klisiewicz initiated a long-range sensor scan of the *Dulcinea*'s last-known position. Only then did he realize that the civilian ship's last coordinates lay in the path of the approaching Klingon ships.

At the communications console, Estrada shook his head. "No response, sir."

Klisiewicz glanced into the blue glow of the hooded sensor display, then looked up as Khatami turned toward him. "No sign of the *Dulcinea,* Captain."

Stano and Khatami traded worried looks. The first officer asked Klisiewicz, "Is it possible they warped out of sensor range?"

"Not unless they can move at warp eleven."

Khatami leaned forward. "Mister Neelakanta"—she pointed dramatically at the main viewscreen—"engage."

14

In all his years of piloting small starships, Quinn had never heard anything like the din surrounding him as the *Dulcinea* hurtled in a mad spiral through the wormhole. The ship's hull moaned like an angry ghost, her engines screamed like frightened children, and her consoles crackled and spat sparks every which way.

Despite his best efforts to control the ship's wild pitching and rolling, it grazed the blinding, blue-white swirl of the wormhole's membrane and then caromed off, its movement made even more erratic by the fleeting impact.

A hiccup in the inertial dampers or artificial gravity (or some other system Quinn always took for granted until it was gone) knocked Bridy on her ass. Clawing her way up from the deck, she growled, "Dammit! Keep her steady!"

He glared at her. "Great idea, sweetheart! Why didn't *I* think of that?"

"Watch our yaw!"

Quinn keyed compensating maneuvers into the helm faster than he'd ever done before, but the ship reacted like a turtle slogging through mud. No matter how hard Quinn tried to get ahead of the wormhole's horrendous gravitational distortions, he remained fractions of a second too slow to prevent the worst from coming to pass. He grabbed his armrests. "Hang on!"

Dulcinea careened off the side of the wormhole's throat. A screech of stressed metal was drowned out by a deafening boom of collision. Overhead lights and console displays stuttered and went dark, leaving the cockpit illuminated by the spectral blue radiance of the wormhole.

Bridy stretched past Quinn to reach the copilot's console, her movements strobed by the wormhole's flickering light. Then she patched in the ship's auxiliary power, restoring the lights and most of the controls. "Mains are fried," she shouted over the howling chaos. "Losing antimatter containment!"

Dead ahead, the terminus of the wormhole was little more than a pinprick of white light at the end of a churning maelstrom. "Just give me a few more seconds!"

"We won't make it!" She armed the fuel-pod-ejection trigger.

"Don't! We're almost clear!" Space-time distortions rocked the ship as the wormhole's far mouth spun open, spat it out, and sent it tumbling madly into a firestorm. All Quinn could see outside the cockpit was half-molten rocky debris, glowing-hot clouds of ionized gas, and multihued flashes of lightning.

Every gauge in the cockpit redlined. "Containment's failing," Bridy said as she ejected the ship's antimatter supply.

"All power to shields!"

"Patching in reserves."

The universe flared white, and then a thunderclap pummeled Quinn like a sonic hammer. All around him, the ship's onboard systems let out sad, whimpering noises before expiring with a slowly fading hum. *At least the helm's still responding,* Quinn consoled himself—before it, too, began deteriorating. Coaxing every bit of performance possible from his wounded vessel, he guided it through a passage between two quarters of a shattered planet whose scattered chunks were gradually being pulled away from one another. *Dulcinea* trembled as boulder-sized hunks of rock and ice were deflected by its navigational force field.

Without taking his eyes off their perilous environment, Quinn said to Bridy, "I need a damage report, a-sap."

"On it." She got up and moved from one cockpit console to another. "Warp drive's down. We've got a few minutes before the impulse coil fails. Life support's barely there. And we lost the subspace antenna."

"Yeah, yeah, yeah. What about the cargo?"

"It's fine."

"All right, then. We just need to find a place to set down and patch this ol' girl back together." Outside, the haze of radiant dust began to dim. "We're almost out of this soup. See if you can get the sensors running and find us a planet—preferably one with a breathable atmosphere."

Bridy was staring slackjawed into space. "Uh, Quinn . . . ?"

"What?"

"Look."

He followed her gaze. "I don't see anything."

"Exactly."

When he turned his attention back to the view outside the ship, he understood. Then his jaw dropped half open in shock. "There are no stars." Beholding the empty heavens with dread, he muttered, "Where the hell are we?"

Bridy looked perplexed. "No idea. We might be so far from the center of the universe that none of its light has reached here yet, or we might be in a pocket universe branched off from our own."

"A universe with no stars? Eternal darkness? I'm not what you'd call a believer, but are you sure we didn't die and go to hell?"

"No, I'm not." Bridy perked up as she pointed at the sensor

display. "Hang on, correction: There *is* one star—a white dwarf, temperature ninety-seven hundred Kelvin. Bearing one-seven-seven mark one-five-oh, distance one hundred eight-point-six million kilometers." She cast a fearful glance at Quinn. "And it has one planet, orbiting at a distance of five-point-two-four million kilometers, right in the middle of the habitable zone. Atmosphere is M-Class nitrogen-oxygen." Then she called up another screen of data, which showed a familiar energy waveform. "It's the Jinoteur Pattern. And guess where it's coming from."

Quinn swallowed, only to find it difficult because his mouth had gone dry. "What do you wanna bet that ain't a coincidence?"

"You know we have to go down there. We need to track this to its source."

"Dammit, I knew you'd say that. Not that we have much choice. We need to get this busted bird planetside on the double." He sighed, then plotted a heading to the signal's point of origin. "It's gonna be a rough landing, honey. You'd better make sure everything's still tied down and shut tight."

Bridy got up, took one step aft, then stopped. "I've seen you botch normal landings when the ship *wasn't* fried. Are you sure you can do this?"

"Positive."

"Without getting us killed, I mean."

"Ask me again in thirty minutes."

Twenty-nine minutes and thirty seconds later, Bridy was too busy hyperventilating to ask Quinn much of anything.

Turbulence buffeted the *Dulcinea* as it arrowed through the upper atmosphere of the white dwarf's solitary, tiny planet. Critical failures cascaded through the ship's major systems, leaving only maneuvering thrusters and the primary sensors functioning for what promised to be a brutal planetfall.

Quinn shouted over the roar of wind and engines, "How's the signal?"

"Five by five." Bridy checked its origin against the ship's

heading. "Dead ahead, range nine hundred sixty kilometers."

"Right." He started flipping toggles on the helm. "Braking thrusters in ten seconds." The ship pierced a thick layer of cloud cover and then leveled out above a desolate, arctic plain. Massive peaks of jagged black stone made Bridy think of daggers thrust up by a giant's hand through the planet's snowy surface. Studying the wild landscape, Quinn frowned. "Not many good places to land."

"I'll watch the ground, you watch the instruments."

"I would if they still worked." He slammed his palm against the console in front of him, but his attempt at percussive maintenance seemed to have no effect. "How's the ground looking?"

"A lot closer than it did five seconds ago."

He primed the braking thrusters. "Hold on to your ass."

The engines boomed, and the rapid deceleration threw them forward. Bridy winced as her seat's safety harness straps dug into her chest. Outside the cockpit the landscape spun, black rock and white ice melting into a gray blur.

Bridy pointed at a fleeting image of level ground. "There!"

"Too far!" Quinn fought with the ship's controls to little apparent effect. "Main thruster's gone! We got five seconds to set down before we *fall* down!"

"Starboard! Get the nose up!"

She grabbed the console white-knuckle tight.

Quinn pulled the ship through a hard turn that arrested most of its forward momentum. *Dulcinea*'s landing thrusters sputtered erratically as Quinn guided it to a mountainside ledge barely as wide as the ship itself. All at once the engines cut off, and the ship dropped the last half meter onto a deep bed of ice-crusted snow. The thud of impact reverberated and then stopped—enabling Bridy to hear a low, dangerous rumbling from high overhead. She and Quinn looked up in unison through the top of the cockpit's canopy at the snow-capped peak looming over their precarious perch. They waited for several seconds, neither speaking nor breathing, while waiting to see whether the mountain would welcome the *Dulcinea* by burying it. Then the distant tremor faded, leaving only the faint creaking of the ship's overtaxed hull as it settled into its new resting place.

Their wide-open eyes remained fixed on the mountaintop.

Bridy's voice was barely a whisper. "So . . . *that* happened."

Quinn rose from his chair and trod cautiously aft. "If you'll excuse me, I need to go have a short nervous breakdown."

15

Bundled in cold-weather clothing and laden with arctic climbing equipment that had been stowed by SI in the *Dulcinea*'s hold (along with gadgets and gear for just about every other terrain and scenario Quinn could ever imagine), Quinn trudged away from the slope of the mountain in pursuit of Bridy. Screaming wind whipped grains of ice against the few bits of exposed flesh on his face, forcing him to dip his chin and watch his legs chop through knee-deep snow.

He clenched his jaw against the cold. "Are we there yet?"

"If you ask me that one more time, I'll smash this tricorder over your head." She led him across a level and nearly circular plain several kilometers in diameter and ringed by steep black peaks like the one they'd descended after leaving the *Dulcinea*. The mountains hid the sunset, which painted the sky in shades of violet.

Bridy pointed forward. "The signal's coming from underground, inside some caves beyond the other side of this frozen lake. Another hour's walk, tops."

Quinn harrumphed from behind his air-warming face mask. "Remind me not to use you as my tour guide the next time I plan a vacation."

"Do you ever stop complaining?"

"I was fine till you made me leave the ship."

"I didn't *make* you leave the ship. We decided to track the signal."

"No, *you* decided to track the signal. I wanted to fix the impulse coils."

She sighed. "Get serious, they're fried. We'll need a starbase for that."

"That's what you said about the thrusters, but I got those working."

"Yeah, and if you'd used them, you'd have triggered an avalanche and buried us—not to mention the caves where the signal's coming from."

"Which is why we're walking instead of flying. Of course, if we'd fixed the transporter, we could've just beamed over there."

"I don't know how to fix a transporter, and neither do you."

"No, but we have a manual. We could figure it out." He scowled. "Why is it whenever we disagree we always end up doing things your way?"

She glanced back at him. "Because I'm in charge."

"Then why even ask my opinion?"

"To make you feel better."

"Well, it ain't workin'."

They didn't speak to each other the rest of the way across the lake. Quinn tried to keep up with Bridy, but she outpaced him enough to open her lead by slow degrees. By the time they reached the far side of the crater-shaped basin, she was twenty meters ahead of him, and she showed no sign of slowing down as she pressed forward into the mouth of a cave. She was limned by the pale glow of her tricorder and partly silhouetted by the beam of her small flashlight as she forged ahead into the dark.

Quinn was about to shout her name when he remembered that a sudden loud noise echoing off the mountains above them might prove disastrous.

Dammit, he cursed her in his imagination, *don't do nothin' stupid.*

He quickened his pace until he reached the cave, and then he stopped to fish his own flashlight from his jacket pocket. His gloved hands fumbled first to find the device and then to activate it. Its narrow beam slashed through the darkness as he pivoted side to side, surveying the path ahead. It was a wide space populated by stalactites, stalagmites, and pillars of dark-blue ice. He glimpsed another, smaller passage on the cavern's far side, but there was no obvious clear path to it—only routes of greater or lesser resistance.

To his dismay, he saw no sign of Bridy.

Then he heard a weak and distant echo of her voice: "Quinn!"

"Honey? Where are you?" She called his name again, but he wasn't sure from what direction. "Keep talkin', darlin'! I'm comin'!" Bridy repeated his name; it sounded as if it had come from beneath him. He prowled about the cavern, searching its floor with his flashlight beam.

He stumbled to a halt half a step shy of a narrow crevasse. Kneeling beside it, he aimed the flashlight into its depths and called, "Bridy?"

"Down here!"

Targeting her voice, he trained the flashlight beam on her. She was a dozen meters below him and wedged between two walls of rough, black ice.

"You okay?"

"I think my leg's broken."

"Yeah, that first step's a doozy." He removed his pack and retrieved the spare coil of climbing rope. "Hang on. I'll have you up in a few minutes." Fumbling to untie the simple knot on the coil, he silently cursed his bulky gloves for making his fingers so clumsy. As the synthetic-fiber rope unspooled onto the cavern floor, he called back to Bridy, "Try not to move."

"Not much risk of that."

Recalling his mercenary training from decades earlier, Quinn secured one end of the rope with a set of strong knots to the thickest ice pillar within a few meters of the crevasse, and ran the line behind another sturdy pillar to serve as a crude pulley. Then he paid out a few dozen meters of slack over the fissure's edge, lowering it to Bridy. "Secure that around your torso in an X shape, and through your legs if you can reach."

"Under the shoulders will have to do."

"That's fine. Let me know when you're ready to come up."

A minute later, Bridy tugged on the rope. "Let's do this."

Quinn leaned back and started pulling on the rope. Slack gathered in his hands, and he coiled it around his left arm while hoisting Bridy back to the top of the crevasse. Bridy was a slender woman, but the effort of lifting her as dead weight was exhausting. As she clambered over the edge onto the cavern's floor, Quinn gave a few more heroic tugs on the rope to pull her to safety.

Then he fell on his ass and gasped for air. His exhaled breath gathered in a wispy cloud around his head while he waited for his limbs to stop shaking.

Bridy lay on her back a few meters away, clearly in no hurry to move, either. In a droll deadpan she said, "Don't have a heart attack, okay?"

"Tryin' not to, darlin'." After a few more pained breaths, he sat up. "We should patch up your leg. Where's the medkit?"

She nodded at her torn-up backpack. "At the bottom of the crevasse."

"Of course it is."

"Along with my tricorder."

He scowled. "Anything you *didn't* lose?"

"Just my good looks."

"And your sense of humor." He got up and moved to her side. "But I don't think you'll be laughing for long." With a gingerly touch, he examined her injured leg and paid attention to her pained reactions. "The good news is you've got a simple fracture. The bad news is we'll have to treat it the old-fashioned way."

Bridy grimaced. "This is gonna hurt, isn't it?"

"Oh, hell yeah. In a few seconds you'll wish I still carried a flask." He removed his gloves, then clapped his hands and set them in position. "Ready?"

"No. Do it anyway."

"All right. I'm gonna count to three, okay?" Bridy nodded. "One." He jerked the broken halves of her tibia back into alignment with one quick pull.

Bridy's piercing scream of pain filled the cavern. Then she punched Quinn in the shoulder hard enough to knock him down. "Asshole! You said on three!"

"No, I said I was gonna *count* to three. Never said when I was gonna set the bone. Oh, and by the way—two."

"Say 'three' and I'll knock your teeth out."

Quinn recoiled in mock indignation, one hand on his chest. "Is that any way to treat the guy who has to carry you back to the ship?"

"I'm not going back to the ship. Not yet, anyway."

"Why? You got a death wish or something?"

"The source of that signal is less than two hundred meters from here, straight down that passage. I didn't come all this way to turn back now."

"You keep saying that, but I don't think you realize how crazy it sounds."

"If you're willing to carry me to the ship, then a few hundred yards more won't matter, will it?"

He started gathering up the rope. "What if we aren't alone down here? Have you thought of that? If we get into trouble, how can we retreat if you can't even walk?" He stopped and faced her. "Hell, even if we *are* alone down here, what's the point of finding the signal source when we don't have a tricorder?"

"Dammit, I just want to *see* it. Let's do a quick recon. Then we can head back to the ship, fix my leg, and come back with the spare tricorder."

He put away the coiled rope and sealed his pack. "If this all goes wrong, do I get to say 'I told you so'?"

"No."

"Let me rephrase: Do you want to crawl the rest of the way?"

She seethed for a moment. "All right, you can say it *once*. Now, can we please get this show on the road?"

"Your wish is my command." He took her hand, helped her

up, and draped her arm across his shoulders so he could support her weight. They moved together, taking care to synchronize their strides.

Bridy wore an amused expression. "You shouldn't be such a pessimist. What're you gonna say if we end up making the greatest discovery of our lives?"

"That's easy," Quinn said. "*I get half.*"

Ten minutes later, Bridy clung to Quinn's shoulder as they stood at the end of the downward-sloped passageway, facing a wall of ice at least a dozen meters thick.

Quinn frowned. "Hmph. I'd call this a sign."

"Don't be ridiculous. It's just a minor obstacle."

"Honey, it's a *wall of ice.* To me, that says, 'Do not enter.' "

"Oh, come on." She gestured at the dark, semitransparent barrier. "I can see flickers of light from the other side. Whatever we came to find is there."

"Sure it is. But I don't feel like hacking my way through the galaxy's biggest ice cube to get to it"—he nodded at her broken leg—"especially since I'd be doin' all the work, on account of you being a gimp."

She rolled her eyes. "I swear, sometimes it's like you forget we live in the twenty-third century." Then she drew her phaser, set it for wide beam and high power, and fired at the ice. The blue beam lit up the ice for a fraction of a second, and then the frozen wall transformed into a dense cloud of sultry, gray vapor. Seconds later, the hiss of boiling water ceased, and Bridy took her thumb off the phaser's trigger.

He scowled. "Oh, well, *sure.* If you're gonna *cheat.*"

"Let's go."

Quinn helped her forward through the curtains of mist. Eerie, nigh-musical oscillations emanated from the chamber ahead of them, and an unearthly glow pierced the thinning fog as they neared the threshold of a vast cavern.

The first thing Bridy saw was the machine.

Every piece of it was in motion. Delicate elements composed

of silvery crystal spun at many different speeds on a variety of planes, all orbiting a core consisting of equal parts hard angles and fluid curves. Ribbons of prismatic energy snaked through the machine's open spaces, crisscrossing one another's paths, sometimes intersecting in flashes of white light.

Rotating in the center of all that motion was an object unlike any Bridy had ever seen. Made of the same silvery crystal as the rest of the machine, the core element was in a constant state of flux, expanding into dramatic stellations of varying complexity and reverting to a simple icosahedron once every several seconds before repeating the cycle of transformations.

Warmth radiated from the titanic device. As she and Quinn drew nearer to it, Bridy noticed a profound galvanic tingling traveling across her body.

She looked away from the machine only because Quinn pulled urgently on her coat sleeve. "Um, honey?" Bridy turned, looked at him, and then shifted her attention to see what he was pointing at.

Her jaw went slack as she beheld the most beautiful and terrifying being she'd ever encountered: a giant nearly seven meters tall, its body formed from multicolored mist that concealed its lower half. A brilliant glow obscured its face, streams of shimmering motes circled its torso, and a great halo of golden light framed its head. As clouds of vapor rolled behind its back, Bridy saw fleeting glimpses of majestic shapes she was almost certain could only be wings.

Its voice was a stroke of thunder and the roar of the sea. **"Welcome."**

Quinn whispered to Bridy, "Is that what I think it is?"

"I think it is."

The resplendent colossus interjected, **"Yes. I am Shedai."** It spread its arms. **"It is I who summoned you, and who have awaited your coming."**

Bridy took a cautious step toward the towering being. "I've seen your kind before. Which one are you?"

"I am the Apostate."

16

Every nerve in Quinn's body told him to run. Standing in the presence of the Apostate filled him with a sensation of impending catastrophe, as if he were teetering on the edge of an abyss and feeling the first tug of gravity. Bad enough the thing was huge, radiating light and heat like a bonfire, and had a voice that quaked the bedrock under Quinn's feet, but it also looked as if it had been brought to life straight from the pages of the Old Testament.

In other words, it was exactly what he'd been afraid they would find, and he would already have been running back to the *Dulcinea* were it not for the fact that Bridy seemed intent on having a conversation with the damned thing.

"You say you summoned us," Bridy said. "You mean, with the signals we picked up from the wormhole? The ones containing the Jinoteur Pattern?"

"Correct. Of all the *Telinaruul,* your faction has evinced the keenest grasp of our technology. Though your under-standing continues to be limited, I trusted you to recognize my invitation."

Bridy hobbled a few steps closer to the Apostate, dragging Quinn with her much against his will. "Well, here we are," she said. "Wherever *here* is."

"A universe of my own creation—a redoubt forged from the shattered remnants of the Jinoteur system and seques-tered here to shield the last vestiges of its power from my exiled kin."

Growing impatient, Quinn spoke up. "Uh-huh. We were there when you did it. You nearly took us down with you."

"A transgression for which I apologize. However, it was imperative that I prevent the other Shedai from ever returning to the wellspring of our power—and that I deny

you and your rivals access to its mysteries until I was ready to bequeath them on my own terms."

Bridy and Quinn traded anxious glances, then she looked back at the imposing titan. "Is that why you lured us here?"

"I summoned you so that you might finish what I have begun. Your civilization stands upon the threshold of greatness, but there are those among the *Serrataal* who would crush your Federation aborning. For the sake of the galaxy, I believe they must not succeed."

Quinn's brow wrinkled with disbelief. "You want us to start a war with the Shedai? Are you nuts? Or do you just think *we* are?"

"War between your kind and the Shedai loyal to the Maker is inevitable, little sparks. My aim is to provide you with the arms and knowledge your people will need to survive."

Distrust resonated in Bridy's voice as she asked, "Why would you help us?"

"This is not the first time I have sought to rid the galaxy of my kindred. Aeons ago, I allied myself with a great race of *Telinaruul* known as the Tkon. They wielded technologies the likes of which your civilization has not yet imagined. I helped them craft a weapon that would let them contain and eradicate the Shedai threat. Soon afterward, the Maker and her faithful ambushed the capital system of the Tkon, detonated its primary star, and ended that empire in a nightmare of chaos and darkness. I will not see that fate befall your Federation. Never again will I let such an atrocity come to pass as a consequence of my inaction."

High above Bridy and Quinn's heads, a ghostly image appeared. It was a twelve-sided polyhedron rotating slowly. Orbiting it were long, complex strings of data—alien symbols, Arabic numerals, equations, fragments of star charts—all of it distorted, spectral, and ephemeral. Quinn squinted and saw that each face of the polyhedron was etched with a unique alien symbol. He looked away from the spectacle and gazed in awe at the Apostate. "What is this?"

"A guide. Instructions for turning the weapon of the Tkon against the Shedai. With it they can be contained and, when the time is right, destroyed."

Bridy's voice trembled with excitement. "What is the weapon of the Tkon?"

"An array containing hundreds of these objects. Linked in the correct sequence and used properly, each can imprison up to a dozen Shedai."

"All right," Bridy said. "Where do we find it?"

"That I do not know. The Tkon constructed it in secret."

Quinn waved one hand in a pantomime of dismissal. "Hang on—stop. If the Tkon had this superweapon, how'd the Maker get the drop on 'em?"

"I helped the Tkon build it, but I never told them how to activate it."

"Why the hell not?"

"They refused to pledge mercy for myself and my brethren. At that time, I still harbored hope that I and the members of my loyal host might be spared. I have since abandoned such folly."

Quinn pointed at the holographic-style projection above his head. "So, this is the weapon's 'on' switch? And you're giving it to *us*?" He permitted himself a grim chortle. "We're flattered and all, but if you don't mind my asking, why don't you go fight your own war and leave us out of it?"

"Because my strength is fading, little spark. Creating this pocket universe for the completion of my task has drained all but the last of my power. I did not procure this knowledge from memory. Using the machine you see here, I retrieved it from the myriad dimensions in which I had concealed its parts. Only now, after you have found me, have I assembled them in one place. Once I am gone, it will not persist for long—a dozen of your hours, at most—so you must document it swiftly."

The Apostate's radiance dimmed, and his stature diminished. He turned his back on Quinn and Bridy and began to walk away toward a deep, lightless cavern. Bridy lurched after him and lost her balance. As Quinn caught her, she called out to the departing Shedai, "Wait! What do you mean, once you're gone?"

When their host turned back to face them, he had shrunk to a height of only two meters, and his voice, though still a mellifluous baritone, had no greater presence than that of any mortal being.

"My end is upon me, little spark. Death beckons."

A cold wind howled through the ice-walled caverns. The frigid gale washed over the Apostate. His body turned gray and scattered like ashes. Beneath the funereal wails of the wind, Quinn heard the Apostate's voice whisper in his ear, "I give you the flame. Use it well."

Grim silence fell upon Quinn and Bridy. They looked at each other, and then they turned in unison to see the Apostate's secret lingering in the air above and behind them. Beyond it, the mysterious machine continued to turn, its fathomless workings uniting and projecting the pieces of the Apostate's dark secret.

Bridy grabbed Quinn's shoulder. "We have to record this! Right now!"

"With what? A tattoo on my ass?"

"Go back to the ship and get the other tricorder. And bring back the spare medkit while you're at it."

"Screw that, we're both going back to the ship. I ain't leavin' you here."

She seized his jacket by its collar. "Quinn, listen to me! We've just made one of the biggest discoveries in Operation Vanguard—maybe in the history of the Federation! I *need* to stay here and study it any way I can. You can make it to the ship and back in less time than it would take you to carry me up that slope—and you *know* it. So stop arguing with me and *go*, already!"

He frowned to mask his frustration. "Dammit, I hate when you're right." He looked around. "It's freezin' in this hole. You gonna be okay till I get back?"

"I have rocks, I have a phaser. I'll be fine."

"Yeah, yeah." He helped her over to the machine so that she would have something to lean against, and then he kissed her. "If all goes well, I'll be back in six hours. Don't you go wanderin' off on me."

Bridy pressed her gloved palm to his face and flashed him a smile to die for. "I'll be right here. Now go. Time's wasting."

Quinn kissed her again, and then he let her go and started running.

17

Quinn felt like a meat popsicle as he staggered inside the *Dulcinea*. Two steps off the ramp, he dropped to his knees and slumped against the bulkhead as the hatchway lifted shut behind him. He could hardly feel his feet, and his fingers were almost completely numb. All his layers of cold-weather gear had been barely enough to protect him from the brutal cold once night had fallen.

Bridy was right, he admitted to himself. *If I'd had to bring her with me, we might not have made it.* The other saving grace for his return journey had been the clear path they had left in the snow as they crossed the frozen lake. Without the tricorder to lead him back to the ship, his only guide had been their footprints.

Between pained breaths he told himself to get up, but his body felt as if it had been cast from lead. *Move, you lazy sack of crap,* he admonished himself. *Bridy needs you. Get your ass in gear!* He reached up and found a handhold. By slow increments he hoisted himself back to his feet, and then he hugged the wall as he made his way forward to the dispensary locker. He shrugged off his backpack, opened it, and pulled out the shelter kit to make room for more urgently needed supplies: the ship's second medkit, a bundle of compact field rations, a large canister of vitamin-enhanced water, and two fistfuls of heat sticks.

A few of those in our pockets'll keep us from freezin' to death on the hike back, he reasoned. He zipped the pack half-shut, hurried forward, and grabbed Bridy's backup tricorder from the equipment locker near the cockpit. *So far, so good.* He checked the ship's chrono. *Just under three hours. Should be faster goin' back.* As he tried to stuff the tricorder inside his pack, he realized his hands were shaking. And not just a bit—a lot. *Hang on,* he cautioned himself. *If you drop dead rushin' back to her, you ain't gonna be doin' anybody any favors.*

Quinn eased himself into the pilot's seat and scanned himself with the tricorder. Within seconds, its display confirmed what he already suspected: he was hypoxic, borderline hypothermic, and seriously dehydrated. *In other words, a dead man walking,* he concluded. He turned off the tricorder, put it in his pack, and pulled out the medkit. His numbed fingers could barely fit an ampoule of triox compound into the hypospray, but then it clicked into place. He pressed the injector's nozzle to his throat just above his carotid artery and pushed the trigger. A fleeting hiss and a momentary twinge of discomfort were followed by a sensation of profound relief. Quinn's head cleared, and his vision sharpened. *That's better.*

He put away the medkit, then cracked a few heat sticks and stuffed them into the inner pockets of his coat and the pouches on the legs of his pants. *That ought to keep me from freezing on the walk back,* he figured. *And I can set up a tube from my canteen so I can hydrate while I walk.*

Closing the pack, he got up and started aft—then halted as a ping of sensor contact resounded softly in the stillness of the cockpit. He turned back and checked the display, which indicated the arrival of a starship in orbit above the *Dulcinea*.

About time, he mused, fishing his communicator from his pocket. He flipped open its gold-plated grille and opened a secure frequency. "Bridy, you read me?"

"Yeah," she answered over the staticky channel, *"I'm still here."*

"I'm at the ship and about to head back. And I've got more good news: the cavalry's here."

"Thank God. We have to get Xiong and a science team down here, pronto."

"Roger that. We—" Another signal appeared on the sensor display. "Um, honey? What're the odds *Endeavour* brought reinforcements?"

Her reply was freighted with fear and suspicion. *"What's happening?"*

"Multiple contacts. Three—no, check that, five ships on approach vectors."

"Quinn, Endeavour *is the only Starfleet vessel in the sector. If you're reading multiple ships—"*

"Then we've got company." He dropped the pack and ran aft to the weapons locker. "You better dig in, darlin'."

"There's no time! Listen to me: let the Klingons land and then take off and make a break for orbit. One of us needs to get away."

"Dammit, Bridy, don't do nothin' stupid! Let me call the play this time!"

"It's too late for that. You need to—"

"No! Not another word! Lay low till I scope the situation." He slapped the grille shut on his communicator, put the device away, and opened the weapons locker. *I need something with kick that won't give away my position.* From his limited arsenal he selected a semiautomatic .50 caliber sniper rifle with a flash suppressor and inertia-free firing mechanism. He nodded. *This, two clips of spun-duranium rounds, and a pack of plasma grenades should do nicely.*

Rifle in one hand and a bundle of ammunition and grenades in the other, Quinn sprinted to the hatch and elbowed the button that opened it. As soon as it passed the half-down point, he rode it like a slide, dropped off the end, and landed knee-deep in snow. He had dashed a dozen strides toward the edge of the *Dulcinea*'s narrow mountain perch when the banshee howls of the wind were devoured by the thunderous roar of engines cruising past overhead.

The sound wave hit Quinn hard enough to knock him facedown in the snow. When he lifted his head, he gazed in dismay at three Klingon birds-of-prey making their descent to the frozen lake between him and Bridy. Following the trio of sleek warships were two bulky, gray-green Klingon troopships.

Quinn pushed himself back into motion, and he scrambled into a tight space surrounded by jagged outcroppings of black rock. He balanced the rifle in a narrow gap between two boulders, peered through the scope, and focused its image.

Far below, the birds-of-prey had already set down on the far side of the frozen lake, near the entrance to the caves, and the troop transports were only seconds away from touching down. Wide ramps descended from the warships' ventral hulls, and armed Klingon troops poured out of them.

Quinn flipped open his communicator and set it beside him on a level patch of rock. "Bridy? You read me, darlin'?"

"I read you."

"I won't lie to you, sweetie. It's bad. Real bad."

"Give it to me straight."

"Three birds-of-prey and two dropships, right outside your front door. I'd say two full companies of ground troops, another hundred in flight crew."

"Okay. Go ahead and say it."

"You sure?"

"I've earned it."

He sighed. "Told you so."

Bridy lifted the ordnance package from her backpack. It was heavier than she'd remembered from just a few hours earlier. Part of her refused to believe she was really holding her own death in her hands, or that she would find the will to do what she knew needed to be done.

She wanted to believe there was still a way out, but her training told her that was all but impossible. She and Quinn were outnumbered more than a hundred to one, and he was too far away to do much more than bear witness to the inevitable.

"Listen up," Quinn said over the communicator. *"Use your phaser to collapse the tunnel to the big cave. That'll slow the*

Klingons down and buy us some time. I can advance to sniper distance in about ninety minutes."

"And then what? You'll start a firefight with two hundred Klingons? In the open? With no cover? Are you out of your mind?"

Her retort was met by several seconds of silence. She admired Quinn's fighting spirit but couldn't stand the thought of him sharing her fate.

Suddenly, she regretted all the times she'd taken him for granted, all the moments when she'd cut him with sarcasm or pulled rank simply because she knew he would let her get away with it. Only then, when she knew she would never see him again, could she admit to herself just how much that deeply flawed, strangely idealistic, ill-tempered, foul-mouthed, crazy-brave, barely reformed drunkard of a man truly meant to her.

With the flick of a toggle and the press of a button, Bridy armed the ordnance package's detonator. Her only remaining decision was whether to set a countdown or to trigger the device manually.

From the caverns beyond the tunnel, she heard Klingon voices shouting.

"Okay, new plan," Quinn said. *"Collapse the tunnel and give me time to get the* Dulcinea's *transporter working. Once it's back up, you phaser that crazy machine into slag and use your recall transponder to beam out."*

Her fingers trembled above the detonator switch. "We don't have that much time. You need to go back to the ship *now*, Quinn."

"Why? It ain't like they've spotted me."

She wiped a rolling tear from her cheek. "Please—you need to hurry."

"Tell me you didn't bring that goddamned bomb with you."

"I'm sorry."

"Not good enough."

"There's no other way."

"Yes, there is! We just haven't—"

"No, there isn't! If even one of those bastards gets in here with a scanner, they'll relay this intel back to their ships, and that'll be game over. We'll never stop them all in time. I can't let them have this."

"If you blow it up, we won't have it, either."

"I know. But those are my orders."

"Goddammit, screw your orders! Just give me a little more time!"

Footfalls echoed in the tunnel. She had only seconds left. Her voice cracked with grief. "You know I love you, right?"

Quinn's stoic façade crumbled along with Bridy's. *"I love you, too."*

She shut her eyes. "Then for the love of God, *run*."

Quinn looked up from behind his rifle's scope, his eyes fogged with tears. Dread rooted him in place as he picked up the communicator. He didn't know whether he was begging mercy from Bridy or from God. "Please, just wait. . . ."

Over the open channel, he heard a translated Klingon shout: *"Halt, human!"*

Bridy's last words were calm and softly spoken. *"Close your eyes."*

The last sound from the communicator was the screech of a disruptor, angry and close. Quinn winced, his grief a reflex. His breath caught in his chest, trapped behind a choked-back roar of fury and sorrow.

The night flared red. An apocalyptic booming split the frigid air and buried his angry screams. Quinn ducked behind his rocky cover a fraction of a second before the detonation's shock wave hammered the mountainside with heat and brute force, kicking up clouds of snow and ice and churning them into spindrifts. Thunder rolled and echoed without end.

He peeked over the rocks, in the direction of the blast. A mushroom cloud of black smoke and ruddy fire climbed into the sky, and the formerly frozen lake had shattered and boiled, swallowing the five Klingon vessels instantaneously.

Then a more present rumbling snared his attention.

It was behind him. He turned. The snow between him and the *Dulcinea* was churning like a muddy river, but it wasn't the origin of the sound. He looked up.

The mountain's snowcap was plunging toward him.

He abandoned his rifle and ran toward the *Dulcinea*. It had been hard enough slogging through the knee-deep snow before; now it shifted and slid like an ocean's riptide and threatened to sweep his feet out from under him.

Stumbling and staggering, he fought his way back to the ramp and clambered awkwardly inside the ship. He slapped the button to close the ramp on his way forward. The ship heaved to starboard, throwing him hard against the bulkhead. Fighting for balance and momentum, he pushed off the wall and lunged toward the cockpit.

He was three steps shy of the pilot's seat when the avalanche hit the ship.

The vertigo of free fall was arrested by his first brutal collision with a bulkhead. Then the nose of the ship pitched upward, and Quinn fell nearly the whole length of the ship into the main cabin. One jarring impact after another threw him in random directions, and the only sounds were the omnipresent roar of the collapsing mountainside, the monstrous groans of wrenching hull plates, and the high-pitched shriek of metal being torn asunder. Every loose object inside the ship was tossed into a maelstrom with debris smashed free from the *Dulcinea*'s broken frame.

Entire sections of the ship were torn away as it rolled down the mountain. Something unseen sheared through the main passage-way. The bow of the ship disappeared, and for a moment Quinn glimpsed the sky.

Then a final, bone-jarring impact brought the main fuselage of the ship to a halt—and a wall of snow and ice rushed in like a river. Broken and stunned, all Quinn could do was shut his eyes as he was entombed in bone-numbing cold and suffocating darkness. He thought of Bridy as his world went black, and hoped the universe would spare him the pain of awakening without her.

18

"Over here!"

Katherine Stano turned to see who had called out over the baleful cries of the wind. Several meters away, Lieutenant Paul McGibbon, the *Endeavour*'s deputy chief of security, waved over the rescue team, which consisted of engineers, medical staff, and a pair of security officers, all of them bundled in awkward combinations of cold-weather gear and dusky red radiation suits. Stano, attired in the same clumsy double outfit, jogged with the others to join McGibbon.

Doctor Anthony Leone, the ship's chief medical officer, was the first to reach the security officer. "Report."

"One human life sign, weak." McGibbon held out his tricorder so Leone could see its display. "Buried about four meters down, inside part of the ship."

The team circled Leone and McGibbon. Stano pushed through the line to join the surgeon and security officer. "Can we get a transporter lock?"

"Negative," McGibbon said. His tricorder's screen was hashed with static. "Still too much radiation from the blast. It wouldn't be safe."

Stano waved everyone away from the entombed fuselage. "Move back!" She flipped open her communicator. "Stano to *Endeavour*."

Captain Khatami answered, *"Go ahead, Commander."*

"Lieutenant McGibbon is sending you some coordinates." She nodded at McGibbon, who started the data upload from his tricorder. "We need you to beam out a layer ten meters square by three-point-five meters deep. It's sitting on top of a buried survivor. I'm sure I don't have to tell you time is a factor."

"Understood. Move your people clear and stand by."

"Acknowledged." She turned to see the rest of the landing

party had already withdrawn to a safe distance, and she joined them in a hurry. "McGibbon, have your men stand by to help excavate the survivor for Doctor Leone and his team."

"Aye, sir."

The mellisonant drone of a transporter beam filled the air, and then a ten-meter-square patch of snow shimmered with golden light. Seconds later, the radiance faded—and took the snow with it.

Stano pointed at the pit. "Someone cut us a slope, pronto."

McGibbon and his men drew their phasers, adjusted their settings, and took aim. "On three," McGibbon said. "One. Two. Three." The security team fired wide-dispersal, low-power beams of blue energy and melted one side of the pit into a thirty-degree slope. McGibbon lifted his hand. "Cease fire!"

Chief engineer Bersh glov Mog stepped forward and scanned the slope with his tricorder. "Ground's solid," he said. "Engineers! Let's go!"

The engineering team deployed into the pit and went to work melting snow and ice and excavating dirt, rocks, and debris. Within minutes they had unearthed the main fuselage of Cervantes Quinn's ship, the *Dulcinea*. Its hull had been twisted, crushed, and shredded. Mog emerged from the wreck and beckoned Leone. "Site secure! Ready for evac!"

Leone was already in motion and hollering for his team of equipment-toting nurses and paramedics to keep up. "C'mon! We don't get paid by the hour!" On their way down to the wreck they passed Mog, who climbed back up to join Stano.

"Data banks are gone," the Tellarite engineer said, his gray-maned, porcine face a portrait of bitter disappointment. "It's just a husk. Nothing left to salvage."

Stano nodded. "All right. Pull your team out and fall back to the shuttles."

"Yes, sir." The engineers followed Mog back to the landing party's pair of shuttlecraft, the *Tyson* and the *Murakami*.

Minutes passed while the medics worked out of sight inside the battered fuselage of the *Dulcinea* and the security officers lingered at the edge of the pit. Then Leone and his team emerged carrying Cervantes Quinn on a stretcher. They were moving on a direct path toward the shuttles when Stano intercepted them. She nodded at Quinn as she told Leone, "I need to talk to him."

Leone shouldered past her and waved his team onward. "He just spent five hours buried alive, Commander. This is no time for a debriefing."

"I just need to ask him one question. Please."

The doctor rolled his eyes and said to his team, "Hold up." He and Stano caught up to them and stood on opposite sides of Quinn's stretcher. "Mister Quinn? This is Doctor Leone from the *Endeavour*. Can you hear me?" One of Quinn's eyes fluttered weakly half open. He said nothing. Leone arched his brow skeptically at Stano. "One question."

Stano leaned close to Quinn and modulated her voice to a dulcet tone. "Quinn, where is Lieutenant Commander McLellan? Where's Bridy Mac?"

Quinn looked to his left, and he pushed one trembling hand out from under his thermal blanket to point into the distance— toward the smoldering crater and slowly dissipating mushroom cloud on the far side of an ash-covered lake. Then he pulled his hand back under the cover and shut his eyes.

The first officer turned back, her demeanor somber. "Thank you, Doctor."

As usual, Leone sounded mildly annoyed. "You're welcome." He waved his hands at his team as if fanning flames at their backs. "Okay, show's over. Move!" They resumed their hurried trot toward the shuttles.

Stano called out to McGibbon, "Paul! Let's go!" As the security team double-timed across the snow to catch up with the rest of the landing party, Stano flipped open her communicator. "Stano to *Endeavour*."

Khatami answered, "Endeavour. *Go ahead*."

"Request permission to use the *Murakami* to reconnoiter the blast area for signs of Lieutenant Commander McLellan."

"*Permission denied. The wormhole's destabilizing. We have*

to leave in the next twenty minutes, so you and your team need to get back here. As in now."

"Understood and on our way. Stano out."

Quinn lay on the stretcher, frozen in both body and spirit. Through the shuttle's open hatchway, he saw the pit from which he'd been exhumed—the open grave that held the broken pieces of his ship, his life, his hopes, his future.

Around him, people spoke in voices of authority, taking refuge in their command of technology, as if it would defend them from the hand of fate. He had nothing to say to them. What difference would any of it make now?

The hatch was closed, and steady vibrations from thrusters and impulse coils pulsed through the shuttlecraft as it took off. Out of the corner of his eye, Quinn saw the planet's horizon curve subtly as they gained altitude. Then the planet dropped out of view as the tiny spacecraft turned toward the orbiting *Endeavour*.

He knew that in the hours, days, and weeks to come, more than one person would pepper him with questions in a futile attempt to make sense of what had happened on this desolate orb in an empty universe that would soon fold in upon itself and vanish forever. All their queries would be for naught. There were no answers to be found here, no wisdom to be gleaned from this catastrophe. In the name of duty, Bridy had given everything, and Quinn had been left with nothing to show for her sacrifice.

The shuttle circled around to *Endeavour*'s aft quarter and began its approach toward the main shuttlebay, whose doors yawned open ahead of them. Beyond the *Constitution*-class starship, the nameless orb that Quinn would curse forever eclipsed the fading glow of its white dwarf star. The best part of him, he was certain, had been left behind on that godforsaken ball of ice and stone.

As *Endeavour* swallowed up its shuttle, Quinn wished the rest of him had been left behind, as well.

FOUR WEEKS LATER

19

Ming Xiong had never been comfortable as the bearer of bad news, and he had never had to deliver a more heartbreaking message than the one that had brought him back to the *U.S.S. Sagittarius.* He had thought he might have the luxury of doing this via subspace, or perhaps even in a letter, but as the *Endeavour* returned that evening to the main hangar of Starbase 47, Xiong had seen the small *Archer*-class scout ship berthed in the adjacent bay and realized he would have to fulfill this obligation in person.

On the gangway that led to the *Sagittarius,* Xiong stopped walking. *I really don't want to do this.* He bowed his head and looked at his olive-green utility jumpsuit. It had his name stenciled over the left chest flap, and its right shoulder was adorned by a *U.S.S. Sagittarius* patch. It had been given to him by the ship's Deltan commander, Captain Adelard Nassir, as a token of their friendship. *I shouldn't have worn this,* he scolded himself. *I don't deserve it right now.*

Ahead of him, Captain Nassir stepped through the ship's open port-side hatch. "Xiong! You're here. Good."

"Yes, sir," Xiong said as he resumed walking and put aside his regrets about wearing the jumpsuit. *Too late to change now.*

Nassir beckoned Xiong. "We're all waiting in the mess."

Xiong followed the captain inside the *Sagittarius.* The ship's narrow main corridor and low overheads gave it a claustrophobic quality. They followed the ring-shaped passageway aft, past the ladder up to the transporter bay and engineering deck, to the mess hall, which served as the ship's conference room.

Waiting inside, mostly seated at the two long tables, was the crew of the *Sagittarius.* As a tiny scout ship, her crew consisted of only fourteen personnel including the captain, and they all wore the same utilitarian olive-green jumpsuits, which were devoid of rank insignia or department designations.

At the front of one table sat Commander Clark Terrell, the

first officer, a muscular man with brown skin and big hands. Across from him sat the ship's chief medical officer, Doctor Lisa Babitz, a svelte blond germophobe.

Behind them, sitting opposite each other, were the ship's petite and kooky red-haired science officer, Lieutenant Vanessa Theriault, and the brawny and bearded chief engineer, Master Chief Petty Officer Mike Ilucci. At the end of the first table sat Lieutenants Celerasayna zh'Firro, the Andorian senior helm officer, and Sorak, the middle-aged Vulcan chief of security and lead recon scout.

At the other table, Senior Chief Petty Officer Razka, a young Saurian who served as a field scout, sat across from medical technician Ensign Nguyen Tan Bao. The engineering petty officers—Salagho Threx, a burly and hirsute Denobulan, and Karen Cahow, a tomboyish young woman with dirty blond hair—sat together opposite engineering crewman Torvin, a gawky young Tiburonian.

At the back of the compartment stood two officers Xiong didn't recognize, a man with distinctive spots along the sides of his face and neck and a young Orion woman with close-cropped raven hair. As Xiong noticed them, Nassir made the introductions. "Ming, allow me to introduce the newest members of the crew." He gestured first at the man. "Lieutenant Dastin, our new tactical officer." Then at the Orion woman: "Ensign Taryl, our new recon scout."

The two officers nodded at Xiong, who returned the gesture. "Hi." After a brief pause, he added, "I don't mean to be rude, but what I'm here to say doesn't really concern the two of you. But you're welcome to stay if you like." No one made any move to leave. Xiong took a deep breath. "It's been a while since I last saw you all. I'm sure I don't need to explain why." The *Sagittarius* crew members nodded gravely, needing no reminder of their intimate involvement in Operation Vanguard or their harrowing encounter with the Shedai. "The reason I asked to talk with all of you is that I have to tell you something. . . . Bridy Mac's dead."

A pall settled over the room. Grief moved like a wave across the crew's faces. Theriault turned away and hid her eyes with one hand; Threx bowed his head and let his long hair conceal his face. Cahow and Tan Bao both appeared shaken by the news that their former shipmate and second officer was gone. The only unaffected visage was that of Sorak, leading Xiong to envy the Vulcan for his completion of the emotion-purging *Kolinahr* ritual.

Cahow asked in a small voice, "What happened?"

"I'm sorry," Xiong said. "All the details are classified."

Babitz cast a teary-eyed stare at Xiong. "Will there be a memorial service?"

"Not in public. The brass doesn't want to call any attention to her death. Her family on Deneva's being told it was an accident." Xiong's composure began to crumble; tears welled in his eyes, and his voice shook. "But I wanted you all to know it *wasn't* an accident. She died bravely. In the line of duty." His last vestige of control disintegrated, and he bowed his head to hide his tears.

Nassir draped a comforting arm across Xiong's shoulders. "It's okay, Ming."

"No, it's not," Xiong said, choking on the words. "It's my fault. I sent her there." He palmed his cheeks dry. "I'm sorry."

Terrell stood and clamped a hand on Xiong's shoulder. "No one here blames you, Ming. Nobody except yourself."

Babitz joined Terrell and Nassir. She cupped Xiong's face in her hands and lifted it to force him to make eye contact with her. "You know she loved you like the little brother she never had?" Xiong nodded, and Babitz gave him a sad smile. "And you know we think of you as one of us, right? And we always will."

Despite their assurances, Xiong's face burned with shame. "How can you forgive me for this?"

"There's nothing to forgive," Nassir said. "It's called being in command."

Sheltered in the embrace of his friends and peers, Xiong felt as if he had no right to their consolation, no place accepting their comfort when he was the one most directly responsible for their shared loss. And, for the first time, he believed that no matter how valuable Operation Vanguard's discoveries might be, they would never be worth the price Bridy's family and friends had just paid.

20

Quinn's journey back to Vanguard had felt like time spent in limbo. Aside from one short debriefing session, no one had asked to talk with him, and that had suited him just fine. He had limited his contact with the ship's crew to its chief medical officer, who had done a superlative job of healing all of Quinn's wounds except the ones that really mattered, the kind that didn't show up on medical scanners.

Now the ship was back at its home port, and Quinn had been "put ashore" on Starbase 47 to make his own way. Unfortunately for him, he had nowhere to go.

He drifted across the manicured lawn of the starbase's terrestrial enclosure. Despite being surrounded by thousands of people, he felt utterly alone. His friend Tim Pennington was off the station, chasing down some story or other for the Federation News Service. There was no one else Quinn wanted to see, no one who knew him well enough to understand his loss, no one else he could trust.

Ahead of Quinn, the cluster of buildings—some commercial, some residential—known as Stars Landing grew slowly larger with each step he took. Somewhere in that small warren of civilian life tucked inside a Starfleet military base there was an apartment with Quinn's name on it, accommodations arranged by the grace and generosity of Starfleet Intelligence.

I guess this is home for now. He stuffed his hands into his pockets. In one was a credit chip good for a few months' living expenses and, if he was willing to travel like a piece of luggage, maybe even passage back to the core systems of the Federation. Aside from that, he had nothing but the clothes on his back.

The report from the *Endeavour* had said no part of the *Dulcinea* had been salvageable, and his rescuers had found no sign of the treasures he had amassed in his cargo hold. For the first time in his adult life, he had no job, no ship, and no prospects. He thought about trying to find a poker game with an open seat. *A few lucky hands and I could go home first-class instead of in steerage.* The idea almost took root, and then he chortled ruefully. *A few lucky hands? Who'm I kidding? Lady Luck might be smilin' on someone right now, but it sure as shit ain't me.*

He felt aimless as he wandered the narrow lanes of Stars Landing, passing familiar storefronts without bothering to look at any of them. *I thought I'd had it all figured out,* he brooded. *My life had purpose. Meaning. Hope.* He looked up at the holographic simulation of a dusk sky projected on the ceiling of the terrestrial enclosure. *I thought my karmic debt was paid. Didn't I suffer enough? Or do enough good deeds?* Quinn felt as if the stars themselves were looking down at his dreams and calling them delusions. Turning his gaze back toward the cobblestone road under his feet, he felt like a rat in a maze and wondered if he had only been fooled for a moment into believing he'd chosen his own path in life.

Then he stopped. There was no point taking another step. Where was he going? What would he do when he got there? Why did he care anymore?

He looked up and realized he was standing in front of his old watering hole, Tom Walker's place. Inside, the atmosphere was muted—quiet conversation mixed with low music, subdued lighting, and no vidscreens or other distractions. Just ordinary folks minding their own business and letting others do the same.

All my paths lead here. They always have.

Quinn stepped through the door and made his way to the bar. He found his favorite barstool empty and waiting for him, so he planted himself on it.

Behind the bar, Tom Walker looked over his shoulder at Quinn. The lanky, fair-haired Irishman smiled. "Cervantes Quinn! It's been too long, man!" Quinn smiled back and nodded at the shelf along the wall. Good ol' Tom, that was all the cue he needed. He knew just what to do. He grabbed the bottle of Anejo Patron and poured Quinn a generous double shot. "To celebrate your return!"

"I'll be staying awhile," Quinn said. "Leave the bottle."

Tom set the tequila on the counter. "*Sláinte.*"

Quinn picked up his shot glass and studied the pale golden liquor. It caught the light and made it beautiful, and the facets on the outer surface of the shot glass gave him the impression he was handling a liquefied jewel.

Twenty-five years a drunk, two years sober—what's the difference?

He knew the drink wasn't the answer to his problems, but his latest ordeal had granted him an epiphany: there were no answers to his problems.

Or to anyone's problems, he decided. *There are no answers at all, and never have been. Just pain, and then oblivion. It only hurts when you care . . . and I don't want to care anymore.*

He lifted the glass to his lips.

And stopped caring.

The saga of

STAR TREK®: VANGUARD

will continue in

WHAT JUDGMENTS COME

Fall 2011

ABOUT THE AUTHORS

DAYTON WARD. Author. Trekkie. Writing his goofy little stories and searching for a way to tap into the hidden nerdity that all humans have. Then, an accidental overdose of Mountain Dew altered his body chemistry. Now, when Dayton Ward grows excited or just downright geeky, a startling metamorphosis occurs.

Driven by outlandish ideas and a pronounced lack of sleep, he is pursued by fans and editors as well as funny men in bright uniforms wielding tasers, straitjackets, and medication. In addition to the numerous credits he shares with friend and co-writer Kevin Dilmore, Dayton is the author of the *Star Trek* novels *In the Name of Honor, Open Secrets,* and *Paths of Disharmony*; the science fiction novels *The Last World War, Counterstrike: The Last World War, Book II,* and The *Genesis Protocol*; as well as short stories in the first three *Star Trek: Strange New Worlds* anthologies, the Yard Dog Press anthologies *Houston, We've Got Bubbas* and *A Bubba in Time Saves None, Kansas City Voices Magazine,* and the *Star Trek: New Frontier* anthology *No Limits.* For Flying Pen Press, he was the editor of the science fiction anthology *Full-Throttle Space Tales #3: Space Grunts,* and he has a story in the latest *Full-Throttle* collection, *Space Horrors.*

Dayton is believed to be working on his next novel, and he must let the world think that he is working on it, until he can find a way to earn back the advance check he blew on strippers and booze. Though he currently lives in Kansas City with his wife and daughters, Dayton is a Florida native and maintains a torrid long-distance romance with his beloved Tampa Bay Buccaneers. Visit him on the web at http://www.daytonward.com.

KEVIN DILMORE has found ways to make a living from his geek side for a good while now.

It all started in 1998 with his eight-year run as a contributing writer to *Star Trek Communicator,* for which he wrote news stories and personality profiles for the bimonthly publication of the Official *Star Trek* Fan Club. Since that time, he also has contributed to publications including *Amazing Stories, Hallmark,* and *Star Trek* magazines.

Then he teamed with writing partner and heterosexual life mate Dayton Ward on *Interphase,* their first installment of the *Star Trek: S.C.E.* series, in 2001. Since then, the pair has put more than one million words into print together. Among their most recent shared publications are the novella *The First Peer* in the anthology *Star Trek: Seven Deadly Sins* (March 2010) and the short story "Ill Winds" in the *Star Trek: Shards and Shadows* anthology (January 2009).

By day, Kevin works as a senior writer for Hallmark Cards in Kansas City, Missouri, doing about everything but writing greeting cards, including helping to design *Star Trek*–themed Keepsake Ornaments. His first children's book, *Superdad and His Daring Dadventures,* with illustrations by Tom Patrick, was published by Hallmark Gift Books in May 2009.

A graduate of the University of Kansas, Kevin lives in Overland Park, Kansas. Keep up with his shameful behavior and latest projects on Facebook and Twitter at kevindilmore.

MARCO PALMIERI is honored he was invited to be a contributor to *Star Trek Vanguard: Declassified.*

A lifelong fan, Marco began his professional involvement with the *Star Trek* mythos as an editor for Simon & Schuster, where he developed numerous projects for the *Star Trek* book universe, including ongoing series such as *Vanguard* (in collaboration with David Mack), *Titan,* and the *Deep Space Nine* novels set after the end of the television series; "miniseries"—*Section 31, The Lost Era, Crucible,* and *Terok Nor;* anthologies—*The Lives of Dax* and *Myriad Universe;* standalone novels such as *Ex Machina* and *Burning Dreams;* and many other projects too numerous to name here. Marco is a contributing editor to *Star Trek Magazine,* published by Titan.

More recently, Marco launched Otherworld Editorial, a private consultation service for writers of fantasy and science fiction.

A native New Yorker, Marco makes his home in Brooklyn, together with the love of his life, Doris, their two amazing boys, Jeremy and Benjamin, and their shamelessly cute feline, Tink.

Follow Marco online at www.otherworldeditorial.com, and on Facebook at www.facebook.com/mxpalmieri.

DAVID MACK is the national bestselling author of more than twenty novels and novellas, including *Wildfire, Harbinger, Reap the Whirlwind, Precipice, Road of Bones, Promises Broken,* and the *Star Trek Destiny* trilogy: *Gods of Night, Mere Mortals,* and *Lost Souls.* He developed the *Star Trek Vanguard* series concept with editor Marco Palmieri. His first work of original fiction is the critically acclaimed supernatural thriller *The Calling.*

In addition to novels, Mack's writing credits span several media, including television (for episodes of *Star Trek: Deep Space Nine*), film, short fiction, magazines, newspapers, comic books, computer games, radio, and the Internet.

His upcoming novels include the *Star Trek Mirror Universe* adventure *Rise Like Lions* and a new original supernatural thriller.

Mack resides in New York City with his wife, Kara.

Visit his website, www.davidmack.pro/, and follow him on Twitter @DavidAlanMack and on Facebook at www.facebook.com/david.alan.mack.